ROAD TO FEARLESS

Lisa Annette Powell

Library of Congress Control Number: 2017913759
Lisa Annette Powell, Hamilton, OH

ISBN: 978-0-9906428-5-5

Cover art design by author; graphics by Brian Busse

My Grandma, T.C. Ahlam and Helen- LIGHTS on my road

MR.CAT

LOVER CAT

To GRANDMA and HELEN

for LIGHTING my road

To GINGER, my protector

To MR. CAT and LOVER CAT for curling up with me when I
needed it most

And to my hero, RONNIE

A prisoner devoid of books, had he a Tarot of which he knew how to make use, might in a few years possess a universal science, and discourse on all possible subjects with an unequalled doctrine and inexhaustible eloquence.

Eliphas Levi

Every rock, every stream, plant and animal has a unique spirit of its own. If you're quiet and listen to what draws you, you have the opportunity to learn somethin' new about the world, yourself, and whatever draws you.

Bridie O'Connair

1

DOWN! DOWN! DOWN! Reilly's psyche-saving word game hit dead-on describing the latest. . .home. No, you couldn't rightly call this a home, she thought. Abode? Even that was too nice a euphemism for what her single, alcoholic mother had brought them to.

And she'd cheated with the first words that came to mind.

16 and a half-year old (and that half was extremely important) Reilly's gut cringed as a flood of horrid, mud-gray flashbacks, stirred by the deplorable trailer in front of her, zig-zagged through her mind. . .

A succession of her mother's boyfriends- more than Reilly could recall the names of, more F-words than anyone should be subjected to and more drunken fights- a few knock-down-drag-out ones- than a child should have to witness or hear. The worst memory tightened Reilly's chest- her insides bucked as she too-vividly recalled the sight of an inebriated, naked 'friend', who claimed the mother looked at another man and proceeded to drag the mother by her hair. . .

The teenager's stomach revolted. Please, not yet. Reilly clutched at her stomach and took a deep, less-than-hopeful breath.

"Don't start that breathing shit," the mother flatly admonished, sucking on her cigarette.

The girl bit her lower lip, tasted blood, but at least the flood of horror faded.

Why did horror always remain more stark, create more run-for-the-bathroom moments, than the few good memories could chase away? Holding her stomach, Reilly didn't receive an answer from the cosmos, and she knew better than to ask her mother.

Three moves inside a year. It was rare for them to roost longer than 6 months in any one place; Reilly had long ago given up hope for any semblance of stability. Too hard to find convivial drinking buddies for longer than the 'magic' 6 month term? No, more likely it was a matter of money that had her mother driving away. On to another guy. . .

Dismal, Despicable, The Dump! Technically, the last descriptive didn't count.

Lisa Annette Powell

The object of this particular coping mechanism was three different words- the first ones your brain spit out with the same first letter.

The 'the' cancelled out the validity of the third word. Reilly supposed it really didn't matter a 'hill of beans' as her Grandpa used to say, and the way her brain had gone numb at the sight of move #3, a bit of leeway was probably due.

She sucked at her lip as her mother made a few inane remarks. A year and a half to go- Reilly's mantra steadied her, somewhat.

To give Red Wing Trailer Court an inch of credit, the trailers facing front at the entrance, one being the manager's, were well-cared for, if not very new.

All pieces of siding were still intact, unlike the monstrosity they had parked in front of.

The cared-for homes had windows unbroken and curtained, trimmed grass and two of those three, not the manager's, had flowers gracing sidewalks, window boxes full of blooms and a bird bath. Several birds cheerily basked in the spa. Reilly wasted a second wishing she were one of them.

Beyond the clean façade, as with most things in life, the girl mused, the trailers deteriorated steadily as her mother drove to the rear. The worst of the small community of 40 homes despaired in the back along a creek bank. And that's where her mother had parked the old, rattletrap car, checked her make-up in the rear-view mirror and stepped out.

"You could leave her here, you know," Aunt Sarah, the mother's only sibling, stated as she heated beef stew for lunch.

"And give up the best part of my welfare check?" The mother searched the refrigerator.

"You're pitiful. . ."

"Yeah, yeah, and look what I'm doing to my 'poor daughter'. Give it up, Sarah. Either she'll make it or she won't, same as everybody else in this world. Beside, you've got enough to pay for without adding another mouth to feed."

"Reilly deserves more than being shuffled around constantly. She needs the chance to make friends. . ."

Reilly heard every politely-spoken word of her Aunt Sarah, even as her mother cut off her sister with a choice curse word.

But then, she'd heard it all before. And her widowed aunt did have two rambunctious boys to contend with.

After Grandpa's funeral, Aunt Sarah had stayed in the house she'd grown up in- she'd spent the last two years taking care of her father, while Reilly's mother played vagabond.

Grandpa's stroke had left him incapable of caring for himself, and spiritually he wished to die- rejoin her Grandma, Reilly figured. It was all too evident to see. At times, Reilly empathized, doting on the prospective release of death. To Aunt Sarah, Grandpa had willed the house, and he'd also left a small sum of money to his other daughter and a bank account for Reilly.

The mother quickly found ways to blow her inheritance on an apartment, clothes and a boyfriend she couldn't afford. Using the skills of a consummate con-artist, she'd wrangled Reilly's inheritance from the bank's care and used it for move #2 of the year.

As it turned out, the lodging was cheaper, but the boyfriend more expensive. Now that everything but the welfare check was gone, they were down to 2 suitcases of her mother's clothes, a single, black backpack with all Reilly's possessions inside and the rusty, but paid-off, ever-complaining Chevy.

The mother decided to move in with some other guy she'd just met. Nothing new there. Reilly remembered only one of her mother's guy friends that Reilly herself had liked. He didn't drink- the mother did. And that sealed the death of common ground.

Reilly never knew her father or his relatives. She understood she was the consequent mistake of one of her mother's indiscretions at 15 years of age.

Her mother didn't hide any unfortunate, realistic bits of life from her daughter. Often, Reilly would lie awake wondering why her mother had bothered to keep her. Fortunately or not, with the complications at Reilly's birth, the girl would have no siblings to share the misery with.

The drinking, a major factor in the disappearance of cash, increased over the years. It was a wonder the mother could manage the drive to move #3, two-plus hours from the last place, but she seemed to have a knack for staying sober when necessary.

The mother always seemed to be able to bar-hop at night with next to nothing and come home slap-happy, usually with company. Reilly had learned at an early age to keep out of the way, stick to her room, and especially, to be quiet.

The only time the girl received encouragement from her mother and sometimes the resident boyfriend, was an inducement for Reilly to pick up bottles and cans for recycling and of course, deliver the money promptly to the mother. Food stamps didn't cover the beer bill, but for the industrious Reilly, gathering recyclables became a way to stay out of the way.

And out of the house.

Only one thing of value had Reilly managed to hold on to for any length of time. She still envisioned. . .a heart-shaped watch on a red leather band with red stones for 12, 3, 6 and 9, a gift from her grandparents which had fallen victim to the cash inadequacy and her mother's wily machinations.

"I'll just wear it to look pretty. I'll bring it back." The mother could tear the heart out of the most crooked politician with her clever act. So naturally, the young girl, ten at the time, had believed her and hence, never seen the watch again.

But the lesson stood fast. Reilly would never trust her mother with anything ever again. Not that anything remained to trust her with. A dead zone replaced the feelings such as normal mothers and daughters experienced.

'Less than 2 years,' became a mantra, changing with time- another coping mechanism.

A medium height, ball-capped, beer-bellied, beer-in-hand, tippling-a-cigarette-in-his-lips guy tromped down the rusted steps of the trailer. Slob, Slovenly, Save-me-Reilly's brain raced in recoil. The queasiness returned.

The new boyfriend ground her mother's body to his, noisily kissed her and offered his beer. He proudly patted an immaculate, new pick-up truck and glanced into the car, surveying with less-than-delight the teenage appendage.

"That your girl, huh? Must take after her father. She sure don't have your looks. Ha, ha! How's about a little hug, darlin'?"

Drunk. Deadbeat. Devil.

"Just leave her alone, Chet. She's real quiet. Won't be any trouble, and she can cook and clean. Bring in our bags," she addressed Reilly.

Chet adjusted his jeans, smoothed his rumpled 'Fords Forever' t-shirt, tossed his half-smoked cigarette, gave the girl a disdainful look and ushered the mother inside with rushin' fingers.

Reilly always considered her mother to be beautiful. Guys tripped over themselves doing double takes when her mother flashed sky-blue eyes and turned on the charm. How could her mother settle for. . .this?

The storm door sported a taped, broken window. It sagged on its hinges and the guy slammed it hard so it would catch. How far down does down go? The girl wondered, pinching herself and taking deep breaths as her gut gurgled a threat.

"Utterly, Ugly, Unholy," she whispered.

Chet's trailer exhibited wear beyond its age and a complete lack of TLC, unlike the truck. Mold grew up the vinyl siding, unhindered by missing pieces. Overgrown weeds brushed against the siding and nearly reached the window sills.

Several windows sulked behind half-hanging duct tape strips attempting to cover cracks- fashionably matching the storm door. Broken shades hung in one window. The original scalloped trim on the yellow trailer had faded to an ashy-white hue. Many siding pieces were hopelessly askew- given up the ghost. The garbage cans overflowed with noisy flies, beer cans and worse- cans of RAID. Huge tree limbs hung over the top of the trailer with many smaller, dead branches lying on the roof. The trailers to either side were in slightly better condition. Slightly. In general, the trucks were much better taken care of than the homes. Strange.

Exiting the car, holding onto the lifeline of her backpack, Reilly looked around. 360 degrees. A cul-de-sac community. Why did the people up front, who cared for their homes, stay here? Why did the manager allow this part of his tenancy to get so run down? With a hop, skip and jump she could knock on the manager's door or one of the well-cared for neighbors. Her brain refused to process the logic of it all.

Imminent dusk. An older model, souped-up Camaro rumbled into the court, parked on the single driveway back of the nicest trailer. Two men got out, by the look of their clothes- mechanics. The younger of the two inclined his head towards her.

"Looks like old Chet's got himself a new house mate." To which the father just shrugged his shoulders.

"Pretty young," the younger one frowned.

"That's not her. Chet was whining about the woman having a kid. I reckon that's the child," he didn't betray a true father's fatherly feelings, but inside he winced.

"How many does that make this year?"

"I think that's number four. Don't know where he finds them. The way he talks, this one is a real looker," the father shook his head, sighing.

"Probably advertises on Craig's List," the son smirked. Upon giving the staring, forlorn girl a studious second, he sensed her despair and gritted his teeth. A flare of rage battered at the battened hatches inside, but he clamped down on it with a silent curse- it had been awhile since. . .

"What does a real looker want with that dump?" Flummoxed, the father and son laughed uneasily. The girl couldn't hear them, but nevertheless. . .

The son took a last glance at the girl, her backpack dragging against non-existent hips, for all the world looking desperately lost; he grimaced and joined his father heading into their well-cared for home.

A group of boys, of disparate ages but similar clothing, smoking and hassling each other, put on a show for two girls sitting on cement steps. The girls paid them no mind; their attention was on the Camaro and the youngest man- the driver, home for the night.

"Hey, you gonna cook or not?" broke into Reilly's reverie. "C'mon, bring our bags," the mother shouted out the door.

Reaching inside the car, Reilly wound up the windows, grabbed the suitcases, and with heavy heart and equally heavy footsteps went inside.

2

Chet, easily amused, put on a tour-guide act. "Now, this is the kitchen," he laughed.

Cracked linoleum floor, cracked counter top, food-splattered range, grease-streaked cabinets, sink full of dishes- some with mold growing atop leftovers.

"Before you get to cleaning up and cooking, your room is the last one down the hall. You got your own bathroom. What do you say about that, little missy?"

'Cleanliness is next to Godliness,' her grandma used to say. Reilly thought she'd landed so far from God that this must be hell. What would happen when she died? If you'd already been to hell was heaven a sure thing? Was this some kind of convoluted logic?

Reilly obsequiously nodded, handed her mother the suitcases and went to drop off her backpack- dreading every step. Long ago she'd adopted a blank, facial expression. It mirrored her numb-struck heart and was the single evidence of the bastions Reilly had built up for her own self-preservation. Her lips, for the most part, had forgotten how to smile. What was there to smile about?

A closet-sized room with a simple cot for a bed, small scarred chest of drawers, a door-less insert bearing twisted, rusty hangers- refused to roll out a mat of welcome. No curtain hid the years of dust and dried bug fluids on the single window; the opening was high enough not to provide much light or a saving breeze. Reilly noted the air conditioning didn't reach the room either.

She stood on the worn bed covers and tried to look out. Impossible. Using her fist she scrubbed, barely clearing enough grime to achieve vision. The trailer backed onto a creek bank, but trash defiled the woods. No surprise, she recognized an inordinate number of Chet's brand of beer in the disparaging litter.

The door's lock was broken. Ditto the bathroom slated for her use. In washing her hands, she discovered no cold water- the faucet, crusted with lime, fitfully sprayed its complaints. It could have been worse- there might have been no hot water. Thank God for small favors, Reilly remembered.

In keeping with the rest of the décor, the bathroom belched filth, too.

No telling the last time the tub had been cleared of layers of grime. The floor, luckily it was tiled, taunted stains from those who'd missed the toilet. That repulsive odor and the prevalent eau de cigarette had Reilly grabbing at her stomach as it revolted anew.

"Down, Downer, Downest," she muttered, and the heck with proper English.

She found a clean towel stuck in the rear of a drawer, mentally composed a list of all she'd have to do before sleeping would be a possibility. The list was familiar, although this time it seemed never-ending.

Soap and a chair ranked high on the list of necessities: soap to clean her personal space- did enough soap exist in this place? A chair to wedge under the door handle of the bathroom and of her bedroom door knob- if she expected to feel any modicum of privacy.

Reilly had never been considered pretty by anyone other than her grandparents and Aunt Sarah. Wiping at the mirror crud, she took a fleeting glance at her heavy, straight blondish hair, dead-pan eyes, cut lip and bony face. No one would bother to give her a second look. But there were desperate, nasty individuals. . . Not pretty is safe, she thought.

Aunt Sarah had pulled her into her arms before her mother drug her away, "If it gets too bad, call me. I'll try to work something out."

Saint Sarah, always doing for others- that's how her mother described her sister. The beauty shop welcomed her back after the funeral. Sarah's clientele clamored for her; they loved her optimism, her listening to their problems, her art with their hair, her work ethic. But Aunt Sarah had two boys of her own- huge handfuls.

Reilly's mother was right. Sarah couldn't feed another without adding more weight upon her shoulders. There was no husband to help her- death in the service. Lawyers were still looking into the whereabouts of his pension.

Hours later, after clearing the sink of a particularly grisly stench amid the filthy dishes, cooking a hamburger hash meal which she couldn't stomach due to the chain-smoking-laden air- even the hamburger tasted of cigarette smoke- Reilly felt near to collapse.

Tapping an unknown source of endurance to keep her on her feet, she continued to straighten the kitchen, did the supper dishes, took out the garbage- tried to stomp it into the can, glanced up and wished on her star.

Wishing and praying- all she had left. Hard to find hope. She wasn't sure why she bothered to keep wishing and praying, but she believed her grandparents must be looking down on her and she didn't want to totally disappoint them. Even though faith was getting terribly difficult.

With the last bit of strength she could muster, she'd tackled the cleanliness of her appointed bath and bedroom. Wedging a chair under her door knob, she fell into bed. Only to spring up in disgust. The entire bed and covers stunk horribly.

Stripping the bed, she threw the offending bed attire outside- except the stench had permeated the stained mattress!

For late fall, it was awfully hot. Not a breeze stirred from the small window. But Reilly put on her school jeans and a long sleeve shirt, and physically and mentally exhausted, she lay on the bed, sweated, and closed her eyes.

In the middle of the night, her smoke-tortured throat begged for a drink of water. Clammy clothes were testament to the amount she'd sweated- her body required fluids.

Gratefully, she eyed the still-burning bedside lamp which she'd placed on the floor.

Reilly never slept in the dark. Monsters reigned in the dark. She shivered, recalling her mother's warnings when Reilly was very young about wolves under the bed and how you must be quiet when you go to bed so you didn't wake them. And if you kept the light on maybe you'd be safe- at least, that's what Reilly grew up believing. The gist of that early admonition still held sway.

She un-wedged the chair, stumbled into the air-conditioned hall and to the kitchen.

The mother and Chet had retired after an evening spent trading laughs and kisses, ignoring the girl and convivially dispatching two 6-packs.

The hall and combination living room/dining area/kitchen were dark. Anchoring her lower lip, Reilly searched for a light switch- feeling along the logical walls. There. Snap!

And just as she expected and feared and dared to hope against, a sundered parade of roaches, blindsided by the light, scurried for the cover and safety of darkness.

Rotten, Revolting, Rut.

In her list of fears, roaches ranked pretty high. The thought of one or more in bed with her. . .

Shuddering, she retrieved a glass, washed it thoroughly with hot water and soap and filling it, she sucked the water down. Three refills.

Rummaging through doors and drawers she searched for. . .

Leaving the kitchen light on, she took her treasure and a glass full of water back to her delegated prison cell.

'In adversity comes strength,' her grandpa, a retired brick layer and avid gardener, had often quoted to her. Adversity. Hmmm. . . Adversity had no concessions for age. I'm 16, and a half, she made sure to add.

Hell, Horror, Hades.

Reilly wrapped the tape, sticky side out, near the ground of each of the bed's legs. She made sure the bed didn't touch any wall. There'd never been any evidence that the sticky side of the tape kept roaches from crawling into bed with her. But, religiously, Reilly had used the tape for years- everywhere except for her grandparents' house. If it wasn't foolproof, at least it gave her a small semblance of security. She had to do something.

Reilly bit at her nails. Not much left to grip with her buck teeth, but even simulating the security measure gave her a moment's peace.

One thing about Reilly- a flicker of hope banked deep inside. She feared to let it loose, but the hope that there was something better to come, for her, lingered like a window-shopper. At times, that flicker was the only thing she had to hold on to. The backpack not withstanding.

I'm 16. And a half. Less than 2 years, she thought. And then her mother would have no hold on her.

Resting her backpack for a pillow, Reilly curled up and silently cried herself to sleep.

3

Same, Silly, School, Reilly thought, disembarking the bus, but she was forced to retract her words. Granted, it was an old, brick building with a plethora of noisy kids jostling to enter before the bell rang. However, instead of the same over-used industrial colors on the walls, this school's paint spoke of an inordinately cheery place- in a school of all places.

Reilly shook her head, surprised to be surprised. She felt the brush of students carelessly elbowing her, but otherwise ignoring her, as they made their way to class.

Despite the blithe, blue walls, it was a sure bet most of the kids hadn't a clue as to their futures. Talk about nursing, electrician, beautician, etc.- that was par for the course, but not set in stone. Or was it possibly different for these students?

Reilly knew absolutely, from an early age, what she would be- the polar opposite of her mother. She'd never known who her father was; the mother never talked about him.

Aunt Sarah, when incessantly prodded, mentioned she believed the most likely candidate for Reilly's father had been killed in a bar room brawl. Probably over the mother, who could bait two guys easier than a cat walking between two chained dogs.

Polar opposite. All she had to do was survive one and a half more years. One and a half years without breaking.

Unlike her mother, who always ran out on bills owed, Reilly believed in paying debts. And she believed in work, also unlike her mother. Reilly would find a way to take care of herself. She'd promised her grandparents and more importantly herself, that she'd never taste alcohol or cigarettes.

The note on the clean kitchen counter indicated which bus Reilly should take to get to the high school. Pick-up time 7:15 at Red Wing Trailer Court sign. No sign of Chet, for which she was grateful.

She fried an egg for breakfast, searched for bread to make a sandwich for lunch. Nothing. The welfare check and food stamps would work out for someone here. Not Reilly. Even though Chet supposedly had a 'great' job.

From experience, she knew her mother would eat steak and ice cream and Reilly, the cook, would suffice with peanut butter, if the mother remembered to buy it at the store.

Only there was no bread. Peanut butter, yes. Bread, no. Reilly did happen across a zip lock sandwich bag, so she pocketed a spoon, after thoroughly washing it, scooped peanut butter with another well-washed spoon into the baggie and headed for the bus stop.

Reilly had enough experience with going to new schools alone. She knew the specifics behind registering and had learned to negotiate new hall routes in record time. Out of school on Tuesday, in a new school on Thursday. Routine. Even to being the middle of a school quarter.

She passed the two men getting into the brilliant, red Camaro. They nodded as she walked by, her hands tucked under her arms, backpack armored on her chest, eyes furtively aware. The car was beautiful and she would have liked to admire it, but not when anyone was looking.

Reilly tried to remain unobtrusive, keeping to the outskirts of the group of boys smoking and shoving each other at the bus stop.

There were three girls absorbed in conversation, but they didn't glance at her. And Reilly posed no threat in her old, hand-me-downs. She followed the gang up the bus steps. The trailer court kids strolled to the back. Reilly took a front seat, watched the bus driver shove it in gear and drive off, impervious to a new student.

"Why didn't your mother call and tell us to expect you?" A harried counselor searched through drawers while giving Reilly the third degree.

Reilly mumbled a safe, "I don't know." Wouldn't due to tell the truth.

"Here's a schedule similar to your old one. I hope you can pick up. . ." The counselor's words died as she stopped and finally attended the quiet, unimpressive girl at her desk. To buy time, she fiddled with loose pens, rustled with papers.

Pale complexion, green-gray eyes, crooked teeth- no, make that crooked buck teeth, much too thin a frame, clothes too big for her body.

"You're staying at. . ." the woman checked the registration form Reilly had filled out. "Oh, Red Wing."

A flit of compassion crossed the counselor's face. "Good luck," she glanced down at the printed name, "Reilly. If you have any questions. . ."

"Thank you," Reilly firmly believed in polite behavior. She accepted the schedule and went in search of her first class.

She was used to adults feeling sorry for her. She'd endured all the kids' snide remarks growing up- bucky beaver, etc. Somehow, welfare didn't pay for dental visits- so her mother claimed. But Reilly continued on, her armor intact as well as her mantra- one and a half years. . .

In algebra class, her neighbor students leaned away from her, crinkling their noses. Reilly blushed, bit the inside of her mouth.

Stupid, Stinking, Smokes. She must not forget to hang her clothes outside tonight. The odor of cigarette smoke permeated everything she wore, including her hair. As always, she endured, mind racing over lists of things to do.

At the bus stop that afternoon, she recognized one of the trailer court boys. Low-hanging pants, tucked in t-shirt, book bag dragging the ground. He elbowed her and asked her name.

Despite her near empty backpack, Reilly clasped a further shield of textbooks to her chest and kept her eyes averted as he leaned into her.

"Reilly," she sighed and stepped away into one of his friends.

"Hey, I'm Reg."

"Name's Tom," the equally-garbed friend offered.

"Whew, you got the perfume on, Babe," Reg smirked.

Reilly frowned up at him, puzzled.

"Smokes- you smoke? Here," he pulled out a pack of cigarettes.

"No, no thanks. My mother does."

"And that Chet smokes a fortune every day. You wanta hang out with us?"

Reilly surreptitiously assessed the two boys. Same age, height. Tom wore a gold bracelet, Reg a leather one. Just kids. No, not just. Reilly had learned to read people fairly quickly- a short lifetime's procession of guys through her mother's door.

These two weren't the most trustworthy. Bold, Brash, Boys.

As the rest of their number joined in, the trash talk began, yet they hadn't ignored her. An excuse came easily to mind.

"Uh, thanks, but I have to make dinner an…and get school supplies. . ."

Bus door opened- saved by the bus.

"Well, OK. Catch ya later," and laughing and harassing each other the boys jumped up the steps. Reilly waited a safe interval and followed. She heard a couple of the boys snicker about her clothes and teeth.

Bad, Bigots, Buttheads.

The mother grumbled about school supply expenditures, like all the times Reilly needed something.

"C'mon then. Chet said there's a Walmart next town over. Let's go."

Reilly stared out the window as her mother drove. Ryan was a small, old-fashioned town. Turn of the century- 1900 or older- brick buildings lined the downtown Main street. An imposing rock courthouse with a gazebo stationed alongside, library, elementary school, high school, diner, florist/gift shop, hardware store and other necessary shops with bright flowers outside immaculate shop fronts gave one a sense of the town's never having lost its heyday. All the buildings were occupied and seemed to be doing good business.

Many of the ornate old structures housed offices. Ryan's Pub announced an Irish Ceali- whatever that was. A double-screen movie theater with its old-time marquee advertising the shows, a jewelry store, beauty shop. . . Reilly didn't catch all of the offerings even though she craned her head as her mother hurried down the main street.

Near the end of town she noted the Camaro parked in front of a mechanics' garage- a revamped two-stall building that originally was an old gas station. Inside the glass front posed the original gas pump with a red flying horse painted on its glass bowl top. The older man was discussing something with a customer outside and the younger one was bent over the open hood of a blue pick-up truck.

Several miles outside town her mother pulled into a gravel lot. Ah, yes, the local watering hole. Ted's Tavern.

Nights spent alone, from the time she was very young while her mother went in search of amusement at the local bars, flashed through Reilly's mind.

Sick, Scared, Sad.

The mother licked her lips. Reilly, glancing at the fastidiously applied made-up face, couldn't figure out why her mother chose the path she had.

The ignition key prepared to shut down the rattling Chevy when Reilly quickly pointed out, "I've got homework and Chet will want dinner."

Spewing gravel, the rattletrap sped out of the parking lot under irate cursing.

Inside Walmart, Reilly received a ten dollar bill.

"Make it count," her mother advised as she headed off to shop in a different direction. Reilly gathered pencils, a cheap pack of pens and tablets and a calculator to replace the one her mother had borrowed and subsequently lost. Over the limit, she prepared her arguments. She'd need them as much as she needed the school supplies.

Her mother's arms were full of candy bars, special facial products and a bright pink sweater.

4

Reilly missed the bus on Friday afternoon. On purpose. The weather happened to be quite an improvement over the bus's clientele. Snickers from the gang in the back of the bus were more than she cared to hear, even though she told herself she was used to such.

If she calculated correctly, and she'd had practice, the dump wasn't more than 8 miles from school. Her shoes were in reasonable shape, contrary to her grumbling stomach. Reilly knew she could handle the distance. At ten years of age hadn't she carted empty pop bottles over two miles, returning them to the nearest store for rebates, and then carried back to her mother a full, heavy carton of pop? Woe betide her if any bottle broke.

Tired, Trips, Tough. Another topic, please, she mused.

At one time, Red Wing Trailer Court must have deserved its pretty name. Maybe the woods in the neglected rear had once sponsored plenty of bird life- red wing black birds. Come spring, she'd find out if any still dared to hang around. If they were still there come spring.

Proceeding down the main street, Reilly fully appreciated the cleanliness of the town of Ryan. Shop owners obviously cared for their buildings. Pristine windows displayed merchandise checked by window shoppers and walkers carried bags of goods. Fall flowers stuck their necks out of planters, waving vibrantly colored heads- mums, leftover petunias and hardy pansies. Reilly was unaware such neighborhoods existed outside old movies.

She skirted passers-by, eyes wary but averted. Nearing the end of one side of the Main Street shopping strip, she spied the scintillating, red Camaro parked outside the mechanic's garage.

A young man swished through the old screen door of the antique garage office- it slammed congenially in his wake- long stride, toolbox in hand. He rounded the jacked-up rear end of the vintage sports car, glimpsed Reilly, head down, backpack clasped to her chest, walking purposefully on the sidewalk. He checked his watch.

"Hey, you miss the bus?"

Reilly stopped, nodded, kept her eyes on the car and avoided his. Out of the corner of her eye, she covertly regarded her neighbor.

Tall, muscular arms and chest- his black t-shirt enhanced his upper body features. Grease streaks stained his jeans. Her chin rose slightly- raven black hair (a year late for a haircut) framed a strong face with beard-shadowed, square jaw.

She allowed herself a straight-on glance at his face and immediately looked away. He was frowning at her.

Hard, Hurting, Handsome- her summary.

She nodded again and resumed her walk. "Nice car," she whispered a compliment, afraid of being heard.

"Thanks," he sent after her. Thoughtfully, carefully, he slid into his pride and joy. Grimly, he wasted a second before starting the ignition. With her haunted look, crooked teeth and thin frame she didn't stand a chance, yet something about her dredged up. . .

Other side of the street. In passing, Reilly noted the library's hours. Reading, and she was a diligent, quick reader, provided another coping mechanism. From the time she could sound out words, Reilly had sought out books to take her on adventures away from her own. As she improved her reading skills, she checked out the thickest books on the library shelves. If someone took the time to write all that, Reilly believed it must be worth her time to endorse the authors' efforts. Eventually, she learned to read the ending first- no use going on a trip if the ending wasn't appealing. After all, she read to get away from nowhere-near-good.

She picked up her pace- had to be back in time to fix dinner and listen to complaints. But a sign on the glass of Dave's Diner compelled her to stop. HELP WANTED

Before move #3, she'd contemplated getting a job, but hadn't worked out all the details- like the arguments she'd need to get her mother to agree.

Musing on the length of walk, the need for better shoes and a rain coat. . .

A bell clapped, like a congratulatory pat on the back, as she opened the door. Sitting at the counter, a man in a suit sipped coffee while studying a casually-clad individual flipping a burger on the grill. The cook decorated a sesame-seed-topped bun from the stainless steel condiment bar, raised a basket of fries from hot oil, gave them a shake, and plated the meal, set it before the counter customer and refilled his coffee cup.

Reilly stood, hesitant, shyly waiting for acknowledgement- if she didn't back out the door first.

The diner room was long and narrow. Six bar stools at the counter, seven booths lined the opposite wall. A large table with eight, brown naugahyde-upholstered chairs matching the booths, graced the rear of the room, newspapers scattered on the table top.

Old, farm advertisements decorated the knotty-pine-paneled walls, along with a cocky, white rooster painting. A woman bustled in from a side room, headed for the restroom door.

"Dave, the meatloaves are in," she called.

"Something I can do for you, Miss?"

Reilly bit the inside of her mouth, anchoring courage, and as if pushed, stepped up to the counter.

"I'd like to see about the job," she left her eyes on the counter top and tilting her head, indicated the sign in the window.

"How old are you? I don't believe I've seen you around before," the cook, a slim man, maybe early 50's with graying hair, wiped his hands on a white towel, rounded the counter and perched on a bar stool, arms crossed.

"I've. . .just moved here," Reilly quietly admitted, trying to keep pluck stoked as her knees began to feel shaky.

Dave, the owner, studied her.

Hamburgers, Hungry. . .

Reilly valiantly forced her knees to still, shored up her backbone. "I can cook, clean. . ."

Dave nodded thoughtfully, "You ever work in a restaurant before?"

"No, sir," Reilly's fingers tightened on her backpack, afraid her stomach would begin to applaud the smell of food. At this moment, for some reason, getting this job had become very important.

"I'm 16. I'm not afraid of hard work. . ." one of the few things she was not afraid of.

"Well, that would certainly be a switch from the kids around here. I have to tell you I'm known as a slave-driver. No unlimited cigarette breaks, no quitting early, no texting or cell phones, no standing around- you got time to lean, you got time to clean."

"Listen to him, Honey. Better yet, don't listen to him. Dave, we do need some help. My name's Martie." A plump, tired-looking but nicely smiling, short, red-haired woman dressed in polyester slacks, sturdy shoes and a turquoise uniform shirt with two hip-side pockets carrying pens and order tablets, with a gold angel pin on the lapel offered her hand.

"Reilly," after drying her sweaty palm on her jeans, she shook Martie's hand.

"When could you start, Reilly? We're closed on Sundays. Open Monday through Friday 6 a.m. to 6 p.m. Saturday 7 to 2. You could work after school- say, 3 to 6 and all day Saturday."

Martie rolled her eyes at Dave, "Honey, she's a teenager and you want her to work 6 days a week?"

"No," Reilly hastily broke in. "That's fine. I'll do it."

"Well, well now," the surprised Dave stumbled over his words.

"You want to come back to the office and fill out some papers? I'll need your parents' OK. Guess you'd like to know about pay?"

Reilly followed Dave into a cluttered, but clean kitchen.

Shelves fully stocked, stainless steel table loaded with cooking utensils and large mixer, an assortment of sizeable pots hanging overhead, a huge, black iron gas range with the biggest iron skillets Reilly had ever seen. At the far wall, a three basin sink and drain board, various gallon dispensers of soaps, towel rack, and more shelves loaded down with stacks of plates and cups. Silverware lodged in separating containers.

To the right, a walk-in refrigerator, and to the left, a tiny office with boxes stacked near the door. Dave sidled in and fiddled with papers in a drawer. Reilly waited, shock-thrilled and quietly congratulating herself. She'd just got a job!

The high of elation slowly began a downward spiral. On the walk home, she'd have to contemplate an arrangement of her best arguments so that she could keep the job and more important- find a way to keep her pay.

"Here, Reilly," Dave handed her paper and pen, pulled a chair up to an ugly, olive green, serviceable steel desk with papers pinned in several stacks next to an adding machine. A large block calendar with myriad notes hung on the wall, a clock above.

"You can use one of those lockers for your stuff."

"Lockers?" Reilly looked up from her writing.

"Yeah," Dave scratched his bare neck. Clean-shaven, dress shirt with collar unbuttoned revealing white t-shirt, khaki Dockers and a speculative smile.

Honest, came readily to mind as Reilly glanced from him to the three, gray, standing lockers.

"You know, put whatever- a change of clothes, purse. . . Somewhere. . . Here we go," he sifted through a bulging basket, pulled out a bag.

"Got a few combination locks here. Take your pick."

Surprised again, Reilly retrieved a brand new, never-used lock; she turned it over and over in her hands as if it were a key to happiness.

"Memorize your combination. Nobody will bother your stuff. You'll mostly be working with Martie and me. We have a lady, Laurie, who helps out with lunch and clean-up."

Dave wondered why a teenage girl, and this poor girl looked like she really needed a job, had such a fascination with a combination lock.

He'd never begin to understand a girl growing up with nothing to keep and call her own- nothing her mother couldn't con or steal away from her and make a buck off of.

5

There's that kid again, the younger mechanic noted, revving his 350 engine as he drew near. At the rate she was moving, it would take her hours to get to the trailer court. He thought about offering her a ride, but his father had called. Mr. Gentry's water pump had died- no water=priority.

The girl seemed to have a different bearing about her, almost a day-dreamy look.

Reilly had her arms crossed. Lost in reverie, she didn't hear the Camaro's hail. She had a job, a locker with a lock, something to look forward to that would happen in just 3 days. How it would help along the one and a half years left!

The mechanic hit the horn twice, waved in passing. Belatedly, Reilly turned and lifted a hand.

Now, the hard part. She rehearsed the debate she'd designed to convince her mother. Reilly hated confrontation, but preparation such as would do a courtroom attorney proud was definitely called for in this situation. One thing she determinedly vouched- absolutely nothing would keep her from working at Dave's Diner.

Suddenly, Reilly began to enjoy the day. Inexperienced in that regard, she tried to listen for different bird calls, list the flowers she knew from working with her grandmother in her garden. Pull pictures out of clouds.

There. Fields on the left. Ryan's Nature Preserve on the right. Breaking the Preserve in half, a gravel road led back to. . .

Reilly paused, thought about walking down the gravel drive a ways. Trespassing was one of those things a good person didn't do. Her grandma and grandpa had always told her she was a good girl. She only hoped she lived up to their expectations.

But it was such a pretty day and there were no NO TRESPASSING signs. At the end of the lane, a small, fairy-tale cottage of stone, besieged by multiple blooms across the front and flanking the sides, beguilingly beckoned. For some reason, the small house made her smile- at least, attempt that unfamiliar expression. It looked so homey, yet kind of lonely, too.

She'd eyed the mailbox before starting down the lane, searching for a name.

Late blooming Clematis, she knew this because her grandma had the same vining flower on her mail box pole, hid any vital information.

But staked next to the mail box, backed by autumn-colored, high grasses, a sign offered a source of information. Garage Sale Saturday 10-4.

Instinctively, Reilly knew what she was doing Saturday- a chance to check out the interior of the lovely cottage had presented itself.

How Reilly loved the thought of having a home as precious as the little house surrounded by happiness in the form of flowers. Maybe, she'd even find some sweaters. Walking to work would require warm gear.

"Mother, look at me," Reilly trembled, she'd never confronted her mother with such dogged determination and a trace of fear ran up her backbone.

Somehow, she dredged up enough tenacity to carry on.

"I'm 16 years old. I want to go to college." This was a slight stretch of the truth; Reilly wasn't certain about the type of continuing education she wanted, or would be able to afford. But the argument for college reinforced her need for a job. "And I need to see a dentist."

"What do you mean, look at you? I look at you all the time," her mother huffed, knowing this was a great stretch of the truth.

The mother confronted her daughter through the backdrop noise of soap operas turned up rather loudly on the TV. Chet hadn't returned from work and she was left alone to trudge through a scene similar to ones she watched all the time. But the irony was completely lost on her.

Thank God this guy has a job, Reilly mentally quipped. Maybe he was one of those binge drinkers- only imbibed on weekends. No, that wasn't right- they'd arrived on Wednesday. She guessed he must save the beer for after work; certain sure, he'd not be allowed drunk on the job, would he?

"I need to have money to get my teeth fixed, to save for my future," Reilly pursued the topic like a dog scenting a pork chop.

The mother frowned. Who was this gawky girl she'd brought into the world? Reilly had always been the quiet, do-as-your-told kid. Not this thin faced, unprepossessing girl standing up to her over a job.

The mother's daughter should be pretty like her mother, shouldn't she? She licked her lips buying time.

"I'll be able to buy my own supplies. I'll eat at the diner. . ."

"You can kick in money for the rent," the mother put her foot down.

In answer, the daughter metaphorically stomped her own foot, only much more vociferously.

"The welfare takes care of my share of the rent," Reilly shot back, adamantly- shocking herself. She turned away from her mother, shaken, trembling. Head swimming. Stomach. . .

"I've got to fix supper," she fumbled with utensils, but her gut directed her to the bathroom. And hurry!

Housekeeping and meal preparation were standard Reilly chores. Unlike most kids her age, Reilly retained a work ethic that hearkened back to the proverbial roots of America. For that, she was glad she'd never had a choice. She breathed a sigh of relief when her mother silently returned to her soap opera. Probably, her mother hoped to stave off any more retching- after all, supper needed to be fixed.

"That girl, always walking," the younger mechanic mused to his father while driving home Saturday after a half-days work at the garage.

"Son, if I were her and walking kept me out of Red Wing and Chet's trailer, I'd walk all day," his father grimly replied.

"Yeah, I guess you're right about that."

3 p.m. Unfamiliar hopes bubbling within, Reilly finally trotted down the gravel lane to the scenic cottage. Her mother had insisted on adding several unnecessary chores, seeing as how Reilly wouldn't be available much after Sunday.

The girl crossed her fingers. Not much left on the tables at the sale. A few knick-knacks, a box of novels, left-over unwanted clothes- outdated, well worn.

An overdressed-for-the-occasion, attractive woman minded what remained of the yard sale goods. Reilly eyed the sales' items with dismay. Nothing useful for her needs.

Her attention turned longingly to the house. A storm door couldn't hide the Kelly-green door with its huge brass knocker- a roaring lion's head. A bay window decorated with flowers inside and out, becomingly stretched to the right of the door and was framed with Kelly-green shutters- the old wooden kind that actually folded shut.   The window on the left was similarly embraced.

"Not much left," the woman broke into Reilly's fascinated study of the house.

Reilly longed to bury her nose in the man's hand-sized, yellow roses gracing the cottage's stone walls.

"You wouldn't happen to have any sweaters, would you?" Reilly dared- no harm in asking.

'Saints be praised!' a lilting voice rang in Reilly's head.

The girl swung about, searching for the source of the jubilant exclamation.

"Did you say something? Uh, about. . .saints?" The puzzled Reilly turned to the woman.

"No," the lady replied putting her hands together, index fingers to her lips.

Reilly wrote off the exclamation as imagination, or lack of lunch.

"This may sound silly, but please, tell me your name," the woman gave Reilly a strange look.

Reilly paused, wondering at the strange request, "Reilly."

The woman gasped, stumbled as if shocked.

"Uh. . . Ummm. . . Wait right here, please." And she quickly entered the cottage; Reilly so longed to follow her.

The lady exited the front door bearing a sizeable cardboard box, set it on the table. Heather, lavender and moss-green colors- sweaters. Heavily patterned, wool sweaters. And on the topmost one, a piece of paper pinned with *Reilly* written in large, fanciful script.

Now it was Reilly's turn to quiver in amazement. "What?" She was afraid to touch the contents as she waited, hoping for an explanation to the mystery. But the lady only shrugged her shoulders.

What kind of an adventure had Reilly unwittingly stepped into?

She finally allowed her hands to investigate the soft, wool sweaters and finger the crisp white paper with her name written in the calligraphy style of long ago.

"My. . ." the woman paused, swallowed, continued. "My great, great Aunt Bridie passed on recently. She was 117 years old. A remarkable woman. She had all of her smarts, lived alone until the day she. . .died.

Aunt Bridie was a local legend known as a wise, sometimes crotchety, healer, gardener, advisor. . . She never lacked for giving advice, but only when it was asked for."

"I remember when I was a small child I was very sickly. Doctors hadn't a clue as to what my problem was- only that if I didn't improve in a certain period of time. . .

Well, they didn't hold out much hope for me. My parents, as a last resort, brought me to Aunt Bridie. At her request, they left me in her care."

The woman's eyes misted as she reminisced the events of her early years. Enrapt in the story, Reilly desperately longed for some clue as to her name pinned on the topmost sweater. No one could possibly have known. . .

"Aunt Bridie had all the facial expressions. I believe she could stop a General in his tracks with one of her looks- certainly with one of her commands. But she had the kindness of a saint, too.

She'd make up these teas for me, laced with honey so they tasted good- all herbs she picked out of her garden."

The woman indicated a section to the side of the house- an area that received sunshine all day. Strategically placed rocks and white, picket fence, separated various plants, and brass hangers, like miniature flag poles, were staked everywhere. Tiny nameplates tinkled from them with the slightest of breezes.

"She played cards with me; we worked puzzles together. One night I asked her if…if I were going to die, like the doctors said. Do you know what she told me?" The woman smiled through a trickle of tears.

"'Now, just what would the good Lord be wantin' with a mite of a girl like you? Saints be praised if I've not been entrusted to tell you that heaven's not ready for the likes of you, right yet.' I'll never forget that. . .her sweet nature and healing ways. And here I am today."

"You were close to her, then?" Reilly didn't want the story to end- sure there were many more highlights.

"We moved away. Once I'd grown, I'd visit now and then, kept in regular contact by phone. . .

Anyway, getting back to this note- Aunt Bridie had all of her arrangements made as if she knew to the day when she was slated to join the angels.

Her shelves were bare of food except for cans of cat food. . . That reminds me, there's a kitten around here, somewhere- a gold kitten with a white bib and white paws. Righteous, she named it."

The woman looked around as if saying the name would induce the kitten to put in an appearance.

'Ask to see my house,' a clear command in that sing-song, lilting voice sang in Reilly's head.

"Did you hear that?" Reilly's head swung right and left.

"Hear what, dear?" The woman eyed Reilly, curiously.

"I. . .uh. . .nothing. Is it possible to see inside the house?"

"Well, I don't know. . ." the woman hesitated.

"It's just that it looks so much like. . .a home," Reilly whispered, wanting very much to cadge a glimpse inside.

'Good girl!' the voice rang supportively.

For some reason, Reilly felt an unfamiliar tug at her lips- a smile, and for her, that was extremely rare.

Her crooked, buck teeth were not attractive and closed mouth smiles were difficult. But, something about being here. . .

This house, this home. . .the great aunt had loved her picturesque home. It was plain to see the love invested in every aspect of cottage and surrounds. Maybe it was a magical place. Maybe Bridie's ghost didn't want to leave, and hoped someone else might like, love the cottage, as she had.

"What will happen to the cottage?" Reilly asked as the woman beckoned her inside.

Stopping, tilting her head, the woman said something very strange. "Aunt Bridie put the house in trust for 2 years. The lawyer has all the details. Even I'm not privy to all of Aunt's arrangements."

She gave Reilly a quick tour of the home. A sitting room with fireplace and rich paneling in the bay window room. The shelf of the bay window was rife with plants, flowering and vining up and around the glass. A heavy drape hung tied back at the side.

"Aunt Bridie only drew the drape on the coldest of nights- after re-situating the plants. She always said light and plants were better for people than blinds and curtains."

An antique couch with high rounded sides and ornately, carved ball and claw feet rested opposite the bay window. It was upholstered in shades of olive green foliage with red blooms against a cream background.

"A beautiful couch," Reilly admired.

"Hmm. . ." the woman didn't quite agree.

"Aunt Bridie, not to frighten you, but you have to be wondering, also had the reputation of being, well, a witch. Not a bad one, mind you," the woman hastily clarified.

"But, she knew things, had the second sight, a fey woman of the old country. Aunt Bridie came over from Ireland when she was a young girl," the woman continued, "Pursuing a job opportunity."

Reilly nodded thoughtfully. She felt not an iota of fear, another rarity for Reilly. She followed her tour guide up a staircase in the entry and into a light and plant-filled bedroom. A brass bed's headboard set so that the dawning sun would awaken its tenant.

"I like her taste in furniture," Reilly stated.

'Of course, you do, Sweetlin',' the voice unexpectedly zinged from nowhere. But Reilly didn't jump, or look around this time.

I'm hearing Aunt Bridie's ghost, she marveled. Wow! Intrigued and surprisingly at ease- more curious than the proverbial cat, Reilly hated to leave.

A quick peek in the kitchen. More plants vining around the windows. There was an indication of a root cellar, and a work room with jars of dried herbs and an interesting piece of furniture with numerous drawers, and heavy books lined up restfully on shelves.

"Who will take care of the plants?" Reilly wondered aloud.

"Would you happen to be needing a part-time job?" The woman ushered Reilly outside. "At the most, probably an hour, maybe once a week. . ."

Reilly blushed and her heart fluttered. More than anything she had ever wanted, she wished for a continued acquaintance with the cottage.

"I could do it."

A deal was struck. The woman told Reilly where she'd find a key and to please not take the key with her, but replace it in its hiding place.

"Per Aunt Bridie's orders," the woman finished.

Reilly helped her close up the sale. The leftovers, which Reilly declined, were put in the woman's SUV to be donated to a free store.

"The lawyer will want your address to send your check."

"Thank you. Uh, maybe he could just send the money here." Reilly sincerely expressed her gratitude, picked up her box of sweaters and headed back to the dump, as she derogatively referred to Chet's trailer.

Every life should have a bit of serendipity. Reilly was long overdue.

6

Recriminations from the mother as Reilly entered the dump, box in hand. Not unexpected.

Non-agreeable, non-supportive, non-motherly, Reilly cheated as she staunchly bit the inside of her lip to maintain a semblance of balance. Would that the mother might do the same Reilly mused, despairingly.

"What do you want with those ugly, old clothes?" The mother turned up her nose; her cigarette dangled from long, red-coated fingernails, loaded ash, ready for free-fall. No matter- the clean-up crew had arrived.

Reilly looked down at what she was wearing, gathering thoughts. Did her mother miss something? Old clothes were Reilly's lot in life- always had been since the passing of her grandparents. Chet laughed, derisively, in passing.

"I'll need something warm to wear to walk to work, unless you're going to drive me?" Reilly amazed herself with her new-found backbone- where had it come from? Was it presaged by acquiring a job and a mystery box? Hastily, she withdrew to her room.

'Long time comin', Dearie,' a lilting chuckle rang in the girl's head.

"Oh, my gosh!" Reilly almost dropped the box. The voice- it was still with her! Could ghosts travel wherever they wanted? Why would a ghost bother with her? Reilly knew nothing of the paranormal.

And most astonishing to her chicken-little self- she was not afraid of the prospect.

The other side had to have something to recommend it- her grandparents were there and they were the best people she'd ever known.

Biting her lip to stave off the 'something' burgeoning in her chest, she gently placed the box on her excuse-for-a-bed. Investigating the contents would have to wait until after she fixed supper. Would the ghost wait? Reilly certainly hoped so.

Chet and the mother had Reilly hopping with inane requests- more butter, another spoon- larger one, refills, ad nauseum. It was late before she finally escaped to her room.

As bare of anything remotely resembling pretty or happy as the small space was, it did provide a sort of sanctuary. This night, the adults were going out- good riddance. Reilly wished they would take the other denizens of the dump with them- namely the roaches.

She unpinned her name from the top sweater which had lovely, muted colors and was heavy with a tree-like pattern. Under it, neatly folded, was another deep green, thick wool sweater with intertwined circles running the length of the sleeves.

Reilly admired the workmanship, wondered if Bridie had knitted them. Below the green sweater was a cape- a long, heavy wool cape with a hood and deep pockets. The cape had shades of lavender, gray and light blue threads running through it and black braid borders and loops for closure. If not exactly waterproof, being wool it would, even when wet, keep her warm.

At the bottom of the box were four cans of cat food.

"How odd," Reilly thought aloud. She remembered the kitten- where could the creature be? Poor thing, all alone. . . A tiny, amused laugh rang in Reilly's head. It sounded so very real, the girl barely staunched the impulse to look around.

She set the cans of cat food on the scarred dresser, refolded the sweaters. In handling the cape, she heard a crinkle in one of the pockets, the other felt slightly bulky.

Pulling out the crinkly content, she discovered an envelope with her name in the same beautiful script as the note pinned on her new sweater. She fingered the ornate calligraphy- the kind of writing you found on old letters when penmanship was an art and letter writing constituted the main means of communication.

Reilly's response wasn't to curl up in bed and pretend her life was normal or cadge onto a dream of wonderland, as she usually resorted to in the evenings. Instead, a thrill of anticipation fluttered in her gut- and this feeling did not send her running for the bathroom. The cottage had brought a bit of whimsy into her erstwhile, cold, despondent life.

Carefully, as if handling a precious breakable, she unfolded the letter.

Dearest Reilly,

Please do not be alarmed at this letter or the box of sweaters or my voice or any other inexplicable happenings. I've known of you for quite some time before my time to go. We are kindred spirits. I knew you would like my home and plants. I knew you would care for them. I'm sorry we never had the chance to meet physically. But, I can talk to you, if you wish, and if you are brave and really want me to, I may appear to you. I think. I'm working on this possibility. You may call me anytime. Don't be concerned if I can't come right away. This is a new prospect for me and untried. I will always answer you vocally. I know your life is difficult. I will help you. You don't have to feel alone ever again. Remember, you can always call me. Please do. I look forward to your friendship.

> *Bridie O'Connair*
> *P.S. Righteous needs a friend*

By the time Reilly finished the letter for the third time, goose-bumps had risen over her entire body. Trickles of tears ran down her cheeks and basted her lips, dripping lower.

Is it possible? I'm to have a real, change the word real, no don't change it- friend? She wiped at her eyes, her wet lips quivered. A friend is a friend- ghost or not.

Gently, Reilly re-folded the letter. She reached for and hugged the tree-patterned sweater.

'It's called the tree-of-life pattern. An Aran Island sweater. If you like I'll tell you more,' the lilting voice chimed.

"Bridie?"

'Yes, Sweetlin'?'

"Thank you for your offer of friendship," Reilly's eyes swept the tiny room, half-expecting to see. . .something.

'You're welcome, Reilly. There is another gift for you in the other pocket. I'll explain them to you later. Get some rest. I have a project for you tomorrow. Good night, Sweetlin'.'

Reilly got ready for bed, wondering how she'd be able to sleep with all the questions beleaguering her brain, the excitement of. . .befriending a. . .ghost. Oh, my gosh! A real, live, talking ghost! It didn't concern her that, technically, the live part was a little over-descriptive.

As she pulled the covers aside, she heard a faint "meow". Standing on the bed, with great effort she hoisted the window open as wide as possible, peered out.

"Meowwww," a little louder and more insistent, drawn out, repeated- "Meeeowwwwwwwwwww".

She looked up, nothing in the tree branches. Glancing down, a wild rosebush twined in a honeysuckle bush besieged her window- valiantly seeking ingress.

"Here kitty, kitty, kitty," Reilly called. For answer she received a pitiful cry.

Reilly raced to the kitchen, grabbed a broom, hurried back to her room. Earlier she'd left all the lights on so she didn't suffer the panicked possibility of squishing any creepy-crawlies.

Using the broom head, she thrust the brush from the window. There at the base, sitting on its roots, sat a gold kitten, plaintively meowing, eyes pitifully beseeching.

She decided the best way to help the kitten would be to go outside- something she never did at night when she was alone. For some reason, the thought of walking home from work at night hadn't yet assailed her thought processes.

But the kitten needed her. Buckling on courage, or a reasonable facsimile of such, Reilly ran outside, around the dump, skidded on a flattened beer can, went sailing for a few feet; regaining her balance, taking a deep breath so as not to scare the kitten as much as to calm herself, she slowed to a walk.

Kneeling near the base of the bush, she ducked under the thorny rose branches, felt her hair catch. The kitten gratefully accepted her proffered hands, licked at her fingers, stepped into her palms and began to purr.

"Righteous?" Reilly asked.

"Rrrrow," the kitten replied and upped the velocity of its purring.

Unmindful of anything but the tiny bundle in her arms, Reilly skirted the edge of the dump and made her way back to her room.

She settled the little creature on her bed. Sun-gold fur, white bib, four white paws— the kitten fit the description and answered to its name.

"Meeeeoooow," the little puss with overwhelmingly large green eyes looked up at her, expectantly.

"I bet you're hungry. You stay here," Reilly patted the bed and retraced her steps to the kitchen. A few brave bugs withstood the light to search for snacks on the kitchen counter which she'd left immaculate— probably take a while for them to discover they weren't in Kansas anymore. Reilly swept them into the garbage disposal with a discarded envelope and flipped a switch. Revulsion vied with fear. Why did the dark bring on terrors?

Greedy, Gross, Grubbers. Reilly briefly speculated that the last word probably wasn't correct— as in listed in an accepted English dictionary— while she searched for a small, suitable bowl for water and a saucer for cat food.

In turning, she nearly stepped on Righteous who'd stealthily followed her.

"I see you're not one to follow orders, are you?"

The kitten pattered about, jumping, crouching, crab-scuttling, busy swatting a sizeable bug that skittered like a tiny hockey puck on ice. Locating a newspaper, Reilly rolled it up and dispatched Righteous' toy.

The kitten winked at her and voiced an opinion.

"Come and eat," Reilly bestowed a smile on the kitten, as tail flagged high, the scampering feline led the way.

As if starving, Righteous cleaned her plate, lapped a sip of water, hopped to Reilly's bed, curled up inside the curve of her arms and purred both of them to sleep.

Litter box— Reilly's last thought.

'Don't worry, Dearest, Righteous is house-broke. Leave the window open. Tomorrow, you can adjust her exit.'

7

Reilly woke to an Irish tune humming in her brain.

"Bridie?" she whispered. Righteous stretched, head into her armpit and tail-end high, licked the girl's face, hopped to the window and sidled out.

'To quote Hollywood, a top of the mornin' to you, Dearie,' Bridie's lilting, extravagantly cheerful voice greeted her. Reilly saw no reason not to address a ghost as you would a. . .well, a more alive person.

"Good morning, Bridie."

'You'll have to be careful not to talk aloud to me in public. Life can be difficult enough without others thinkin' you're not the full shilling. Up! Up!' The ghostly voice urged overenthusiastically.

Reilly tossed aside her blanket, feet took to the floor; she hurriedly dressed, excitedly anticipatory. Bridie had mentioned a task. . .

'While you live in this sorry excuse for a pig sty-meanin' no disrespect to 4-legged pigs, you'll feel better if the pig sty, excuse me, trailer, doesn't look so tatterdemalion.'

"You want me to pick up the garbage outside?" Reilly's face fell at the enormity of that senseless task.

'Tidy up as best you can. Hurry, the other part of today's assignment, should you choose to accept,' Bridie cackled, 'excuse me, Sweetlin', I was remembering a show called MISSION IMPOSSIBLE. Seemed appropriate.'

'We'll, er, you'll go to the creek-side out back and tidy that spot, too. It will get you away from the poison inside here.' Bridie made ghostly, gagging sounds over the cigarette-saturated air. Who knew ghosts could smell?

"Well, I'll be damned!"

"What's up, Dad?"

"Will you look at this?" The young mechanic joined his father out the back door of their home, looking toward the worst half of Red Wing Trailer Court.

Reilly had just finished picking up the trash, mostly beer cans haphazardly tossed about the dump's yard and overflowing from the garbage can. Recyclables had been relegated to separate bags.

She'd torn the weeds from the trailer's siding and scrubbed the moldy sides. Now, she perched precariously on an overturned bucket, trying to replace a piece of trim which had lost its moorings. Shaking her head, she gave up in frustration.

Father and son watched in amazement as she cocked her head, eyeing her accomplishments.

"That is one industrious child," the father touted, "as my grandfather would have said."

"Yeah, and how long do you think it'll stay that way," the son shot back. For some reason, he felt himself getting seriously irritated.

"Sometimes a great notion," the father rejoined, recalling a book he'd especially enjoyed by Ken Kesey.

"That about sums it up," the son replied. He'd read the book, too.

Reilly emerged from the dump, sandwich in hand, a thermos full of water and a box of garbage bags under her arm. She headed around the trailer to the creek bank.

If Dave considered himself a slave-driver, he'd certainly appreciate Bridie, Reilly thought. The ghost had remained pretty much incommunicado while the girl worked. A simple 'good girl' cheerily sufficed to encourage here and there.

"Now what is she up to?" The son swore under his breath, aggravated at himself for feeling. . .aggravated.

"Son, why don't you do that little girl a favor and go introduce yourself? Maybe help out? It would be nice for her to know somebody decent lives here. It'll answer those questions that keep you staring out the window and gritting your teeth."

"What do you think you're doing?" An exasperated, but sharp question startled Reilly, who'd crawled under an enormous honeysuckle bush to retrieve beer cans, glass and paper.

Righteous lounged, sphinx-like, on a tree limb, batting at late season, flying insects and provided back-up to Bridie's inspiriting impromptu calls.

"A Sisyphean task," Reilly grunted, crawling out, dragging a half-full, garbage sack with her.

"Hmmm, Sisyphean. Don't see any rock-balls or mountains, unless you're counting the creek bank?"

"Haven't got there, yet," Reilly averted her eyes from her interrogator. What was he doing back here?

She sought the easiest route of escape- prepared, just in case. After all, she didn't know this guy. A beautiful car didn't guarantee a beautiful owner. Handsome, maybe, but not necessarily beautiful in the trustworthy sense.

Leery, Lone. . .

"I bet you didn't think I knew who Sisyphus was," the young man broke into Reilly's unease with a challenge.

At a loss, Reilly flushed under his scrutiny, stood there tongue-tied, feeling stupid, but oddly mindful of her dirty clothes and sweaty face.

"Better be careful not to cut yourself. Don't want to die of tetanus from this worthless sh…job you've saddled yourself with." Poor kid. Sweating, wearing the filth of. . . Just standing there with a. . . Something about her. . .reminded him of. . .

A flash of pain stabbed through his head- one hand flew to his temple.

"Are…are y…you alright?" Reilly looked up, curious about the sudden silence.

A calloused hand rubbed his head without alleviating. . ., "Yeah."

He would be nice looking if he smiled, Reilly thought.

'Wouldn't he?' Bridie quipped.

Reilly blushed and dropped her eyes. Bridie was certainly a trip, and how had she read her mind?

"My name's Trinity O'Ryan. What's yours?" The mechanic agreed with his dad's suggestion.

This kid could use a friend- not that he was going to help pick up papers and sh…stuff.

"Reilly Brooke," she whispered, resting the can and glass engorged bag against shaky knees, surreptitiously studying Trinity.

Why had he bothered to come back here and talk to her?

'Never you mind that. Ask him about his name,' Bridie steered a course of action.

Reilly bit the inside of her lip to keep from responding to Bridie's voice. That would really make her look like an idiot.

"Uh, Trinity. Th…that's an interesting name," Reilly managed.

Pain gone in an instant, Trinity couldn't completely stifle a grin. A glint of amusement fired his dark blue eyes, enlivening his entire face.

Tanned, Trim, Trust-worthy, slid through Reilly's head. If the first thoughts a person had concerning another came from intuition, why was she so disconcerted? Why should he make her feel uncomfortable? Bridie seemed to know him- he must have some honest qualities. . .

Filthy hands caused her to drop her eyes, take in her appearance. . . Well, just look at me, she felt like crying.

"My dad's favorite western had this carefree gun-slinger in it- a superfast draw- the cowboy's name was Trinity. Sometimes he pops the old movie in and. . ."

Trinity broke off, thumbs hitched in jeans riding low on his hips. Now, why was he sharing this information?

"You shouldn't be here, it's not safe," he scrutinized the wooded creek-side, misused by the trailer court's partiers- when the weather complied.

"Are you g…going to h…hurt me?" Reilly stuttered. A creepy feeling began to override her initial intuition.

"Nah, you're not my type," the hardness returned with shuttered eyes.

Reilly had seen more than her fair share of this type of attitude, from both drunk and sober men. Type. . . She guessed her looks, indeed, endorsed an iota of safety- she should be grateful, right? Who would want her? Crossing her arms, she donned her shield, strangely unrelieved, and hurting.

What an ass! Trinity could have kicked himself. Here he'd come out to introduce himself and make friends, sort of, and now he seemed to have insulted the poor kid- she had no idea of his true meaning, his past. . .

"I didn't mean that. . .like it sounded," he rushed to fill the void and put her at ease.

Reilly hitched her shoulders. Familiar terrain.

"It's not safe in there, either," she murmured, indicating the dump behind her.

"Welcome to the club, kid." An idea occurred to him that brought out the 'protective hero' ingrained within. As. . . Oh, God. . . She used to call him. . .

His jaw clenched in a flare of anger and remembrance.

"Chet bothering you?" Trinity walked right up to the girl, so fast she hadn't seen it coming. Couldn't run. Despite registering her unease, he let his forefinger raise her elfin chin, so he could gauge her eyes, which tried every-which-away to duck his.

It took a flustered moment, what with Trinity terribly close, for Reilly to glean just what he asked.

"N...no," she fiercely stammered, face flaming, mortified.

Trinity's eyes held hers for furious seconds- a lifetime to the girl in which she simply wished to. . .disappear.

"If he ever looks at you cock-eyed, you come and tell me. Do you hear? Promise?"

"O...OK," Reilly didn't believe she'd ever been this embarrassed.

Trinity let go of her chin and retreated, his drooping pants caught under his shoes, but he quickly reestablished control, and harnessed his 'hero' instincts.

"It would be pretty out here if people took care of it," he attempted a neutral topic.

"C...can I ask you something? I m...mean you w...won't take offense?"

After what he'd inadvertently implied about her looks, and Chet, how could he take offense? "Ask away."

"Why do you wear your pants like that? I mean, if you had to run (a possibility that relentlessly preyed on Reilly) you wouldn't be able to. Your feet. . .they'd catch up in your pants and cause a fall." It had almost, disgracefully, happened.

Reilly flushed anew at her impertinence, but she'd always wondered about this strange male fashion, pants lower than user-friendliness or propriety smiled on- underwear showing, really?

Trinity grinned in relief, for a whole three seconds.

"My dad asks the same thing. I don't have to run. You've not been here long enough to know, but I'm the top of the food chain around here."

He could be cocky, too, Reilly thought. Didn't suit him.

"There's always someone higher," Reilly spoke from watchful experience.

"Kid, you think too much," he replied, on a knife's edge between amusement and renewed aggravation.

"My thoughts are the only things that are all mine," she bit her lip at this personal admission, and desperately searched for more cans to pick up.

Too much like. . . Trinity's jaw turned to stone; he felt a resurgence of discomfort in his head, and this time it gripped his chest in a vise, too.

"There you are," a pretty blonde skipped to Trinity's side, blithely avoiding trash; she gave a condescending nod to Reilly, which Trinity missed, and proprietarily hung onto his elbow.

Without looking at the girl clinging to his arm, Trinity said, "I guess I'll see you around. Bye."

Oddly enough, he felt as if he'd just as soon stick around here- as if he were deserting. . .

Shrugging off the uncharacteristic discomposure, he half-wished Erika hadn't shown up, but he'd make time somewhere to get to know more. . . Why? Because the poor kid could stand a friend, came to mind. His sister. . . She'd expect it of him.

"Thank you," Reilly spoke to his departure.

Frowning, Trinity stopped dead, about-faced, "For what?"

"For being kind," Reilly replied, sincerely.

And that really stumped him, set him back, remembering. . .

Reilly and Righteous were readying for bed, the girl hitching a chair under the door knob and the kitten bathing her paws and face, belly and tail.

"Good night, Bridie," the exhausted girl offered, thinking of tomorrow, school and her first day of work at the Diner.

'One more thing, Sweetlin'.'

"Bridie, anyone ever tell you you're a slave-driver?"

Bridie giggled, girlishly, 'Stand in front of a mirror and practice a smile.'

Reilly's eyes betrayed horror.

'Now Dearie, that's not a smile- try again,' the ghostly voice ordered.

"Why?"

'Warm responds to warm, but someone must start the fire,' Bridie enigmatically stated, watched the girl fret her lower lip, and the wise woman proceeded to clarify.

'Because as your friend and advisor, I'm here to tell you a smile in your line of work will earn you more money. Tips, Dearest. The big tippers like happy faces, not shrinking violets. And I've got something else up me sleeve. C'mon now.'

Just why Reilly thought her new job only involved cleaning and cooking, she couldn't say. Waiting on people. . . She did it at home. . .

With the greatest reluctance, Reilly stretched a smile, tried to keep a closed mouth, hide her teeth.

'It's OK, Sweetlin'. It's only for a little while longer,' Bridie's voice soothingly swathed her bony shoulders.

To appease her new friend, Reilly gave it her best shot. Bridie squealed her approval which seemed to come from above Reilly's head.

In optimistically glancing up, she caught a transparent image of a tiny, elf-like woman with a beaming smile, dancing a jig in the corner of her ceiling. The dancing leprechaun wore a greenish sweater, long skirt and muck boots- muckers. And she giggled, hummed and cavorted all at the same time.

"Bridie?" Righteous meowed and vaulted up as if her old friend might catch her- Reilly provided her own arms as a failsafe for the ambitious kitten. With a purring song ringing in her ears- Righteous wreathing her neck, Reilly stood immobile, amazed and awed, teary, and grateful-incredulous emotions surging together, wakened after lying in rust-bound trunks, waiting. And the most startling of all, for some inexplicable reason, no fear accompanied the ghost's appearance to her.

'Will you just look at me, Sweetlin'? Saints be praised if I'm not half-bad as a ghost! What d'ye think, lass?'

"I think you're a sight for tired eyes. Beautiful," Reilly was suddenly wide awake. She could see. . .a ghost! Her new friend seemed more alive, now. A thought occurred to her.

"C...can others see you?" Reilly had to restrain her hands from reaching up to touch her. Could she receive a hug? How long it had been since anyone had touched her as if they cared!

Bridie seemed to mull this over. 'I'm here for you, Dearie, so I'd have to say. . .maybe not. Take a true sensitive to actually see a ghost, let alone talk to one. Righteous, my dear little one, sees me.'

The kitten attempted to stand up on Reilly's shoulders and offer a paw; Reilly helped balance the trilling endeavor.

Bridie's hand reached toward the white paw, 'Righteous, my dearest, you take care of our mutual friend.'

The kitten's paw pawed through Bridie's twiddling fingers- a handshake of agreement.

Exhaustion re-seeped in to claim Reilly and she couldn't fight it. Her last question wasn't voiced as her eyes closed- her head resting on the pillow, Righteous lovingly cradled in her arms. Why hadn't her grandparents come to her? As ghosts?

The spell of an Irish lullaby serenaded Reilly's sleep as Bridie figured out how to get off the ceiling and sit/hover by the bed, her see-through hand resting atop the girl's, and moving to affectionately caress the kitten's head.

'Ah, Sweetlin', tis a grand colleen y'are. I'd've been proud to have you for me daughter,' the ghost fondly reflected.

8

"Don't try to take it all in at once, Honey," Martie mistook Reilly's bemused look. "You'll catch on."

Reilly had completed her tour: learning where the condiments were so as to fill the sugar, salt and pepper dispensers on each table, how to funnel catsup into every catsup bottle, how to make coffee and have filters filled and ready ahead of time, where the dish towels hid out, how to use the 3-basin sink with its quaternary disinfectant rinse, keep the ice flowing, where the bathroom supplies were kept, how to stack the coffee cups, saucers and plates, roll the silverware into napkins, fill the creamers from the milk dispenser, and take the plated orders as they came up to the proper customers.

"Most folks are here pert near every day. They know the routine. If you get stuck, they can answer questions as well as Dave or me."

Reilly politely nodded- hoping she would pass muster; she placed an order pad and pen in her pocket. Martie had pulled out a week's worth of uniform shirts- ones she'd outgrown and others left behind by previous waitresses, and relegated them to the new help.

The older woman made sure to give Reilly only the ones she thought might compliment her fair coloring. She'd also provided Reilly with pretty ribbons to tie up her long hair.

"Abbreviations for the orders come in handy. Find something that works for you that Dave understands, else he'll be hollering over at you to interpret. As an example, OE for over easy eggs, got it?"

"Dinner crowd begins early, around 4:00. It starts kinda slow. If you watch me a table or two, I'll bet you can take over. We split tips, 'cause dishes and clean-up are shared. Don't let anybody give you a hard time!" Martie winked, "I don't. Establish your rights, Honey. Questions?"

"Not right now," Reilly fingered the order pad in her pocket, not relishing the idea of waiting on strangers, not daring to believe she might do this without making disastrous mistakes.

"Will I be cooking, too?"

Martie plumped down on a stool, "You really can cook?"

"Yes, ever since I could reach a stove standing on a chair," Reilly averred.

"Well, not right away. Say, have you eaten?" Grimly, Reilly shook her head- there hadn't been anything to spoon into a baggie or put on bread for her lunch. An air sandwich didn't go very far. Grocery shopping had never been high on the mother's list of things to do. Why should it, when eating out was easier? No trouble sweet-talking some male into buying her a dinner. . . Her mother never seemed to eat breakfast. Who knew what Chet did for breakfast or lunch- who cared? And with Reilly now conveniently absent at dinner time. . .

"Then, what would you like? Get you shored up and ready," Martie indicated the blackboard specials and handed Reilly a paper menu.

The new waitress devoured a lunch special. Monday's offerings were sauerkraut and metts, mashed potatoes, green beans and choice of salad. She hadn't had a meal that didn't reek of cigarette smoke since they'd arrived at the dump- her stomach was most grateful.

"Thank you, Dave," Reilly stacked her dishes in a convenient bus pan and washed her hands.

"Seems like a nice girl," Martie poured a cup of coffee for herself and her husband.

"Time'll tell," he cautiously replied. Too many girls had come and gone for Dave to get enthusiastic about the latest try-out. Though, intuition kicking in, he secretly held out special hope for this girl.

Reilly hovered at Martie's elbow as she took an older couple's order: grilled ham and cheese, French fries, cole slaw and a plate special- house dressing on the salad and rye bread.

She followed Martie as the orders were clipped to the board above the grill and Dave attended to business. Martie let Reilly dress the salad, dish out the cole slaw and take them to the table along with drinks and the bread.

Remembering Bridie's warning about smiling, Reilly tried one on for size, but felt too self-conscious to pull it off. Her frozen facial muscles were not amused, so she ducked her head all she could and intently studied her order pad.

"You're new here," the man grunted.

"Y…yes," Reilly assented.

"Hmm. . . Wonder how long you'll last," he un-wrapped his silverware; his wife sweetly berated him and kindly smiled and thanked Reilly. He muttered a 'good luck' to her and attacked his salad.

Not knowing how to respond, Reilly simply turned, checked for something else to do.

The old cowbell at the door banged out a warning- literally. Two older men in dirty coveralls slid into a booth, ignored the blackboard's daily offering- the days never changed, turned up their coffee cups and hollered over at Dave.

Martie had whisked off to the kitchen, leaving Reilly to take the initiative. She picked up the coffee pot and approached the customers.

Dave looked in the mirror above the grill's order board. The girl didn't just stand around, had to give her that. Other than the short time she took to eat, she'd been busy wiping, sweeping, rolling silverware, spying out things that needed to be done, and all without asking. What do you know? Dave stifled a grin.

"Would you like coffee?" Reilly asked, ready to pour.

"Is the pope Catholic?" One of them laughed.

She accepted this as a yes and filled their cups, set the coffee pot down, pulled out her tablet and pen.

"What would you like?" She tried to sound friendly and smile- things that were definitely not second nature to her. Hiding in a book, or at least behind the tiny order pad would have been the more comfortable thing to do.

"A slab of ribs," the crew-cut farmer enthusiastically avowed.

Reilly looked startled. She'd not seen anything remotely resembling ribs identified on the menu.

"And a beer," the farmer added.

"Same for me," his buddy agreed, straight-faced, adjusting his John Deere ball cap.

'Tell him you're fresh out, Dearie. I know this 'un and he's a dunderhead.'

Nearly dropping her pen in surprise, Reilly blurted without thinking, "Sorry, but we're fresh out." She blushed, wondering if Bridie was behind her- didn't dare turn around to find out.

But Bridie was way ahead of everyone. She clipped the crew-cut farmer upside the head with a sugar dispenser and then poured.

'Smart ass,' Reilly heard the clear appraisal, and the elfin ghost conspiratorially winked at her.

Crew-cut turned in his seat to see why sugar was falling over his shoulders.

But Bridie had set the dispenser down in its proper place- no evidence. He gave Reilly a speculative frown.

She hitched her shoulders, "Ghosts, I guess."

With utmost glee, Bridie cavorted on the table tops. 'I had no idea being dead could be so much fun!'

Busy with the grill, Dave had missed the sugar act.

"Well. . .," the farmer hemmed, brushing at the sugar shower on his coveralls in thorough mystification.

"John, can't you see she's new? Order," Dave finally noticed the stand-off and reprimanded him.

"Did the ghost eat all the ribs?" John wasn't finished kidding the new kid. His equally shocked companion held his peace- just to be on the safe side- did check over his shoulder for signs of other vagabond containers, though.

'Tell him the pig's ghost wanted them back,' Bridie egged on the scenario.

"N…not exactly," despite herself, Reilly felt a chuckle coming. "The pig's ghost wanted them back."

For a second, John's jaw dropped in utter astonishment, and then he chortled, slapping the table, sending sugar scuttling, coffee sloshing.

"Pig's ghost," he cried. "I suppose the pig's ghost needed a beer, too, eh? Ah, here's a smart one, better watch this one, Dave!"

Reilly took their reformed order and hastened off.

"What's for dessert?" John caught Reilly with plates in one hand and coffee pot in the other.

"Apple pie," she called over her departing shoulder.

"Store bought?"

That stopped her. "I…I don't know. Wait a second."

She caught Martie exiting the back room kitchen. "Martie, is the apple pie home-made?"

"That John," she shook her head. "He knows better. No, but it's edible. Wait, I'll tell him."

How could a hometown diner not have home-made desserts? Reilly struggled with the lack of logic.

At clean-up, Martie explained that they used to have a wonderful baker make the pies at home (in-between watching kids), and bring them to the restaurant to sell, but the state board of health- some new guy from the big city without a lick of sense in his head, had told Dave he couldn't use the pies because they weren't prepared in an officially licensed facility.

"'As if everyone poisons themselves by cooking at home! Licensed facility my. . .' Dave had a few choice words for the fellow, after he left, of course."

The bell had clanged continuously until 6:00- locals knew not to enter past 5:30 and expect to eat.

The town of Ryan closed up early, especially during the week. For the most part it was a small, farming community. The adults still believed in 'early to bed, early to rise.'

"See you tomorrow, Reilly?" Dave asked as he calculated the day's receipts, totaled bills, balanced the drawer and prepared supply orders.

Reilly finished locking up her tips- all of them. Wouldn't do to take a cent to the dump. Except she was getting short on cat food. . .

"Yes, thanks, tomorrow. Good night, Dave." She waved to Martie as the door clanged behind her.

Bridie fell into step, or rather, drifted like fog, as Reilly walked home. Night and being alone outside would have especially disconcerted Reilly- if she'd been alone. Night had always scared her and disrupted her system.

'A nice night for walking. Did you enjoy your first day at the diner, Dear?' Bridie seemed to ken the girl's fears.

Reilly mentally ran through a few aches in muscles that hadn't experienced that kind of use before, but they were good aches. She adjusted her backpack and actually surveyed the darkness the few lights didn't bridge.

"Yes, Bridie, especially when you sat on that man's lap," Reilly found herself grinning- she might get used to this unfamiliar stretching of her lips. Several times she'd nearly dropped plates at Bridie's quirky antics- she'd have to be continuously on guard and extra quick on her feet to ensure the dishes' survival.

'Mick O'Ryan,' Bridie drooled. 'Aah, he's a handsome one! Wasn't bold enough when I had me 'physical' to bounce on his lap. Wouldn't a done me reputation much good, either.'

Reilly joined in with Bridie's raucous snickering.

9

Friday defiantly cooled off through the course of the day- a harbinger of winter's approach; Reilly found herself relishing the wonder of someone- Bridie- caring enough to considerately suggest taking one of the wool sweaters along. She figured ghosts must have a connection with the weather gurus above. And she was quick to thank her new friend for her solicitude.

Having to endure only one bus ride in the morning was doable. She looked forward to a decent meal at the diner, and her waitress job was growing on her- she was beginning to enjoy the influx of regulars and getting to know their peculiarities.

All of the customers seemed to appreciate her efforts- they saw she was serious about her work- unlike the shiftless kids at the trailer court or the previous, fly-by-night waitresses. Office workers, farmers, shop owners, a local plumber, electrician, travelers and others were a daily treat, and Reilly couldn't believe her great luck in obtaining her job. And her best friend.

She hadn't seen the mechanics, the O'Ryans, but Mick O'Ryan and others of the clan O'Ryan dined regularly and Bridie always seemed to have a hug and kiss, not to mention flirty eyes, for the completely unaware Mick. Bridie also accompanied her to the dump's doorstop without fail- her amusing vignettes kept Reilly's mind from relentlessly seeing monsters in the deep darkness. And then there was her nighttime companion, Righteous, who always timed her arrival.

Familiar noises emanating from the dump destroyed her sense of well-being as she approached the steel grate steps. Here she'd anticipated a quick clean-up and curl-up in bed with Righteous. Not happening.

"Reilly, finally," no 'hello', no 'how was your day?' Reilly had been impressed with how the time walking home flew in Bridie's company- only to come to. . .this.

"Fix a pot of that chili like you make," her mother ordered.

Reilly's spirits plunged through the floor. It was 8:30. Her normal routine would have been a quick homework endeavor and then, bed. But this was Friday and the dump was hopping.

Chet and three beer-guzzling friends were obnoxiously cursing and shouting at some game on the TV- turned up loud enough the whole neighborhood was probably tuned-in to the decibel-defying contest. And all were smokers.

The mother and another heavily made-up woman kept the beers passing in the horrid smog. And of course, no one seemed to have been genteelly designated to clean up or cook. Waiting for her. The garbage can overflowed and various substances and snacks littered and congealed on the floor.

Chili, Chumps, Chimps.

Reilly eyed one of the gangly guests as he stumbled from his seat, grabbed at a lamp for balance, only to have it collapse under his weight. Riotous laughter snorted.

He bumped into her, slung an arm over her shoulder, "Hey, kid!"

Reilly quickly ducked out, revulsion spread up her backbone, bringing on shivers.

She made her way to her room, dropped off her bag. No sign of Righteous, but she dished out a can of food just in case the kitten returned before she did. The window stayed open for a kitty door. From her pocket, she drew out a piece of catfish- Friday's once-in-awhile special, and placed it alongside the canned food.

Two hours of cooking and dodging drunks later. . .

Tired, Tacky, Ticked-off. Technically, the last word wasn't admissible, but at this point, she was fatigued enough not to care. Could she help it if her brain faltered?

Reilly washed up and headed for bed, wondering how she'd ever be able to sleep through the grating din in the front room. And she had to leave at 5:00 a.m. Saturday morning to be at work on time.

"Better take up running," she muttered.

'Those blithering eejits,' Bridie seethed.

"Blithering, Blathering, Buttheads," Reilly agreed aloud.

'That's the spirit, Dearie,' Bridie cheered, hiding her grim dissatisfaction with the state of things.

About to climb into bed, Reilly noticed the cat food, untouched. Odd. A cheering racket exploded outside her bedroom window and a frisson of foreboding impaled Reilly's gut.

"Oh, great," Reilly felt like crying.

'Best go outside, Reilly,' the ghost advised, impassively.

"Outside?" Reilly echoed, apprehensively.

"Got 'em," a voice cracked from the outdoors. Curses of applause followed.

A flash of fear overrode her hesitation. She bolted from the room, full-out running, pushing at various wavering bodies, jumped the steps and tore around the dump to the creek bank behind.

A small bonfire permitted the extension of Friday night parties, despite the damp chill. Reilly didn't notice the garbage strewn about the wooded area she'd spent last Sunday cleaning. She didn't take into account how many bodies idled about, cursing and hollering endorsements.

All of her focus was for the tiny flash of gold high in the creek-side sycamore. The tiny meow of terror, and the ogre pitching rocks and beer bottles at the kitten.

Unbeknownst to the few people alive that knew Reilly, she had been gifted with a tremendous lung and vocal capacity. More like that of a Banshee in Bedlam.

Reilly, herself, didn't know her own capabilities, but the scream she let out- a scream born of years of tightly held self-control, pierced the ears of everyone in Red Wing Trailer Court. Whether inside or out. Whether TV watching or not. Inebriation was no safeguard.

Scream number two outdid scream number one. And it was reported the next day that several windows had actually cracked.

Reilly barreled into the fat pitcher, clutching his ears, knocking him off his feet. She stood over him, not a weapon-in-hand, other than a fight-to-the-death-to-protect 'motherly' resolve.

"Meowww," a plaintive ratification from above. Righteous' gladiator had come to her rescue.

The perpetrator rolled and scrambled up, shouting obscenities at Reilly. His chin was bleeding and so were his hands- compliments of the broken, beer bottle glass spewed on the ground.

He drew back a fist to hit her. Reilly ducked and swept in. Running on a fury she would not have recognized if she'd been in her right mind, Reilly instinctively clasped both hands tightly together and chucked him under his chin and then kneed him where it counts.

By this time the audience had expanded. A scream of such striking pitch tended to draw tenants from their erstwhile dormancy. Maybe something extra-terrible was happening. Could be entertaining. . .

Her opponent fell again under her onslaught. She stepped around the downed flotsam, headed for the sycamore.

But a hand grasped her shoulder, spun her around. Adrenalin raged in Reilly's blood. She kicked out at the latest assailant.

"Get her," wheezed the fat body curled like a fetus in the glass-bedecked dirt.

"What did you do that for?" Reilly recognized one of the kids from the bus.

"It's only a cat, for f**'s sake," another voice sneered.

"Only a cat? And you're only an ass," Reilly spit back furiously.

"Roll her down into the creek," a suggestion came from one of the cronies. His suggestion was embellished by others' flagrant chants.

"LET HER GO." Three words backed with the threat of civil war cut across the tumult of the heckling partiers.

Instantaneously, Reilly was released. With the sudden removal of the bruising grasp of her shoulder, she nearly fell, back-peddled into a stalwart tree trunk. The adrenalin began to peter out of her system; tremors filled the vacuum.

"Hey, Trinity, we were just havin' a little fun. . ."

"Shut up!" Trinity, in his uniform clothes of black t-shirt and black jeans, eyed every male and female in the vicinity with a murderous gleam. His hands ached to follow through. . .

"Meeeow," Righteous figured the order for silence did not include her. "Meoooowwww."

"I'm only going to say this once. Every one of you, get the hell out of here! If I get a single hint that Reilly or," Trinity looked up at the kitten gazing down adoringly on him.

Trinity cursed violently, "A cat, has suffered the slightest inconvenience. . ." Trinity stood, hands on hips, belligerently defying anyone to brook his orders. His body sizzled with the desire to pummel the shit out of someone. Please, let just one of these asses backtalk.

But no brag resided in his admitting that he was the top of the food chain.

"No problem. . ."

"Hey, we're outta here. . ."

"Sorry, man. . ."

"Didn't know she was y. . ." This last earned a significant glare.

Whipped into line, the malefactors hastily melted away. Two of them aided their fallen comrade.

Reilly's body trembled with the aftermath.

She barely recognized herself, but her digestive system reflected on the event, the essence of odious conflict- though this incident was horribly magnified- and let its contents erupt. She fell against the sycamore, turned from her savior, retching and gagging, body heaving.

Trinity kept his distance- still wishing for something to beat the hell out of. He offered her a shop rag from his rear pocket, waited out the dissolution of rage which dissipated with her every heave. Embarrassed, she accepted the mottled cloth.

Steadying herself against the sycamore, she held up her arms, cooing to the kitten, but Righteous refused to budge a descent, and paced back and forth on the thin limb. Struck with fear or. . .

"Leave it alone, Reilly. It'll come down when it's ready."

"But, what if she's hurt? Scared?" Knowing fear firsthand, Reilly's voice betrayed her vulnerability. The adrenalin rush all gone, as well as her dinner, she was left tottering, exhaustion in every bone. And Trinity noticed she was shivering.

He cursed again, eyed potential grips and began climbing the tree. His low belted pants were a distinct hindrance.

"F…Damn!" he swore, took off his belt, readjusted his jeans and re-belted them. He booted himself up the sycamore trunk, took the compliant kitten in hand and descended.

"Here," he tried to un-velcro the kitten from his shirt.

Righteous put all of a kitten's wealth of cuteness in the look she bestowed on Trinity and purred, rubbing her jaws along his thumb.

The most hardened criminal might have difficulty resisting a kitten playing up cute. Trinity, though hard, was far from a criminal and he felt a tug inside his chest.

"Thank you, Trinity," Reilly accepted the kitten and buried her face in the gold fur. Righteous' sea-green eyes slowly winked volumes at Trinity.

The sight of that pinched face sunk in the tiny kitten's body, the flashback of Reilly ready for battle without a snowball's chance, and hadn't he heard, yes, he had- a giggle when he was forced to adjust his pants to climb

- all of this sent tentacles across the armor of Trinity. . . and they found a chink.

"Any time," he mumbled and stalked off.

Bleary-eyed, Chet accosted Reilly at the door. His group had peered outside at the screams, but wasn't interested enough to decipher if someone was being murdered or not.

"You're not bringing that in here."

Reilly glared her response in a way Bridie later chortled reminded her of one of her own General-stopping expressions.

10

'Righteous, best do your part. The darlin' girl has got to get up for work.' Ghost and kitten exchanged conspiratorial looks.

The kitten, claws sheathed, walked across Reilly's chest and face- no response. Kneaded Reilly's arms and wrapped her front legs, hug-like, around the sleeping girl's neck, purring all the while- no response. Went nose to nose and eye to eye complete with sonorous mewling- no response. As a last resort, Righteous tried piercing Reilly's ear lobe. That did it.

"Oh, gosh! What time is it?" Reilly exploded up, raced to the bathroom, returned and threw on her clean, work jeans and shirt she'd left hanging out the window so they wouldn't stink of cigarette.

Bridie soothed her with, 'You've got plenty of time, Dearie. Yer a right spirited lass when the call comes and I'm that proud of ye, I am,' Bridie sniffled into transparent hands.

Reilly tried not to rehash the previous night's goings-on, fearful of her gut's reprisal. She kept Bridie's compliment in mind, though. Kind words were pretty scarce in her life. She hoped her ghostly friend was right about Righteous being OK.

'Dearie, I've enjoyed many a cat's company in me life and I'd be willin' to bet on old St. Pat's bell that Righteous is the culmination of all me old friends' smarts. Don't worry.'

Righteous seemed to approve of this commendation for she stopped eating long enough to give a hearty purr and proud wink- her body wreathed Reilly's arm.

Reilly was beginning to get used to Bridie when they were alone. But in public the ghost's popping in and talking to her was quite disorienting. Reilly worked on pins and needles, afraid of saying something aloud in response to Bridie and appearing ridiculous to the diner's clientele.

The girl set the cowbell clanging as she rushed into the diner with ten minutes to spare. With no watch to guide her, she didn't dawdle on the eight mile jaunt to work.

As early and as late as Reilly walked to and from her job, dark presented a prevailing issue of unease. But if a ghost accompanied one, then technically, one wasn't alone, right?

At least, Reilly depended on Bridie to smooth the way on the long trek. Conversation with transparent company seemed to hinder the fear that lingered like an elusive aura or wraith-like second skin on the girl.

"Slow down, Honey," Martie gently admonished as Reilly hastened to her locker, greeted Dave taking biscuits from the oven and stirring brown, bacon gravy and pale, sausage gravy for the diner's breakfast special- biscuit and gravy, eggs and home fries.

Unlocking the god-send, Reilly retrieved a uniform shirt, hurried to the bathroom to change, and joined Martie in the dining area.

"Better have a bite to eat, Reilly. Saturday's a might busy. Why don't you help yourself to the grill?"

Reilly liked to cook, when she wasn't exhausted, and had a clean kitchen (i.e. bug-less) to work in.

She'd intently watched Dave every spare second during the week.

Several times he'd offered her the use of the stainless steel grill to fix her own meals, if she wanted something other than the plate specials kept warm on the steam table. It was easier to make certain things on a grill than in a space-impaired skillet and she relished the new experience.

It was a good thing Dave had got Reilly started on a Monday afternoon and not a Saturday morning. Not that it would have stopped Reilly, but Saturday breakfast rush didn't let up- more like a hurricane of the hungry. It mingled with a few lunch enthusiasts and only died down around 1:30.

Reilly nearly dropped the coffee pot as Bridie literally swept through the closed door and through Martie taking table number eight's order.

The ghost's high-spirited greeting of 'God bless all here' went unacknowledged by unaware breakfasters. Reilly barely controlled an inane smile at Bridie's antics.

Until ROCKY TOP played on the radio and Bridie began to clog dance. The sight of an Irish leprechaun kicking up her muck boots and holding her long skirt high, dancing atop stacks of hotcakes and through the steam of hot cupped coffee, let alone the Moulin Rouge can-can maneuvers aimed at the many ball caps, some of which went flying. . .

Reilly bit her lip to maintain and focus on what she was doing.

After her illustrious parading through the breakfast patrons, Bridie sat across from Mick O'Ryan and made calf-eyes at the handsome pub owner who obliviously ate his stack of heavily-indulged-with-syrup hot cakes with great gusto.

Reilly had just delivered a four plate line-up of breakfast specials perched along the length of her arm- a recent skill- when Trinity and his father slid into a newly vacated booth.

Martie was occupied so Reilly bussed their table.

"Well, hi there, neighbor," O'Ryan Senior greeted her.

"Howdy," she answered self-consciously, retreated with the dirty leftovers, assiduously wiped the checked table top, and brought clean silverware, coffee cups and coffee pot.

Trinity eyed her dark circles, the ribbon tying back her hair.

"Get any sleep last night?"

Blushing, Reilly avoided his eyes, "A little."

"With all that noise, it must have been damn little," Trinity left off perusing the girl, idly flipped the menu. He mused on how she had been anything but shy in taking out the fat kid the night before.

"Coffee?" she asked.

Pat O'Ryan nodded, gauging his son's reaction to Reilly. He'd dragged the high lights of last night's screaming incident from his irate son and was equally angered at the fiasco.

Irked at his father's speculation, Trinity rattled off his order before Reilly brought out her guest check pad.

"Special- eggs over easy, two sides of bacon, extra crispy, large orange juice and a glass of water. Get that?"

The hard is back, Reilly thought, and repeated Trinity's order verbatim, "Spec OE, 2b xc, Loj, h20. Got it. And for you, sir?"

"Call me Pat," Senior chuckled. "I'll have the same."

Trinity busied himself with his silverware until Reilly left. And then surreptitiously watched her in action.

Pat admired how Reilly filled coffee cups as she bustled to acquire the juice, always busy looking for areas needing attention. Taking empty plates, wiping up spills. . .

"Hey, you gonna wait on me or do I have to wait all day?" Farmer John, her very first customer on Monday, grunted.

Trinity eyed the crew-cut customer. John Stalbridge gave everyone a hard time. Most took him with a grain of salt and turned away. Some avoided him altogether. Trinity bristled. The locals were used to the obnoxious jerk's tactics, but Reilly. . .

Arms loaded with dirty dishes, Reilly flew by.

"Hey, you!"

"Back in a second." She was off by three.

"That girl is a hustler," Pat tried to stave off his silent son's rumination.

"Good morning. Specials are on the board. What would you like?" Reilly asked the normally disgruntled farmer while bussing his table. His friend helped stack the dirty dishes.

With grave sincerity, Stalbridge vowed, "If you were younger I'd either marry you or adopt you. Any homemade desserts, today?"

Bridie hovered at her side. Since the table behind him had the sugar dispenser in use, she whispered in Reilly's ear and gigged the girl.

"You know if you'd married the woman who used to do the baking, you'd have homemade desserts all the time," Reilly surprised herself at her effrontery.

But Bridie kept after her. Reilly hoped the ghost didn't get her fired.

"Why. . .," the farmer blustered, "The woman was 75 years old! And babysat a dozen kids! You're a brassy girl!"

Trinity was half out of his seat, "Damn Stalbridge, giving her a rough time."

"Son, you don't want to get the girl fired. Sit down. If that's the same girl as put fat Al on his butt, I'm betting she can take care of herself."

'Reilly, quick! What did your grandma used to call fussy, old farts?'

Reilly's eyes widened and she blurted out, "And you're a fuss budget!"

"What did you call me?" John Stalbridge got all huffy. His friend tapped his arm with a dirty knife. Trinity was a second from bolting and tearing into the cranky, old farmer.

"A fuss budget," Reilly blushed. "Now, are you going to order or sit here and be crotchety all morning?"

Stalbridge's friend was rolling on his side of the booth, tears wet his eyes. It wasn't often anyone got the better of Stalbridge.

"I ain't been called a fuss budget since I was a kid. Where'd you get that from?"

"My grandma called crotchety folks fuss budgets and you seemed to fill that bill," Reilly stood her ground. She had no choice. Bridie had backed into her like an oak.

'Good lass! Give 'im the old what fer,' Bridie sang out as she proceeded to perch atop the counter while plates slid through her ghostly form to the counter customers.

Crew-cut relented, ordered, and Reilly rushed off.

Another customer grabbed at her arm, "I need an egg sandwich in a hurry."

"I…I'll see what I can do." As she approached the grill with orders, Dave handed her an egg sandwich.

"I saw him come in. You'll get used to all the regulars. Most have the same thing every Saturday. Some eat the same breakfast every day," Dave gave her a pat on the shoulder and grinned- pleased as all get-out.

Reilly lined up her left arm with plates full of biscuits and gravy, eggs, home fries, sausage, bacon, hot cakes, omelets, coffee pot in right hand, and delivered the orders to their prospective tables.

"Here you are," she set down Pat and Trinity's plates, refilled Pat's coffee and swept away, calling to Martie that she'd do some dishes.

Clean cups and plates stacked, Reilly turned in time to ring up her neighbors.

"Thanks again for…for your help. . .last night," she shyly offered.

Trinity wordlessly nodded and followed his father out.

'Now, there goes a fine figure of a man, now that you can tell he has an a…'

"Bridie!" Reilly forgot herself and admonished the ghost in a hiss.

But Reilly had noticed Trinity's jeans as he exited the diner, well-fitted and belted the way jeans were meant to be worn.

'Can tell he's an O'Ryan, that one,' Bridie continued to extol the merits of Trinity's physique.

Reilly eyed the two stacks of bills on the counter at 2:30. One was her share of the tips and the other her pay for the week.

"What are you fixing to do with your first pay check, Honey?" Martie inquired as she took out the register drawer, and headed to the office.

Dave, addressing the grill with a black grill brick to scrape off the day's accumulated grease, stopped to listen.

Reilly fingered the bills, added them up in her head, tallying in the rest of the week's tips. She sat stunned. All this- hers, and for a job she didn't consider 'work' as she knew it from her 'chores' at the dump. Not a cent would she keep with her, except to buy cat food on the way home. Her mother was not above rifling through her things, hoping to acquire funds. She'd hinted all week about Reilly's bringing home rent money or food money or an endless list of other money 'needs'.

Her locker would serve as her bank account until she could legally have her own. One her mother could not touch, no matter how sordid the tale she might contrive to gain access.

"I need a good pair of shoes for. . .work." Reilly felt sure Martie and Dave had no idea she walked to and from work.

"Talk to Skip down the next block at Lad-n-Lass Shoes. He'll have just the thing," Dave instructed.

"Thanks, Dave," she rose to lock up some of her money prior to going to the shoe store.

"See you on Monday?" Dave couldn't help the buoyance in his voice. She seemed content with her job, but once paid. . . You never knew.

"Sure," Reilly affirmed, agreeably.

As the girl waved out the door and turned toward the shoe store, Dave picked up the phone.

"Skip, how are you? Do me a favor. Do right by the little girl headed your way. Name's Reilly. Put the balance on my account. Make the sale seem like a special close-out or something. I don't want her to know. Thanks."

Bridie regarded Dave, 'Good as yer gravy, that's what yer are, Dave.'

11

'Aye, Righteous, let the Sweetlin' sleep. Those bleedin' eejits up all night with their shenanigans, keepin' a hard workin' lass runnin' their errands- the filthy bollocks.'

Righteous re-curled up in the curve of Reilly's arms, purred and watched her new warm friend as, ears twitching, she glanced up at her old friend.

Bridie flitted her ghostly, elfin self from the corner of the room's ceiling to rest at Reilly's bedside. She trailed her supple-in-death fingers, free of old-age arthritis, through the kitten's golden hair.

It was to be expected, but one never counts on exactly when a guillotine blade falls. Reilly walked right into an ambush.

"I need ten dollars," the mother said without any preamble. No good morning- that would have been totally out of character.

"I don't have any money," Reilly replied, her gut cringing on instant stand-by.

"Don't give me that, you got paid yesterday. I need cigarettes," as she spewed smoke from the stick in her mouth.

"It's already been slated for the dentist. I've got to go," Reilly sidled by, clutching her stomach, as her mother huffed.

"You better not have any filthy animal in this house," the warning struck.

Filthy? Reilly looked around at the less-than-pristine living room.

"You need to give Chet some respect- giving us a place to live, and you better get this place cleaned up. There's laundry needs done. . ."

But Reilly heard no more as her insides revolted. Her body adamantly objected to the anguish the mother's constant harangues throughout Reilly's life brought on. Anymore, the slightest altercation with her mother incurred violent repercussions. She cupped her hands to her mouth and rushed for the closest receptacle- the kitchen sink.

The mother retreated as a new stench filled the room. "What's wrong with you? D. . ."

Reilly wiped her mouth, rinsed and fled.

'Walk along here, Dearie, and stop if any plant speaks to you,' Bridie instructed, shocked to her invisible core at how Reilly's mother accosted her daughter.

Righteous in tow, they were slowly making their way down Bridie's drive. Reilly rubbed her grumbling stomach, anxious to stop its potential for further eruptions or for the need to find a bathroom. Bridie's strange request sifted through her misery. Her brow donned a puzzled frown.

'Just try,' Bridie serenely urged.

At first, Reilly wasn't sure if she were hearing plant talk or simply feeling the aftermath of the morning's vomiting and subsequent faintness.

She stopped, walked a few steps, stopped and backed up, peering at a particular plant, trying to ignore Righteous gambling about like a March hare.

"Bridie?"

'Take a few of the green leaves and chew them. It's peppermint- will settle your stomach, lass.'

In total trust, Reilly acquiesced, slowly chewing, savoring the taste and texture. The results weren't immediate, but there definitely was a surcease in her gut's discomfort.

'Remember that plant. Come along, we've some to do. Can't have you feelin' poorly.' Bridie thoughtfully drifted beside Reilly.

How weird to see through a person, Reilly mused, watching the scenery pass by.

'Cead Mille Failte, Reilly,' Bridie sifted through the locked door of her cottage and waited for Reilly to unlock the door and accompany her.

"What does that mean, Bridie?" Her only friend's impromptu appearances and disappearances were growing on her, although it still tended to give her goose bumps when Bridie actually walked through another person.

Reilly had nearly learned the art of ventriloquism, too.

Bridie mentioned communicating with her mind, but Reilly didn't quite have the hang of how that worked. So, she kept her lips almost immobile and spoke in a hushed tone with her ghost friend, whose hearing was impeccable.

Customers at the diner wrote off Reilly's constant head movements as simply checking to see what needed to be done- when what she was really doing was turning to answer the ghost or catch the latest frolic.

'A thousand welcomes,' Bridie beamed. 'Ah, me poor plants, they miss me,' the ghost lovingly eyed her assortment of house plants.

"Bridie, can the plants see you as Righteous and I can?"

'Ah, now aren't you the smart one! I reckon they can at that!' Appeased, Bridie began to sing an Irish lullaby, all the while flitting from plant to plant, checking leaves with the soft breeze of her passing through them.

On a more physical level, Reilly filled a pink elephant watering can and provided each plant with its liquid requirements. Gently, she removed dead bits.

'Too ra loo ra loo ra,' Bridie hovered, literally, feet in the air, supervising Reilly's expertise. 'You have a way with plants, lass.'

"I love these clovers. Do they bloom all year?" Four clay pots held shamrocks with pink flowers and one large clay pot sprouted four-leaf clovers with tiny, white flowers.

'But of course! What would an Irish house be like without this fine symbol of Ireland a'bloomin'?'

Once the plants were all tended to, Bridie asked Reilly to sit with her on the high-sided couch.

"Will you tell me about yourself, Bridie, and this fairy-tale cottage?"

Bridie's finger tapped into her transparent lips. 'I'll reckon to start at the beginnin'.

I was born in Ireland, the west side, more than 117 years ago- the seventh woman in my lineage to have the second sight. A fey woman, Bridie O'Connair of County Clare- me. You know the history of Ireland with our many troubles.'

'The O'Ryan, more on him in a minute, had been here in the U.S. of A for a number of years and he'd made himself a goodly fortune. He was wantin' Irish lasses for takin' care of his new mansion.

You've seen the grand community center- that's the house he built for his family. A lot of bricks for not much.

See, it was one of those marriages without love and affection- prime requisites, if I do say so m'self- although O'Ryan, that fine figure of a man who deserved so much more in a wife, doted on his sons. A great lot of fine strapping men they turned out to be.

I answered his advertisement. He sent me passage and so I came to work for the handsomest man I've ever seen.

He'd married his Yank wife late in life, took her riches and doubled and tripled them. Folks around here began calling him The O'Ryan, like he was a clan leader. This town, he founded it. His land became the county of Ryan.

Yer man, Trinity, is a great, great grandson. I'm not sure if I've got all the greats, but you get me meanin'. Mick O'Ryan, of the pub, is a brother to yer man Trinity's father. Looks more like the grand old man himself.'

"I've noticed how you can't seem to keep your eyes off of him," Reilly wasn't trying to be impertinent, even if it sounded that way.

'Aye, I wasn't lucky enough to have me a fellow when I was in me 'physical', but I can stare as much as I like, now. Gettin' back to the story. . .

The O'Ryan acquired a gamblin' fever.'

'He built a racin' stable founded on a divil of a stallion. Finn McCool, he named the beast and The O'Ryan bet him heavily, too much so.

The day of his last race. . . I remember, ah so clearly. . .

By this time, I had me own reputation as a healer and a fortune teller of sorts. I read cards so as to give a body something to think on- the future is one's own to make, not anyone else's to foretell.

Seldom did I use my second sight, and never for personal gain. I come by me cottage and land honestly, I did.'

Reilly studied the faint features of Bridie's earnest face. Wavy, short hair swept back- a wraith with only the slightest bit of color in her wool sweater, long skirt and boots. She didn't seem older than, maybe 60's.

'Lass, once you get so old, you don't get any older.' Caught out in her thinking, Reilly blushed.

"What happened at the last race?" Reilly pictured the huge mansion with its array of uniformed Irish maids, farm lands, pastures, racing stable, and a chestnut stallion nearly impossible to handle.

'Ah, lass! I knew you had the gift. You're right, that beast was monstrous persnickety! But he and I had an understandin' betwixt us.

The night before the race, the beast was feelin' poorly. I've no doubt a lyin' groom pocketed some extra coin for a dirty deed- slipped a poison in the stallion's feed.'

The O'Ryan was fit to bust a gut. The doctor couldn't do a thing for the horse. He might die, it was said.'

'And the O'Ryan, in his cups is all I can think, had pert near bet the farm on him for the coming race. No backing out. Ah, the brash boyo and his boastful betting.

The O'Ryan sat up by his ailin' horse, a rifle in his hand. Plain as yesterday, I remember strollin' into that fine, brick stable, basket of herbs in me hand.

I was in me twenties by then and wantin' somethin' for meself. You kin glean me meanin'?'

Reilly nodded, she could certainly fathom wanting something to call your own.

'I asked the O'Ryan to sign a paper for me. A right legal one. If I healed his horse and it won the race, I was to have land for m'self- 25 acres, and a stone cottage built to my way of thinkin'.

You see, lass, I knew, and this is how the sight works- you know as you know yer own hand. I knew what to do for the beastie and I knew he'd win.

The O'Ryan didn't waste a second, he signed. To him 25 acres and a cottage was a wee drop in a giant bucket. Brought in two of his sons for witnesses, he did, at my request.'

"What did you do, Bridie?"

'In good time, Dearie, I'll be showin' you, but for now it's all you need to ken is that Mr. Finn McCool so bested his competition the next day that no one else ever cared to run against him. He retired a champion and spent the rest of his days playin' with the ladies.'

"And you got this home."

'Aye. I loved this place for all the years I was here in me 'physical', and I love it still.' Ghostly tears flowed into an invisible world.

'I saw you, Reilly, a few years before me leavin'. I saw you comin' down the drive, esteemin' my home and flowers. I saw you askin' if there were any sweaters.'

"That's why the box with my name on it," Reilly felt she should be shocked. But it was more of a warm awakening of an elusive something inside of you which you could not explain. And were heartily grateful and amazed to feel. You knew it to be true, but it was almost like you'd simply forgotten- whatever this feeling might be called.

'You're gettin' a ken now of what second sight is, me girl,' Bridie approved. 'An awakenin' is as good a way to describe what happens.'

"Can you hear my thoughts, Bridie?" Reilly wasn't so sure if she liked the idea of such an intrusion. But then, she didn't really have any privacy to invade.

'Only in so far as my intuition and second sight take me. Don't be concerned about private feelin's, although it's not hard to decipher you now I've seen your mother in action. God and all the Saints preserve us!

My legal man has explicit instructions. My great niece had to keep the box aside, and only if you asked could she bring it out.'

"I heard your voice. I thought I was imagining it, or it was just flying insects or something," Reilly said, recalling her bewilderment.

Bridie howled, stood up and danced a few steps reminiscent of Riverdance, only she used her arms like wings.

'It was that excited I was, Reilly, that you'd come to. . .care for my plants,' Bridie hedged. Wouldn't do to let the darlin' girl know too much too soon.

"I've never met a ghost or anyone who could see things in the future."

'There's a strong feelin' I've got that you have the gift, lass. Too much trouble in your young life to develop properly. But I'm here to. . .guide you, if you'll let me.'

Reilly reflected on what a tall order that was. Would she be up to the ghost's expectation?

Bridie patted through Reilly's thigh, lovingly looked around her parlor. 'We've all the time in the world, lass. Many's the hours I spent on this couch with a fire in the grate. Happy hours.'

Righteous had followed Reilly and Bridie and was curled between the girl and the ghost on the antique sofa. But the kitten scrambled up at Bridie's next suggestion.

'Let's stroll outside. The three of us takin' advantage of the sun.'

12

"What are these tall, colorful grasses?" Reilly, being ground-bound, was dwarfed by thick, russet and gold grass that towered over her. The seed heads, bent in the draught, tickled her exposed skin.

Righteous bounded into the 'forest' looking for cat toys- tiny, moving things. Bridie rested horizontally atop the foliage, her head propped through her elbow.

'Prairie grass, the original grass of this great country. The best of grazing fields, an ecosystem in itself. Most of the dear grasses were taken out by the dunderhead farmers from the old country- how dastardly! I'll not get started. See along the edge? Me onions- they replenish every year. Garlic, leeks- it's a wonder the gracious goods nature provides. If you walk further, you'll come across wild asparagus.'

"Asparagus?" Reilly made a face.

'You won't be makin' that face come spring when the asparagus peeks out of its hibernation- I'm bettin'- so good, you'll eat it freshly picked, never mind steamin' it.'

"Hmmm. . ., I'll try," Reilly wasn't soundly convinced, but she remained open. Might be the height of idiocy to bypass a ghost's recommendation. . .

'Now, before we meander into me herb garden, I'm settin' you a task.' Bridie checked the girl's reaction to this proposition.

"OK," how could she refuse, Reilly wondered?

'I want you to walk slowly on the rock path, similar to when we first walked the drive. Don't stop to read the names of the plants.'

Reilly had glimpsed the brass name tags suspended from brass stalks among the herb garden tenants.

'Let your mind be open and quiet and when you feel a calling, stop and touch whichever plant seems to have a message for you.'

The most unusual assignment she'd ever been given, Reilly considered. She took a minute to breathe deeply of the aromatic air, reveled in the last of the autumn sun. She opened the white, picket fence gate, and without consciously focusing on any particular plant, Reilly slowly walked the flag stone path.

In winding her way amid the various standing, dried plants, she initially felt nothing more than the occasional kick-up of the breeze from the west. She tried to ignore the scent of rain. . .

Something. . . Reilly rounded a curve and was brought up short- a slight twinge of. . . She let the twinge pull her to a dried plant, some 4' tall. Its fanciful foliage splayed like small fans. Must have been very pretty when green, she thought.

The plant issued an invitation to Reilly's fingers. She obliged, and as her thumb and forefinger barely touched the leaves, the twinge deepened into a sigh. A sound that had nothing to do with the wind.

Frowning, she searched around for Bridie and an explanation. Bridie was delightedly kicking up her heels-green muckers rising along the picket fence. The ghost held her transparent skirt up and out of the way of her busy feet.

Reilly couldn't help but smile.

Whatever else Bridie brought into her life, the girl had to admit she'd not smiled so much since being in her grandparents' care when she was really young.

'I knew it! I knew it!' Bridie sang out. 'D'you know the name of that plant, darlin' girl?'

"No, I don't believe I've ever seen it before."

'Its name. . .'

Reilly bent to read the hidden, brass name tag.

"Mugwort?"

'Yes! Every rock, every stream, plant and animal has a unique spirit of its own. If you're quiet and listen to what draws you, you have the opportunity to learn somethin' new about the world, yourself, and whatever draws you,' Bridie played professor.

Reilly paused to reflect on this.

"My grandparents were great gardeners. My grandma had the best tasting tomatoes I've. . ." Reilly turned her head and pretended to cough at the few, good, poignant memories she had.

'It's alright, dearie,' Bridie sympathized.

"They. . .told me plants could call you but they never intimated what you're saying. I just assumed it had to do with the plants' needs. . ."

'Not everyone reads all the aspects of the plants' spirits. I've had more years than most to learn various spirit languages. This plant called to you for several reasons. One, mugwort will repel insects.'

Reilly got excited about this, "Roaches?"

'Better than RAID, Dearie! And better for your health. Not havin' to breathe those horrid fumes. Two, mugwort will put a little spring in your tired tootsies- a sprig in your shoes'll do you.'

Bridie left off her picket fence dance and hovered in a sitting position atop the mugwort. Reilly contemplated putting bits of dried herbs in her shoes.

'Three, mugwort is an herb for protection. It will help banish negative influences.'

"I have plenty of those about me," Reilly cringed.

'But the most wonderful of all, me girl- mugwort signifies your body is ripe to open the door, to use your intuition. Gifts! Your sight is ready to waken and connect you to your inner strength. Now, what do you have to say for yourself?'

Reilly found it fascinating that every aspect of the plant she chose related to what was happening in her life. The drunks in the dump, the roaches, her feet tired from all the walking, her readiness to befriend and seek guidance from a ghost.

She hoped Bridie was right about the second sight- not that she wanted to win a lottery or anything along those lines, but to provide an advance warning to keep her feeling safe. . . To keep the fears at bay. . . At least for the next year and. . .

'It will be with you for always, Dearest, if you let it,' Bridie confided, sincerely. 'With these gifts you must stop wishin' time to fly- there is no magic in 18.'

Reilly fought the mistiness blocking her vision- wishing for. . . She wiped her eyes, and under Bridie's tutelage gathered a few cuttings.

'Now mind, it should have been harvested in mid-summer. But as it's called you today, it must have reserved enough power for you. Under your doorway it will keep out unwanted visitors. It must be renewed after a time. You won't need much.'

"What is that girl up to now?" Trinity wondered aloud.

Earlier, he'd seen her vacating the trailer court, looking a bit green around the gills.

He almost ran out to see if she were sick, needed anything. But she quickly blew by, clutching her stomach. Tail high, the kitten led the way.

Mid-afternoon, he'd gone to town, and there she was at Bridie O'Connair's place. Most folks would deem this odd, as everyone avoided Bridie's, unless personally invited. Gone or not, Bridie's influence lingered. In the past, those who trespassed always ran away, scared to the proverbial death.

It was heavily rumored that Bridie was a witch and would protect her cottage, even from the grave- probably haunted the place. Although Bridie had a mysterious side, Trinity knew better, as did the ones she had helped over her many years. More of a quirky saint than a witch.

In all of his encounters with Bridie, she always had a twinkle of fun in her eye, like she was always ready for a great new adventure, and she was the most vivaciously interesting conversationalist.

No topic was too sacred for Bridie to tackle. Trinity donned a reluctant grin, missing his old friend.

His family had held her in the highest regard. After all, if you lived to be 117 years old, there must be something damned special about you.

He recalled her walking to town one evening, near 8 years ago. How many 100 year olds walked several miles to town?

Trinity had stopped and offered her a ride in his Camaro. Damn, if she hadn't flirted with him the whole way to the local IGA grocery store!

He patiently waited for her to select her groceries, took her home and carried the bags into her whimsical cottage. As he remembered, the inside of her home smelled heavenly.

What was that girl doing?

Trinity considered stopping and offering Reilly a lift, but he wasn't too thrilled about a cat in his Camaro.

If he didn't know better, he'd think Reilly had a companion. She constantly turned her head, looked up, like she was talking to someone. But there was no one there. Probably using the cat for conversation, except the cat was on the ground. . .

"Bridie, it's going to rain," Reilly could almost feel the second the rain would break.

'Ah, that it is. Did you happen to see yer man, Trinity, keeping an eye on you today?'

"Why do you call him 'my man'? I don't really know him, except he helped save Righteous," Reilly thanked God for

Trinity's help that night.

'It's just an Irish expression,' Bridie responded, but the ghost had a gleeful gleam in her eye as she watched the Camaro slow in passing and then speed off.

13

'Reilly, Sweetlin'?'

"Oops," Reilly nearly drenched Mrs. Snider with her beef stew special as Bridie's unexpected voice and transparent appearance startled her.

Recovering in time, Reilly successfully delivered the meal, and Mrs. Snider spooned her lunch with great satisfaction. Bridie stood on the slurping woman's head pointing at a bearded customer entering the diner. With newspaper in hand, he retreated to the furthest booth from the entrance.

'Study that man,' Bridie ordered at the same time Dave greeted the newcomer.

"Usual, Steve?"

"Yes, and throw a few extra pickles on today, if you would."

Dave pulled out three hamburger patties from the cooler, plopped them on the hottest side of the grill, pulled off the in-between papers, dunked frozen onion rings into the deep fryer and decorated a bun for the sandwich, studiously humming the country song playing on the radio.

Bridie jibbed and heckled Reilly to remember the fellow's face, conveniently hidden by the sports section.

Reilly gave the ghost a questioning look which the few late lunch patrons missed, but Bridie wouldn't reveal her purpose. So the girl memorized his face as she poured his coffee.

As always, she tried to smile without subjecting anyone to her embarrassment over the state of her teeth. That meant a strained, closed-mouth effort.

Unfortunately, this man seemed too curious about her mouth. He put down his newspaper and regarded her thoughtfully, which unnerved her further. Coffee pot in hand, she hastened away to other tasks.

The diner's newest waitress bussed tables, checked condiment levels, avidly reconnoitered for things needing to be attended. Turning with her eyes focused on Bridie, she stepped into. . .

"You work here every day?"

Ketchup splattered plate digging into his chest, Trinity wryly regarded his neighbor. Reilly's eyes hastened to catch up with the bulk of the mechanic blocking her path.

Those same eyes widened at the stains she'd added to his black t-shirt.

"I…I'm s…sorry," she blushed, but with both hands full she hadn't a napkin to offer to clean up his chest.

"My bad, don't worry about it," Trinity side-stepped and took a seat at the counter.

With Martie on break, Dave dropped off Steve's sandwich and called out to the blushing girl, arms full of dirty dishes, "Reilly, think you can handle it?"

Lately, Dave and Martie both enjoyed some well-deserved free time. Between 2:30 and 4:00 the diner was easily managed by one efficient employee- provided the lunch rush dishes had all been done.

Her eyes struck in the headlights of Trinity's attention, "I…I'll be fine, Dave."

Dropping the dishes off in a bus pan, Reilly hastily wiped down the table and arranged the condiments against the wall.

Wiping her hands on a dry dish towel, she skirted the counter to wait on Trinity.

"Does this mean you're cooking and waiting on me, Reilly?" The mechanic grinned, eyeing the menu after glancing at the board-touting specials.

Disconcerted, she nodded, eyes plastered on her order pad instead of on Trinity's grease-streaked body perched on a counter stool.

We'll have to fix that, Bridie thought, drumming her fingers on the counter and watching the lack of interchange between Trinity and Reilly.

"Bridie," Reilly seethed as well as anyone could while covertly whispering. The ghost was openly, ardently, practically salivating over Trinity's well-fitting jeans and the muscular biceps extending from his short sleeves. Bridie hugged herself with star-struck rapture in her faint eyes. One of them winked at the flustered girl.

Buying time, Reilly went to obtain and deliver a glass of ice water to the counter customer, trying not to look at the ghost. Or the customer.

"What do you recommend?" Trinity closed his menu and was immediately frustrated at Reilly's shy, intimidated mien. He couldn't know it had as much to do with Bridie's frivolous antics as with his presence.

"You're kind of late for lunch," Reilly murmured.

"Had to finish a brake job," he explained.

"There's still beef stew," Reilly suggested.

"Nah, I'd rather watch you cook," Trinity boyishly teased.

This always seemed to bring girls around, but Reilly wasn't even looking at him so she missed his efforts.

"Can you fix me a ham and cheese omelet with peppers and onions, crispy home fries and English muffins?"

With a dramatic swoon gesture, ghostly fingers gliding across Trinity's backside, Bridie peeped 'good bye'. Trinity scratched at his lower back and wondered why Reilly imitated seeing off a non-existent, exiting customer. Shrugging, he took a long haul on his water and waited for her to acknowledge his order.

"Sure. Do you like your omelet well done or soft?"

"Well done," Trinity unrolled his utensils. "And an orange juice, too."

Ordinarily, Reilly felt comfortable enough in her grill cook abilities, but for the first time since tackling the large, hot stainless steel expanse, she splayed a tad of eggs out of the bowl as she scrambled them.

Pulling off a paper towel, she ducked to the floor and cleaned up her mess, only to rise and find Trinity eyeing her every movement. Flustered, she washed her hands.

Her brain belatedly spewed: Muddled, Mess, Mechanic. The words hadn't come as quickly to mind. Now, why would her old coping mechanism falter?

Probably something to do with Bridie, Reilly figured. The ghost's faint appearance in her life had provided a spell-binding, serendipitous stage that eclipsed most of the negative impacts of her life. Maybe it was the mugwort, too.

Bridie certainly gave Reilly things to ponder. How many other teen-age girls had ghosts in their lives? For that matter, how many people period had ghosts in their lives?

Bridie had said she'd seen Reilly coming. It was terribly kind of her to care enough to stick around and befriend a friendless girl.

She set Trinity's late breakfast in front of him, eyes furtively casting about for something to do. But everything was in order. . .

"Have you eaten? Why not sit with me, if you can?"

"Uh, n…no. . . I…I'm sure there's. . ."

Saved by the bell- the diner's cow bell clanged.

Crew-cut Stalbridge strode in with his typical, "Any home-made desserts today?"

This she could deal with.

"No."   But one of these days I might surprise you, Reilly weighed the issue. She had an idea to run by Dave and Martie.   As soon as she found the courage to bring up the subject.

"Good omelet, Reilly.   Hey, John," Trinity politely hailed Stalbridge.

"You got my brakes finished?"

"Yeah, car's ready.   Don't wait so long next time. The wear almost damaged your. . ."

"Yeah, yeah. . .   Coffee to go." Stalbridge's curt, obnoxious reply grated on Trinity. Reilly also felt peeved for Trinity.

Crusty old Stalbridge complained about the bill waiting at the garage and left, sipping too fervently at his hot coffee and almost spilling it as he burned his tongue.

Trinity re-focused on Reilly.   The girl didn't seem quite as scrawny, although the 2-pocket uniform shirt hid any idea of a figure.

If she only did something with her hair. . . Her sun-bleached locks were pulled tightly back with several strands falling, curtaining her eyes and framing her pale face.   And he ached for her, considering her teeth.

At least, the diner provided food in a clean environment, Trinity speculated. But her overall countenance still bore the guarded, downcast eyes of one waiting for the next weight to fall.

Trinity could only guess how hard it must be for her, living in Chet's hellhole. By the looks of the girl, who never seemed to smile that he'd seen, probably because of those teeth, life before Chet hadn't been a picnic, either.

Trinity tried to strike up a conversation with her. He wanted to know what she was doing at Bridie O'Connair's cottage, but the diner's business picked up and waylaid his intentions.

There'd be another time.   Trinity left a ten dollar bill at his plate. Maybe a sizeable tip would perk her up. If she at least smiled on the inside. . .   Well, that would be something.

Trinity waved as he left. His memory flipped to. . .

Gritting his teeth, he whispered, "No, don't go there."

Of the long list of fears Reilly carried like a ton-weight on her shoulders, roaches vied with few others for top billing- one of those being alone in the dark.

The mugwort, tape and Righteous seemed to be working on the creepy-crawly issue. Not a bug had crossed the mugwort-sporting threshold into her bedroom since she brought the herb home.

Reilly wished, but figured there wasn't enough mugwort in the world to keep Chet's party pals from mis-using the bathroom slated for her use. She was tired of the vomit and misplaced urine left for Maid Reilly to clean up.

Revolting, Rotten, Wretches. Technically, that last wasn't correct, but it sounded just right.

As for being alone in the dark. . . Reilly had imagined the walk to and from work would be especially terrifying, but having Bridie as her escort had alleviated most of her worry. The ghost's sweeping along like an accompanying breeze with extensive topics for conversation belayed most apprehensions Reilly's mind diligently sought to conjure up.

The girl couldn't decide what a ghost might be able to do in a confrontation and didn't dare to ask- just in case the answer wasn't something she wanted to hear. She held to her heart, though, that with Bridie by her side, the long walk would always be safe.

14

'You're restless tonight, Dearie,' the elfin ghost hovered in a sitting position atop the dresser, studying Reilly.

The TV blared from the living room. Chet and her mother were watching an inappropriate movie and eating spaghetti and meatballs that Reilly had prepared.

No matter what hour she arrived at the dump, orders awaited her. Waiting for a load of clothes to finish its rinse and spin cycle, she sat on the bed absently petting Righteous with one hand and thumbing through her text book with another.

Some of her assignments required the use of the Internet. Somehow, Reilly figured, she'd have to get to the library. Reilly wanted to do well in her schoolwork. She certainly felt she couldn't afford to flunk any subjects, not that she was close to flunking, but that might interfere with escaping. Must leave with a clean slate. A good school record was an important first step away from her mother's world. Reilly ardently believed this.

'Reilly?' Bridie settled into the bed.

"I'm sorry, Bridie," the girl murmured.

'Sweetlin', you've devoted entirely too much time either thinking about the mess you think your life is or avoiding thinking about it altogether. You're like a racehorse, heart pounding to cross the finish line. Eighteen is not magic. You must not wish your life away. Name three things you like about yourself,' Bridie set a task.

Reilly bit her lip and frowned.

'Now don't burn your brains up,' the ghost warned.

"Well," Reilly hedged. "You- Bridie, Righteous and...and my job at the diner."

'That's not quite what I wanted. Three aspects-traits, unique to you.'

Reilly's eyes misted. "I'm not a great student. I'm not pretty. . ."

'That's enough, Reilly,' the ghost broke in with a bit more leverage in her voice. 'Three positive, personal traits, or else I'll be takin' me leave of you tonight.' Bridie started to drift above the bed- her head disappeared through the stained ceiling.

"Don't go, Bridie," Reilly sniffled.

The ghost wrapped her arm about the girl's shoulders. Reilly leaned in and promptly fell through the transparent image to lie inside Bridie's lap.

This sudden tromp on the mattress dislodged Righteous, who harrumphed in that superior manner that only a cat can pull off. Reilly sat up and the kitten resettled herself-casting a sidelong eye to her benefactors.

"Rrrow," Righteous chastised the girl.

'I'm waiting, Dearie. Would you like a clue? What happened when those blitherin' eejits attacked our darlin' Righteous?'

Indignation in every word, Reilly answered, "I screamed and knocked that fat bully on his butt."

'Aye, and what does that say about yerself, lass?'

Reilly sat discomfited- never had she considered extolling the prospect she might have good points.

'Begins with an L,' Bridie urged.

"Loyalty?" Reilly managed after a loaded minute.

'Yes, that's a mighty powerful, positive, personal trait. I'd like another, please.'

Going with the flow, "I like plants and animals," Reilly admitted.

Bridie nodded, fingers beckoning for one more. Reilly seemed stumped. The ghost rolled her eyes and muttered, 'Like pickin' ticks out of a dog's hide. What do you like about your work at the diner other than the money?'

The diner chipped at Reilly's inherent shyness, but that wasn't what Bridie asked for. She shrugged a shoulder.

"I...I like to cook. I...I'm a good cook."

'Bravo! That's m'girl. I think it's time you brought out your other gift.' The ghost's eyes sparkled in anticipation.

"Gift?"

'Remember the cape. My letter to you was inside a pocket and the other. . .'

"I forgot!"

Thoughtfully, Reilly gathered Righteous, who'd given the girl a superior half-open eye, settled the gold kitten on her pillow and unfolded the cape from its box.

She groped the pockets, pulled out a small package. Carefully unwrapping the brown paper revealed a silk drawstring pouch.

Its façade depicted a gold cat walking on its hind feet, wearing a hooded, purple cape. The fantastical cat-shades of Righteous, held a candlelit lantern in one paw and used a walking staff in its other white paw.

The fairytale, feline hermit trod a path bordered by gray rock walls, similar to a castle's arched doorway or a haunt-guarded Irish sidh, and the goal seemed to be a stand of ancient twisted oaks- a beautiful, mystical scene of a journey.

Reilly admired the silk bag and fingered the gold tassels with crystal beads which hung from the drawstring. The contents were heavy. She glanced up at Bridie, who smiled and beckoned impatiently.

Reilly withdrew a deck of cards from its silk carrier. A sense of 'magic' sizzled- these were not ordinary cards. Their edges barely retained a glint of original gold gilt and her hands tingled as the cards rested in her palm. They seemed anxious to make her acquaintance.

A flash across her eyes pictured many hands reverently shuffling and then arranging the cards one at a time in various patterns.

'What did you see, Reilly?' Bridie didn't miss a thing.

Reilly described the moving picture montage she'd seen.

"My hands are tingling, Bridie. What are these? Fortune telling cards?"

Bridie's fingers kissed the deck in Reilly's hands.

'These cards have been gifted to the women of my family- one fey woman to another, old to young, for over 200 years. Before these, there was another deck lost to a fire- a sad but appropriate endin'.

These are a means to a journey of discovery of your true self.'

'Each card holds worlds of meanin', but it's up to you to decipher what the card might mean in relation to you. What lessons it might impart.

They are simple tools to help you study on becoming your best self- similar to those self-help books one sees crowding the shelves. Only these contain infinite ideas.

The alchemists of old held self-transformation to be more worthy than any lead to gold notions spouted by ignorant louts.

If you turn over the deck, the first 22 cards you see have pictures and symbols with many layers of meanin'. The other cards are similar to an ordinary deck of cards in that there are suits.

Over time, I will show you different ways to use them, if you are interested.' Bridie waited, hopefully.

Reilly hadn't moved the deck since releasing it from its protective pouch. The tingling continued- a pleasant feeling- an invitation of sorts, not to be denied.

'Use me,' flitted through her head and it wasn't Bridie's voice.

Wonder enthralled Reilly; her senses sizzled. Her best friend was a ghost that she'd met via a yard sale at the most enchanting home she'd ever seen- a cottage that exuded the 'homey' feel she associated with her grandparents when they'd been alive.

Bridie's home held that sense of living welcome even with Bridie as a ghost. How alive it must have been when Bridie lived there in her 'physical', as the ghost termed her living body.

And now Reilly held in her hands an ancient deck of cards. She wasn't sure how they might work. . . Like an Ouija Board?

'Dearest, the cards have less to do with telling the future than helping a person understand their present. In preparin' for a journey, you take one step, then another. I've never purported to use these tarot cards, as they are called, to tell one's future. One's future is their own.

If I were presented with a question by a worried person, I might lay out the cards and lead the querent- the person with the question, to figure things out for herself. My second sight is aside from the cards, and generally I receive messages at random- predicated by the goodwill of the Blessed God.'

Reilly listened, fascinated. Her restlessness had faded and in its place a sense of taking the right step forward emerged. Like the wonder of picking up a great new book from the library. Beginning a new adventure.

As intense as the feeling to walk the drive to Bridie's home had been, she knew the cards were at home in her hands.

"Bridie, shouldn't these go to a woman in your family?"

'Of my relatives here in the U.S.- my sister came here to work, married and stayed- I know of no one called to this deck. So, I've adopted you, Reilly. I believe the cards agree with me- they like you, otherwise you would not feel a pleasant sensation. If they wished to be elsewhere, at the most you'd feel nothing. At the worst, they'd probably self-destruct or disappear, if not prick you.'

Carefully, reverently, Reilly fingered and splayed the cards.

The worn pictures of ancient sites, people of olden times and animals flickered at her- enticing, yet patiently waiting to be called on.

"Thank you, Bridie. Please, tell me what to do?"

'To begin, for the next 22 full moons you will journey through the deck. The first card on the bottom is the beginning- your first step. Set aside the journeyman/forest man.

Now, carefully shuffle the other cards. You may also lay them on a clean flat surface and mix them up as a child would. It's OK if any of them decide to overturn.'

The card side opposite the pictures was a simple, worn, green-gray background with 4 symbols touching each other: a sword, a spear, a shield and a goblet, all golden as if doused by sunlight.

"What are these symbols, Bridie?"

'They refer to the Celtic Gods and their magic weapons and to the four directions, east, south, north, west. Each holds intrinsic meaning as you journey.

No one lives in a vacuum. Plants, animals, people- all of the earth is an inter-connected web. If you've seen Celtic art, it is a celebration of this principle. In trying to hold yourself together through the trials of your young life, you've distanced yourself, set yourself apart, in order to hide. It is time for you to come out of limbo and retake your place in the wonder of the circle of life that never ends.

I hope these cards will help you think along those lines. Help you recognize aspects you may wish to change.'

'I will be here to help you, Reilly. But, I'll not supply you with answers. They must come from you as you realize all the wonder of you and what is around you. And I'm not speaking of bleedin' eejits,' the ghost scowled at a particularly strident uproar from beyond the closed door of Reilly's bedroom.

Reilly couldn't help herself, she felt giddy and at Bridie's see-through scowl and waggling brows, she giggled.

'Ah, lass, I hope to hear more of that delightful sound. Allow your fingers to select- be drawn to, one of the cards. The first card you set aside- the forest man, will be your study partner. The other card you choose. . . Well, see what it may have to tell you. Ask it.

At random times through this cycle of the moon, you may wish to replace it in the deck, reshuffle and choose another to guide you along with the woodsman. In asking the card what it might teach you, you are basically asking to tap into the knowledge of the entire connectedness of all around you.

If you receive an answer, an intuition or recommendation, be grateful. This is not rocket science. Anyone with pure heart and intent may learn, taking cues from the cards. Be quiet. Be open and listen. Remember, these are only simple tools to use. Good night, Reilly. Choose.' And Bridie faded away.

15

Reilly fell asleep with several images rolling on the screen behind her eyes. In one, an enigmatic, resolute man peered at her from a forest, incongruously wearing the colors of all four seasons. His appearance was not separate from the trees and foliage. He blended in with his surroundings, better than camouflage, and his eyes welcomed her.

The other image was of a high tower- a fortress lit by the moon, under siege by lightning and a resultant fire as the lightning struck the tower and sundered rock and ancient timbers. Right before she succumbed to the depths of dream-saturated sleep, Reilly felt the bastions she guarded herself with, shift.

She stood inside a grove of trees. Not one she recognized as ever seeing before. In slowly turning and admiring the huge oak trees heavily laden with acorns and burnished leaves, she began to decipher faces.

Watchful gazes, patient. Within each tree.

"Be one with us," bees droned a musicale.

Here, it didn't matter that she saw herself as imperfect, as cut off. This interconnected world accepted her as an integral part and patiently waited for her to accept herself, acknowledge her personal skills and play her role in the web of life. The energy inherent in the forest world was palpable- a vibrant living force.

After minutes spent searching the various trees' encouraging faces, Reilly closed her eyes, held her arms out.

From the soles of her feet, she felt pores open and toes lengthen- extensions rooting in the soft layered detritus of many seasons' cast-off foliage.

She could feel the soles of her feet grow roots and tunnel into the warm earth, by-passing earthworms and grubs on the way. Her legs fused and she grew taller. Her arms grew out and the hairs on her arms leafed.

Her elbows and fingers branched, sprouted smaller limbs. The tie that kept her hair pulled back dissolved and her locks took on a Medusa-like greenery.

Strength flooded her entire body- now that of a young oak tree. The pulse of the tree had become indecipherable from her heartbeat. Although Reilly became anchored within the form of an oak, she didn't feel imprisoned, but empowered by the energy all about her- the energy of a complaisant, alive, important, growing host of trees.

Her face, eyes open, was now in line with the other smiling facial features of the friendly oaks.

"You see, Reilly, you do belong."

And for once in her life, Reilly had no negative memories, only a sense of acceptance and of completely belonging somewhere.

Spring storms swept through. The appendages of Reilly's tree body swayed with the wind and the rain. Soaked up the sunbeams of summer. Befriended birds, squirrels, insects. Created a lair where her navel once was- housing for a family of raccoons.

Fall changes beckoned her to produce acorns and she watched her leaves turn russet and break away from her, leaving a hint of seasonal sadness with their whispered good-byes as they fluttered away.

Winter iced and froze her limbs, but they remained steadfast as her bloodstream slowed and slumbered. A yawn of a long winter's nap overwhelmed her senses.

A burst of enthusiasm, a rise of elation greeted the return of spring. Her blood coursed through her trunk and enlivened the emerging shoots on her branches. She was presented with a wealth of green leaves once again.

"Accept the seasons and the changes as they emerge in your life. Nothing remains stagnant. Grow and be at peace with the now, and one with all. We will always be here to remind you, if you let us. Carry us with you when you return."

From this last encouragement, Reilly gathered her time in the grove was ending.

"But I don't want to go," she cried.

"You must, your journey is just beginning," the sweet voice faded.

Reilly rolled over in her sleep only to find herself back in her own body on a dark path.

"Remember the strength you felt with us," a faint whisper confided as she hesitantly walked forward.

Alone in the dark- perhaps her worst fear.

"Remember. . . Remember. . .," she repeated for her own benefit and to hear anything at all in the brazen darkness fraught with. . .

The sound of footsteps behind her startled her and when they seemed to be drawing near, Reilly didn't think twice.

She ran. One of her worst fears- being chased. . .

Ahead, a tower with a crown of moonlight stood, forbidding. Nevertheless, Reilly believed she'd be safe if she could reach the tower. But it seemed unattainable. The faster she ran the further the tower seemed to drift from her.

A hand grasped her elbow. Reilly nearly screamed. She fought her way out of the hold, ran on, her breathing ragged with her efforts.

"Reilly," someone was calling her name. "Reilly, stop!"

Lightning coursed through the night. Strobe lights of power slaying the moon. The haven- the tower, was struck and rocks were harangued from their mortar. The entire structure began to disintegrate. From its turreted top, the fractured walls gathered speed as they burst from their moorings and obstreperously toppled to earth.

Reilly fell back in shock. Nowhere to run. Too hoarse from her heaving to scream, she backed away. . . Into the arms of her pursuer, who protectively turned her away from the shocking cataclysm. She had nothing more to fight with.

A sense of strength- the strength she'd felt in the oak grove emanated from. . .

'Reilly, Dearie! Best do your worst, Righteous,' Bridie issued the alarm.

A low growl in her ear pulled Reilly from the most vivid dreams she'd ever experienced. Reluctantly, she allowed Righteous to induce her to wakeful status- the kitten continued to prance on her chest.

"Bridie! Now I won't know how it ended," she exclaimed to the grinning ghost.

'Silly lass. Did you think you could finish your journey in a single night? Up and off with you.'

16

"Bridie, what's the significance of pigs?" Reilly was physically tending to Bridie's indoor plants, while the ghost ran her faint fingers lovingly through vines, leaves and flowers.

'A fair question,' Reilly's friend gave her a searching study. 'You wouldn't be after knowin' the Celtic philosophy concernin' pigs. You drew the card of the Underworld.'

Reilly felt kind of shy- remembered the oaks' advice, "You said I might choose another card."

'Well, of course, Sweetlin'. Tis yer own journey. Pigs. A pig is a guide to the Underworld. He'll force you to face. . . Pigs can also be destructive. . . I'll not be supplyin' all yer own answers, mind you.'

Reilly muddled over Bridie's enigmatic words.

'Do you need a clue?'

"I don't think so. Between the cards and my dreams lately, I've got plenty to think about," Reilly chewed her lip, serious in her puzzling.

'Yer dreams aren't troublesome?'

"No, well. . . Maybe for seconds at a time, but then, exciting things also happen. It's better than a movie. I hate to wake up," Reilly admitted.

'Don't be usin' your dreams as a 'scape goat. Your journey takes place on a physical level, I'm remindin' you,' the ghost warned.

"I know, Bridie. The cards don't frighten me. Unlike many other things in my life. And the dreams, I can deal with them- they're part of my journey, too, right?"

'Tis so. Take the cards and dreams with a tad of salt. Remember, they're tools. Not to be taken overly serious. More like helpful tips for yer personal adventure.'

Bridie had fixated on one of the clovers. She didn't see Reilly chewing on her lip and the advice, too. But knowing the girl, she sensed her moods.

'Dearie, run and get a small clay pot from the back shed. It's time to be separatin' this here clover. Gettin' a mite crowded in there.'

When Reilly returned, Bridie instructed her on gently taking out a few clumps of clovers, separating and replacing the remainder. Two rooted plants, flowers swaying, went into the new pot with fresh soil.

'Now, you take this wee plant with you.'

"Oh, no, Bridie, I shouldn't." How to explain?

The cards in their silk pouch and a sweater and a change of clothes were already in her ubiquitous, black backpack- always with her. Everything she needed- most of what she called her own. Never knew when her mother would sweep her away or when the owner of the dump might evict them. She didn't want to take the risk of not being able to take the plant with her or return it to Bridie's cottage. Because when her mother called, there was no time for retrieving anything. If it wasn't on your person, it was lost. The mother planned their exit in time to pack her things, not a thought was expended for her daughter.

And the plant wouldn't survive in the backpack. Neither would Righteous. . .

'There'll be no such talk, Sweetlin',' Bridie admonished her.

"What if I have to move? Bridie, will you still be. . .?" Reilly felt her eyes tearing. Of the top fears, unexpected change was one of the worst. And now the very idea of leaving Bridie was too much to bear; and who would take care of the kitten?

'Don't be courtin' trouble. Study hard on the meanin' inherent in the card you picked. A very important lesson. And you will take this plant. The darlin' will be lonesome for close company, now that it's lost its family.' Bridie hushed Reilly's misgivings with a raised, transparent brow- the stop a general look.

'Look at these 3-leaves of the shamrock. I'll give you another lesson. Live. Love. Laugh. A bit of St. Paddy's trinity teachin's, but here you go.

Live your whole life, Reilly. Every second, every minute, every hour. There will be sad times, hard times. It's that way for everyone, in different measures, but you live through and go on to enjoy all the pleasantries, too. Even if you have to scout them out.

Love. Find somethin' you're passionate about, and indulge. Anythin' from chocolate to books to a grand fella. Even somethin' as simple as. . .this wee plant.

Laugh. Because laughter is the very best medicine. Never take anythin' too seriously. Speakin' of medicine. . .'

Bridie passed through walls and Reilly scooted to keep up, only through open doorways.

'Music, me bonnie Colleen. Music ties with laughter in me book as the best medicine. Turn on this old record player and we'll give a listen to some of m'favorite boyos, The Irish Rovers.'

Reilly's grandparents had had a record player and had used it frequently. She knew exactly how to operate this one, although it was even older than her grandparents' old Zenith.

'Ah, tis one of me favorite tunes, STAR OF THE COUNTY DOWN,' Bridie exulted.

As the uplifting, lilting music brooked the quiet, old parlor, Bridie swayed, and in no time the ghost lifted her skirt and boisterously danced about- kicking up her muck-boot heels in utmost alacrity.

Reilly's feet began to tap. Couldn't help it, the music was so. . .happy. Only the dead, she thought, could abstain from movement with this lively song playing. Oops, Reilly blushed. Ghosts, technically are dead, aren't they?

'C'mon, lass, join me,' Bridie called. Seeing Reilly's reluctance, she took hold of the girl's shirt tail, took the lead and guided Reilly, swinging her around the room. Like an erratic puppet, the girl tried desperately to keep up.

If Bridie had been there in her 'physical', there would have been collisions. Reilly's shy introspection had never let her give in to dance, or anything else, either. But the music cast its spell and no one could top or stop the exuberant Bridie in her floating, flying, animated maneuvers.

In spite of herself, Reilly felt her lips break into a snip of a smile. Smile gave way to laughter. Her feet were moving in time with the beat; her arms were playing along.

'Ah, now! Tis yer man, Trinity- a likely dance partner, indeed!'

"Wha. . .?"

Reilly spun around without benefit of ghostly arms and stared horrified at Trinity, outside the bay window, peering in with a goofy grin on his face.

'I think we'll turn the music down a wee bit, so you two can talk, Sweetlin'.'

Trinity shook his head, utterly amazed, walked around, and knocked on the front door.

"Oh, God," Reilly wailed.

'Now, Dearie, I know that lad is one good lookin' fella, but it's not reverent to call him, God,' Bridie objected.

The ghost promptly swung open the door as Reilly stood petrified in the hall.

Bridie peeked over the top of the door, scanning Trinity up and down as if he were a candidate for Mr. Universe.

"I'm surprised the electric's on," Trinity grinned at Reilly, his head cocked, listening to DONALD WHERE'S YOUR TROUSERS.

"Reilly, can I come in?" Trinity felt a hefty shove from behind. Frowning, his head swung about, checking for the culprit.

"Uh, oh. . . The electric is. . .for the p...plants," Reilly stammered a reply.

"Hmmm. . . I see Bridie's left her records on, like always," he mused.

"Like. . .always?" For a moment, Reilly thought, maybe Trinity could see Bridie, too. Her eyes swept the room, searching for Bridie's whereabouts.

"I've been here before. Once Bridie reached 100 or so, she stopped walking to the IGA. I'd pick her up. Help her with groceries, any other errands or chores. She was a great fan of music," Trinity explained.

"You knew her, then," Reilly repeated, feeling like an idiot. Hadn't he just said so? What was he doing here?

"Everyone knew Bridie. Either loved her or were afraid of her. No fence sitters where Bridie was concerned. I can still feel her presence," Trinity glanced around.

'Why, so you can, you great Dunderhead! This is my house, so why wouldn't you?' Bridie struck a glancing blow upside the back of Trinity's head.

Reilly's jaw dropped, watching Trinity's hair brush off his head. He nonchalantly scratched at his errant locks.

"You alright? Look like you saw a ghost!" Trinity joked at Reilly's wide-eyed face. "Or at least a big spider. . ."

As he said spider, Trinity's cheerful demeanor sank, bobbed and drowned. Spiders. . .reminded him of. . .

"Trinity? Trinity?" Reilly had to repeat his name twice to bring him back to present. "What's wrong?"

"Wrong? Nothing. Nothing. I've been wondering what you do here. . ."

Hands hitched in his jean pockets, Trinity walked to the record player, replaced the arm and its needle back on STAR OF THE COUNTY DOWN.

"Care to dance to Bridie's favorite song, or do you prefer dancing with ghosts?" A half-grin returned, raising the corner of his mouth and unleashing a beguiling dimple.

Trinity wasn't sure where the invitation had come from, but he'd been pleasantly surprised watching Reilly dance around.

To see her having fun for a change brought a momentary lightness to pierce the blighted armor of his chest and the harder bands encumbering his heart.

"Uh. . .," Reilly hesitated. He'd mentioned ghost again. . .

"Oh, c'mon, I won't bite. Bridie would probably dump one of her compost pots on my head if I tried something inappropriate in her house," Trinity put on his best, girl-bedeviling smile.

And this time Reilly saw it. She gulped, choked, but with Bridie nodding and cheering her on and finally shoving her, and the image of the oaks. . . To refuse would pin her as a bigger idiot.

Reilly allowed Trinity to place one of her hands on his shoulder, quite a stretch for her, and gently took the other. Awkwardly, she tried to follow the pressure of his directive movements.

Bridie retired as audience, sat with crossed knees, spinning on top of the record player, laughing and clapping. Earnestly concentrating on putting her feet anywhere but on top of Trinity's toes, Reilly pursed her lips. And continued to trip around, feeling like an awkward, embarrassed, clumsy ox.

Trinity wished her smile would peek out again. Reluctantly, he released her when the song ended.

He sank onto the high-sided couch, his eyes studying every square inch of the room.

"You liked her," Reilly turned off the record player and sat on the far end from Trinity. There were no other chairs. She was alone with him, should be leery, but with Bridie on guard. . .

Trinity's voice snatched her from 'borrowing trouble'.

"She was a grand gal. Intuitive. Some people claimed she was a witch. I thought she was closer to a saint."

'Ah, Trinity, me lad, if I were a 100 years younger and alive. . .' Bridie stifled a giggle as faint tears rolled through her cheeks.

94

"She kept this place tidy as a church. If anyone ever needed anything, she was ready to offer, but she never minded other people's business, never butted in, never preached. . ."

Trinity rubbed his hands together, eyed the fireplace laid with logs as if Bridie would suddenly. . . A fire would be nice. . .

"I'm really glad for the time I spent with her. The town of Ryan will miss her lively, lovely, extraordinary self."

His hard closed look melted as he spoke of Bridie, as it had when he'd danced.

Saints preserve us if these two ain't a sorry pair. One hard as a rock needing a bit of soft. The other, insecure as a feather loose upon the wind- needin' an anchor to befriend and secure her, Bridie cogitated.

A blast rattled the bay window.

"It'll be a cold one tonight- that time of the year," Trinity addressed the pick-up in the wind.

Reilly was stupefied that she wasn't overly nervous and even more bewildered that she'd actually danced with her neighbor. Her very good-looking neighbor. Could Bridie be the reason? Or maybe it was this cottage. . . Magic?

"This house is. . .homey and warm," Reilly leaned against the high side.

Trinity faced her for a moment. "The both of you are suited," he realized after a lingering reconnaissance, hoping not to disrupt this new easiness flowing between them.

"Both?" Had he seen Bridie? "Do you believe in ghosts?"

"Ghosts, no. Not at all," he said vehemently. His eyes narrowed- the hard recurred. Why?

"Trinity, why are you sad?" She dared ask.

Abruptly, he rose, paced, opened his mouth to speak, decided against it.

Go on, lad, tell her, Bridie prayed.

"Need a ride home?"

"I'm sorry. I didn't mean to. . ."

"No sweat," he rolled a considerable, magnificent shoulder.

"I…I was thinking how nice it would be to be here, to be home. This is what home should feel like. And as it got dark, have a fire in the fireplace and homemade, chocolate chip cookies coming out of the oven and a glass of. . ."

"Did you say homemade, chocolate chip cookies?" Trinity emphasized every word as if he couldn't believe what he'd heard.

"Yes," she shyly blushed.

Think oaks, she told herself. "Sounds pretty good, huh?" Reilly tapped her knees and rose too, wishing she were in her grandparents' kitchen. The idea of the cookies was futile. . .

"Can you make them?" An eager spark of hope kindled in Trinity's eyes.

"Sure," the blush deepened, self-consciously. It felt kind of funny to tell someone she could do something. . .nice.

"Do you have to get back?"

Reilly shuddered, "I try to stay away all I can."

"Can't blame you there. Tell you what, if I buy the ingredients will you bake?"

"Here? I don't think I should," she hedged. She didn't really know her neighbor. . . She wasn't exactly alone with him, here. . . Bridie was all ears, perched on the couch. But. . .

'Oaks,' Bridie shouted.

"Nah, at my house. It's just Dad and me. You'd have two slaves for life or at least for a week. What do you say?"

'Yes! Yes! Yes!' Bridie chortled, doing an Irish jig on the record- spinning it without benefit of electricity.

Reilly's fascinated eyes fastened on the ghost, blocking Trinity's view of the record player.

"Reilly?" Trinity couldn't help but wonder at the loss of Reilly's attention, almost like she really was spying a ghost. Wouldn't put it past Bridie, he thought.

Part of Reilly remained uncomfortably leery. In her neighbors' trailer, just her and. . . Bridie, Bridie would come, surely. Face your fears. . . Oaks. . . Trinity seemed honest and excited about cookies. Bridie certainly approved of him. That had to count for something. And part of her craved homemade, chocolate chip cookies. How long had it been? The craving won out.

Trinity watched Reilly place baking ingredients in the cart. Flour, sugar, eggs, some kind of soda. . .

"How many batches can you make?" He didn't want to sound greedy or anything, but. . . How long had it been?

"I have some homework- would two batches be OK?" She studied the chocolate chip selection. Always get the best ingredients, her grandma had said.

"Great!" Trinity wheeled the grocery cart to the checkout, putting in a gallon of milk on the way.

"You have a dog named Wrench?"

Trinity had told Reilly not to pet the Heinz 57 pound puppy. Which had grown into a 45 pound beast.

"Let him come to you. He's not overly friendly with strangers. Once he offers his paw, shake, and then you're a new friend."

Wrench had other ideas.

He practically crawled into her lap as she knelt to shake.

Slobbery dog kisses had her giggling and desperately attempting to fend the large, overly friendly dog off. Trinity stepped in after a flabbergasted minute, pulled the reluctant Wrench off, offered Reilly a hand up.

"Somebody dropped him off at the garage, starved, full of ticks and fleas, missing a lot of hair. Poor pup. You know that old expression about throwing a wrench in the works? Seemed to fit. He's always got his nose in a job."

Wrench's whole brindle pit bull body shook with excitement- tail beating percussively. Reilly couldn't pet enough of him fast enough to suit him.

"That's odd. Wrench barks at everybody and is generally stand-offish. Everybody except. . ." Pat Sr. dropped the last words like a burnt potato.

She caught the faint change in the air, saw Trinity grit his teeth, stumble over Wrench and take the grocery bags to the kitchen.

"I'm here to make cookies," she cut through the whiff of tension.

Pat O'Ryan greeted this news with the same enthusiasm as his son. Even without the enticement of cookies, Wrench enthusiastically clung to her side. Reilly's disconcert melted away.

"We probably have a recipe around here somewhere," Pat clue-lessly opened and closed cabinets and drawers as Trinity un-bagged the groceries.

"That's OK, Pat, I don't need a recipe," Reilly said.

"You've got the recipe on you?" He eyed her backpack.

"No, I memorized it. Through all the moves, I wasn't able to save a cookbook." Father and son exchanged looks and then tried not to put Reilly on the spot with the sympathy that doused them.

She held up a bag of chips. "I could always cheat," she pointed to the recipe on the back of the bag.

"Wow!" Trinity shadowed her, tripping over Wrench, until Reilly requested cookie sheets, bowls. . .

Pat eyed his son and the industrious girl. 'All the moves,' she'd said. This hammered at Pat's heart. He believed wholeheartedly in family and stability.

Wrench issued a low growl and vigorous barking as he raced to the door before the bell rang.

"I'll get it," Trinity sauntered to the door, waving at Wrench to chill.

"I hoped you were here," a sultry girl's voice cut into Reilly's batter-beating.

Cookies for four, she thought.

Trinity blocked the entrance. "Why are you here?" He curtly grilled the model-material visitor.

"I tried to call. . ." The girl didn't sound too happy at her reception.

"Look, I'm busy here. We've got company. I'll call you sometime," Trinity tried to brush off the girl without any attempt at finesse.

The girl batted her eyes, to no avail, tiptoed up to kiss him, but fell short as Trinity backed into the trailer. Her swinging hips were wasted on the closing door.

Pat shut down his computer as a delectable scent absorbed his concentration. He joined his son at the table, both men as expectant as two kids on Christmas.

"Why don't you bring your homework over here and do it? We've got Internet," Trinity offered. God knows, that Chet probably didn't have a computer.

Reilly blushed, "Uh. . . I do have an assignment that. . . It would be helpful to use the Internet, but I'm not. . . I…I don't have any. . .computer skills."

"No big deal. We'll have you up and running in no time," Trinity poured milk- three glasses.

Pat added his two cents, "Reilly, this house has two laptops hooked up. You're welcome to use them whenever you want. We'll even leave the door unlocked. Wrench already thinks you belong here." The dog promptly thumped his tail in agreement.

"N...no, I. . . Could I come, maybe, on Sundays?" A twinge harkened in her chest at this unanticipated, sincere offer, yet she felt weird about accepting. Oaks...oaks, she mentally recited, mantra-like.

"Any time," Pat declared, definitively.

Trinity and his dad downed the hot cookies as fast as they left the oven- more like starving kids than well-fed adults. It was a wonder to Reilly that they didn't burn their tongues. The numerous accolades gave her a sense of unfamiliar well-being. Almost like being part of a family.

Reilly was reluctant to leave the warmth of the clean, but lived-in trailer. But she had her school work and Righteous. . . Oh, my, she thought- I almost forgot her.

As Trinity walked down the hall, she studied the pictures on the living room wall. Family pictures.

One, especially, drew her. Trinity seated, a guitar in hand, and a small, cheerful girl- all smiles, with her arms wrapped around his neck. Trinity's face was turned to her, but his smile mirrored the little girl's.

"My daughter," Pat sadly explained. Caught off guard, Reilly could only nod.

Next to this picture was a family portrait. Pat, with his arms around a tall, graceful, shiny-eyed woman, stood behind two older boys- Trinity's brothers, both resembling their mother. Trinity and his little sister obviously took after their father. The family looked like a family should- all happy to be together, though one sensed mischief lurking in those Irish eyes.

By the tone of Pat's voice and the grim look on Trinity's face as he returned and saw what they were looking at, Reilly knew the sister and mother were no longer alive.

Embarrassed, Reilly felt as if she'd been caught poking her nose into something she shouldn't. Pat cleared his throat to clear the emotion-laden air and gently tapped her on her shoulder as Trinity stalwartly tried to regain balance. Neither witnessed the soft, loving look Pat bestowed on his son.

The force of the howling wind outside broke up the reverie the cookies had instigated.

"I'll walk you back," Trinity said as he brushed by his dad and the girl, headed to the kitchen. "Why don't you take some cookies with you?"

"N...no, thanks. I'd rather know you were enjoying them."

"We'll certainly do that. Thank you very much, Reilly, and remember, our door is always open to you," Pat said by way of good-bye.

Reilly picked up her backpack, donned the sweater from inside it and gathered the small, newly potted shamrock. Wordlessly, she walked next to Trinity, back to the dump.

"Like mother, like daughter," Chet rudely remarked, eyeing Trinity with Reilly in his doorway.

Seething, Trinity threw a glare of reprimand at Chet, backed with a physique to do real damage, thanked Reilly again, and grimly turned to go.

Reilly sidled around Chet. Her mother, wondering, silently waved.

Reilly set the plant on her bedside table. The state of her drawer, slightly opened, caught her attention, as did the state of her few clothes hanging haphazardly in the tiny closet.

Reilly smoothed sleeves, noticed a torn pocket. She should have been angry. Other teenagers would have been furious to know a parent had rifled through their belongings.

But Reilly knew her mother and/or Chet would be checking for money- Reilly's wages. She expected this, nothing new here. It emphasized the importance of her locker at work. Brought home her well-earned 'smarts'. Unfortunately, she also knew she would be subjected to constant cajoling and guilt trips regarding her pay.

The mother wouldn't relent.

The image of the oak sinking roots, dancing with the seasons, enduring the harshest winds, came to Reilly.

This time she would not give in to her mother. This time she would stand fast- she promised herself.

Righteous scrambled over the partially open window's ledge, jumped to the bed and sat gazing at Reilly as she tried not to feel hurt.

"Sorry, I don't have a cookie for you," she conversed with the purring kitten as she opened a can of cat food.

In turning back to the bed, Reilly saw Bridie minding her and Righteous.

'You had a good time with yer man, Trinity,' she stated.

"Why do you call him my man? He is a man, not mine, and I'm just a kid," Reilly scowled, cross-grained.

But Bridie merely laughed, 'Remember, it's an Irish expression, Dearie, and kids do grow up. Confess, Sweetlin', you do find him handsome. . .'

"And look at me," Reilly avoided the pockmarked mirror, bit her lip to stave off tears.

'Aye, that reminds me. I've put a letter inside your bag. Remember that man I told you to memorize? Give him the letter the first time you see him.'

18

'The cards are presenting in an unusual way,' Bridie scrutinized what Reilly had drawn.

"Am I such a mess?" Reilly was still smarting from Chet's surly remark about her being like her mother. Even though she knew it was a lie, she liked it better when he ignored her completely, as was his regular habit.

'Not at all, Sweetlin'. Tell me what lessons you are learnin'.'

This drew Reilly's frowning focus. She felt put on the spot, especially since she was not one who ever offered to answer a question in class. For one thing, she didn't want to be called on- have attention directed at her, and for another, she might be wrong even when she thought she was right- how embarrassing! Always stay under the radar; don't invite circumspection- that was Reilly.

Just another one of a long list of fears. Was I born this way? She ruminated briefly on her current state, or am I a circumstance of how my life has played out? Is it possible for me to. . .?

Bridie patiently, empathetically, waited out the silence.

"The forest man card tells me I have strengths I never thought of. I never considered myself as strong, but I guess I move with or hide under the changes, the awful things, without breaking. Not yet, anyway," Reilly finally allowed.

'Good girl, Sweetlin',' Bridie encouraged.

"Bridie, sometimes it's so hard," Reilly clenched her fists in futile fury.

'I know, Dearie, but that which does not break you, makes you stronger. Some wise person said that.'

Reilly studied the last card she'd been offered by the deck. Bridie called it the Underworld card. A man in a deep-colored robe, staff in hand and a white pig at his feet, stood outside a grass-covered portal into the earth.

"The card tells me to acknowledge my fears. Not to be imprisoned by them. I'd just as soon forget them, but they're everywhere," Reilly gazed at Bridie.

'What conclusion did you come to regarding pigs?'

"Between the tower and the pig, I must not let my fears destroy me or cause me to feel alone or separate. I need to leave the shelter of the. . .armor I've constructed and know that I will be alright. Endure, like the oaks do."

'You'll find willows, being quite supple, are very adept at moving with changes; going with the flow, I believe is the expression- study them in a storm. I'm here to help you, Dearie, although you cannot physically lean on me,' Bridie patted through the girl's shoulder.

Righteous sat up in Reilly's lap and pinned her with an immutable stare. The kitten had a sense of the girl's distress level bearing down on her with the next question and wished to calm her new friend. One white paw reached up and lovingly stroked the girl's cheek, a muted 'meoow' in its wake.

"And if I leave?" Reilly's voice quavered. If Chet and her mother were arguing already. . . Her mother was such a grand flirt. . .

'Another fear for your list? Don't borrow trouble, lass, it comes soon enough. And don't confront your fears- no battlin'. War is pointless. Say hello to your worries and walk on. Take your cape today. I feel storms coming- look for willows. You'll be on your own tonight.'

Reilly blanched, alone! That long walk. . . in a storm, by herself?

'Sorry, lass, but ghosts don't do well out in a storm, at least, I'm not sure I would.'

Either do I, thought Reilly. The only safe place in a storm was in bed and heaven help her if the lights went out. . .

'Keep that letter with you and don't forget to deliver it,' the ghost instructed.

The thundering and heavy rains took their toll on the diner's customers. One of the brave happened to be Steve- the man Bridie told her to memorize.

Reilly poured coffee, took his order and pictured the oak as she withdrew the letter from her pocket.

"Sir, I'm supposed to give you this." She set the letter on the table with his scrolled name showing.

Steve put aside his newspaper. From behind his glasses, he first studied the new waitress, whom he definitely admired for her work ethic.

When his eyes turned to the envelope with his name in fanciful calligraphy across its surface, a shock rippled through him. No one else wrote like that.

"Where did you get this?" he whispered, but Reilly had retreated to the comfort of the grill to prepare Steve's usual order.

    With shaky fingers, Steve opened the envelope.

Dear, I'm calling in my favor. Please see to Reilly's teeth. Many thanks,

                    Bridie O'Connair

    The letter vibrated in Steve's hands. He had to set it down and steady himself. He looked around as if he almost expected Bridie herself to be sitting across from him. Steve took off his glasses and rubbed his temples. Memories steamrolled over him.

    Ten years had passed, but the outcome of Bridie's aid, which he'd so diligently begged of her. . .

    The love of his life still lived, beyond any doctor's explanation. They were completely stymied. Pooh-poohed the dentist's testament of Bridie's advice, her suggestions.

    He'd gone to the elderly, wise, healing 'institution' of the town, as a last resort- what had he to lose? He'd absentmindedly recalled the legends of the woman's prowess, and they were legion, told and retold for a hundred years. He had to feel like he'd addressed every possibility. The doctors said his wife was going to die.

    The kindly, sage woman had offered several, simple suggestions and remedies, had not asked for a cent, contrary to the hospitals and doctors' offices which had nearly bankrupted him.

    Bridie, unlike those same doctors, had been overjoyed and grateful to God for his wife's recovery and return to perfect health. Her sole request- the return of a favor at some undetermined time.

    Dr. Steve Desatnik, orthodontist, and his wife, had prospered over the past ten years, always quick to tender continued thanks to Bridie. They had kept in contact with her in case she needed anything- how he missed her!

    He didn't know how it was possible for a woman to request a favor after death, but Bridie. . . If anyone could do it, the mysterious, lovely Bridie would. He'd never really thought of it before, but certainly would not put it past her, and here before him was proof.

    Steve folded the letter, definitively written in Bridie's handwriting, replaced it in its envelope and carefully pocketed it. He swiped at his eyes; he would keep his promise, gratefully, gladly.

Reilly delivered Steve's usual, tried to hurry away.

"Reilly?"

"Y…yes," she wrung her hands, eyes searching for an outlet.

"I…I don't know if you know what I do for a living. I'm an orthodontist. It seems we have a mutual friend in Bridie O'Connair."

His warm, brown eyes surveyed the young, self-conscious girl with heightened interest.

"I'd like the opportunity to fix your teeth. Could you and your parents come to my office this week for a consult?" He handed her a card with his office hours listed.

"I. . ." Reilly hesitated. Yes, she'd love to get her teeth back in her mouth. All of the childish jibes had pelted any semblance of self-esteem she might have had to smithereens since her adult teeth had grown in. Her crooked, front teeth made a travesty of attempts to smile. Keeping her mouth closed and eyes down was a direct submission to the self-deprecating fear of being ridiculed, constantly embarrassed. How she envied all the whining kids who'd been provided with braces at an early age.

"I work every day after school," she said.

"That's good. How about Saturday? Around 3:00? I share an office with Dr. Mardis, two blocks west."

Absently nodding, Reilly mentally tallied her earnings. Surely with her job, he'd let her make payments?

Reilly tried not to focus on the downpour as closing time approached, or the fact she'd be all alone. Oaks, she chanted to herself, bolstering her courage.

She'd certainly get wet, but she wouldn't freeze. Not only had she brought the hooded cape, she had an extra sweater, too.

"Good night, Dave, Martie," and she slipped out. If they knew she had no ride they'd be quick to offer transportation to the dump, but she didn't want to put them out. What must it feel like to have caring parents to pick you up when the weather was horrendous? Or even when it was nice?

Reilly joked with herself about looking forward to the challenge.

Night and alone and storms- three of the worst on her list, and what did Bridie mean about not being good in storms? Would lightning disagree with a ghost? Odd. . .

"I can do this," she braced her backpack against her chest. The promise of Saturday and the prospect of finally getting her teeth fixed. . . Her mother had never seen fit to use the welfare benefits to take her to a dentist. Always some excuse.

These thoughts almost succored her backbone as she walked into the light-stealing, rainy night. Almost.

Reilly stayed far from the side of the road as she hastily negotiated her way to Red Wing Trailer Court. The few vehicles flying by would have further saturated her if she'd been within range of the rooster-tails of spray they launched.

If that were possible. Her old shoes were soaked. She'd put her new work shoes inside her backpack and this, she'd ensconced in a big plastic bag.

She tried to muse on the cars going by, hurrying home to. . .families sharing meals. She wondered if Trinity and Pat had eaten all the cookies.

Silly, she chided herself amidst her running commentary which sought to dispel imaginary monsters. That was three days ago- no cookie could have survived that long.

A car's headlights grazed her.

Cautiously, fully alert, Reilly walked faster.

The car slowed.

She caught the make out of the corner of her eye as she picked up speed. Not a car she recognized.

No Bridie at her side.

With split focus, Reilly minded what the car did and began to run- hard to accomplish when your shoes sank into mud with every step.

The small vehicle pulled off the road, headlights on bright.

Fear stroked her chest and stoked her adrenalin. She gathered her cape about her and raced best she could, splashing, slipping and sinking into the wet ground.

Please, don't let me fall, she prayed.

She heard the car door open, tried to picture the oaks, called up that strength she was supposed to be capable of, accelerated, slipped. . .

"Reilly?"

Fear overrode her senses. Run! Run! Her adrenalin-fired cells clamored.

"Reilly!"

She barely registered the voice hollering something and then pursuing her, splashing footfalls close, too close.

"Reilly! Damn't! Stop running! Reilly!"

Something about the voice clicked, she slid to a stop, gasping, trembling, nearly fell, but caught herself.

"Reilly, get in the damn car before we both drown!"

19

"What the hell were you running from?" Trinity cranked the heat as the two of them drenched the front seats of an old Ford Escort.

"I…I didn't r…recognize the c…car," Reilly stuttered.

"Yeah? Well," Trinity shuffled through the contents of the back seat, looking for a grease-free towel. Irritated with himself and her cowering body and slow-to-settle-fright-stricken eyes, he continued to explain.

"The Camaro's put up for the winter. This is my bad weather vehicle. Didn't you hear me calling you?"

"N…not at first," encumbered, she kept ducking his gaze— her eyes out the window hoping to see an oak or a willow. Her fingers, clenched with cold, struggled to reach for the heat blowing from the vents.

"You cold?"

"N…not r…really," she huddled close to the door.

"You're not afraid of me, are you?" When she didn't answer, he swore under his breath.

"I. . . If you were me. . .in my shoes. . .you might have run, too," she tried to make him see it from her point of view. Explanations were awkward.

Trinity sat dumbfounded. He made an effort to look at it from her shoes. What little he knew of her. . .

If he'd been uprooted all his life and had been forced to live in a roach-infested pit like Chet's place, with drunks in and out. . .

Yeah, he'd probably run, too, if anybody pulled over. In this day and age, small town or not. . .

"I'm sorry, Reilly, I didn't mean to scare you. Why didn't your mother pick you up from work?"

Reilly hesitated, not wanting to lie. How should she answer?

"She has. . .other things to do," the girl murmured.

"Right," Trinity swore again. He wasn't born yesterday. "You walk home every night? Alone, no matter what the weather is? Are you crazy? Winter's coming, sheesh!"

"I…I have no choice. I need to work."

"What? To supply them with more 6-packs?" He refrained from an outright smirk, barely.

Reilly froze. She pushed back her hood and for the first time Trinity could recall, she really looked at him, in fact, stared him down.

"Is that what you think?" A lick of fire raced up her backbone. That same fire lit up her eyes.

"I'm working so I have something. . .some means to get away from them. As soon as I'm 18. I do not give them my money. I hide it. They search my room every day, hoping I'll bring home my tips or something. I'm not like them!" This last ended on a crying note.

Reilly bit her lip, forced one fingernail under another. She would not cry in front of him. She would not.

"Jaysus, Mary and Joseph, Reilly! I'm sorry. I know you're not like them. Jaysus! They actually rifle through your things?" How awful did he feel?

Trinity had a few choice descriptive words for Chet and the mother, which he rehearsed, silently, under his breath. He waited for Reilly to get control. In another situation, he might have pulled her into his arms, but here, now, it would probably alarm her even more. Aggravated, he thrust his hand through his sodden hair.

"I think your walking home by yourself in this freakin' weather is the bravest thing I've ever seen," he said with utmost sincerity. Also the dumbest, he kept to himself, as thunder reverberated, lightning flashed across the sky and descended to ground, presaging another torrential downpour.

The ensuing silence of his passenger told him she'd retreated into herself again. Urgently, he sought some means to solace her. Poor lonely, scared shitless. . .

"Hey," he gently offered into the car's stillness.

Tit for tat. She'd bared her soul to him. Given him a nasty glimpse into the misery inherent in her life. He admired the inner strength she exuded, but couldn't for the life of him imagine how it was fueled.

Reilly apparently had no support. Zilch. She had a will, a job, a kitten- he'd seen the two of them together. If he wanted to take the first step to a real friendship. . . It would require. . .

He glanced out his window. What the hell.

"The sadness. . .in my heart. . .stems from the loss of my little sister. Ivy Rose."

Trinity drummed his fingers on the steering wheel, wishing the hum of the engine made the telling easier.

Hell, everyone in Ryan knew how close Trinity and Ivy Rose had been. But Reilly was an outsider. In more ways than one. . .

"Ivy Rose was sunshine on a cold, rainy day. Always cheerful, always smiling. Even when she was picked on. Even when she was sick. . ."

The bands constricting his heart for the past five years rattled and the awful tightness in his chest shifted.

He sighed, gritted his teeth, forced himself to continue.

"Six years separated us, but it was nothing. We were very, very close, loved all the same things. She was my greatest fan and I hope she felt I was hers. I. . . I was her hero in. . .spider dispatching, bully beat down. While other 18-year olds were making out with girls, I sat by her bedside and watched her die. Bit by bit, that f… disease stole her life, took her away. The one bully I couldn't defeat for her. But to the last, she smiled. Said she wasn't afraid, told me. . .told me. . .Mom was waiting for her. . .and. . .and," his eyes watered.

He gripped the steering wheel, but not hard enough to break it, like he desperately wanted to. . .like he tried to break so many heads, walls. . .his brother. . .

"Trinity."

It took a minute for Trinity's cells to shuck the numbness in his hurt-scorched brain. Reilly's hand softly rested atop his and she was speaking to him.

"I wish. . . I would have loved to meet her. Make cookies with her. . .," Reilly's voice trailed off.

She wanted to absorb the suffering paining this nice, nice young man who had showed her nothing but kindness. More than anything she wanted to help him feel, be, OK.

"I. . . I can't imagine having someone to care for like that, who cared about me, too," Reilly whispered into the poignant stillness.

"Yeah, I did have that. . .for a while. Maybe it would have been easier if I hadn't. . .," he grimaced. He'd not opened up like this to anyone, not one family member. Not even Bridie could get it out of him, though for some reason, he felt she understood all the emotions tearing at him.

"Don't say that, Trinity," Reilly pleaded. She knew he still ached, terribly. How does one go on without hurting when a love is taken away?

Trinity's jaw clenched. His teeth bit hard on the inside of his mouth until he tasted blood.

"Now you know. If you listen to the stories around town, you'll hear I went a little crazy. . .after. The crazy is still inside; mostly, I keep it under control." He'd not scare her with how he almost killed his own brother.

The implacable shell surged anew as he regained his composure. He didn't feel Reilly take her hand from his; he didn't see the gentleness in her eyes.

"You probably have homework. Better get you back," he reached for the gear shift.

"I wish we could just stay here. Let it rain. Wash all the hurts away. All the fears," she barely whispered.

Trinity by-passed the gear shift, held out his hand.

"Hi, my name is Trinity O'Ryan. I'd like to be your friend."

Reilly stared at Trinity's hand, his open invitation. Momentarily, he disguised the hardness from her, but she knew of its inevitable return. Hopefully, not for forever. . .

She placed her hand in his. "Hello, my name is Reilly Brooke. I'd like to be your friend."

They shook hands. No agendas- simply the beginning of a friendship.

"And by the way, I'll be taking you back to the trailer court every night. No ifs, ands or buts."

"Reilly, lend me enough money for a carton of cigarettes. I'll pay you back once the check comes in," the mother waylaid her.

The girl gritted her teeth, felt a sickening rumble in her gut. Reilly knew her mother as a champion of persistence. Especially after coming up empty handed from searching Reilly's room.

Funny, this time she'd actually mentioned repaying- a new tactic? But Reilly knew her mother better than that. The expression, 'it would be a cold day in. . .' came to mind.

The guilt trip was act 2.

"You know I can't get by without my cigarettes," her mother had a way of softening her tone, the better to cadge sympathy. "I'll go bonkers."

But Reilly had learned many lessons the hard way. She'd been her mother's pawn for as long as she could remember- a means to a government check instead of her mother's getting a job. Her mother had also used her daughter to con money from Reilly's grandparents- the mother's own parents. Reilly needs this, Reilly needs that, tell Grandma you need. . . And when they did hand over any money at all, the mother hastened off to a bar, or a beauty appointment, or. . .

Reilly's insides threatened to reveal themselves.

"I don't have any money. It's all with the dentist, and whatever else I might make is going in a college fund." One you can't get at, Reilly reminded herself.

The wages and tips were adding up quick. Reilly exchanged small bills for large ones, even though there was plenty of room in her locker. Every day she expressed her gratitude to whoever might be listening- up there.

"I'm your mother. The least you can do is lend me a little for cigarettes."

With Reilly remaining intransigent, her mother's tone left off its nicety.

"Can't do it. Why don't you ask Chet?"

"You're not getting smart with me, are you?" Her mother had never hit her- there were easier ways to exert control and build fears.

Reilly clutched at her stomach, began to cough. The mother backed away. Wouldn't do to spew over the mother's new, turquoise sweater.

"I better do my homework," the girl rushed to the bathroom. Why did her pretty mother act like this? She'd given up ever receiving a logical answer.

'Ah, Sweetlin' you're gettin' stronger. I'm that proud of you. I'm knowin' it's hard, lass,' Bridie lent balm into the emotional turbulence. It wasn't her place to deride the mother, as bad as she wanted to.

Reilly's stomach slowly regained peace in her room, away from her mother; she chewed on a dried slip of peppermint and opened a can of cat food, enduring the familiar sense of being lost after every confrontation.

Muddled, Messed up, Morbid.

Ignoring her turkey entrée, Righteous rubbed her body against Reilly's hand and arm, trilling all the while, arching her back, tail straight up. The kitten sensed her friend's distress and tried to bring her 'round.

Reilly took a deep breath, stroked the golden Righteous. "I think I'll pick another card, Bridie."

'The cards are pushing your journey by givin' up the picture cards early. That can be hard to face. You have a strong friend in Trinity. Don't be afraid to lean on him. He can take it. I'd dearly love to hold you, me girl,' Bridie wrapped her thin ghostly arms into Reilly.

"Bridie, I . . . I can feel your. . .energy," the surprised girl startled; sadness shifted to a back burner. Bridie had poured every powerful ounce of love she could muster into her apparition and the touch she enveloped Reilly with.

"I'm so grateful you're here. Without you and Righteous, it would be easier to sink. . .to just sleep."

'I know Sweetlin'. Now, back to Trinity. He'll be a good friend to you. He's exceptionally strong. And he and Pat love home cookin'.'

"I guess you're hinting at something?" Reilly studied her mentor. How could this woman be 117? If anything she seemed to be getting younger. No longer looked the sixty-something Reilly had surmised at first meeting the ghost. It seemed as if she'd lost another twenty years. Was that possible? She guessed if one was a ghost, a lot of things were possible.

'Never yer mind 'bout me age. I bet those two O'Ryans would love chicken and dumplin's on a Sunday afternoon,' Bridie heartily suggested.

"Bridie, I can't just barge into their kitchen. . ."

'But Dearie, you'll already be there- doin' yer homework,' the ghost acted totally innocent, wide eyes and all.

Reilly rolled her eyes, "Bridie, honestly!"

The girl shuffled the cards, carefully. The deck spit one out; the card landed on the floor.

'Ah, the cards have decided,' Bridie watched. She was used to the cards taking on a life of their own.

Reilly stared at the symbol. Upright on a russet plane with flickers of fire all about the edges stood. . .what looked like a twisted walking stick with a mysterious gold circle on top of it. In the midst of the circle, greens sprouted, intertwining.

"Ace of Wands? Bridie?" Perplexed, she turned to the ghost.

'What is your first reaction to what you see? Your very first reaction.'

"It takes a lot of energy to keep a fire burning," Reilly's brow furrowed. "I know at times I lack str. . ."

'This has less to do with strength than it has to do with the expression of your own fire.'

Confused, Reilly fondled the card.

'You've had an idea since you started to work at the diner,' Bridie hinted.

Astonished at Bridie's insight, Reilly set down the Ace of Wands and fiddled with her fingers. Why should she be surprised? After all, Bridie did have the 'sight'.

"I'm. . . Well. . . It's hard to think of a diner having home-cooked meals, but not any homemade desserts," the girl finally voiced aloud what had been on her mind.

'And just what do you intend to do about it?' Bridie challenged.

At Bridie's instigation, Reilly had gathered and hung several dried plants which her mentor had beribboned and hung to dry in her gardening room- a small room off the kitchen which acted as a mudroom and wash-up area. It contained a small sink and counter to trim, repot and prepare garden produce and flowers.

Between Bridie, the cards, and the aromatic scents of lavender, basil and mints, Reilly fell asleep the second she hit the pillow. Righteous curled in her arms every night, after her customary lullaby purr and kneading action on the girl's bicep nearest Reilly's heart.

Reilly walked through a sun-flooded, wildflower meadow. Sunflowers, most of them bigger than her head, towered over her. Deep purple blooms on long stalks, red flowers, orange trumpet vines, white Queen Anne's lace- all summoned and fed more butterflies than Reilly had ever seen in her whole life.

They settled on her shirt, hitched rides on her arms and hair. A beautiful sensation filled her as she felt their tiny movements. She couldn't help but be filled with joy.

'Hello there,' a merry voice startled Reilly from her butterfly watch.

She turned toward the greeting. From the woods skipped a girl, maybe ten or twelve years old.

Dark brown hair had sun-lightened streaks. All dressed in pink sleeveless shirt and shorts, the girl had a most amiable smile, a few freckles and big, brown eyes. Something about those eyes. . .

'Isn't Bridie's garden the best?'

"So this is what it looks like in the summer?" Reilly asked. She surveyed the colorful growth and turned back to the happy girl.

The newcomer had her hands behind her back. She swayed with the breeze, just as the flowers did. The smile never left her lips.

Something very familiar. . . Reilly frowned trying to put her finger on the pervading inkling of perception. A resemblance. . .

"Ivy Rose?" An entrancing shiver ran up Reilly's spine.

'I so hoped you'd know it was me,' Ivy Rose clapped her hands, overjoyed. 'When you told Trinity you would like to meet me, I had to try to get you to see me. It's great to meet you, Reilly. I'm so glad you can see me and talk to me.'

The little girl practically bounced/floated up and down with glee.

"Are you. . .are you a ghost, too?" Reilly whispered in her sleep.

'I'm trying to be. Bridie does it without any effort. I find it difficult. Trinity doesn't see me,' she sunk into dejection, but immediately chirruped.

'I probably don't have much time. I wanted to talk to you about my brother, Trinity,' Ivy Rose turned ultra-serious.

"He misses you, something fierce," Reilly told her.

'I know; I've tried to reach him. I keep spreading his guitar picks across his bed. I've tried to talk to him, but he doesn't hear me and I'm not very good at being a ghost. I can't seem to appear to him. Maybe it's because he doesn't hear me. Ooh, I'm about to fade.

I miss his music. He never plays his guitar anymore or sings, even with the radio on. Will you listen for me, Reilly?' The little girl's words came out in a rush.

'You could tell him what I say.' Ivy Rose's body faded, getting fainter and fainter.

"But Ivy Rose, I don't know if he'll believe me," Reilly qualified.

'Just promise you'll listen for me and try to get him to listen, too. I told him before I left I'd come back and talk with him,' the girl's voice pleaded as she nearly vanished.

"Maybe he is too sad to. . .hear," Reilly explained her thoughts on the matter.

'Yes, but now you're here, it will be great! I like you Reilly. To think you're not scared of ghosts when you have all those other scares, wow! You're very special. Ooh, darn it! I have to go, I'll be in touch.'

"Wait. . ." Reilly cried, but the young girl had. . .evaporated.

Wow, is right! Reilly thought, am I to have two ghost friends?

And just how was she going to convince Trinity?

21

'When are you going to talk to Dave and Martie?'

"Uh, I. . . I think I'll wait until after I get my braces on."

'Why put off 'til tomorrow what you can do today?' Bridie trounced, hovering closer-than-close as Reilly watered and thoroughly checked all the house plants.

At times, Bridie was near enough that apparition and live body mingled. Reilly had grown used to the tingle of Bridie's ghostly impact- similar to how the cards titillated when Reilly released them from their pouch. A dose of mild electricity- tingly and mysteriously magical. Wonderfully fascinating.

"Bridie, it's Sunday."

'Why, so tis and tomorrow is Monday. . ."

"If I. . . If they want me to bake pies or cakes I don't want to get started and then need a day off. I mean. . .in case they have to pull some of my teeth."

'Ah, I see. That's usin' yer noggin',' Bridie approved.

Reilly was more than ready to broach the next subject. "Bridie, I saw Ivy Rose last night in my dreams."

'A very sweet child, that one.'

"You couldn't help her?" Reilly wondered. Why she expected Bridie to be an infallible healer, she didn't know, but she had a whole lot of faith in her ghostly friend.

'Dearest, sometimes the Good Lord's decisions are final. He called Ivy Rose home,' Bridie sighed.

"It doesn't seem fair for Trinity to lose his mother and then his little sister, too. Especially when they were so close," Reilly sizzled with emotional upheaval recalling Trinity's pain.

'Ah, to see the two of them. Amazing siblings!' Bridie reminisced.

"Why didn't you tell me. . .about. . .Trinity's loss?"

'It's Trinity's story to tell, Reilly, not mine.'

"She said he never plays music anymore. I don't understand. Is she always around him, kind of like you being here for me?"

'Loved ones are always around those they love. That love never ceases. I loved you simply from seeing you in my visions. Sometimes, a body can't get through the sad to see. Now, it's getting near dusk and I've a task for you before you go. Inside my flower room, in the chest with all the little drawers. . .'

Bridie sifted through walls and waited for Reilly.

'Three across right and three drawers down,' the ghost instructed.

"What an interesting piece of furniture," Reilly admired the chest of many drawers.

'Right handy for storing packets of dried remedies, seeds and such. A veritable filing cabinet.'

Bridie floated to the top of the chest as Reilly opened a long drawer. A row of envelopes dwelt within.

'Take a packet with you, Dearie.'

"What's inside, Bridie?"

'Us old timers would call it a 'physic'.'

Reilly cocked her head thoughtfully, hitched her shoulder in ignorance.

'I'll just say, it's to work the evil…er, bile out of a body, and leave it at that,' Bridie tendered a vague explanation.

Reilly fastened her cape, pulled up the hood, slung her backpack over a shoulder. She didn't mind winter, except it might put her in closer contact for longer periods of time with her mother and Chet.

Walking quickly would keep her from freezing.

Restlessly, Trinity had ventured outside the celebration going on inside his home. Reilly hadn't returned yet and it was getting dark. In a minute, he'd go looking for her.

Being at Bridie's, he felt, was perfectly safe. Trinity believed Bridie, herself, kept her home guarded better than a regiment of pit bulls. Even from beyond the grave.

In the single instance he'd heard of anyone trespassing on Bridie's turf, those two teenage troublemakers had suffered digestive problems and nightmares for weeks.

The town of Ryan took no pity on the wrong-doers. Bridie was a revered institution- a much admired and sought after counselor, healer, teacher and more. But there was always the walk to and from Bridie's. . .

A caped figure turned into Red Wing, long woolen folds flapping around purposefully striding legs.

Trinity remembered that cape.

Somehow, Reilly had acquired it and now she strode, looking for all the world, like some Goth version of Little Red Riding Hood. Who would be the big, bad wolf?- idly flitted inside his head.

The door opened behind him and he felt Sharrod's arms encircle his waist. His hand registered the warmth of the single beer he'd nursed all afternoon, not the human warmth of the female.

Sharrod stirred the hair on the back of his neck, murmured suggestions which irritated him. In fact, the girls he'd regularly seen for some time all irritated him.

He was tired of them. They were all the same. They wanted sex right now, or to get married, right now, or to move as far from the town of Ryan as possible, right now. Always wanting something, and not hesitant about besieging him, right now.

Trinity liked living in the town of Ryan, liked being Mr. Fix It. Maybe he didn't aspire to much. Peace, yes. A peaceful heart would be nice.

The loss of his little sister had constricted his heart, bound it with a numbing density like a tumorous cannon ball stealing life. Trinity couldn't excise it, and wondered some day if his heart would simply implode with the aching weight. Get it over with.

He sipped at the warm beer, untied Sharrod's arms and stepped to the porch rail.

"Reilly!" He hailed the girl, walking with her head down. She wouldn't have known he was watching her.

"Reilly," he called again.

Reilly pushed back her hood, glanced up. Beer in hand, Trinity was calling her. Loudly calling her.

He grinned at her, waving his beer bottle.

She gave him a look Bridie would not have been at home with. Horrified, Reilly glanced from Trinity to the bottle in his hand to the sexily-clad blonde stroking his arm.

Trinity- drinking, drunk- calling her.

Her chest tightened with a strange remorse. She bit her lip and ran. He was no different than the others. Not really. Just another drunk, in this. . .this damned dump!

"Reilly? Now, what the hell?" Trinity vaulted the porch rail and took off after her.

The parking area in front of Chet's trailer was double- and triple-parked. Reilly had no desire to run the gauntlet of Chet's jeering friends.

She sidestepped between parked cars and trucks and headed to the creek bank.

"Reilly," Trinity hailed her to stop. What was she running from? What caused her to move hysterically through the brush?

"Reilly," he fruitlessly called, once more in pursuit. Swearing, his arm snaked out, grasped a fold of the cloak, halted her forward momentum.

Trinity repositioned his hand, grabbing at Reilly's arm and spun her around.

Chest heaving, Reilly cried, "Get your drunken hands off me!"

Futilely, she batted at his t-shirted chest.

"Reilly, settle down! Jaysus, Mary and Joseph and all the Saints!"

"No drunk touches me. I'd rather die!" Chin high, eyes on fire, spitting-mad and scared, serious as a heart attack, she confronted him.

He felt her shudder through the heavy cape. Unbelievably, he gleaned the fear behind the fire, glanced at the beer bottle in his hand, released her, swore under his breath.

"Why. . . Why do you think I'm drunk?"

"Well, you're drinking, aren't you?" She shot back, tears flooding her cheeks. Fear vied with disappointment.

"Reilly. . . Reilly, one beer, no, a half beer doesn't make one drunk. Look, this bottle is half full and it's been open for around 3 hours. You don't have to be afraid of me. Jaysus, I'd cut off my head before I'd hurt you," his eyes were stark with sincerity.

He watched a dawning erudition rear in her eyes and she closed in on herself, hugging her chest.

"This is. . .weird. I seem to be racing after you, lately," Trinity's jaw clenched. What a mess! He looked at the offensive bottle and proceeded to pour out what was left.

"Weird fits right in with my life," Reilly murmured, clearing the moisture from her eyes, humiliated, wishing she could just disappear. She heard Bridie gently rebuke her from up in a tree, but her eyes initially avoided ascending that high.

"Look, there's a difference between having a few beers and getting hammered. I know. I used to. . ."

"Hell, even Bridie enjoyed a pint of Guinness now and then. And I'm not talking about the American size pint; I mean a real Irish pint. Bigger than her elfin self," Trinity smiled, fondly recollecting.

'Ah, that's right, lass. Nothing like a pint and a basket o' fish-n-chips,' Bridie perched in a tree limb, and sitting next to her, thin legs swinging with delight. . .

Oh, boy, Reilly thought, eyeing the two of them- Bridie and Ivy Rose. Ivy Rose waved, excitedly, bouncing on air.

"Earth to Reilly," Trinity tried to regain Reilly's attention, wondered what she stared at up in the tree. He didn't see the kitten.

Good. He didn't feel like climbing trees right now. Reilly's fears, especially those concerning him, were disturbing as all get out. In fact, they truly made him feel. . .just feel. . . He needed to get to the bottom of this, right now.

"Reilly, can you tell me your most frightening experience? Put everything in perspective- recognize I'm not. . .some kind of monster."

Reilly paled, "Aren't you cold?" She looked for a way out, maybe just apologize and go in. . .

"No changing the subject," he firmly said.

'Reilly, tell him you will if he'll listen to what I have to tell him,' Ivy Rose spoke up.

Great, thought Reilly. I'm in a 4-way conversation with two of the conversationalists being ghosts. How do I pull this off without looking like I need to join the funny farm?

"May I ask you something first?" Reilly fiddled with the cape's folds.

"Sure," Trinity replied without really thinking first.

Reilly crossed her fingers.

'Ask him if he ever hears me,' Ivy Rose bounced through the tree limb.

"Do you. . . Do you ever hear. . .your sister?"

The hard came back fast and extra hard.

"Hear her? She's. . .dead. Do you ever hear your grandparents?" Trinity flared, his eyes half-shuttered, lambasted with disconcerted anger and confusion. How in the hell. . .

"Yes, I hear their voices all the time," Reilly admitted, only not like Bridie's. She searched Trinity's face for signs of his thinking she was crazy.

'Ask him about the guitar picks,' filtered down from above.

Reilly concentrated on keeping her eyes on Trinity. He'd already spun around to check out the tree.

"Don't you wonder about the guitar picks spread all over your bed?" Reilly braced herself.

Trinity harshly sucked in air. "How in hell did you know about that?" His jaw ached with his fervent clenching and his heart was double timing- running a marathon unprepared couldn't have produced more strain.

"I…I. . ." Reilly stammered.

Trinity backed up, reluctantly stepped forward, "Who the hell are you?"

His eyes narrowed. Was this girl pulling a fast one? Was she psychic? Did she see ghosts? Couldn't be, could it?

"I'm nobody. Nobody at all," Reilly moved to go around Trinity as Bridie and Ivy Rose remonstrated with her. She'd thrown it all away, a possible friendship with this nice, young man. . .

"Reilly, damn't! Reilly, stop running from me! Tell me. . .what you know." He figured the only way to get her to stand still was to let her talk, no matter what she talked about.

"You're going to see her again, Ivy Rose. . ."

"Yeah, if you believe in heaven and all that. . ."

"Would it be so bad to believe in something as good as heaven and seeing. . .?"

"Listen, you're a nice kid. You're kind. Maybe a little mixed up. Probably too much time alone at Bridie's. . ."

'Tell him_____.'

Reilly closed her eyes. I can't do that, she thought.

'He's my big brother and he hurts. Please, tell him,' Ivy Rose begged.

"Kindness waters the seeds of the human heart," Reilly whispered.

"What did you say?" Trinity gasped.

Reilly repeated, "Kindness waters the seeds of the human heart." This time she studied Trinity's features.

His close-guardedness, the granite shield, previously staunchly in place, which shuttered his warmth, suddenly fell away. He stared at her astounded. Shock and anger battled for possession of his mind.

22

Trinity slumped against the trunk directly under Bridie and Ivy Rose- his chest burning and his brain a whirligig.

"Our...our loved ones are always around us. Ivy Rose misses you playing your guitar," Reilly felt like some kind of a preacher, hoped she didn't sound too whimsical and that he'd not write her off as being. . .

"You're saying," Trinity gulped, studied his empty bottle and wished he'd left at least one drink. "You're saying. . ."

"I can hear her sometimes. . . when I'm around you. She told me. . ."

"About the guitar picks. . .which I do find scattered on my bed. Her favorite saying," Trinity's chin jutted up, he peered into the tree, completely at a loss.

There was no way Reilly could have known. Absolutely no way.

"God help me," Trinity ran his fingers through his hair. "I. . . I don't know what to say."

"If you stay open to the prospect, you...you might hear her."

"Yeah, well, uh. . ."

"Just think about it," Reilly rushed on, afraid she might lose Trinity altogether. "You asked me about my scariest memory."

Trinity ducked his head; his hair provided a hide-out. He needed an anecdote of Reilly's life to help him regain his equilibrium. Little did he know, Reilly's story would not fit that bill.

"When I was very young, maybe 5. . . One night, my mother wanted to go out. My grandparents and aunt weren't available to babysit and. . .I was too young, then, to be left alone in the apartment. It was cold that night, so my mother took blankets. . .and. . .my stuffed lamb. My grandparents had given me a stuffed lamb for Easter- from the Easter Bunny, they told me."

Reilly's eyes misted recalling her toy. "The lamb was soft, cuddly, small enough for me to wrap my arms around. Big enough for a kid to feel safe with. She had a white, fluffy body, black-tipped ears, black face, gold eyes, pink nose and smiling mouth and black legs and feet and a little white tail," Reilly paused, bit her lip to keep from crying full-out at what had transpired.

Trinity's attention hooked on a sense of impending doom; he studied every emotion as it played across the stage of Reilly's face.

"You remember that pretty good," he said in an effort to break the ice Reilly seemed froze inside.

Reilly's mouth twisted, "It was the first thing I remember loving and losing."

Trinity frowned.

"She parked the car in the shadows of the bar's parking lot. Didn't want to chance anyone seeing a little kid in the car. Told me to be quiet. I hugged my lamb, sucked my thumb, rocked myself."

Trinity's jaw panged as he set it, picturing the scene as Reilly spoke, felt the overwhelming urge to punch the life out of something steal through him. An exigency strong enough to counter the feeling of helplessness he'd had just minutes ago.

"I got cold and. . .I began to cry. Some guys. . .must have heard me. I remember faces peering in at me- ugly faces, like Halloween masks. Scary faces. I tried to shut my eyes, but then, they tapped at the windows to make me look.

One of them tried the door. It was unlocked. She told me to be quiet- I screamed into my lamb's body. . . I remember the smell of the man as he opened the door, leaned over the seat and tore my lamb from my arms.

I screamed and screamed. He thought it was funny. Laughing. . .laughing at me. . . One of his friends. . .told him to leave me alone. But he took my lamb. . . They began to fight. All the noise. . .

I never saw my lamb again. I cried myself to sleep," tears sidled down Reilly's face.

In his anger and at his impotence to make it better for her, Trinity swore violently and his fingers closed tightly about the beer bottle. It shattered in his hand.

Reilly bit her lower lip, wiped her face. "Look what you've done. Your hand is bleeding," trembling, she reached for his hand.

"F*** my hand! God, Reilly, I'm so, so sorry. . ."

More than anything he wanted to pull her into the safety of his arms as he used to hold Ivy Rose after the bullies made fun of her limping. Hold her and comfort her until he got his hands on the sons of. . .

"Let's take care of your hand," Reilly desperately

needed the diversion. And the sight of Trinity's blood certainly distracted her in a faint, queasy kind of way.

Bridie advised from above, 'Hydrogen peroxide, Dearie. Make sure you don't bandage any glass inside the cuts.'

Ivy Rose smiled through tears and waved at Reilly and her brother as she faded away.

"Why are all the people at your house?" Reilly asked as they walked back to Trinity's. Her reminiscing. . .well, she was just glad she had someone to talk to, something to do, otherwise, she might cry herself to death, dredging up that horrid night.

The motherly instinct in her took over as it would have if a child needed tending. She made Trinity keep his hand elevated until she could get a good look at it. And told herself she could and would handle the blood.

"It's my dad's birthday."

"Oh, I…I wish I'd known. Maybe, I could've baked him a birthday cake," she offered.

"Can you make pineapple upside down cake?"

"Sure, that was my grandpa's favorite," she mentally bored down on a pleasant memory.

"My brothers married career women, nice, but they can't cook much, and I abhor bakery cakes, no real taste, nothing but sugar. How about next Saturday?" Trinity didn't care to wait for next Sunday, hated to wait for Saturday.

"I…I have a dentist appointment," Reilly hedged.

"Great, I'll pick you up and we'll get the ingredients. . ." Trinity broke off. Was he forcing this girl into. . .?

"OK," Reilly agreed, greatly relieved they were still friends. It would be fun to make Pat's favorite cake.

And Trinity certainly seemed to have turned around for the better. She set aside the horrible memory, hopefully for good.

Reilly was fleetingly introduced to Pat Junior- a doctor, Sean- an accountant, their wives, Kate- a nurse, and Sandra- a florist, and Sandra's and Sean's baby- Maria, as Trinity made his way to the bathroom with Reilly in tow. Blood running down his arm.

His family hollered at Trinity for being stupid.

"You know, most people just down the beer and smash the bottle instead of squeezing it dry and cutting themselves. Didn't you teach him better than that, Dad?"

The harassing followed them.

Pat Jr. managed one scholarly look at the injury, snickered 'you'll probably live' before he was rudely banished by his younger brother.

Sharrod tried to bustle her way to Trinity's side and play nurse, but he cut her short with one derisive glance. In a huff, she tossed her hair and left, but no one was interested in her histrionics.

Brothers, wives, cousins and all were eating, conversing and speculating on who the girl in the odd clothes was at Trinity's side.

Trinity shut the jeering out by closing the bathroom door. He wasn't a whining patient. He didn't flinch as Reilly cleaned his wounds, checked closely for glass particles hiding within, and then expertly, via Bridie's advice, bandaged his hand.

"I . . . I think you were lucky. I don't believe you need stitches, but I think it's going to hurt," Reilly dared a glance up into the warmth of Trinity's eyes.

Bridie, studiously supervising, confirmed Reilly's prognosis.

"You know, if I were my namesake, you'd be tearing up your petticoats to bandage my hand," he grinned at her- a hint of mischief on his dimpled face.

Flustered, Reilly stepped back into the closed door.

"I'll have to watch that movie someday. See if there's any resemblance," she tried to make light of the rush of feelings he stirred in her.

"How about Saturday, while the cake's baking?"

That night in bed, Trinity reviewed what Reilly said about Ivy Rose. He didn't have to focus on Reilly's tale of her scariest incident. It was forever scarred into his brain. If he could only smash in the face of whatever SOB had treated a scared kid like that and taken her toy.

Trinity pictured the lamb. An idea formed. In this day and age it was possible to find anything, right?

His thoughts turned to Ivy Rose. With hope and a tad of unease in his voice, he whispered, "Ivy Rose?"

The weighted bands on his heart creaked.

He didn't hear her voice, but he felt something light rain down on his blanket. Trinity's fingers found a single guitar pick on his chest.

Ivy Rose's tears mirrored her big brother's, only on a different dimension. Trinity, her big brother- Reilly was bringing him back.

23

From the moment Reilly entered the dump, intuition clamored like the cow bell at Dave's Diner. Only there was no welcome, here.

Several guys at the counter, munching clumsily on snacks and downing shots, hushed and eyed the girl. One of them shot a warning to Chet.

Oblivious or purposely ignoring her entrance, Chet continued his tirade, "I hate cats. Sneaking b____! One's been hanging around my trailer. I left poison out earlier. That ought to take care of its sorry hide." He raucously laughed. Mr. Comedy.

When no one joined in, he glanced around and winked at Reilly. Why not? She had no rights here. Dumb, sorry looking girl. If the mother wasn't such a looker. . .

Horror, Hell, Hades, blasted through Reilly's mind a second before her shocked system comprehended the full import of Chet's words.

He leered at her over his beer. Bleary-eyed, he couldn't understand why no one else thought he was clever or funny. Protecting his turf. That's all he was doing. Stinking cats.

"Now, Chet, really," the mother said, catching Reilly's expression which seemed somewhere between readying for war and fainting.

"Don't look at me like that! You know better than to bring an animal home. This isn't your house, you know," the mother further tormented her stunned daughter.

A shock of silence reigned. Even a few of Chet's hard-core buddies were perturbed at this scene.

Reilly rushed from the room. Let the outside door slam with added vehemence. If anyone had blocked her path, her adrenalin-surged body would have knocked them flat. As Fat Al could testify to.

"Righteous! Righteous!" She called frantically as she raced around the trailer and into the woods.

No answering meows. Only blurred party sounds, not even wind. Cold. A wraith of cold flaunted in her chest.

Reilly pictured the golden kitten lying helpless, suffering, hurt, dy. . .

"Righteous," she cried. Shivering with angst, she searched under brush, kicking at leaves, checking under upraised tree roots. Where would a sick kitten go?

"God, help me," she begged.

'Easy, Sweetlin',' Bridie appeared at her side. 'Easy.'

"B…Bridie," the girl succumbed to hysterical tears.

"Meowww," tail high, Righteous trotted into view.

"Oh, Righteous," Reilly swept up the kitten and dissolved to the ground, crying for all she was worth, near drowning the un-protesting creature.

Bridie gave the huddled girl and purring kitten a moment together before breaking in.

'Dearest, listen to me. You apparently forgot. I told you Righteous is the smartest cat I ever was after meetin'. Believe me, lass, she can tell the difference between poison and an acceptable meal.'

Bridie, herself, was near to tears watching her two charges.

'I can see I'm going to have to take a more direct approach, here. Listen, Sweetlin'. The bleedin' eejit has temporarily suffered a spate of amnesia. We'll make short shrift of the likes of 'im.'

Reilly sniffled and looked up, hopefully, at the ghost.

'You've got the packet, do ye?'

Reilly nodded.

'Years ago, the bollocks took a shot at me friend, Brimstone,' Bridie's eyes twinkled.

"Brimstone?"

'Tis. You know the expression 'raining fire and brimstone'? Brimstone was the bull-in-the-china-shop version of a cat. He'd be after stalking above me on some shelf or t'other, as casual as yer please, knockin' things off. Not that he was meanin' to, mind you. It's mighty good I always had an otherworldly sense of self-preservation or I'd be after havin' me head bashed in right and left, in the days of me 'physical', that is.

Was a sad day when Brimstone lost the tip of his tail to that eejit's aim. But I'm all for those needin' comeuppance gettin' it, and the sooner the better. I tinkered with his firearm and the next time he used it the bleedin' thing shattered in his hands.

Such a fine sight! All those bits of shrapnel in his hands and chest and him squealin' like a stuck hog.

Later, I sneaked up on him in the IGA. Him pourin' over how many beers he might be wantin', but with his hands wrapped up he couldn't pick them up. A glorious sight!'

'I tapped him, none too gently mind ye, on his injured hands and gave him one of those wicked witch of the west looks. I simply said, 'Bridie remembers'. Should 'ave seen the look on the bleedin' eejit's trap!'

"Reilly, make a pot of chili for Monday night football," her mother ordered.

"It'll be late," Reilly tersely replied.

"That's fine, we'll be up late. Chet said to make a list of what you need and to make sure it's spicy."

Oh, it will be spicy, Reilly deliberated.

Nobody ever minded her, so it was easy for Reilly to place the entire packet of 'physic' in Chet's chili. She used the amount of jalapenos he wanted- all the better to mask any taste peculiarities.

"Damn, that was good," he hooted.

Chet, nor her mother, mentioned one word about cat poison. Neither did they ask if she'd found the kitten. Nothing about Reilly was worth talking about, unless they needed something. In which case they placed their order- as her room never seemed to reveal anything worth having.

Half an hour later, Chet was married to the bathroom sink and toilet. Both ends spewing bile, as Bridie had predicted.

"What in the hell was in that chili?" Reilly heard him ask her mother in between bouts of hacking and vomiting and full-blown diarrhea.

"Chet, we all ate the same. You had more jalapenos. Probably, you just picked up some kind of a flu. You'll feel better tomorrow."

The mother quickly exited the stench-filled master bath in their bedroom suite. The one with the working door. And air conditioning in the summer and plenty of heat in winter.

"Reilly, take Chet the Pepto Bismol," her mother demanded, accosting the girl in the living room while drawing on a cigarette and inhaling deeply.

Reilly, glee rising in her heart, handed in the pink bottle from the other side of the half-closed bathroom door.

Her mother was well out of earshot. Bridie hovered, winked at her, 'Give him his comeuppance, lass.'

"Chet?" Reilly waited for a break in the hacking and groaning to assure he would hear her.

"Yeah," the hoarse voice moaned.

"The kitten was Bridie's friend. Bridie remembers," Reilly clearly stated. "And so will I," she added.

"Wha. . .?"

Bridie cackled as she described the terrified look on Chet's face. Right before another stinking blast erupted from both ends.

Dr. Desatnik, orthodontist, and his partner, Dr. Mardis, dentist, conferred on the best means to right Reilly's misaligned teeth.

"When's the last time you saw a dentist?" Dr. Mardis asked her as she sat fearfully in the dentist's chair, under the spotlight.

Bridie danced on the dentist's tools attempting to keep Reilly calm. Not a tool stirred, nor did tranquility best the girl's discomposure.

"I've never been to a dentist," she managed around probing fingers in her mouth.

The dentist had a hard time with this information. "Never?"

"My mother said welfare didn't cover dentist appointments," Reilly hated to repeat what she inherently knew was a lie.

Dr. Mardis exchanged looks with Dr. Desatnik. Not hard to read their thoughts.

Reilly didn't mind the teeth cleaning, but the doctors decided she had to be relieved of her upper wisdom teeth and two more beside. This was getting more than a little scary, she thought, but Bridie gave her a huge smile and did an especially grand launch off the dental instruments to land on, first, Dr. Mardis' bald head and then, Dr. Desatnik's, stirring his graying hair- no matter her upper body went through the ceiling and all Reilly witnessed were the muckered feet imitating the can-can. Bridie would have been a perfect circus act, except most everyone would miss the event.

"We could pull these at your next appointment, Reilly."

"If we did it today, could I get my braces this week?"

"Depends on how fast you heal. Better to wait another week. We'll check on your progress in a few days and you be sure to call us if you have any problems or questions," the dentist tried to be reassuring.

"I know you're anxious to get this procedure started," Dr. Desatnik said. "Do you have time to pull these teeth, Mike?"

"Are your parents picking you up today, Reilly?"

"No," Reilly murmured. "My friend, Trinity, will be here to take me. . .back." She would never refer to the dump as home. In fact, she'd been sneeringly advised it wasn't her house to bother calling home.

"Well, let's get started." Dr. Mardis instructed his assistant as to his requirements.

Reilly's list of fears had not included needles in the past. She'd had no experience of them. But as the shots of anesthesia drew near her mouth, needles moved to the top of the list, even though the dentist had placed a numbing substance on her gums first.

Bridie made faces, kicked up her heels, sang a funny burlesque song about a man and a girl in the heather. . . Pulled out all the stops to steady Reilly's blood pressure and help allay her run-away anxiety.

I can and will do this, Reilly chanted to herself. Oaks. . .ow. . .

Trinity waited, wondering. What in the world were they doing in there? Standard dentist appointments didn't take this long.

Dr. Mardis, momentarily leaving Reilly's side, spied the waiting Trinity and explained about the surgery. Trinity winced. He'd no fondness for going to the dentist. Thank God, he had great teeth.

By the sounds of the gadgets they were using on poor Reilly, and the idea of sharp instruments in one's mouth. . . Well, he was only human.

Doctor Desatnik explained why the surgery was necessary. Reilly simply had too many teeth in her small mouth, at least on top.

"She needs to rest today and tomorrow. As far as eating goes, broths- nothing hot, yogurts, mashed potatoes, a milk shake would be nice. We'd prefer if she slept sitting up tonight and Sunday night."

The list of instructions went on and on. Thankfully, they provided him with a copy of them and an appointment card for Wednesday, a telephone number for emergencies and another one for questions and a prescription for pain meds.

Trinity rang his dad. Pat suggested calling Kate to stay with Reilly at their house.

"I wouldn't put it past Chet and her mother to start something if they knew Reilly was with just the two of us. We both know they won't take care of her," Pat rang off, prepared to call Kate.

Kate graciously complied and told Pat she'd call on Reilly's mother as a nurse and present the situation as the best way to keep an eye on Reilly. Just in case of unexpected breakthrough bleeding- that ought to cover it. Kate didn't imagine the mother would want to deal with her daughter's blood loss. Never mind all the rest of the dentist's counsel for Reilly's care.

"Hey, Reilly," Trinity took in the ice packs tied to Reilly's jaws. Her dazed look. "Let's get you home."

Her eyes saddened at his offer.

"To my house. Kate's going to come and spend a few nights. She'll talk to your mother," Trinity explained.

Reilly couldn't bite her lip in alarm, but she quavered- Trinity's house? Too weak to worry much, she indicated her clothes.

"Don't worry about anything. Kate'll take care of it. You stay quiet, sleep if you want."

Unsteady on her legs, she nevertheless tried to walk unaided.

"None of that, lass. Wrap your arms around my neck. I'm going to carry you to the car," he moved closer to her.

Reilly began to shake her head, winced, caught herself. She readjusted her backpack, which Trinity promptly relieved her of.

"Now what did I say about staying quiet?" He whisked her into his arms.

"That woman has no right to be a mother," Kate ranted to Pat and Trinity once she had Reilly ensconced in a comfortable recliner and had drug the two men out of the girl's hearing.

"She actually told me I'd have to get any money I needed from Reilly. Can you imagine that?" Kate was thoroughly ticked-off and bore no compunction about letting anyone in on her raging disgust. A few choice words flew, searing the air.

Unfortunately, Trinity already knew most of it. He watched Reilly nap as he, Kate and Pat, played cards. They kept the game as quiet as two Irishmen and a woman possibly could. The TV stayed off.

Ivy Rose took turns sitting at Reilly's side and peering at Trinity's cards. It was getting easier for her to remain in transparent form for longer periods of time. She held out hope her big brother might yet see her. Resorting to guitar picks was getting old.

When Reilly woke, she tried to talk. Trinity gave her a mock-fierce eye and a pen and paper. Kate provided soft Jello and runny mashed potatoes.

Bridie reminded her about the packet of herbs for a healing tea. Reilly indicated her backpack from which she drew out a homemade tea bag. Kate, who'd known of Bridie's healing talents, recognized the tea bag, boiled water, allowed the tea to steep for a decent interval, and then put it in the refrigerator to chill.

Reilly wrote, Righteous, and appealed to Trinity.

"I guess we'll find out if Wrench likes cats," he said, hitching a shoulder, displaying a dimpled grin. Now, just where might he find the little con artist? He'd not forgotten the tree-climbing rescue attempt he'd been cajoled into by the kitten.

24

Wrench had assumed responsibilities- guarding Reilly like a dog guards a bone. He became her foot stool, at least until Trinity returned with Righteous pinned on his shoulder.

"Damned if I didn't have to climb the same tree and get this little player. Sittin' up on a limb, looking pathetic, pretending she didn't know how she could possibly have got up a tree, let alone have any idea about how to get down. Sheesh!"

Wrench gave a short huff and sat up to figure out what this new creature was doing in his house.

Righteous had yet to meet anything worthy of fear. Weighing only a few pounds, the kitten took on the large, exuberant Wrench with all the natural bravado her 'big head' contained.

Nose to nose, she allowed the dog one sniff, vaulted and raced across the dog's back. Wrench took this in good heart as an offer to play.

Righteous and Wrench conducted a whirlwind game of chase. If the dog got too close, the kitten ducked under a chair or hopped atop one. The kitchen table made for great fun, filling in as a merry-go-round for pets.

Righteous' special tactic, which had the house rolling in hilarity, involved racing around the kitchen table chairs at lightning speed- too fast for Wrench to catch or follow with his bulk.

The dog ended up chasing imaginary cats around the chairs while Righteous sat out of range, sphinx-like, on one of the chairs, watching and wondering just what that dog was looking for.

"This is better than a stand-up comedy routine," Kate laughed, tears rolling down her cheeks.

"The difference between how a dog thinks and how a cat thinks, amazing," Pat chuckled. Righteous accepted her due and winked at her admirers as poor Wrench exhausted himself.

"Little player," Trinity mused.

When the out-of-shape Wrench decided he needed a break and Righteous deemed otherwise, the kitten would throw her front paws around the dog's neck and chew on poor Wrench's ears until the dog rolled over on top of her.

One mewling squeal and Wrench hastily displaced himself; he thoroughly scrutinized the kitten with a diligent tongue-licking.

Righteous soon bore a striking resemblance to a drowned rat, but nevertheless retained her affronted dignity with a flag-high tail and disdainful sniff.

Initially, the humans were concerned for the tiny kitten's well-being, but dog and kitten figured out the parameters.

Bridie and Ivy Rose enjoyed the playground antics as well as the humans in their 'physicals'. Reilly, finding she was unable to laugh- she still could not feel her mouth, ended up crying instead. Happy tears for a change.

Finally, the episodes of chase and wrestling came to an end. Wrench panted and dropped under Reilly's feet. Righteous hopped to the counter looking for. . .

"We haven't got any cat food. Do you think Righteous- what a name, would like a cheese burger?" Pat pretended to ask the kitten about her menu preferences. Righteous looked him dead in the eye and trilled her response.

"I swear this cat understands every word I say," the astonished Pat said.

'Of course she does. The impertinence of humans,' Bridie rolled her eyes, swung her heels back and forth, perched next to Righteous on the counter.

"Cheese burgers sound good, Dad," Trinity realized he was starving. He pulled out a package of hamburger and went to work.

Pat went out to light the grill as Kate hollered, "I like mine well done. I'll make Reilly a milk shake."

Trinity's pretty and efficient sister-in-law had Reilly write down her favorite flavor. Luckily, she'd surmised as much and had picked up the shake-makings on her way to Red Wing.

Not since both her grandparents were living and Reilly stayed with them had she felt so warmly tended to and part of something- a family.

She had two ghosts, Trinity, Pat and Kate at her beck and call. Not to mention a live, warm footstool and a lap warmer-in-waiting. There wasn't time to feel shy or worried. This family accepted her as a guest- a welcome guest. Kate had even provided pajamas- a set of pink sweats. There was no pain and Reilly knew she'd sleep better in her recliner than she had in. . .she couldn't remember.

A knock at the door barely brought Wrench out of his doze. With a half-hearted attempt, he rose, taking Reilly's feet with him, woofed and promptly collapsed back to sleep.

Kate opened the door.

"Is Trinity here?"

"Come on in," Kate motioned and delivered Reilly's milk shake.

"Trinity," a silky, female voice crooned to the young mechanic as he cut onions and peppers for the hamburger patties. With a flourish of horseradish and scattering of spices, he formed the burgers and set them on a plate- ready for the grill.

"Erika, what are you up to?" He cast a disinterested glance at the highly made-up girl.

"Did you forget?" She seemed puzzled to find him in his work clothes making hamburgers. Apparently, he had.

She flashed him a smile, "The concert? Are we still going?"

"Completely slipped my mind," Trinity forearmed his hair from his eyes.

"Are we babysitting tonight?" Erika eyed the swollen-cheeked girl in the recliner, spooning a vanilla shake.

No competition there, she tilted her chin surveying the disheveled kid.

Bridie's brows rose. Ivy Rose stuck out her tongue and Righteous arched her back and hissed at the pretty blonde before jumping to Reilly's lap for a taste of ice cream.

Trinity paused in his patty forming and glanced over at Reilly. Her white-socked feet rested atop Wrench's worn out body.

Reilly avoided the blonde's perusal- she was used to 'those' looks. She knew Trinity had many girl friends. She had no dreams or pretensions about her chances of catching his eye in that department. Having him for a friend was too good to be true.

Trinity looked from Reilly to the Diva wielding concert tickets. Easy decision.

"How do they feel?" Trinity and Pat glanced up at Reilly as she approached their table, guest check pad in one hand and coffee pot in the other.

Reilly hesitated, cautiously answered around a mouthful of unfamiliarity, "Achey."

Her hand shook as she poured Pat's coffee. Very unlike her. Pat took the pot from her.

"What's wrong, Reilly?" His fatherly instincts superseded all else.

"I…I guess I'm shaky because. . .I haven't eaten, yet," she mumbled, bashfully.

"Not at all? It's 5:30," Trinity eyed the wall clock with a surge of angst.

"I got here late from the orthodontist. . ."

Trinity slid out of the booth. "Get in," he ordered.

"I've got to…to work," she managed, her lips having a weird time working around the strange contraptions girding her teeth.

"Not like this, you don't. Stay here," Trinity motioned. He walked over to Dave, who grimly nodded at his words.

Turning back to his grill, Dave pulled burgers off the high heat section and grievously subdued, called over to his waitress, "I'm sorry, Reilly, I forgot all about your missing dinner."

He busied about the steam table and contritely delivered a plate of soft foods- meatloaf, mashed potatoes and gravy, and applesauce to her, proceeded to ask the O'Ryans for their order.

"Take your time, Reilly. We're fine. Martie and I will finish up. You've had a trying last few days," Dave patted Reilly's shoulder.

Slowly, mindful of the feel of wire and metal against the soft tissue of the inside of her mouth, Reilly spooned her meal.

Trinity dropped his dad off at their house and drove the short but flagrant distance back to Chet's trailer. Reilly had profusely thanked Pat as he exited- for taking her in, for being kind. . .

She tried to find a means to sit longer with Trinity-anything to prolong the time before entering the dump.

"You and your family have been so nice to me, watching out for me. . ."

"It wasn't simply a matter of altruism- that pineapple upside down cake was brilliant!" Trinity put the car in park.

"I can't believe your dad ate half of a cake," she marveled and promptly winced at her overly-enthusiastic expulsion which nearly cut her lip. Braces. . .

"Well, I have to tell you, if it weren't for Kate and my brother I'd have eaten the other half." Realizing he sounded like a pig, he qualified his remark, "Except for saving a piece for you, of course."

"I guess I'll have to make a bigger cake or two of them, next time," Reilly sincerely hoped there would be a next time.

"I like the sound of that 'next time'." Trinity wasn't in any hurry to leave.

"You know, I think Wrench misses Righteous. He whines around the house like he's trying to find the kitten and then, sinks disconsolately, kind of like Eeyore, when he can't find her.

Bring Righteous with you on Sunday. Be like a family reunion. It's a grand riot to watch them play."

Trinity leaned back in his seat, head turned to his passenger. He knew she didn't want to go in. Couldn't blame her.

It was nice to have her talking again. Watching her sleep upright with swollen jaws. . . Brought back the memories of other, hard nights.

"How long is the doctor saying you have to wear these braces?"

"He's impressed with my healing abilities, but he's not sure if. . . He thinks maybe 18 months, two years. I have to wear this creepy contraption at night," Reilly shivered.

"You cold?" He cranked the heat, but Reilly shook her head.

"What?" Trinity asked.

"I think I'd scare myself at night if I looked in a mirror while wearing it," she said by way of explanation.

"Kid, you think too much. It can't be that bad, and if it helps shorten the time you have to wear those braces, then hell, wear it all you can," Trinity offered his support.

"Trinity," Reilly hesitated. She wanted to bring up a subject, but didn't want to seem nosy or, worse, have him rebuff her.

"Ask," he stated, bracing himself.

He had questions for her regarding Ivy Rose, wanted to tell her about the other night and the guitar pick, but it was getting late and once that particular conversation got started, he didn't want any disruptions.

"You said…you said you went crazy. . . I've not heard anything from anyone," mostly because she didn't talk with anyone else. "I mean about. . ." she broke off. It really wasn't any of her business.

And the ghosts wouldn't tell. It was Trinity's story to tell, according to Bridie, if and when he wished.

Trinity swept his fingers through his hair, exhaled loudly.

"I'm sorry; I shouldn't have asked," Reilly's hand went to the door handle.

"No. Wait. It's alright. . . I was pushing a date with a penitentiary– for murder. After my sister. . ." Trinity had a difficult time swallowing, breathing.

"I only wanted to fight. To beat the hurt out of myself by inflicting it on others, I guess. Better yet, I prayed for someone to beat me senseless. . . No one stepped up to that plate.

I earned my top-of-the-food chain reputation by taking down all comers. I went searching for fights and if I couldn't find one, I'd start one. I went after every f…idiot that ever made fun of her.

Maybe, you don't know this, but she was born with a club foot. Had an odd way of trying to run– a real clumsy gait. That made her a target, until I divvied out the bloody noses, broken ribs. . ."

Reilly considered telling Trinity that Ivy Rose could run now, and skip beautifully, too. No more handicaps.

A soft hand settled into Reilly's shoulder. A tingling sensation emanated from it. Reilly glanced back and saw Ivy Rose in the back seat, eyes on her brother. Eyes full of love, empathy.

Reilly tried to contain herself. After all, Bridie had been jumping in and out of her life for quite some time. Trinity felt the jolt as Reilly startled.

Misinterpreting her reaction, he said, "If this is too much for you. . . You did ask."

"N…no, please go on. What happened?"

Someday, Reilly hoped Trinity would see Ivy Rose, only on this side of heaven. The prospect of him not a part of her life, even if only platonically. . .

"At a family reunion, some summer holiday or other. . . I almost killed my brother," Trinity admitted, ruefully. His jaw clenched in vivid remembrance.

Reilly felt a tear at her heart. Surreptitiously, she glanced at Ivy Rose, who knew all of this. Hadn't she told Reilly she'd always been at her brother's side? Trying to get him to notice her.

Reilly began to comprehend Ivy Rose's motive in attempting to get her brother to 'see' her, now that Trinity was relating the extent of his suffering.

"I'd kept to myself through the party. It was easy enough to do. Why I'd even gone, I can't tell you. I didn't want to talk to anyone. Didn't want to hear advice or old clichés.

Toward evening, my brother, Pat, asked me to play my guitar. Unbeknownst to me, he'd brought it along. It had been three years or so and I hadn't touched my. . .guitar.

Pat, I guess. . .I guess he thought it might help me if I would just pick it up and try to play."

Trinity had turned hard again. It was in the tone of his voice, the rigidity of his countenance, the splurge of veins in his temple and neck, the gulp of Adam's apple, the clench of strong fingers on the console, as he reflected on the events of that day.

"C'mon, Trinity, play for us. Look, I brought your guitar," Pat Jr. held out the instrument with sanguine expectance in his eyes.

"Yeah, Trinity! C'mon, play for us," partying cousins, aunts, uncles avidly pushed.

That's what it felt like to Trinity- being pushed. Foreplay to a fight. Trinity succumbed to the now all-too-familiar volcanic rise in his gut. The desire, the desperate ache to inflict pain. To use his fists to destroy. . .

Pat Jr. laid the guitar on the picnic table in front of Trinity.

"C'mon, Trinity," he whispered and tapped his younger brother's arm.

Trinity erupted- volleyed into Pat Jr., who at 5 years senior to Trinity, was bigger, heavier and much stronger.

But Trinity had the lodestone of his pain and 3 years of practice behind his explosion. All the skirmishes. . .

Pat Jr. was in trouble from the beginning, fending off Trinity's furious fists. He refrained from striking his younger brother and kept saying he was sorry, to no avail. Trinity was in another world, where only anger existed and that anger must be assuaged in the only way he knew. The few men big enough to jump in to try and restrain Trinity got pummeled bloody for their efforts. A cornered wild animal-Trinity.

At the denouement, Trinity ultimately found himself not himself, astride his brother, choking him. Choking the life out of his brother. Not really seeing or caring who it was his hands throttled.

"Trinity," his dad screamed. "Trinity, he's your brother! He's your brother! Do you think Ivy Rose would want this?"

"And like a light switch flipped inside my head, it was done. I. . . I released Pat, wishing someone would knock me unconscious. Anything to take away the. . .

I managed to apologize to every one bloodied at my hands and I ran. I had to get away.

As if I were in a dream, I found myself walking down Bridie's drive. For some reason, I always ended up at Bridie's after a fight. She'd patch me up physically, never said a word unless I asked her a question- a paragon of sang-froid, Bridie.

Just being near her- it was the only soothing time and place I could find."

"She was the wisest person I ever met. I haven't been in a fight since then, but everyone knows my capabilities. With one look, I can make anyone back down. I guess that comes from not caring if you win or lose, live or die."

Reilly wished she were brave enough to wrap her arms around Trinity. Brave enough to reach out a hand. . .

"I understand what you meant now, about how you are pretty high up on the food chain," Reilly murmured. She understood plenty, now.

Trinity barked a laugh. He'd forgotten that introductory meeting. Reilly and her Sisyphean task. He turned to his pale passenger.

"You and Bridie have a lot in common," he complimented her.

Reilly ducked her head, embarrassed. Ivy Rose giggled.

"I mean that as a great compliment."

"Thanks. Thanks for so many things. Picking me up; you're always on time," Reilly said with a hint of surprise in her voice.

"Believe me, being on time is one of my pet peeves. If I'm ever late, by so much as one second, you know something is wrong," he sincerely declared.

Trinity sighed. If he could change time right now, it would be dawn, Sunday, and he and Reilly could talk all day, but. . .

"You better go in, it's getting late. School tomorrow, remember?"

Reilly tried to smile. In general, it was getting easier with the new mouth hardware, except, for the second time in a day her top lip got caught on a wire. She flinched.

"I'm going to call you Smiley Reilly," Trinity grinned.

"Please don't, you almost sound like a parent," Reilly opened the door, a silent 'the kind a girl should have' in her mind, even though she didn't want Trinity as that kind of a relative.

"Huh, well, I am a little older than you," for some reason this irked him.

"Nobody's older than me," Reilly's mumbled exit words seared his soul.

"How's my favorite girl?" Crotchety John Stalbridge blocked Reilly's overladen progress to the bus pans. He hitched his thumbs in his farmer's overall pockets.

"And what you're really asking is 'What's for dessert, today?'" Reilly responded.

She sidestepped the gruff customer and rid herself of stacks of dirty dishes. Weary, but satisfied, she checked on the other diner patrons and refilled drinks.

Stalbridge and his friend slipped into the booth Reilly had just wiped down.

"Well?" A lush, gray brow shot up as the farmer probed. His fingers tapped the formica table top.

"Banana pudding," Reilly answered.

"Pudding?" Stalbridge made a face. "Pudding?" He was sure there had to be a mistake.

He ended up laughing, for want of a better retort. She was putting him on, right? Pudding, that was that stuff that came out of a box, just add milk. That was not considered a homemade dessert in his book.

"C'mon, what's really for dessert? You ain't all out, are you?"

Reilly ignored his exasperation. Stalbridge wildly scanned about. He'd got here as early as he could, for cryin' out loud!

"Do you like banana cream pie?" Reilly countered.

"You bet I do, that's one of my favorites," he beamed. Now they were getting somewhere.

"Then you'll like banana pudding," she pulled out her guest check pad.

She'd grown used to the regular patrons and their idiosyncrasies. Familiarity bred a sense of being at ease, as far as Reilly was concerned. Even the cantankerous ones, like Stalbridge- who was the worst, treated her well, and she looked forward to going to work.

"And if I don't, do I get my money back?" Stalbridge pushed the envelope- he was known for these tactics and Reilly kind of enjoyed bantering with him. More often than not, she surprised herself by getting the better of him. Who was this new Reilly?

"No. 'In for a penny, in for a pound,' as my grandma used to say," she countered.

"Your grandma had an awful lot to say," Stalbridge quibbled and ordered the pinto beans, ham and cornbread special and reserved a banana pudding, peering at Reilly with disjointed brows.

It had turned out better than she could ever have hoped for and Reilly was flustered, over the moon, with the deluge of compliments. For the first time in a very long time, she'd begun to enjoy a satisfaction with herself. Believed she'd done something, well, something good. And big.

Her homemade desserts at the diner were applauded great guns. Monday through Friday, she rushed from school to the diner, prepared several steam table size trays of. . .

She'd started off with a simple peach cobbler, and the look on Stalbridge's face when she'd told him what the dessert was- his jaw turned into a Venus fly trap, he was struck dumb. And when she owned up to making it herself, he proposed after one bite.

This was the first week trying out her desserts.

Dave had liked the idea, but wasn't sure how Reilly intended to keep up. Could she possibly make enough the night before to tide over the customers until she got to work the next day?

Invariably, the desserts ran out, but the response to her efforts was amazing- ecstasy for the lucky early birds and a lot of downtrodden expressions on the faces of the customers too late to acquire one of Reilly's specialties. Dave and Martie chalked it up to growing pains- a learning experience for the diner. They told her not to worry. All new ventures needed time to work out the specifics.

Martie fielded umpteen calls from the regulars wanting to know the dessert for the day. Customers were already used to the Monday-Friday lunch and dinner specials. The Real McCoy desserts joined the patrons' usual orders and the homemade goodies flew without wings. Dave promptly dropped the frozen pies.

"Honey, could I get some real milk for my coffee, unless you have real cream?" An irregular customer in an incongruously expensive suit and tie interrupted Reilly.

"This is milk," she accepted the proffered stainless steel creamer with misgivings.

"No, it's not. I know milk," the suit debated.

'Bleedin' featherhead! He doesn't know doodly squat! Look at his socks, one blue and one black,' Bridie elbowed Reilly. Luckily, the jibe passed through her or said creamer would have spilled on said arrogant, elegant suit.

Barely refraining from laughing in the oh-so-serious suit's face, Reilly patiently replied.

"I'm sorry, but that really is whole milk. I poured it myself," she set the creamer back down and bustled away as the guy rethought his argument.

"Martie, the man in #4 says the milk in the creamer isn't milk," Reilly sought aid from the more experienced Martie.

The woman snorted, "It takes all kinds, Reilly. You can tell he's not from around here. Pour him a fresh creamer and be nice- that's all you can do."

'I bet he wears purple underwear, the dickey dazzler, color-blind bollocks,' Bridie danced a jig on #4's head, purposely disturbing his costly hair style.

He ran a hand over his head, smoothing down the uplifted strands of hair and surveyed the surrounds quizzically for the source of the draught.

"Oh, Bridie," Reilly carefully grinned, shaking her head.

'Now, that's what I want to see more of,' the ghost peered over the banana pudding Reilly rushed to deliver.

Reilly hadn't mentioned her ideas about homemade desserts in the diner to Trinity or Pat. Instead, she waited for their visit to Dave's, buoyantly anticipating their pleased expressions.

They didn't eat out every day and she'd missed seeing them Monday, Tuesday and Wednesday, although Trinity picked her up promptly at 6:30 every night.

When Trinity asked how her day had been, she had to check herself not to spoil the surprise. She'd never had a living friend to trade events of the day with.

Too many moves and unsettled conditions at wherever she happened to be living, kept friendships at bay.

"Busy tonight," Pat said hello and took a seat at the counter, surveying all the crowded tables.

Martie tilted her head for Reilly to wait on Pat. Dave's wife usually took the counter customers- less walking, especially after the long days she put in. But she knew Reilly liked her neighbors and they liked her.

"Hi, Pat," Reilly's eyes swung to the door, but no Trinity.

Pat didn't miss the disappointment creeping into the set of Reilly's shoulders. He had to give it to her, though- she knew how to keep a poker face. Pat tried not to read too much into the friendship of his youngest son and this much younger girl.

Reilly pretended to ignore Trinity's absence, so Pat informed her, "Trinity's gone ice-fishing for a few days. I hope you like Walleye."

"Fish, yes. Are there frozen lakes around here?" Reilly puzzled.

"Nah, Pat Jr., Trinity and a couple friends, went north- to Lake Erie. What do you recommend, today?"

Reilly brightened with this question, "Banana pudding for dessert."

"Banana pudding? I don't care for those frozen desserts," Pat opened a menu.

"This is homemade," Reilly found herself stifling a cat-out-of-the-bag smile.

Pat's eyes widened, "You?"

A blush tinged her cheeks as Reilly equably nodded.

"Well, in that case, I'll take 2, along with the dinner special."

"Hey, Little Girl," Stalbridge hollered across the dining room. "I'll have another one of those puddings. Sam will, too."

"Hold on, I have to see what's left," she called back.

Dave tapped the counter top in front of Pat. "That Reilly," he wore the biggest smile.

"Good worker, huh?" Pat asked, unnecessarily.

"Good doesn't begin to describe her. Boy, can she cook! You missed the peach cobbler and apple crisp," Dave poured himself a cup of coffee.

"Peach cobbler and apple crisp, did you say? I'm going to have to get after her. She didn't tell us! Of course, you missed the pineapple upside down cake she made for my birthday. Just wait until Trinity gets back," Pat mused.

"Fred, how are you?"

A fifties-something gentleman in flannel shirt and jeans eyed all the full booths and sat next to Pat after hanging up his sheepskin coat.

"Awful," Fred grunted.

The townspeople of Ryan were pretty well accustomed to this kind of reply from Fred. The proprietor of the hardware store never had a pleasant moment if he could help it. Doom and gloom- that was old Fred.

"Anything especially awful or just awful in general?" Pat wondered aloud.

Dave rolled his eyes at Pat as if to say, you had to ask.

"Some damn so and so broke in my back door. Couldn't just break the lock, oh, no.

Had to break the lock and the hinges, not to mention the hole they left in the middle of the damn door! I hope whatever axe he used falls on his neck.

Tossed all my receipts around like confetti on New Years in New York, broke into my knife case- I mean busted all the glass. Took all my best knives, then the SOB busted up my cash register and cleaned me out of the day's take. Tore my phone off the wall, to boot."

Fred saturated his coffee with a cup's worth of sugar, which never seemed to sweeten his prevailing attitude. His normal hang-dog look bore extra hanging as he stirred his coffee pudding.

"That's pretty awful," Pat and Dave empathized. "Find out who did it?"

"Not yet. Bill's working on it. Says it's probably some out of town troublemaker. Which means they'll never find him," Fred looked fit to bawl.

"Well, at least you have insurance," Pat said.

"Insurance? Those crooked SOB's. Wanted to know about my alarm system. Hell, who around here has ever had an alarm system? Then he gives me a bunch of hoo ha about the cost of the knives. Blah, blah, blah. They're refusing to reimburse me for the money in the cash register. Said it's my fault! Can you conceive of the. . .? I should have deposited it in the bank! Who in the hell needs insurance? You pay your premiums, and on time, mind you, and then the SOB's fight you on a claim."

"So what I want to know is, if I'd put my damn money in the night deposit and some crook hits me over the head before I complete my deposit, would the insurance company smart alecks pay for my hospital bills and the lost take, too? No, you better believe they won't. Drive you into the mad house, fighting them, is more like it," Fred continued to rattle on, cynically.

"Here, Fred," Dave cut in. "Try this," Dave placed a dish of banana pudding in front of Fred.

This not only shut up poor Fred, but a smile almost graced his lips. Almost.

Until Bill, the local law, dropped in. Fred started up all over again to whoever was within listening distance. Bill warned Dave and Pat, as he was warning all of the local shop owners, to keep an eye out and deposit the day's receipts in company or call him for an escort.

"You're kind of quiet, Reilly, tired?" Pat drove Reilly to the dump.

Actually, she'd been thinking about Dave's suggestions concerning the money he discerned she was keeping in her locker. Her pay was adding up quickly. In four months, she'd made nearly $3000. Martie touted how much better the tips were with Reilly working.

When Dave expressed his fears for her locker deposits, she'd told him there wasn't another safe place to put her earnings. And Dr. Mardis and Dr. Desatnik refused to let her pay. Reilly bit her lip with the emotion this elicited.

She didn't go into details, but when Dave recommended the bank, all Reilly had to say was, "I'm a minor."

As he tried to glean what she tried hard not to say, his expression changed to stark bewilderment, and he'd walked off, mumbling under his breath.

"A little. You really liked the banana pudding?" Reilly came back to earth.

"Like isn't the word for it. Wait 'til I tell Trinity what he missed," Pat enthused.

"Will he be back on Sunday?" Reilly had accepted the O'Ryans' offer of the use of their computers. In exchange, she often baked cookies or prepared a meal.

Wasting their breath, they'd tried to convince her she needn't think she had to repay them, but it gave her a sense of propriety and something harkening on the 'happiness' scale to see them jostle each other for cookies or drool over chicken and dumplings. And Wrench and Righteous provided entertainment. Father and son in a real home. . .

"He should be. I'll fry us up some fish, if he catches any."

Funny, Reilly thought, Trinity never mentioned being away. But then, why should he?

'Ah, just look at you! Yer all ag borradh!' Bridie spun around, clapped her hands like an Irish Flamenco dancer and hovered next to Reilly on the high-sided couch.

Brutal cold had lambasted the air on this particular Sunday and Reilly nestled in her cocoon of Aran Island sweaters and cape on the walk to Bridie's.

She'd paused briefly at the O'Ryans- no sign of Trinity. If he'd returned late Saturday, then he probably slept in, or maybe he wasn't home yet. Reilly tried to stifle a twinge of loneliness, but the feeling continued to riddle her chest.

Like a modern fairytale zealot, she'd allowed herself to count on seeing him, count on his conversation.

Silly, Stupid, Set-yourself-up-for-pain. Technically, that last one didn't meet mustard, being a phrase and all- Reilly's mind rambled. She switched topics.

Her mother seemed to be doing well, but all of her mother's boyfriends started out 'suitable'. If true to course, the honeymoon would end- abruptly. And new living quarters, i.e. new boyfriends, would be arranged. Kind of like a maître 'd, but instead of aiding reservations in a restaurant the mother was plugged into an invisible dating hotline.

Reilly had learned over the years to armor herself against these inevitable, whirlwind disruptions. Without fail, they happened, facilitating a dead zone around her heart.

Typically, she'd refrained from close contacts, not only because it was embarrassing to bring anyone home, but also because the break-offs were never cauterized with 'good-byes' or 'I'll keep in touches'. Reilly simply disappeared from whichever school she'd been temporarily enrolled in. Grab and go. She'd lost a decent winter coat that way. It had been in the apartment and Reilly had been walking home from school when her mother said 'get in', and they'd left. Hence, the backpack always at hand.

Trinity's absence and not telling her he'd be away brought all this up. What if it happened while he was away?

Bile roiled, waiting an opportunistic release to scald her all over again. That's the price she'd pay for becoming friends with Trinity, and Bridie and Ivy Rose, too.

And for getting a job she loved. . . Reason didn't fit into Reilly's mood. When her mother decided to go, all this would disappear. . .

'Sweetlin?'

"What's that. . .ag borradh, mean?" Reilly returned to the moment.

'Tis a lovely Irish expression similar to 'busting out all over' in American slang,' the ghost remarked, smiling and kicking up her muckered feet.

Reilly stared- impossible to ignore the effusive antics of her mentor. Bridie definitely seemed younger, years falling away- maybe it was a ghost trait? And how did Bridie come up with. . . At that moment, Reilly teetered on the verge of depression- another numbing mechanism. Nothing about her right then felt. . .like a lovely Irish expression.

Down, Down, Down. . . Stop it, Reilly mentally shouted at herself. Think of all the good. . .

'Dearie, I sense yer borrowin' trouble.'

"Sorry, Bridie. I guess. . . What happens if I have to move? I know I've asked you before. . . Will I still see you?"

'Why, of course you will, Sweetlin'! I'm a ghost. I go wherever I wish. If I move too slow for you, just keep callin' and I'll lift up me skirts and come runnin',' Bridie tapped Reilly's thigh.

'I'm right proud of you, I am. Those wonderful cobblers and such, and comin' up with the idea for hot fudge cake on Mondays when you didn't have time to make a special dessert- ooh, I can almost taste it. You put yourself into every one. Good food is only great if it's prepared with love and I watch you, lass. You love to cook. It's bred in yer, no pun intended.'

Reilly didn't fathom how, but Bridie was bringing her up, lifting her spirits, no pun intended; she half smiled at the ghost's compliments.

'You have other ideas, too.'

"I don't want Dave to think. . ."

'Believe me, that good man will appreciate yer suggestions, especially after the way his business is poppin' over yer desserts. Don't rest on your laurels, Dearie- charge ahead!'

Reilly thought about her other ideas, why not? She'd pick a slow time and see if Dave was interested. He wasn't hard to approach.

She reckoned if she had a chance to pick her own father, it would be a toss-up between Pat and Dave. Along with her grandpa, they were the best men she'd ever known.

When Dave paid her, he always slipped in more than her earnings. The first time she counted her wages, she'd thought he'd made a mistake.

"No mistake, Reilly. You earned it." She remembered fighting tears on the way to her locker- Dave's words ringing in her ears, the finest congratulatory applause.

'It's time you had appreciation, Dearie. Never forget. Don't lock yerself up ever again. Change always happens. Troubles always come. You've lived through them and soon the only troubles you'll have will be those of yer own makin',' Bridie wrapped Reilly inside her ghostly arms.

Just some over a year left, Reilly thought, then, I'm 18 and away from all the dumps.

'Live these moments, lass, and relish them. Good or not, they're all learning experiences. Did I catch you hummin' while you whipped up that meringue?'

Reilly blushed.

'Do you sing?'

"Not really," the abashed girl flushed.

'Nonsense! Someday I'm going to have you sing for me,' Bridie vowed. 'Meanwhile,' Bridie mulled over something, tapping her chin.

"What is it, Bridie?" Her ghostly friend wouldn't allow her any time to brood in withdrawal mode. With all of her ideas and not to mention the card she drew last night. . .

'I'm hopin', lass, that you'll be tendin' my garden.'

"I'd like that. Come summer, if I'm still here, I intend to work full time at the diner.

I could take care of your garden on the way home. I bet Trinity and Pat would like fresh vegetables. . ." Reilly broke off, biting her lower lip.

'Ah, yer missin' him, is it? It's only natural,' Bridie's grin was wider than the room.

"He said he used to come here when. . ."

'We'd sit together after I asked him for a few repairs or such. Troubled, he was. Seems he gained a semblance of peace, here, in me cottage. At times, I'd patch up his cuts and bruises, but the real scars were his to medicate. The inside ones,' Bridie explained.

"He told me he almost killed his brother." Reilly understood how horrific that time period must have been for Trinity.

Bridie remained silent. Reilly knew the ghost wouldn't divulge stories that were not hers to tell- one of the reasons Trinity had spent so much time here. He had gained warm, peaceful sustenance from Bridie, as Reilly, herself, did.

'A garden would be just the thing for you. I'll teach you about the plants you're not familiar with. You see, Reilly, the land remembers those who love her and she loves a loved garden as well as the wildness of her wildernesses. Everyone needs to feel productive and appreciated and loved. Whether left wild and free, or used organically, the land is happy.

I've plenty of seeds and good ground.

Soon we'll start the tiny seedlings; I'll teach you how to revive the garden soil, and you'll get to know me wild critters, especially the mafia godfather of possums!

Always allow some of the bounty for the dear critters,' Bridie had adroitly changed the subject.

Reilly sensed the stir of looking forward to something. Something beside 18.

"The godfather of possums?"

'Ah, you'll see, you'll see, me impatient lass.' And Reilly tried to picture a waddling master of opossums and his entourage, intent on mischief, to no avail.

"Bridie, what's a ceili?" Reilly passed O'Ryan's Pub frequently. A sign announcing Saturday's Fish and Chips and Ceili, always hung in the window.

'Pronounced with a hard C, Dearie. A ceili is a lovely musical, Irish party. A traditional get-together with sweet toe-tappin' tunes and dancin'. Songs similar to the ones on me record player. Reminds me, you'll have to listen to THE CHIEFTAINS and THE DUBLINERS, too.

Ah, the pub on Saturdays, I never missed a one and once I got a little wobbly in me 'physical', yer man, Trinity, would pick me up and take me. That young blade could charm the knickers off a saint with his voice and his playing.

Trinity plays real music, not like that noise that'll blister yer ears- blabbin' from eejit cars with their radios so loud you'd think a tornado was on its way, not to mention the cars themselves vibratin', fixin' to rocket off.'

Loquacious to the extreme when voicing her opinion once she was on a roll, Bridie struck an obnoxious, jittery pose, pretended to drive with a gangster lean, turning up the radio full blast. Reilly empathized; she didn't care for those overly-loud cars, either. She hoped to hear Trinity play, hoped it would happen before. . . No, don't borrow trouble, she silently chided herself.

"Ivy Rose said she misses his playing. Why don't I see Ivy Rose all the time? Do you think Trinity will see her someday?"

'She stays close to Trinity- like an optimistic guardian angel. As do I with you. Time will tell with the other, lass.'

"Did you never marry, Bridie? Or want to?"

'Sweetlin', I never married, but I had the love of my life and I had a grand affair with life. I love so many things. . .'

"Who was he?" Curiosity struck Reilly.

'You'll not catch me spillin' beans, lass. No, no,' Bridie adamantly huffed.

That was OK with Reilly. She thought she knew who he was, anyway. Someday, she'd find a picture of. . .

'Weren't you going to ask me about the new card?'

Leave it to Bridie to keep Reilly from over-speculation. She opened her backpack, carefully withdrew the caped-cat silk pouch and showed Bridie the latest tarot card to make itself known.

'What does it say to you?' Bridie's fingers graced the ancient deck in Reilly's hand.

The top card depicted a woman in a white, flowing ethereal toga-style gown. Upon her forehead rested a silver, crescent moon. In her upraised hand was a large, crystal ball. At her feet, a swan with outstretched wings and a tiny, rock-lined well and willow trees. The picture was hauntingly alive with moonlight- as a full moon lingered above.

"I. . .," Reilly always felt uncomfortable answering questions in class and while this was not high school. . .

'C'mon, don't dither,' Bridie urged.

"What comes to mind is the phrase, 'see the light'. I mean, the lady and the well and the swan, the crystal and even her gown and. . .tiara are…are blessed by the moonlight," Reilly tried.

'Go on, Sweetlin'.'

"If one sees the light, it's an acknowledgement of. .
.a coming to the realization of some intelligence. . ."

'And how do you think this might apply to you,
Reilly?' Bridie's twinkling eyes settled on her protégé.

"There's something for me to learn, er understand,"
Reilly was confused and eager to have this cleared for her.
"Bridie?"

'The priestess is a conduit or wake-up call to listen
to your intuition and dreams. Never deny anythin' your inner
self tells you! It might be imperative.

Without knowing the symbology of me Celtic ancestry,
you wouldn't ken all the meanin's.

Wells and springs were sacred places, where the world
of sacred and earthly happenin's met.

Often in the old country, folks would place ribbons
and trinkets at these sites- Brigid's well, for one, and ask
for healin's or some other important thing. Underground
waters, considered holy, were natural places of healin',
inspiration, a speak with spirits.

The tiny, white flowers at the priestess' feet are
heralds of spring- a stir of renewed life- your ag borradh.
The willow branch strengthens your intuition. You may
perceive very important knowledge by listenin' to your inner
self.'

"Like your second sight, Bridie?"

'Yes, lass. The swan is related to prophecy. I
thought you might have the gift. The cards do, too. Second
sight and intuition are a grand match. Always take heed,
Sweetlin'.'

It was rather scary for Reilly to think she might have
'the sight'. Her regular sight was frightening enough, but.
. .

'Do not be afraid, Reilly. Remember, these are only
suggestions for filling your life as it was meant to be.
Feel gratitude- these gifts can be developed or ignored, but
they are yours to do with as you wish.'

"With the well in the picture, does that mean I might
be able to help folks like you did?"

'That's for you to decide, Dearie. I'll not live
vicariously through you, but I will help you every step of
your way in whatever you decide to do, if you wish.

The moon is also related to female energy- a moving
with the seasons, a cycle.

This card is a call to wisdom and strength through inner recognition. I would not be surprised if you are called in the near future in a way you've not been called before. Listen, and know that I am here with and for you. I could not be more proud of you if you were me own daughter. In fact, I consider you me own,' Bridie placed a ghostly kiss on Reilly's forehead.

Reilly barely had time to replace the cards in the drawstring pouch before great yawns overtook her and a feeling of undeniable weariness claimed her.

"Bridie, I. . .would you mind if I took a nap?"

'Not at all, Sweetlin'. Many's the time I curled up here and look, here's Righteous, all fit to join you.'

Trinity crouched down, the better to see Reilly's face, all snuggled into the curled-up Righteous' fur. The kitten's paws formed a necklace around Reilly's throat.

Bridie's heavy cape blanketed her. In a fetal position, she was fast asleep, her shoes on the floor. He'd have to remind her to lock the door when she napped here, alone.

But maybe, Trinity looked around, felt something brush against his hair, as if a hand caressed the crown of his head- maybe she wasn't alone, here.

His fishing buddies, Cory and JT and his brother, Pat- they'd all grown up together. Cory and JT hadn't suffered as much as Pat when Trinity moved through his crazy stage. They'd come through it intact and remained friends.

But the topics of conversation on the long drive had been innocuous. Nothing deep, nothing personal. They were still leery of him and he couldn't blame them.

Cory was great with jokes and there had been laughs and the fishing was super. Inside their toasty cabin drug out on Lake Erie, the fish had acted as if they were starving. They'd practically jumped into the coolers.

So why then, why the further they drove from the town of Ryan, had the hardness chinked up again around his heart? Why was it, only now watching this girl sleep, that his breathing seemed to ease? The weight seemed to lessen? Why?

He remembered Bridie advising him, "Trinity, lad, when you're ready to be healed, the means will come along." Was Reilly his path to. . .?

Lisa Annette Powell

Reilly snuggled deeper under the covers. Her grandpa had returned with a mess of blue gill and her grandma was busy frying up the fish. She could smell the cornflake coating as it browned in the old iron skillet her grandma always used.

Someday, I'll have iron skillets, the girl dreamed, just like Grandma's. Her grandpa was calling her.

"Reilly, come on, girl! Dinner's almost done. Don't want to miss any of them blue gills."

Reilly stirred, felt movement under her chin.

"Reilly? Hey, Smiley Reilly, wake up, oops, sorry-you said you didn't like that name. Dad's frying up a mess of Walleye. C'mon, don't want to miss out."

"Sheesh! Wonder what the diner's giving away?" Trinity and his dad bumped into the local deer control and 6 other customers waiting in line right inside the diner's door. The cow bell clanged relentlessly.

Myron and Bryan Stanislaus, twins, deer hunters in and sometimes out of season, nodded at the O'Ryans.

"You haven't been here in a week," Pat idly attempted to explain the standing room only crowd.

"What?" Trinity asked over the noise.

Trinity and Pat were tall enough to look over the heads of the other customers, so Pat tilted his head at Reilly.

Mrs. Snider had a hold on Reilly's arm- the coffee pot sporting arm; Reilly's other arm had a line of plates arrayed on it.

"Dear, this pie reminds me of being a little girl. My mother used to make it this same way."

"Thank you, Mrs. Snider," Reilly blushed and bashfully smiled at the enthusiastically reminiscent, elderly woman.

"Hey, Reilly!" Stalbridge crowed. Reilly delivered the orders she carried, checked coffees and other drinks on her way to seeing what the crusty farmer wanted.

"What's for dessert tomorrow?"

"It's a surprise," Reilly said, topped off his coffee and walked off.

"Ah, c'mon Darlin'," Stalbridge whined.

"What's been going on around here?" Trinity surveyed the abnormally boisterous diner, bewildered at the crowd and the change in Stalbridge. "Is that Reilly?"

The waitress he thought was Reilly had her hair in a pony-tail with a tortoise-shell headband keeping all stray hairs, the usual curtain she hid behind, from hanging in her eyes. And damned if she wasn't smiling!

Two openings at the counter were hastily taken by Myron and Bryan. The big table in the back was minus two satisfied, exiting customers.

Pat indicated the seats to the suited men in front of them, but they told Pat and Trinity to go ahead. The business men required a table for their entire group- not all currently in attendance.

"Executive table for us, Son."

"Great, maybe we can help them out with some of those major and worldwide indecisions," Trinity replied, tongue-in-cheek, eyeing. . .

The so-called executive table was often used as a conference table for political discussions ranging from the local to the international. More voices were raised than problems solved, which made the table a good imitation of all governments everywhere. A local race horse owner accepted bets at this particular table, which he placed at the track for the regulars of Dave's Diner, including Dave.

Contractors mixed with farmers, shop keepers, delivery men and bank presidents at this table. They shared not only bets and conversations, but also free donuts- provided by the bakery delivery man, book exchanges and in the early hours, newspapers.

Before Pat could explain the recent changes in the local eatery, Trinity's eyes fastened on 4 pieces of pie in Reilly's hands. And they didn't look like anything other than homemade.

"Desserts? Dad?"

"Reilly's the star of the diner, Son."

"Well, I'll be. . ." He watched the girl garner and soak up compliments right and left as she approached them.

"Hi," Reilly shyly greeted her neighbors.

"You didn't tell me," Trinity griped.

"I…I wanted it to be a surprise. Seems I'm the one surprised. I never realized so many folks were craving homemade desserts," Reilly admitted.

"Please tell me there's some left for us," Trinity said as Martie brushed by with, "Down to 3 pieces, Reilly."

"Reilly," Trinity beseeched.

"I…I set 2 p…pieces aside for you and Pat, j…just in case," Reilly blushed and stammered.

"Hallelujah! What are they?"

"Peanut butter pie."

"Peanut butter?" Trinity's brows rose under his long, ragged-excuse-for-bangs.

"Trust me," Pat ordered the special and pie.

Reilly, Dave and Martie were still learning about how many dessert trays Reilly needed to make to carry through the evening and the next day's lunch. Before leaving on Saturday, Reilly made a tray of chocolate cake, sans icing, which kept in the walk-in refrigerator for Monday's hot fudge cake.

As soon as Reilly arrived at work after school, she prepared her dessert of choice in the huge steam table trays. Cobblers were simple. Without fruit in season, she used canned peaches or frozen blackberries, and made her own biscuit topping. Apple pies required the help of the clean-up woman to peel apples and have them ready for Reilly, who then made the pie crust.

Cream pies, banana pudding with fresh bananas and real meringue, all went over with tremendous vivacity. Reilly wanted to try a special cake her grandma loved to bake- it ranked high with other possibilities on her list. Luckily, she retained all the recipes inside her head.

Calculating the increase in ingredients involved pencil and paper, but wasn't difficult. Reilly inherently possessed a knack for the culinary arts.

Dave spent time with her to show her how to price individual servings. If and when the hoopla settled down some, she had a few more ideas for him.

Bridie perched on the butcher block table, sticking her fingers in the whipped cream topped peanut butter pies, wishing her ghostly taste buds would allow her to taste the confection.

'What did yer man, Trinity, say?' Bridie eyed her fingers with exasperation.

"He liked it. Wanted another slice, but. . ."

'Sold out! Ah, lass, I'm right proud of you.'

Reilly rolled up the compliments and stored them in the back of her mind. The prospect of quick changes, and from experience they were never good changes, weighted/waited there. Somehow, she wished the compliments would out-balance the ugly.

Every night when she reached the dump, she ironically hoped to find her mother and Chet continuing on good terms.

She could stand her miniscule room without air conditioning and little heat; she could fend off the bugs, thanks to Bridie, but what would she do if her mother suddenly decided to move on?

This town of Ryan, Bridie, Righteous, Ivy Rose, her job, Trinity. . . If she were forced to leave. . . She'd be 18 in a little over a year. . .

Hold on, she prayed. She knew with all her heart that she'd return to Ryan- if they'd let her back in after her mother drove them away without any goodbyes, because this place felt like home, and Reilly desperately wanted, needed a home.

"You OK?" Trinity couldn't decipher Reilly's quiet demeanor Friday at dinner.

"Dr. Desatnik adjusted my braces. My mouth aches," Reilly answered.

"Back to soft foods, huh?" Reilly nodded.

Pat and Trinity ordered extra slices of the Italian Cream Cake- her grandma's specialty cake, and then complained, "We're going to get fat eating like this every day!" Agreeably, they stacked their used plates.

"Well," Reilly wasn't sure how to reply, "there's no dessert on Saturday, or Sunday."

"Unless you're cooking Sunday?" Pat rejoined as they rose to leave.

"See you later, Reilly. Dad's hanging out with my uncle tonight," Trinity said before exiting.

"Should I bring a leftover for Wrench?"

"Nah, been too chilly for Wrench lately, to be sleeping on the concrete floor all day. If you want to box something up, we'll let him and Righteous divvy it up at my house, later."

With Trinity and Pat providing her a ride after work, the kitten could often be found waiting on the O'Ryans' porch. To the extent that Pat had stuffed a box with straw and old towels- in case the kitten got cold. Reilly wouldn't put it past Pat to put in a kitty door just for Righteous.

Since the 'Bridie remembers' incident, Chet had not only steered clear of Reilly, but also all cats, period. Being ignored in this instance was a blessing Reilly was grateful for.

Trinity was religious about being at the diner's door at 6:30 sharp and he waited patiently for Reilly if she wasn't quite finished.

But this Friday night, for some reason, Reilly found her eyes constantly checking the big diner clock with its picture of a huge white rooster. The bird's feathered wings were the time-teller arms.

At 6:25 Reilly experienced an unusual crick in her neck and a pressing head ache. Her braces had never done this to her after the previous adjustments. She rubbed the back of her neck, thoughtfully.

At 6:32, a weighted sense of doom pushed to the forefront of her thoughts. Reilly's heart and every other cell of her body seemed on the edge of revolution. Her hands refused to carry out their assigned tasks. Tremors. What was going on?

'Intuition is a powerful sense- never ignore it,' Bridie had advised her when the tarot deck presented Reilly with her latest lesson.

Bridie wasn't at the diner, right then.

Reilly operated solely on her own recognizance- her whole body electrically erratic, the ache around her heart became unbearable. . .

6:34

"Martie, something's not right!" Reilly cried and bolted out the door, sending the cow bell into anxious overdrive. Twenty degrees outside, Reilly didn't stop for her cape. She ran as if her life depended on it.

The diner's cowbell echoed tumultuously- heralding Reilly's racing form, constraining her heart. Its rattling clamored on a level commensurate with her clamoring intuition.

HURRY! HURRY!

She didn't think to call on Bridie. Other than running, she didn't think at all. Turning right out the door, she put on the speed, slipped on a trickle of ice, used the forward momentum- hands out in front of her- to gain all the speed she was capable of mustering.

The garage.

HURRY!

"Dave," Martie interrupted her husband going over the books, balancing the register, tallying the day's receipts in the tiny office.

He looked up, a pleased expression on his face. Martie's worried frown quickly alerted him.

"What's wrong, Martie?"

"I don't know, but I think you better follow Reilly- she ran out of here like a house afire!" Dave shot up, papers flew.

Reilly skated into the garage perimeter. Trinity's car was parked out front, but the lights were off inside the building. Why? She knocked on the door, tried to open it- locked, but she could hear something running within.

HURRY!

All of her senses fired volcanically.

"TRINITY! TRINITY!" She screamed repeatedly, and fisting her two hands together, she broke the pane of glass in the door.

As her right hand scrambled violently for the lock, she barely felt a stinging on her arm and the back of her wrist. She switched the lock to open, fumbled with opening the door and locating the light switch, all the while calling, praying. . .

'Take a deep breath before you go inside,' she heard clearly in her head.

Dave heard the sound of shattered glass in the still, frigid air as he exited the diner. Unlike Reilly, he slipped and fell on the ice criss-crossing the sidewalk, cursed his slippery shoes, staggered up, and shadowing the buildings for self-preservation, he scuttled, hobbling toward the garage.

Reilly flipped the light switch on the right side of the door.

"TRINITY!"

No sign of the young mechanic, but the distinct odor of a running car engine's fumes filled the closed garage. She bolted into the bay area, observed one car with hood up, running. Its passenger door was locked. . .

Her eyes frantically searched, saw familiar booted feet peeking from behind a huge, red tool cabinet!

"TRINITY!" She gagged; the poison-soaked air forced a coughing fit.

GET HIM OUT!!!!

Reilly choked on the exhaust-saturated atmosphere as she rounded the cabinet. Trinity lay sprawled, face down. She gently rolled him over.

GET HIM OUT!!!!! hammered at her dumb-struck senses.

Trinity's ashen-hued face hurled her into a living terror the likes of which she'd never conceived of.

"God help me," she prayed, and hooked her hands under Trinity's arms. Much too slowly, she began to drag the dead weight.

"Bridie, Ivy Rose, God, help me," she pleaded as her oxygen-deprived lungs strove to the utmost. She bit into her lower lip to invigorate her dwindling strength.

In answer, a burst of adrenalin provided just enough power. Reilly used every ounce of it and managed to get Trinity half out the door before she collapsed at his side.

Cradling his head, she felt a lump at the base of his neck where it met his t-shirt clad shoulder.

"Tr...Trinity, Trinity," she cried, sucking in cold, but pure, air.

"Reilly? Oh, God!" Dave knelt, pulled out his cell phone, dialed 911.

"O'Ryans' garage, Trinity O'Ryan down, unconscious, exhaust fumes! Hurry, get an ambulance ASAP and the fire department!"

Pocketing his phone, he felt for a pulse, couldn't find one, spied blood dripping onto the sidewalk.

"Reilly?"

"Trinity, Trinity, come back," she entreated over and over while Dave helplessly clasped Trinity's lifeless hand. Somewhere deep inside, the thought of a world without. . .lurked, teasingly, but she had no time to countenance its jibe.

God blessed the local emergency squad. Within a couple minutes, they were there, unloading a gurney, checking vitals, applying oxygen.

The sounds of sirens stopping on Main Street emptied O'Ryan's Pub.

"Oh, God, my son!" Pat eyed the ambulance outside the garage. He swept through the crowd, his brother, Mick, right behind him.

The EMTs tried to displace Reilly who'd entered a trance of sorts, crying her mantra of, "Trinity, Trinity, come back. . ."

"Jaysus, Mary and Joseph," Pat trembled to a stop, aghast, at Trinity's side as the gurney was lifted into the ambulance. He saw the blood and paled further, his knees weakening.

"What happened?"

"We've got to get him to the hospital, stat. He's in a bad way."

Pat absently nodded, was guided solicitously to the passenger door of the ambulance; a helping hand supported his entry.

"You better take this girl, too. It looks like she's slit her wrists," Dave hoisted Reilly up and into the ambulance.

One EMT took charge of Trinity, another examined Reilly's arm, wrapped a bandage about it and radioed in. The ambulance whisked its passengers to the hospital, sirens screeching.

"Trinity, Trinity, come back. . ." over and over Reilly begged.

"Pulse is weak, lump on the back of his neck, his color- not good, carbon monoxide poisoning," Info and orders were relayed to the emergency room to facilitate preparations.

In between Reilly's gently sobbing mantra, she'd told the EMTs how she'd found Trinity lying on the garage floor, a motor running. Pat listened, head sunk on his chest. His own prayers intently winging from his fraught-with-fear heart, adding to Reilly's pleas- no checking his tears.

Reilly fought the EMTs and nurses who tried to separate her from Trinity as he was wheeled into the emergency room. They physically ushered her to another cubicle of lesser emergencies.

"GET HER BACK IN HERE!" Pat's voice roared as Trinity's condition immediately took a nosedive with her removal from his side.

The initially puzzled doctor enforced Pat's demand as it became readily apparent that the girl was having an imperative effect on the patient.

"Trinity, Trinity, come back. . ." Out of the doctor's way, Reilly intoned loud enough for Trinity to hear over the emergency room bustle. His pulse immediately re-registered and steadied with her voice once more within his range of hearing.

Coma or not, a recognized voice, a hopeful voice, is vitally important to an injured party, transcending all the medical terms flying about, especially if a person might be undecided about staying stateside.

With the oxygen application, Trinity's color improved from death's gray door, but it was far from normal.

"We need to get a better idea of this lump. Let's take him to x-ray. Make sure there is no. . ."

"Trinity, Trinity, please come back. . ."

"Reilly? Is that your name? Dear, let me take care of your arm," a kindly, efficient nurse drew Reilly off to the side next to a wheeled cart, but her ministrations were foiled.

Reilly began to shiver- delayed reaction- onslaught of shock.

"Get me a blanket," the nurse ordered. "Honey, stay with us, this young man needs you," she diligently reassured the stricken girl.

The nurse wrapped a blanket shawl about Reilly's shoulders, provided her bulk to lean on, her arm about the girl's waist, stationing a mobile Reilly at Trinity's side as they wheeled the gurney to x-ray.

"Trinity, Trinity, please. . ." she repeated continuously while the gurney quickly rolled to another section of the hospital. The procedure enacted in record time, Trinity was re-installed in the emergency room- with numerous medical contrivances attached and recording.

"Reilly, dear, I need to ask you some questions. Reilly?"

Lips quivering, the girl's tear-saturated face melted the sympathetic nurse's heart.

"I need to call your parents." Reilly's voice stalled, her brain attempted to decipher which role to fill- the dutiful patient answering questions or the lighted thread of a path for Trinity to follow back to life.

At the girl's sudden silence, Trinity's vital signs also plummeted- checking out.

"CODE BLUE!!" Medical personnel hollered, scrambled for resuscitation equipment.

"Get t. . ." Pat broke from his son's side, fought to keep control, grabbed Reilly's arm. . .

"Talk to him, please, Reilly, just keep on talking, please. . ." And to the nurse, "I'll take full responsibility for the girl, her parents are away."

"Trinity, Trinity, come back. . .please. . ." she coughed, further aggravating her compromised vocal chords, swiped at tear-streamed cheeks, and the industrious nurse placed a cup of water in her hand, guided it to the girl's lips, foisted tissues in her free hand. Reilly's bloodied forearm tremblingly settled on Trinity's.

Before further machines assumed Reilly's place at Trinity's side, his pulse registered again. Audible sighs filled the room.

"Dear God," somebody murmured in reverent awe at what they'd just witnessed.

The previously skeptical attending physician's scrutiny swung from the disheveled, disconsolate young girl with her constant pleading, to his patient; he waved the superfluous equipment out of the room.

"Keep talking to him, young lady. Believe me, he can hear you, and your voice is…is life to him. I can't explain it, but. . .there it is," he eyed the machine recording the essential evidence. He, too, felt caught up in something. . .miraculous.

The nurse asked Pat to switch sides with her so she might assist the doctor as he stitched the lengthy slash on Reilly's arm; she gently cleansed the dried blood from her hand and offered her own prayerful entreaty for the young man's successful recovery.

No one asked Reilly any more questions.

"How does she keep doing it?" Pat's brother murmured in stunned admiration.

Reilly barely sipped water when it was offered to her. Her entire focus, her hands and her voice, were all spotlighted on Trinity- calling him, urging him to stay.

"Trinity, Trinity, please come back. . ."

Pat perched on the edge of a chair on one side of his son, red-eyed from tears, praying. His other sons were enroute. Mick O'Ryan, coming and going with coffee, water and juice, fielded questions from the local police, who were immediately and furiously, on the case.

One of their own, the police car mechanic, had been badly injured, might even die. . . The townspeople of Ryan banded together- the perpetrator WOULD be found.

The local hotline had apprised everyone in the small town, who did not possess a police scanner, of the situation and prayer groups formed as well as a hunt for potential witnesses.

A reward was set to be aired statewide. The town of Ryan didn't fool around when one of their own was injured. They might have looked askance at Fred's doom and gloom loss, but not on attempted murder.

"Trinity, Trinity, come back. . ."

"The lass is a walking miracle, Pat," his brother gripped Pat's shoulder, commiserating, and also feeling a spirit move within him he'd not believed possible.

Only once more were Reilly's efforts proved to be the only course- a veritable, miraculous lifeline. Somehow, her mother had heard of the night's events, dialed the hospital and demanded Reilly be put on the phone.

Trinity again took a turn for the worse as Reilly fought with a new nurse about answering the hospital phone.

Reilly let the phone drop to the floor as she rushed back to Trinity's imperiled side.

"Trinity, Trinity, stay here, please. Please come back, please come back. . ."

At the renewed sound of her voice, Trinity rallied once again. Pat slumped in relief. The awe-struck doctor gave uncompromising orders the girl was not to leave the room or answer phones or anything else- come hell or high water, until his patient was out of dire straits.

The night hours crept unbearably on, only broken momentarily when Trinity's two brothers slid into the room, Kate in tow. Pat Jr. and Sean dropped to their knees at Trinity's side and began praying silently as their uncle explained Reilly's role in Trinity's tenuous hold on life.

As the 20-hour mark approached of Reilly's being on her feet, her voice nearly left her. Wild-eyed, she struggled to form the words.

'Easy, lass,' a familiar voice advised.

Kate thrust a cup of juice into Reilly's shaking hands, cradled the cup to aid the girl to drink.

Hurriedly, she gulped the contents, searched Trinity's face, and there was Ivy Rose at his head, stroking his temples. The tearful, little girl ghost waved and smiled sympathetically at Reilly.

'It's OK, now, Reilly. Can you hear me? It's OK. Trinity will be all right now. Thank you so much. I love my brother, but it's not time for him to join me and Mom.' Ghostly tears reflected in the transparent face.

Pat jerked awake from a momentary slumbering lapse, blinked bleary eyes.

Dear God, the girl was still talking to his son- more like a stymied lullaby at this stage. How did she manage? Where did her strength come from? Why hadn't Trinity's own family been. . .helpful? He glanced around at his other sons and Kate. Sean's wife had to stay with the baby, but progress reports were issued regularly.

All eyes remained fastidiously on Reilly. A strange look was in her eyes which were glued to the side of Trinity's head. What was she looking at? Most exchanged bewildered glances.

"She's exhausted, poor thing."

"Trinity," Reilly croaked, and then she totally mystified everyone in the room as she called, "Bridie?"

Three things happened at once. A draft of fresh air swept through the room, Trinity's vital signs registered perfectly normal and Reilly fainted.

"How is my little hero?"

Reilly, groggy, rubbing at her sore throat, woke to find her mother peering down at her, with a smile, no less. The girl had no idea what day it was, what the time was, where she was or how she'd got there. Only her abject discomfort told her she was not dreaming.

"C'mon, Reilly, rise and shine. I'll make you something to eat. Bacon and eggs?"

Righteous unfurled from Reilly's arms, stretched, arched her back at the strange woman in Reilly's room and hopped to the dresser, rubbing her jaws along the stacked cans of cat food. The noise of their toppling acted as an alarm, driving Reilly's brain to focus.

"Trinity," she murmured, woefully. She winced as her bandaged hand and arm hit against the mattress. Her mother hadn't waited for her.

"Bridie?" Reilly whispered.

'Easy, Dearest,' the ghost hovered into view.

"Trinity?" Reilly's heart was thumping like a percussive war.

'Yer man, Trinity, will be waitin' for you. Call the hospital, get somethin' to eat, don't worry, lass. You are an amazin' girl. You'll see what I'm meanin'. The talk of the town- the star of the town of Ryan! Ah, sure tis, they'll be writin' a song for you! Did you know they wrote a song for me?'

Bridie kissed the astonished Reilly and waved her out the door, after she'd fed the starving, complaining Righteous.

Reilly couldn't remember the last time her mother had cooked for her. Too many of her mother's culinary projects turned out scorched and inedible. The case of the burnt, green-for-St. Patrick's-Day mashed potatoes came readily to mind.

But, at one time, her mother had been good at crispy bacon and hard fried eggs. A long time ago. . .

A newspaper rested on the table. Chet eyed the sleepy girl as if she possessed the evil eye, bussed her mother's cheek and hastily exited the dump. If he needed any more proof of Reilly's connection with that 'witch, Bridie', the morning paper provided it.

In great detail, from numerous admiring witnesses, the story told of Reilly's impromptu race to the garage, how- if she'd been a minute later- Trinity O'Ryan would have died, how she kept him alive throughout the night by calling his name over and over again, how when she was taken from Trinity's side the young mechanic had passed over and how Reilly's voice brought him back to life. . .

But Reilly had no eyes for the paper. She shakily dialed the hospital- needing to hear. . . She didn't know Pat's cell number or even if his phone might be turned on.

"Ryan Hospital," the receptionist answered.

"Y...yes," Reilly's exhausted voice creaked, abysmally. "C...could you tell me h...how Trinity O'Ryan is?"

"Sorry, we can't divulge patient information, other than he's stable," and the receptionist brusquely ended the call.

Struggling to forestall collapse, Reilly felt her eyes shutter and tear. She stood forlorn, phone in hand- a poster child for the description of dejected, yet hanging by a thread.

Her mother dished up Reilly's breakfast, glanced up, and was astonished by Reilly's prostration. Reilly never cried- not that her mother knew, never complained, never registered pain. A strange constriction stabbed the mother's chest.

"How is he?" she asked.

"Th...they won't tell me," Reilly cried, crumbling into a chair, shivering uncontrollably.

A riptide of anger doused the mother, "We'll see about that." Once more the hospital number was dialed.

"Your name, please," she requested after the receptionist answered.

"Jessie Frye," the receptionist hedged.

"Have you read the morning's paper? Reilly Brooke, the girl who saved Trinity O'Ryan's life, sat up with him all night keeping him alive, just called you and you put her off. I'm going to hand the phone over to her and if you don't answer all of her questions, I'll be sure to tell the local paper all about it."

Jessie Frye hemmed and hawed, falling over herself with apologies as the mother turned the phone over to her daughter with a wink and headed to the toaster.

"Th...thanks, Mom," the stupefied Reilly stammered.

"Don't mention it. Read the paper and eat some breakfast." Her mother actually ruffled Reilly's unruly hair in passing.

Reilly took three bites of perfectly crisped bacon and bolted from her chair. With quivering fingers she dialed a number and checked the time on the clock. 1:43.

"Dave's Diner," Dave answered.

"D...Dave?"

"Reilly, Honey, is that you? How are you?"

"Dave, I'm so s...sorry."

It was Saturday and Reilly had missed work and worse she hadn't even called! To Reilly, this was as bad as a mortal sin.

"Nonsense! You listen to me, Reilly. You rest. You are a heroine, do you hear me? An unbelievable heroine! How are your hands?"

"I guess I won't be able to do dishes for a while," Reilly coughed. Her mother forced a glass of juice on her and mimicked drinking it.

"Well, I'll turn the grill over to you and I'll do the dishes. How's that? I hear Trinity's doing fine, thanks to you. See you Monday?"

Again, Reilly tried to apologize before ending the call, but Dave refused to hear it. Reilly contemplated the distance to the hospital. Must be close to twenty miles. . .

Her mother had waved and left for a beauty shop appointment which she was late for. Reilly wondered, too late, if maybe she shouldn't have asked her mother to drop her off at the hospital.

The receptionist said only family could visit. Twenty miles. . .

Though physically and mentally exhausted, Reilly couldn't go back to sleep. She washed up as best she could. I have to see him, kept her upright and functioning. I have to see for myself how he is.

She found her cape in her room. Someone had thought to bring it from the diner. Who? Who had brought her home?

It was cold and blustery out, no snow. Twenty miles. If she'd had some of her money with her she might have called a taxi. No, she wouldn't have.

31

"Dad," a hoarse greeting blessed the room, as Trinity slowly opened his eyes, brushed off the oxygen mask.

"Trinity, Son," Pat was instantly awake. His hand grasped Trinity's- the one without the I.V. patched into it.

Dark blue circles under his eyes, the pallor of his son's face, the hospital gown, the oxygen attachment, the close calls with the Grim Reaper. . . Pat let the relieved tears flow, unchecked.

"Trinity," he stroked his son's arm, emotionally overwrought.

Pat Jr., Kate, Sean and Mick O'Ryan hustled into the room, overpowering the small space. Trinity's head languidly acknowledged one familiar face after another. He basked in the overwhelming love of his family. Wincing at the pressure of the pillow on the knot at the back of his head, he felt an equal twinge at not seeing the one he most needed to see.

"Reilly?" his dark brows furrowed.

"She's fine, Son," his dad assured him.

"Fine, hell! We're going to get her an honorary badge from the fire department and the key to Ryan! The way she pulled your ass out of that garage. . . Talk about your 90 pound weaklings! I don't know how she did it. . . And you, a clear dead weight of some 200 pounds," Sean joked, alleviated at seeing his younger brother awake. . .alive.

"Reilly?" Trinity's eyes conveyed his utter urgency to his father.

"Of course, Son. I'll. . ."

"You stay right here, Dad. I'll go get Reilly," Kate patted Trinity's covered foot, kissed her husband's chin and gripped Pat Sr.'s shoulder.

"Anything else, besides our illustrious Reilly?" she asked.

"Some decent food would be nice," Sean commented.

"Well, the diner's closed. I'll see what I can do. Trinity, a milk shake?"

Trinity tried to shake his head and grimaced with pain.

"I'll take that as no," Kate was nearly out the door when Mick spoke up.

"Stop in at the Pub, if you want. Mary usually has something in a pot that's edible."

Pat Jr., the family doctor, but not Trinity's attending physician, held his brother's wrist, freed his stethoscope from a pocket and listened to Trinity's heart, felt the 'grand' lump, took stock of his lungs upon ordering his brother to breathe, examined Trinity's eyes.

Trinity sluggishly pushed him off, only to have the attending physician step to his side to do the same.

"Hmm. . . Impatience, a good sign. I'll get some broth for you. Nothing more than that for right now. You keep that oxygen right where it needs to be, Trinity, or we'll hog-tie you," Pat Jr. warned.

"You're one lucky guy," the ER doctor grinned, and with a few compliments for Reilly, and advice on the probable time for Trinity's release, he left the family alone.

Trinity rolled his eyes- the only movement which didn't hurt.

"Tom wants to talk to you as soon as you're up for it. The sooner the better, Son, to catch. . ."

Tom Barrett was the local police chief. He had had Pat accompany him to the O'Ryan's garage for a few minutes after Trinity's condition stabilized. If anything was missing and headed for a pawn shop it was important to have this information as soon as possible. He hated to take Pat from his son, but tracking down a potential murderer. . .

Pat understood, and with Trinity resting peacefully hours earlier, he'd done a quick check of the garage's tools and equipment, all of which had imperceptible markings on them. The local people knew the O'Ryans marked their tools.

Several valuable sets of socket wrenches and all the easy-to-carry diagnostic tools were missing, along with some of the day's take from the busted register drawer.

Pat had deposited most of the money as he left on Friday night. The thief would not have known this unless he was a local, as all the shops were being extra careful after Fred's loss. All evidence pointed to an out-of-towner.

The prime suspect would probably hasten to the nearest city of any consequence, where pawn shops awaited those who were genuinely inconvenienced by the state of the economy, and of course, the ever present thieves, too.

Pat brought his son up-to-date on what had transpired after Trinity was knocked out. Reilly's role in talking to him. . .

Pat choked up trying to relate that part, especially when his son flat-lined when she left his side.

To change the subject, he encouraged Trinity to try and recall anything concerning the perpetrators from the garage, but not to talk too much.

Trinity remembered hearing one of the two thieves call the other by name, and also seeing a distinctive type of shoe, before he lost consciousness. With the back door unlocked- he'd forgotten to latch it, and with no Wrench to warn of the intruders, the two had easily sneaked in with the engine and a radio providing cover noise. They'd caught him with his back turned. He hadn't a chance.

The charge of attempted homicide would hold because the two miscreants had deliberately left the car running and had stuffed rags in the outside vents and under the doors. Trinity wasn't meant to wake up.

"From now on, all doors will be locked if one of us is alone, shoot, let's just make it a habit to lock the back door, period. And Wrench comes to work every day. I don't care how cold the concrete floor is, we'll buy him a heated bed- a raised heated bed," Pat attempted a bit of humor.

A nurse's assistant stopped in with a tray containing two cups of broth and a small container of green Jello. Pat Jr. poured water and warned his brother to drink as much as he could, to help flush out the toxins.

Trinity complied grumpily in a creaky voice, "My throat is raw."

"To be expected. Try to drink some of this broth. See if your stomach can handle it."

Trinity made a face with the first spoonful.

"Yeah, yeah, yeah," Sean registered the complaining face. "We'll have to see if your girlfriend is any good at chicken soup. That'll fix you up."

Sidelong glares hushed Sean.

'What?' he mouthed. 'Isn't she one of his girls?'

Trinity ignored them, playing with what they'd given him in place of food, wishing Kate would hurry back with Reilly, wishing Reilly would make chicken soup.

"We got 'em," Tom Barrett poked his jubilant face in. "Pawn shop, west side of Dayton, phoned in a set of tools. Thank God we got that description out. No one can fault Ryan's police force for doing its job.

Two hoodlums, early 20's, records stretching back for years. Upping the ante from petty theft to attempted homicide. With this one, they're going down for a long time."

Mick had dozed off in a vacant chair after assuring himself of Trinity's resurrection and hearing complaints about food, but the Chief's good news roused him.

With a thumbs-up gesture, Barrett departed with, "Saved the town the $10,000 reward." He gave Mick a pointed look. The Pub owner nodded imperceptibly.

"$10,000 reward," Sean whistled.

"Hey, Ryan doesn't mess around. If you had any sense, you'd move back here," Pat Jr. elbowed his brother.

32

A haggard young girl in an incongruous long cape hesitated on the threshold before stepping into the room. Above all, Reilly did not want to intrude, even though she desperately needed to see him. Assure herself he was really all right. Trinity spied Reilly, shoved his tray table away, face distorted with the effort and stared as if his life depended on it.

Kate waved her husband and Sean out. Whispering, she confided, "I found her walking here. Can you believe it? Does the word 'indomitable' come to mind?" The two older brothers shook their awe-struck heads and briefly studied the miracle worker who'd saved their brother's life as Kate dragged them away.

"I'll leave you two alone. Reilly. . . I. . . We, all of. . .," Pat glanced out the door at his older sons and back to Trinity, "want to. . .th…thank you. . ." His voice cracked with deepest emotion.

Reilly didn't hear. She didn't feel Pat touch her shoulder before he left the room. Her sole focus was on the poison-tinged pallor of the young man in his hospital gown sitting up- his deep blue eyes staring volumes. Eyes no longer guarded. Not an iota of severity.

She took in his blue-black hair all askew and his dark beard shadow, all emphasizing the previous night's events dramatically etched on his face. Cracked lips, bruised under-eyes. . .

"Reilly?" Trinity's voice, bereft of the discarded oxygen-deliverer, was rent with the pathos he'd held in check for his family's sake. Now it sundered the distance between them.

Shakily, his arms rose. Without a second's hesitation, Reilly's black bag slid to the floor and she rushed into his embrace, threw her bandaged arm and her good arm around his neck, felt him wince as she inadvertently hit the lump on the back of his neck. As she made to pull away, his arms molded her to him.

Holding her body with one arm, he adjusted his I.V. hook-up line and sucked in the scent of her, tears rolling into her neck.

"Trinity," her own raw vocal chords bleated, "Oh, Trinity. . . I…I was so afraid. . . More than I've ever been. . .in my whole life." She sobbed piteous relief into the crook of his shoulder- sobs that wracked her tiny body.

Trinity clutched her quivering frame to him and released his own pent up tears into her hair.

Time had no bearing as Trinity and Reilly adjusted to a pseudo-return to normalcy. For each of them, in their own way, nothing would ever be normal in the sense of their previous 'normal' friendship, ever again.

Both physically weary, but mentally overwrought with things that must be said, they mutually broke the ferocity of their embrace.

But Trinity kept her close. He hoisted his body to his left to give her room. Gently he perused and held her bandaged arm, lifted it and softly bestowed a kiss. Her other hand received the same treatment, much to her embarrassment.

Annoyed, he banished the uncomfortable plastic nasal canula (the doctor had opted for this in lieu of the full mask) which agitated between them, tossing it from the bed.

He didn't attempt to wipe the trail of his tears, although he tremblingly fingered hers. Her blushing cheeks quivered under the intimacy of his touch.

"You smell like hamburgers," his first strained statement. With difficulty, his fatigued brain tried to prepare, organize, what he urgently needed to express.

"I'm sorry," Reilly ducked her head, embarrassed. How was she going to wash her hair?

"N...no, no! I only m..meant. . . I'm starving and. . .you smell so good and they'll only give me this," his disgusted face nearly had Reilly grinning, "colored water to eat and. . .and green Jello, yuck!" He tilted his head at the leftovers defiling his hospital tray.

"Reilly," Trinity paused. He had so much to tell her, to say, to thank her, and he didn't want to leave anything out.

Reilly sensed a dilemma in Trinity's exasperated demeanor, mirroring her own. Blushing, she dared to directly confront his eyes, expectant, patiently waiting, and he fastened his bleary gaze on the solicitous, infinite healing-green of hers.

"I. . . I saw her, Reilly," tears erupted again. Trinity couldn't control them and the liquid spilled and streamed over his trembling lips. What he needed to say was only for her, only Reilly. Only Reilly would really understand.

"You saw Ivy Rose," Reilly filled in, letting her own tears cascade, matching waterfalls.

"She. . . She was standing next to my mom. Both of them. . .together. In a rainbow of colors, brilliant light. Ivy. . .Ivy Rose was perfect. Her feet, everything- perfect.

She waved at me, jumped up and down. . . Her laugh- just as I remembered. My mom smiled at me, too. I couldn't wait to reach them. I…I felt like I was in a dark tunnel that…that was hard to escape. I just wanted to move toward the light, get to Ivy Rose and my mom.

But. . . But the closer I got. . . Every step was like my feet were weighted, each step heavier. . . The closer I got to them, the more alarmed they seemed. They…they waved their arms at me and pointed behind me.

I…I remember stopping and looking back. There wasn't anything to see, but I heard a voice calling me. This voice accompanied me through the darkness of the tunnel. It kept me from joining my sister and mom.

The call. . . The voice called my name over and over. Once, I think it stopped and I felt a rush of gladness. No one called me and I. . . I walked toward Ivy Rose and my mom. But they continued to point behind me, as if they were telling me to go back."

Trinity swallowed hard, but his water-logged eyes never left Reilly. She nodded ever so slightly. Her hand sought a cup of water and she handed it to him without looking at it.

"It was your voice, Reilly. Why? I wanted to go forward, but your call. . .confused me and. . . I was pulled in two directions. Ivy Rose and my mom smiled at me, encouraging me, waved good-bye and turned and walked into the most dazzling colors. Rainbows flashed around them. And then I also heard Ivy Rose- she…she giggled and told me she'd see me later."

Trinity felt a light touch at his brow. Strands of his hair rearranged, were softly pulled from his face.

Reilly smiled through her tears. She hadn't been wrong to call Trinity to stay here- it wasn't just selfishness on her part- well, not solely. Her intuition had been right- she'd got to the garage in time. 'Listen,' Bridie had said. Thank God, she had. Trinity would fully heal now.

Reilly studied the little girl ghost perched on air near Trinity's head. Her child's transparent body was dressed in the pink shorts and top and she returned Reilly's smile with high wattage. Her eyes, lavished with love, sought her brother as she played with his hair.

Trinity watched Reilly's eyes shift to his left.

"She's here, isn't she?" Reilly nodded.

Slowly, with the greatest, prayerful hope and a leap of faith, Trinity turned his head, unmindful of the pain at the base of his neck.

A faint, familiar outline vaguely filled in and leaned down to peer expectedly at him.

"Ivy Rose," Trinity whispered.

The soft chiming of a carillon giggled in his left ear.

'Hi, Trinity! Is Reilly taking good care of you?'

Trinity gulped, utterly fascinated.

'I get to be your guardian angel, but I'm pretty new at what all to do, so Reilly helps me out. Is that OK?'

Trinity wasn't positive if the voice was solely inside his head or aloud. Did it really matter? He could see and hear his little sister! And he wasn't dreaming. Reilly held his trembling hand. He was definitely awake- no pinch necessary.

"You will hear her in your head as clear as if she were physically sitting next to you," Reilly affirmed, sensing Trinity's quandary.

With all of her recently acquired ghostly experience, Reilly still felt shy instructing Trinity. She felt a shove at her back- Bridie offered her two cents.

"You can respond to her using your mind," Reilly continued.

'You rest, Trinity. I'll see you later,' and Ivy Rose leaned in to kiss his forehead, and then, she dissolved before his astonished, captivated eyes. He rubbed his forehead and swung back to Reilly, full of questions.

"Better rest for now. I'm kind of new to this, too," she said. "It's too much wonder to take in all at once."

Her words floored him speechless. He leaned back into his pillows, completely enervated, yet blissful, closed his eyes, pulled Reilly into his arms, careful of her injured arm, and they napped together.

Pat Sr. peeked in after a suitable interval to find his son clasping his lifeguard to his chest. Both of them fast asleep.

Kate's words rang in his head, "I found her about 10 miles out. She was walking to see him. That's 20 miles!"

Sean broke in, "Just who is this girl?"

"She's an angel," Pat Sr. averred.

"I bet his other girls wouldn't do that," Sean mused.

Pat Jr. hugged his wife and didn't say anything, but he heartily concurred with his wife's description of 'indomitable'.

Trinity's dad refused to entertain the ramifications of 16-year old Reilly and 23-year old Trinity. Grateful prayers occupied all his weary thinking.

33

"Dad, can I borrow y. . .," Trinity's throat tripped repeatedly. A cup of water was thrust in his hand. "Your c…cell phone?"

His brother, Pat, cut in. "Look, Trinity, you're supposed to rest, not stay on the phone all night. Your harem can just w. . . Never mind," he murmured as Kate sideswiped his shin with an effective heel. "You need to rest," he rushed before she dealt another blow.

Trinity felt Reilly freeze at his brother's faux pas. He rubbed her back, conciliatory, but he furiously yearned to cast something heavier than a frown at his older brother.

"It's for Reilly," his admission pierced his father and brother. "In case I can't sleep tonight. Can I call you, Reilly?"

The girl was embarrassed at all the attention and slippage-of-tongue directed at her. She had a hard time relaxing with Trinity's hand on her back, too. Thankfully, her hamburger-scented hair fell like a veil about her face. She wondered if she might talk her mother into washing her hair. Or if Bridie might be capable of doing it. . .

But she definitely would like it if Trinity felt up to talking to her later; she wordlessly assented.

"Dad, if you could take Reilly home? Maybe get some rest, yourself. I'm fine, really," Trinity might not have looked it, but his spirits were definitely on an ascent.

"A hot shower, a cold beer, and my own bed sound pretty good," his dad agreed, scratching at his beard-shadowed chin.

"Uh, Dad, could you maybe take Reilly to Bridie's tomorrow?" Trinity further requested.

"Thanks, but that's not necessary. I…I'll walk," Reilly was the deer caught in the proverbial headlights. She didn't want all of this intense regard- the family had enough to do. Another protest formed, but Trinity quelled it by putting his hand over her mouth. Which further embarrassed her. Nowhere to run, ran through her mind as one of his hands had grasped her long, flannel shirt and the other. . . Oh, my. . . He really put his hand over my. . .

"No, you won't, Honey. I'll take you. I wonder what time you'll be getting released tomorrow."

"Don't sweat it, Dad. I'll make sure he has a thorough going over before I break him out of here," Pat, the doctor/brother, smirked, and suffered another shin-digging remonstrance via his wife for his effrontery.

Trinity rolled his eyes and sank back into his pillows, releasing Reilly's shirt. Although he and Reilly had napped for some forty minutes, he needed another.

"Dad, you think I could get some hamburgers? I'll be wasted away by the time I get home," Trinity's energy and voice were noticeably fading.

"All right, folks. Let's get out of here and let our golden boy sleep," Sean joked, playfully, hiding his immense relief at Trinity's being around to joke with.

Pat embraced his son, kissed the top of his head, fighting off more tears. Trinity pulled Reilly to him for a last hug. Further tickling her timidity.

"Mr. O'Ryan. . ." Pat gave Reilly a sidelong rivet.

"P...Pat, I...I could make. . .some chicken noodle soup. . .uh. . .tomorrow. Hamburgers might be too much for his system, too soon. . ." Bridie winked conspiratorially at her.

"You're probably right about that. You were. . .thinking uh, like, homemade noodles, by chance?" Pat's voice more than hinted at boyish, enthusiastic anticipation.

"Sure, they're easy to make," Reilly shrugged her shoulders.

Pat pulled into the IGA before heading to Red Wing. "Let's get whatever ingredients you might need. I guess cookies are out of the question?"

Bridie made a suggestion from the back seat.

"I...I think it would be better if Trinity didn't have sweets for a few days. Best to concentrate on nutritious meals," Reilly hedged.

"Sounds like good advice, but I think I'll let you explain that to him. I believe he'd be more apt to listen to the cook."

Before dropping Reilly off at the dump, Pat once again tried to express his gratitude. "I...I don't know how you knew, Reilly, to run like you did. . . Maybe Bridie's rubbing off on you, for all the time you spend at her cottage. . . I can't tell you how. . ."

"You don't have to thank me, Pat. I...I care about him, too." Reilly opened the passenger door, climbed out, remembered something. "Pat, I...I don't know how to use this," she held up the cell phone.

"Bridie, did you. . .put the suggestion to me? Warn me about Trinity?"

Reilly attempted to find a comfortable way to curl up in bed. Her arm was throbbing, had been all day. All those stitches. She didn't know what kept her from passing out when the doctor's needle went into her arm- yes, she did- Trinity.

With all the surges of emotion since Friday night, the little sleep she'd had Saturday morning. . . How could a body stay sizzling awake when it was also numb from fatigue? But she had to ask Bridie.

'No, Dearest, that was your intuition,' Bridie floated down to the bed and touched the injured arm.

"Why didn't you tell me? Did you know Trinity would be hurt?" Reilly watched Bridie's faint, ageless features arrange and rearrange as she contemplated what she was going to tell her young friend and protégé.

Bridie knew Reilly's inner turmoil. The dear girl's battle with insecurity was far from won- hence her questioning her own abilities. In the silence, Reilly began to chew her un-bandaged fingernails but stopped when Bridie, 'Tsk'd, Tsk'd'.

'I can only tell you, Sweetlin', that difficult moments are always a possibility,' Bridie started with.

Of course, Bridie was right. Reilly's life was fraught with difficult moments. Why should that change? A difficult moment involving the loss of Trinity. . . Reilly couldn't even begin to contemplate that sort of tragedy or how she'd be able to live with it.

But, really, why should the hard stuff stop?

Because an Irishwoman's ghost decided to befriend her, because the dream of a child had provided her another ghost friend in her life, because Trinity had become a friend, because for the past few months- ghosts aside- there'd been a glimpse of a semblance of what a normal life could be. . . A job, friends- (Righteous meowed and dove under her good arm) a pet friend. . .

'Dearest,' Bridie called Reilly away from her mental ramblings, 'Like the cards, I'm not a fortune teller. My second sight isn't always on point- I can't call it up if it's not willing. The role I've accepted with you is to help bolster your courage, your own 'sight' and intuition, help you not to retreat into yourself, despite all the,' Bridie's nose sniffed as if smelling a great stink, 'not so great goings on here.

I hope you think of me as your friend, as well as a sort of teacher. Ivy Rose may have tried to warn her brother, but he was not tuned into her. As ghosts, we don't always have the power to interfere in the physical world. It takes a lot of energy to displace a physical object in the 'real' world. Ivy Rose would not have had the power to stop the attack on yer man, Trinity. It seems, though, that he might be more of a listener, now.'

"I can't help but think what. . . He might have. . .d…died, if I'd waited. . ." Reilly's face crumpled. Tears surged from sleep-deprived eyes. How could she produce any more tears? She hugged her knees to her chest.

Righteous pawed at her in kitten concern, eager to assuage Reilly's distress; the girl opened her arms to allow a kitten cuddle and busied her fingers tickling under Righteous' chin- much to the kitten's delight.

'Waste of time to think about spilled milk, Sweetlin'. You listened, and that's all that's important. Never deny those silent messages.' Bridie leaned to kiss the weary girl as her eyelids drooped.

Reilly slept with a light burning, as always. Sleeping in the dark was way too scary. Remnants of the times she'd been left alone at night as a little girl stuck with her like a relentless leech, sucking courage rather than blood. The light kept the what-evers away. God help her if the light burned out before daylight. . .

She had enough freedom with her hands to undress, but elected not to. Sleep beguiled her to drift its way and then suddenly, she would startle awake. She'd barely begun to drift to sleep once more when a ringing at 11 p.m. jerked her fully awake.

Bolting upright, she bumped her sore arm. She gritted her teeth and fumbled with the cell phone. What had Pat told her? Oh, yes, push the green button.

She missed the receiver as she said 'hello'. Being used to the old-fashioned type phones, she was surprised how tiny a cell phone was. Reilly tried again as she heard Trinity calling her name.

"H…hello?"

"There you are," an audible sigh, "Were you sleeping? I didn't want to wake you. . ." Trinity's hoarse voice asked, anxiously.

"N…no, I don't have any experience with cell phones. I guess I was talking into the wrong part? Did you get any sleep after we left?"

"Very little. It seems every time you drop off, you're fair game for somebody bustling in to check something, or ask if you need anything. When I say I need a decent meal and sleep, they just laugh. Sheesh! Why bother asking?

Uh, Reilly, I. . . I'm sorry, I never. . . I mean. . . I can't believe I haven't thanked you. How…how did you know? I didn't get the chance to ask. I…I didn't have any awake senses to feel afraid, or to feel anything- they completely caught me off guard. I must have had a second before blacking out. I'm sorry I scared you. But, you. . . How did you do it?"

Reilly explained about filling the salt and pepper shakers and getting a crick in her neck. At first she thought her adjusted braces were giving her a headache, but then the pain actually had her dropping a salt shaker.

And suddenly, silent alarms were clamoring in her system. . .to hurry to him. The race to the garage, breaking the glass to get in, the smell of the fumes, pulling his body out. . .

"I was so s…scared," her voice cracked in his ear. Picturing his body lying on that cold floor. . . She bit down hard on a finger to keep from crying.

"I'm sorry you had to go through that, I mean, be afraid because of me. But I'm really glad you were there. If not for you. . . I'm glad I'm here," Trinity's voice also broke.

"Don't think about it; it's too horrible to think about, but no matter how scary it all was. . . I'd do it all again," Reilly whispered.

And it was true, she realized, she'd walk through the shadows of hell, if he needed her to.

"My sister is sitting with me," Trinity told her. To help alleviate some of the raw emotion, Ivy Rose had told him to change the subject.

"I'm happy for you, Trinity, so very happy." They talked for nearly an hour before both of them were yawning in each other's ears.

"Will I see you tomorrow, Reilly?" She assured him she'd be there.

"Trinity?"

Here it comes, Trinity thought. He'd been jostling ideas concerning how much he'd tell his doctor brother.

Trinity knew he'd not relate all that he'd discussed with Reilly. Pat's logical mind probably wouldn't appreciatively soak up, or begin to understand the mystery of Trinity's experience, anyway. His dad might. But he sincerely doubted his older brother would. As for his number-minded brother, Sean- no way.

"Can you tell me? I've never talked to a patient who…who's died before. . ." Pat's worried regard settled lovingly on his younger brother- their turbulent past long laid to rest.

He'd not been at Trinity's side when his heart and breathing stopped. The attending physician, out of professional courtesy, had confided to him the medical particulars and regaled him with Reilly's effect on Trinity- about her being directly responsible for bringing him back.

Pat didn't lend much credence to the other doctor's miracle explanation. He was much more realistic- miracles had scientific interpretations. Of course, his wife would strongly disagree.

Trinity knew better than to try to bring up Ivy Rose's ghost- that'd earn him a 'you need a psychiatrist' remark. And Trinity wasn't up to fisticuffs. Not anymore.

"There's nothing to fear, Pat. It's beautiful, welcoming, but only if it's your time to be there." There, thought Trinity, that sounds plausible.

"What do you mean?" his brother asked with unfeigned interest.

Trinity thought a moment. "It's like…like a door to another world. If you're expected, the entry is warm, with lights, and you feel as if you're greatly welcomed. . . But, if it's not time for you to be there, the lights remain distant, the tunnel sucks you back; your feet are too heavy to continue walking forward to the light. I…I don't know how else to say it."

Trinity rested his head against the passenger seat head rest, bore the pain of his receding lump, closed his eyes, wished his brother would not pursue the subject. He wasn't sure about bringing up mom and Ivy Rose waiting in the light. . .maybe another time.

"So, who's this little girl? Haven't I seen her before? Kate and Dad think the world of her."

"Dad's birthday party, remember? She took care of my cut hand. She's my friend, and she's an angel," Trinity murmured, pale eyelids shuttered, long dark lashes outlandish against the pallor.

"Yeah, that's what Dad said."

At a stop sign, Pat regarded his brother's closed eyes, a face no longer death-gray, but still painfully white, and for once, unbelievably, perfectly at ease.

The exasperating demeanor of rigid jaws and guarded eyes that Trinity had carried for too many grievous years seemed to be totally absent.

And that WOULD be a God-sent miracle, Pat mused. He bit his lip to stifle the burgeoning emotion in his chest. His younger brother was going to be all right.

"It smells like heaven in here," Trinity took a deep breath, glad to have that plastic obstacle off his nostrils. "You know, they had me ride in a wheel chair to the car?" He snuck around Reilly to see what she was stirring in an enormous pot. His hand glazed her waist in hello.

Blushing, she glanced up at him, "Chicken noodle soup," and returned to separating the homemade noodles, gently stirring them into the aromatic broth.

"Quit your griping about hospital procedures," Pat Jr. fished a noodle from the soup and side-stepped Reilly's hot, swinging wooden spoon.

"Hey," Trinity hustled Pat from the kitchen. "Go sit down brother, quit bothering my cook. I'm the sick person, remember and this is my soup."

"No, you go sit down, and rest," Dr. Pat stood his ground.

"Trinity, you should rest," the cook, impaled by the 'my' remark, said.

Trinity almost tangled his feet with Wrench and Righteous as they raced around the kitchen table. Pell mell. . . If Wrench fell behind, the kitten about-faced and raced across his back to begin a new game. At this rate, Wrench would be ready for a marathon race, if one could be found for dogs, Trinity mused.

"Got a three ring circus going on in here. Crazy animals. Damn, these are good," Pat fished out another noodle while Reilly rolled out more makings.

"I wouldn't know, I'm just the patient," Trinity griped, good-naturedly.

"Sod off, bro! I gotta get going, Kate will have dinner waiting for me, and she'll want a full report.

Reilly, a great pleasure to see you, and my heartfelt

thanks for rescuing my little brother," Pat Jr. grinned at her. "If I can ever do anything for you, don't hesitate to ask."

Tapping Trinity- who actually was taller and outweighed him- on the head, he embraced his father and left.

"Reilly, are you making cookies?" Trinity asked, hope reigning in his eyes, as Reilly delivered a brimming bowl of soup to him. Golden, thick noodles played peek-a-boo with carrots, onions, celery and chunks of chicken.

"No, you need to stay away from sugar for a few days. Your body needs to suck up all the proper nutrients it can get right now," Reilly reddened, feeling silly.

"Funny, I can remember Bridie saying that very same thing to me when I had the flu." Trinity would have other questions once he and Reilly were alone.

He nearly dropped his soup when Ivy Rose appeared at his side. It was very hard not to give himself away and effusively greet his little sister aloud. Reilly smiled in empathy, as Ivy Rose ecstatically waved.

"I guess this means I won't get dessert at the diner, tomorrow, either?" Fascinated, he tried to be surreptitious about watching Ivy Rose stick her finger in his bowl.

"If you promise to stay away from sweets this week, I'll make whatever dessert you want next Sunday," Reilly bargained.

Trinity hesitated, what with a ghost playing in his soup. . .

Misconstruing his hesitation, she asked, "Do I have to invoke the honor system?"

Reilly quailed as the words left her mouth. She sounded awfully bossy to her own ears, but Trinity simply winked at her.

"Son, you're taking the next couple days off to rest," Pat put his foot down.

"Dad, if I stay home for days, I'll end up in a psych ward," Trinity and inactivity did not dance harmoniously.

'I'll stay with you, Trinity,' Ivy Rose giggled into his ear. He almost responded, but quickly caught himself, hid his eyes by watching his fork impale an especially wide noodle.

"Well, at least one day of rest, then you'll stay in the office with the ventilator on full blast, and you will get the book work caught up," his dad relented.

Trinity thought he better quit while he was ahead. After all, he and Ivy Rose had a lot of catching up to do.

"Book work, sheesh," he mumbled under his breath.

Reilly grinned at the family exchange, her face fully on her soup.

It was difficult to bear his pleading, but she stopped Trinity at two heaping bowls, "just to see if your stomach is OK."

34

"Shouldn't you be in school?" With crooked brow, Trinity eyed Reilly Wednesday morning at the diner as she approached to take their order.

Unfortunately, with his feeling completely back to normal, he'd gulped a huge amount of orange juice after asking the question. So when Reilly answered she'd been suspended, shock, disbelief and laughter vied for an outlet and Trinity spewed orange juice from nostrils and mouth- straight across the table, to splatter on his dad's clean uniform shirt.

With an aversion to said uniform shirts, Trinity's own black t-shirt suffered a minor fallback. He'd be sticky until he rinsed his shirt off at the garage.

"Come again?" Scandalizing several napkins, he swabbed his face and shirt and scrutinized Reilly as if she'd just landed from an alien environment while his father considered the state of his apparel with quiet misgivings, speculating on whether a replacement hung in the garage office.

Saturday's edition of the Ryan Tattler, the local paper, founded 1800-something, claiming Reilly as a local heroine, had impressed and thrilled all the mature inhabitants of the town.

They made it a point to stop and congratulate and thank Reilly for her saving Trinity's life. As THE Mr. Fix It, Trinity's expertise was important to all of the townspeople- not to mention the O'Ryans in general were well thought of.

The same could not be said for many of the kids at the high school.

Reilly ducked catcalls of 'here comes the hero' all day Monday and Tuesday. The most immature cretins decided it might be fun to pelt Reilly with raisins and assorted other unwanted lunch items in the cafeteria.

Reilly had struck up a conversation with another recent addition to the town's census- a girl with Tourette's Syndrome. Her stuttering and odd quirks had made her a fair target, too.

The first plump bomb tangled in Reilly's hair. The next one tipped her shoulder and landed on the table in front of her. And the hits kept on coming, accompanied by fits of laughter.

The boys may have been mentally deficient, but they didn't lack in the pitching department. The new girl across from Reilly just ducked her head in submission- she was used to being picked on.

Other students snickered, enjoying the 'stoning'. A few came to Reilly's defense, but were booed down. Reilly's new friend got up and left, resignedly throwing away most of her lunch upon exiting the cafeteria.

Reilly figured if she'd been a popular, beautiful student- outsider or not- it would have been a different story. The transgressors would have been booed down. But Reilly was Reilly- an outsider, ordinary, passive. . .a distinct target.

She tried to ignore them. Without a response, they'd surely quit. A rubber band smarted her bandaged arm as it rested on the table, and suddenly Reilly saw black- a totally new experience.

Like a slow motion movie, she watched herself grab a leftover carton of chocolate milk, swivel from the waist, and throw with all of her sub-consciously induced might.

The cretin pitchers ducked and the chocolate milk rocketed to the pink-clad back of an oblivious girl sitting behind the laughing boys.

Bridie had had just about all she could take. Many different accounts of students watching from different angles circulated for days on what exactly happened next. None of them fully agreed with each other.

The chocolate milk carton stopped just shy of Miss Pink Shirt and upended on the heads of the three male pitchers, who no matter how they tried to move away, suffered the full effects of the chocolate substance as it dripped onto their puzzled faces.

The principal strolled by on the tail end of this scenario, and the three bullies and Reilly were directed to his office to explain.

As evidence of the guys wrong-doing, the principal spied two raisins in Reilly's hair. Her suspension of two days was mild compared to the week's suspension for the instigators.

Trinity gave Reilly a thumbs-up, "Cool!" as Reilly sauntered off to circulate the coffee pot.

"Trinity!" Erika gushed upon entering the diner. She swept to Trinity's side of the table, practically pushed him over with her tight, jean-draped hips.

"Erika," the light of enthusiasm died in Trinity's eyes.

Question followed question as Trinity's female friend petted his arm and altogether annoyed him.

"You should have called me. I could have brought you flowers or something from take-out," she designed a petulant, heavily made-up face for his daring to overlook her. Never mind he almost died- he should have called her.

His lips twitched sarcastically around a suitable rejoinder, and he rolled his eyes at his dad, who gave him one of those 'you're on your own, here' looks, while continuing to eat.

Indignant at Trinity's close-mouthed mien when she had fully turned on her charms for his benefit, Erika, overtly pouting, excused herself to the restroom.

Reilly, arms laden with breakfast specials, glanced up as Bridie manifested, waltzing through the window to a country ballad, and spotted Erika's hip-swaying pageant queen stroll to the restroom.

Erika, too intent on catching Trinity's eye, missed Reilly's advance. Reilly, intent on Bridie, missed seeing Erika. A major collision ensued.

In trying to maintain her feet and rescue all of the plates and protect her sore arm, something had to give. Several plates of steaming biscuits and gravy tumbled, and Erika's pristine jeans were doused with goo.

"Look what you've done, you clumsy twit!" Erika hissed.

Wrong move.

The customers turned at the sound of the plates hitting the floor. Dave swung around from the grill. Martie rushed to the rescue with broom, dust pan and rags.

Everyone was treated to Erika's pretty butt sliding about on the gravy-slick floor as Bridie, rankled to the nth-degree, smirked, 'Excuse me,' and gave her a grand shove.

'There are a few so-called young ladies who are way overdue for comeuppance,' the ghost crowed, stomping atop the subjugated prima donna's head- destroying an expensive coiffure.

Reilly, initially stricken by the incident, and being called a not-so nice name, stifled a giggle. She was alone in that department for every customer broke into hearty guffaws and resounding applause. This included those whose breakfast now plastered Erika's hind end.

"I've been on tenterhooks all day. Tell me about your suspension," Trinity's arm lay across the passenger seat, gazing at Reilly sitting next to his sister in the back seat.

While his dad drove, Trinity grilled Reilly on the specifics.

"Son, I'm not sure you should be encouraging this kind of behavior. . ."

"Dad, think for a moment. What would you have done if you'd been in Reilly's place?"

"Hmm. . ." Pat held counsel upon reflection.

Reilly couldn't bring Bridie into her story. Not with Pat listening. Maybe later she'd tell Trinity how Bridie had 'guided' the chocolate milk carton missile.

With Ivy Rose bouncing ping-pong beside her and Bridie's abrupt appearance lying on the back dashboard, Reilly was surprised to see Trinity's eyes widen when his head swung all the way back.

His jaw fell open as Bridie and Ivy Rose waved boisterously at him.

Reilly grinned and shrugged her shoulders- surprise, surprise! The ghosts had joined them. And Trinity could see both of them! What else could she do except wait for her and Trinity to be alone- ghosts in tow- to talk, sans Pat?

35

"Is Reilly in?" Trinity gave short shrift to the pretty woman who opened Chet's door.

"Why, you're Trinity O'Ryan! Come in."

Trinity hesitated. Entering the premises was not high on his list, but he complied and stood, thumbs hitched in his pockets, not touching anything.

Reilly's mother made it obvious she found him attractive. Trinity was used to older women flirting with him. At one time, it might have given him food for thought, but that was years ago. Before Ivy Rose went to ghost-hood.

Chet strode in from the hallway and faltered, disconcerted, discovering Trinity in his house. He nodded respectfully, skirted the head-of-the-food-chain's personal space, gave the mother a wondering appraisal, and exited without a goodbye. Trinity's reputation for crazy fighting carried a lot of weight, even if one couldn't exactly pin down the last time a fight occurred.

Reilly's mother leaned back against a counter, the better to show off her perfect accoutrements. She seemed to have forgotten something. . .the reason he was there?

"Uh, Reilly?" Trinity thought he'd nip whatever in the bud.

The mother knew when to back away from disinterest, but she'd certainly ruminate on how long her daughter might hold this hunk's attention. Just that whole life-saving business, surely. What an eyeful, she assessed the young man with hungry eyes.

Instead of going to Reilly's room, she hollered the girl's name.

Trinity remained standing, even as the mother offered a seat. Tried to stay impervious to the squalor of the old trailer- knowing old had nothing to do with clean.

"Hey, Reilly, you busy?" He greeted her, took in her old, baggy clothes- the mother was dressed to the nines. What a mess; his gut churned at the ramifications inherent in the whole sordid scenario.

The wealth of surprise Reilly exhibited at finding Trinity calling for her at the dump put a boyish, dimpled grin on his face.

"Got your homework done?" he asked.

Reilly hiccoughed a deep breath, wanted to pinch herself, responded, "Except for a few math problems."

"Good, bring 'em with you.   The local creamy whip opened today.   You like ice cream?"

Reilly was quiet on the 5-minute ride to Ryan's tiny soft-serve institution.   She couldn't believe Trinity was taking her for an ice cream.   She couldn't believe he'd come to the dump and asked for her.   She shyly reveled in the companionable silence- afraid sound might break the bubble she thrilled to be in.

The first day open- no matter the weather- had people standing patiently in line at CURLIES, talking, checking out the menu- which never changed, anticipating the taste of the season's first creamy whip, and overall, simply enjoying themselves.

Nearly two months had elapsed since Trinity's near demise, and another topic had climbed to the top talk of the town- another battle to keep nationwide chains from the town of Ryan.

The huge chain store didn't stand a snowball's chance. Ryan's charter had enough insight when it was drawn up in the mid-1800's to recognize how big business could destroy the charm, health and well-being of a small town and its family-owned operations.

THE O'Ryan had plenty of canny political acumen, and even more money to back him- the town and its surrounding farms would remain sacrosanct.   He'd made provisions for the entire county, which happened to be named after him.   After all, he'd owned the entire section.

The patrons of CURLIES exchanged hello's and cursed the nerve of such and such for wanting to take out a block's worth of original, beautiful, brick buildings and put in a parking lot and some no-good @#@#. . .   On and on, the folk of Ryan defended their local business owners, wide green belt, farming community, and the camaraderie and sense of fellowship that went with it.

"Why do they call it CURLIES?   Is that the owner's name?" Reilly asked, in joyful anticipation.   She loved soft-serve, and remembered as a small child the times her grandparents took her to the local creamy whip. She even remembered the woman, Mary, with her long, red nails, as she handed the dish of ice cream down to the goggling, eager, young Reilly.

"See that tip on his cone? CURLIES prides itself on topping each ice cream with a curlicue. Cool, huh? And if your ice cream is missing its curl, yours is free."

Reilly admired the talent that went into the artistic presentation on all of CURLIES' items and the pride that guaranteed each one would have a curlicue.

Bridie held Ivy Rose's hand in line behind Trinity and Reilly. Ivy Rose jumped up and down, impatient. Just because she could no longer taste the treats, didn't mean she could hardly wait for her brother to acquire his ice cream.

Trinity always ordered the same thing- a strawberry and caramel sundae and he used to share his with her. And she reciprocated by allowing him to bite a chunk off of her drumstick.

Reilly couldn't stop herself staring at the ghostly train with so much transparent exuberance on ghostly faces-waiting in line, of all things!

In mid-sentence, Trinity stopped talking and checked to see why he couldn't hold Reilly's attention. He staggered and gaped, dumbfounded, at finding Ivy Rose and Bridie in the ice cream line. His surprise had him jostling the man in front of him which set up a chain reaction of sorts.

Good-naturedly though, unlike impatient lines in big cities, no frowns, curses, or fists flew.

Reilly wondered at the extent of Trinity's reaction, "Haven't you seen her lately?"

Trinity's brows furrowed. "Ivy Rose. . . It's like. . . Sometimes I think I see her. . . Sometimes I hear her, but most of the time it's so faint, or she's popped in unexpectedly and I'm floored. By the time I recover, it seems like she's fading away. But, Bridie's here, too, in line for heaven's sake! That is. . .this is. . . Wow!"

"The way your sister described it to me, she's still learning. I think with you now ready to see her, she'll improve quickly. Just keep talking to her," Reilly listened to Bridie's advice in one ear, and relayed it to Trinity.

At their first opportunity to talk alone, after Trinity's bout with death, she'd told him how Bridie had found her. Trinity had been amazed to think Reilly had an on-going relationship with his old friend. When he saw her in his dad's car. . . Suffice it to say, the shock had reverberated throughout his entire body. Ivy Rose and Bridie, together- WOW!

This was only the second time he'd seen Bridie. The whole ghost thing was still pretty hard for him to get a handle on. Hard to imagine. He had to watch himself when Ivy Rose appeared at home. Luckily, she usually came when he was by himself. He wondered how Reilly managed it all so calmly. Of course, she did have a head start on him. . .

As for Bridie. . . He remarked on how she looked incredibly younger than the last time he'd seen her- alive. Reilly had been right about that.

Was that how ghosts worked? Could they appear in whatever age they wished?

Bridie had yet to give her a straight answer, and Reilly felt like it really wasn't any of her business. What did it matter, after all?

Trinity half-hoped Ivy Rose would take a bite out of his ice cream, similar to how she'd played in his soup. She didn't disappoint him when she swept the curl off the top, waved, giggled and diaphanously skipped off with Bridie's hand swinging in hers.

"I'm not sure I'm comfortable with you up on that ladder," Trinity eyed the baggy jeans above him. For a second, he allowed himself to imagine what Reilly would look like in some nice clothes.

"I'm OK. It's best to confront your fears," she sent down to him. Be an oak, she challenged herself to buck up her courage. Heights were another no-no in the fear department. She tried her best to focus on Bridie, lucidly perched in a branch above her, pointing out which suckers to snip from her apple trees. Never mind that Reilly was some eight feet from the ground. Oak. . .

"Look, why don't you let me do it? Better than you being afraid and maybe falling," he cautioned. But Reilly shook off his concern with grim determination- carefully shook. Didn't want to rock the ladder.

"Uh, well, if you're positive, I'll start over here, then." Trinity grasped his pruners and walked off, glancing back, solicitously, now and again.

Having learned firsthand, via Bridie in earlier days, he'd given Reilly instructions on which limbs to tend. Either she was a natural or. . . He didn't see Bridie. . .

"How come I can see you right now, but he can't?" Reilly asked her tree-sitting ghostly friend.

'His thinking is on somethin' else,' Bridie mysteriously replied. 'Ivy Rose tells me he's picked up his guitar again.'

Was that an adroit change of subject, Reilly pondered? Something else?

She watched Ivy Rose skip circles around her brother. Of course, his sister. All of his attention would be for Ivy Rose.

The two living humans sat on the grass munching the sandwiches Trinity had supplied. Wrench and Righteous cadged bits and pieces- Wrench with the most pleading, pitiful dog eyes and hushed 'whoofs', and Righteous with quick, batting, thieving paws.

"Do you know how Bridie acquired this property?"

Trinity took his time swallowing. He canvassed the territory, gauging his little sister's proximity. She'd faded into. . .wherever ghosts hung out when not visible to. . .

"Well," he dithered. How should he put this? Reilly wasn't stupid. Once more he scanned the environs. No ghosts. . . Here goes, he thought.

"It's pretty well known in my family that my great, great grandfather and Bridie were. . . That is, uh. . . She was his. . .mistress," Trinity sped through the family rumor, dismayed as Reilly's eyes flashed, shocked.

'The divil, you say!' Bridie erupted. 'Excuse me, Dearest, I'm not sure if it's correct to say divil when yer a guest in heaven. The bloomin' eejits!'

Reilly flagged her hands at Bridie. Too late. A shower of compost landed on the unsuspecting Trinity's head. The aware dog and kitten had adroitly backed away in time to avoid the 'comeuppance'. They patiently awaited the denouement before safely returning for more snacks.

'The impertinence of men! Ah!' Bridie wailed, 'drives me to distraction.'

"What the. . .?" Trinity dusted the dry aromatic out from his thick, black hair.

"You shouldn't go telling tales," Reilly chided him.

"What? I'm just repeating what th. . ."

Reilly shook her head violently and pointed her finger as Bridie grabbed another handful.

"I'll tell you the truth," Reilly offered. This seemed to stave off Bridie's ire and aim.

"The truth? How would you know the truth. . .? Oh," Trinity eyed his despoiled sandwich, rolled a shoulder, blew off the fallout and half-heartedly took a bite.

"Trinity, I can see and talk to Bridie all the time."

That stopped the chewing, almost started the choking.

"Serious?" Trinity's voice adopted the tone of one who has entered a church. His sister's appearances were just now gaining in numbers- how long had Reilly and Bridie been. . .?

"Yes, she doesn't have the fading problems Ivy Rose has, but your sister will get the hang of it, I'm sure."

Trinity set his sandwich down, glanced around, thought he saw something. . .

"Can you see her, now?" he gulped.

"Oh, yes. She's right behind you, by the compost pile."

Rising, Trinity decided to sit closer to Reilly.

"Jaysus, Mary and Joseph, I've offended her, haven't I?" Like a scout on a foraging mission, Trinity's head swiveled to and fro.

'He's not runnin'- that's a good sign, but tell him the truth, Sweetlin'. Spoilin' me good name like that,' Bridie harrumphed.

Reilly recounted, for Trinity's edification, about the stud and its racing career.

"I remember that horse had quite a reputation. There are pictures of it, and Bridie, too, in the community center and at my house, in some old scrap books."

"Then you can understand why she might be peeved if your family spreads gossip like that," Reilly informed him.

Trinity ducked again, just in case.

"I'll have to devise a way to get the family to know the real truth. Shoot, it's a lot more fascinating to think Bridie saved the O'Ryan's prize stud horse. Do you think. . .?"

"I think," Reilly looked to Bridie, who nodded. "I think Bridie and the O'Ryan were great friends. Probably unheard of in that day for an older man and a young woman to just be friends, and that's a darn shame."

Too late, Reilly thought the same might be said of her and Trinity.

"Yeah," Trinity affirmed, speculatively. He was thinking about the difference in his and Reilly's ages. Hell, seven years wasn't insurmountable.

"You see her all the time?"

"Whenever I'm. . .," Reilly hated to admit her continuing fears, but this was Trinity. "Whenever I'm afraid, she's close. Whenever I call, and sometimes when I least expect her, she pops in.

She's the real reason the principal wants me to pitch on the girls' softball team and…and that thing with Erika in the diner. . ."

"Bridie?" Trinity fell over, laughing so hard he had to hold his stomach. "Bridie," he called, "I'm sorry, please accept my apologies."

He rose, bowed gallantly, and peered about, hopefully.

"Do you think I'll get to the point where I can see her all the time, too? And talk to her?"

A breeze from nowhere brushed by.

'Apologies accepted. And an open heart may see all,' Bridie's voice preceded her transparent form's entrance right in front of the astounded Trinity.

36

Reilly stared at the card lying in her hand. Bridie's gift of cards was more like a host of riddles, brain teasers.

'Sweetlin', before we address yer current puzzle, I know you've a question about yer man, Trinity, not seein' me the other day. Tis up to us ghosts if we want a body to see us. He'll be seein' me in company with you, lass, at times. As for Ivy Rose, she tried so hard for her brother to see her when he was hurtin', it like to broke her spirit, so to speak. Now, that he's ready, she'll be in better, uh, er. . .form.'

Bridie's explanation made sort of a surreal sense, and Reilly was grateful her friend tendered it without being asked. She nodded her comprehension and went back to staring at the latest card.

Nine small gold cups streaming water and clover. Reilly assumed the symbolism must have been well known a long time ago. It was lost on her- nothing but a mystery.

Apparently, tarot cards and their symbols used to be fairly commonplace in certain circles in older times, and the suits, numbers and picture cards developed over centuries into the deck of cards everyone recognized and played with now.

With no experience of card games, new or old, the ancient meanings were mostly indecipherable to Reilly. A means to discover yourself and grow, Bridie had revealed in the beginning. Hmm. . .

"Let's see," Reilly thought out loud. "I know the number nine is very significant."

'You're makin' things too difficult, Dearest. Skip everything you don't know. Tell me what you see.'

"Nine little cups of gold- a fortune?" Reilly volunteered, hopefully.

'Good. Go on.'

Reilly frowned in fervid concentration. "The shape. . . How the nine cups are aligned. . . Kind of like the shape of a home. . ."

'Interesting,' Bridie mused. 'What do these mean to you?'

The girl hesitated, not comfortable answering questions- even with Bridie as the teacher.

'Remember, there are no right or wrong answers,' Bridie urged.

"I've felt more at home in this town, even if I have to live here," her nose wrinkled, indicating her feelings for Chet's filthy trailer.

"And...and I'm making good money," she whispered. God help her if her mother knew.

'Did you see what you did there?'

Confused, Reilly bit her lip and looked to Bridie for an explanation.

'With each admission of a good happening in your life, you equivocate by bringing up a negative.' Bridie allowed Reilly a minute.

As the girl's eyes began to water, Bride felt like crying, too.

Get a grip, ye old ghost, the ghost chided herself.

"It's just that I. . . I don't know how long I'll be able to stay here. . . This is the longest time we've spent in one place. I don't want to leave. . ." Tears spattered Reilly's face.

She eyed her nails which had been growing lately as they'd not been food for anxious thought.

'This card is very important for you to digest, Sweetlin'. It represents the happiness you're experiencin'- a time period of stability. But, most important for you to glean from this lesson, is not only for you to be grateful. . .'

A light went on in Reilly's brain. "I need to stop expecting the next guillotine to fall. Live in the moment," she exhaled a sigh.

Bridie's eyes twinkled, 'Good girl! The more time you spend expectin' the negative to come 'round the corner, the less. . .'

"Time I have to be positive," Reilly completed.

'And a positive outlook carries one over the difficulties much easier,' Bridie kicked up her heels.

"Reilly, we've got trouble," Martie bustled around the diner Saturday morning, setting out creamers, starting coffee, filling coffee filters.

"Where's Dave?"

"He's got the flu- bad. He managed to make the gravy for the biscuits and gravy, but he burnt the first batch of muffins. I rescued the second batch, but he forgot the blueberries. There's no way he can run the grill, and in between hacking and. . ." Martie made a face.

"I'm OK with trying to run the grill. We can put the blueberry-less muffins on the board and when we run out. . ." Reilly's mind raced- opening time was bearing down on them.

"I know- we'll put the spare blueberries in pancakes as a special. When they're gone, I'll make apple fritters with the canned apples."

"I sure hope we don't get slammed today. Maybe the nice weather will have folks doing other things." One could always hope.

"Hi, Butch."

A graying man sporting reading glasses and golf attire peered over his glasses at Reilly manning the grill.

"I need an egg sandwich in a hurry," he decreed, and opening the cash register, took out thirty-five cents for the Saturday edition of the Ryan Tattler- his Saturday morning habitual activity.

Upon reentering with his paper in hand, Reilly presented him with a cup of coffee and two slices of bread with a whole egg, shell included, rolling in between.

The normally reserved Butch, who rarely spoke, and ate while perusing the paper from front to back, or conversed with his friend, Hal, if Hal was about, examined his order for two whole seconds before breaking his no-smile rule.

"Tsk, tsk, Reilly," he grinned.

With a quick return to the grill, Reilly turned a frying egg, put it on toast and slid the plate into Butch's hand.

Reilly had fastidiously learned the morning crowd, their regular orders and idiosyncrasies.

The executive table hosted a bakery driver, Karl, who usually presented the diner with a coffee cake or batch of donuts. Uncle Bob gathered bets to take to the race track. Carol traded books with anyone who was interested. Earl, a local contractor, religiously smashed his breakfast goetta and then drowned it in coffee.

Doom and gloom Fred, who never received his knives back or much in the way of insurance money, sank into an executive seat, prepared to massacre his scrambled eggs with lots of catsup. Big Bob came for breakfast and stayed for lunch. The grocery truck drivers were always congenial guys. Zeke, a famous guitarist, and many other locals whom Reilly knew the likes and dislikes of, as well as the regular travelers passing through, were in attendance on this particular Saturday.

As Murphy's Law would have it, the diner got slammed-hard.

"Hey, I need some coffee," crusty Stalbridge grumbled.

Martie rushed by delivering orders. She called over her shoulder, "Can't you see I'm busy, John? Get up and get it yourself, and while you're at it, take the coffee pot around and start another pot."

"Where's Dave?" Stalbridge rose and agreeably did as he was told, sidestepping new arrivals as they calmly, yet avidly, occupied vacated tables.

"Sick. Flu," Martie brusquely confided, bussing one of the dirty booths that a family had slid into and patiently waited for her to clean.

"Should have said so to begin with," Stalbridge grunted.

Reilly couldn't believe her eyes. Grumble-goose Stalbridge was pouring coffee, and another regular was taking dirty dishes to the kitchen sink.

"Reilly, I'd like to try those apple fritters, if you get a chance," he leaned over the counter and nicely asked Reilly.

Guest checks lining the clipboard over the grill might have been intimidating to a relatively new grill cook, but Reilly fell into an unrushed rhythm- flipping hot cakes, scrambling eggs, blotting grease from bacon strips, filling the toaster. . .

"Honey, I've got a go order for," Martie tentatively bit her red-lipstick-tinted lower lip, "Twenty orders of pork chops and eggs."

"OK, Martie," Reilly took a deep breath, eyed the orders yet to be filled. "Maybe 45 minutes?"

Martie spoke into the phone, glancing around. The diner was packed, with more people clanging through the door, forming a line- a regular madhouse.

"We're going to run out of dishes," Martie remarked.

Dave had tried to stay behind the scenes and tend to the dishes, but he couldn't refrain from coughing and other necessities, so Martie uncompromisingly suggested he head upstairs to bed.

"Either we'll get through it or we'll get through it," Reilly murmured, turning a huge western omelet with two spatulas.

At 11 a.m., the gravy was gone; apple fritters took the place of the blueberry-less muffins and the last of the blueberry pancakes.

There were only two plates left on the shelf over the grill, and ten cups remained in the stackable tray. With the radio out of commission, ROCKY TOP kicked up on the juke box- its quick rhythm simulating the furor in the diner, and Bridie can-canned about, kicking up her heels above oblivious guests' heads seated along the countertop in the noisy melee.

Reilly shook her head. If anyone had taken the time to ask her, she would have admitted she was actually having fun.

She stacked the to-go orders under the heat lamp. At the end of Bridie's frenzy to the popular, old country tune, the ghost blew Reilly a kiss and disappeared.

"Martie, I've got to get some plates," the crook of Reilly's elbow wiped at her steamed face. Working the grill, especially at this pace, was a hot job.

"Honey, you stay put. Jasper," Martie tapped a hungry farmer, waiting at the door, on his shoulder. "If you want to eat, I need some clean plates, cups and silver ware!"

Jasper grinned sheepishly, and exchanged greetings with friends on his way to the kitchen, and the piles of dishes.

"Save me some apple fritters," he called, rolling up his sleeves.

At 1:00, Martie thought she'd collapse. Reilly was starving, not having had an opportunity to eat breakfast. She felt like her face bore an inch of grease and her uniform shirt was long past the laundry requisition stage.

The last eggs she'd tried to fry over easy she'd busted the yolks with her shaky hands, but the heaven-sent Jasper never said a word- too busy enjoying his apple fritters on the side, after bringing out stacks of clean plates, cups, glasses and utensils.

"Sheesh! Looks like a tornado hit this place," Trinity and Pat walked in.

"Yeah, and stayed for breakfast," Martie perched on a stool and surveyed the room.

Every table but the two which were still occupied, was stacked with evidence, not to mention the counter.

"The Energizer Bunny," Martie hitched a thumb at Reilly, "did great on her trial by fire. First Saturday at the grill- and as you can see, it was a Doozy."

Pat and Trinity exchanged glances, ruefully surveyed the mess. Trinity winked at the grill-scorched Reilly.

Pat unbuttoned, rolled up his sleeves, "I'll get the dishes, Trinity. You clean up out here. You girls take a break. Get something to eat, if you can."

The best thing about a small town diner- if you needed help, it was always easy to find- walked right through the door, as a matter of fact.

37

"Haven't seen Erika or Sharrod or Peggy or any of your other groupies around, lately." Trinity's dad had inclined himself to his single, indoor, culinary specialty- chili spaghetti.

Saturday night and they were just finishing up. Trinity had made no move to jump in the shower. His cell phone remained silent- no constant, intrusive female calls.

Pat studied his youngest son across the table from him. There was a decided difference, serenity evident in his eyes and in the way he held his broad shoulders. More relaxed, as if the dragons were finally slain.

Thinking back, Pat realized Trinity had not been this at-ease since. . .well, before. . .before Ivy Rose got sick, nearly seven years ago.

Trinity had jailed himself in suffering after Ivy Rose passed on. A long, brutal sentence- totally undeserved. Why his son felt such responsibility- no one could explain it- only that Trinity was Ivy Rose's hero, big brother, best friend. . .

"I haven't seen them either, Dad," Trinity finished a last bite and grinned at his dad. "Good chili!"

"Son," Pat interrupted his son's rise from the table. "I never asked you about. . .your experience. Your brother said you didn't feel like talking about it. . ." Pat's voice trailed off, leaving the door open if Trinity cared to step through. The young man regained his seat.

"Pat, the doctor, wouldn't have understood. He's too logical- A=B, without any question of outside possibilities."

His dad agreed, folded his hands on the table, leaned into the chair back and waited.

Son felt out father. A smile curled. A dimple strutted.

After all the hours he'd spent talking with Reilly about it, and with Ivy Rose's impromptu 'visits' and constant prodding him with misplaced guitar picks strewn in unlikely places to induce him to play guitar again, Trinity felt pretty comfortable with what he was about to say.

The heavy restraints barring the freedom of his heartbeat were gone. The release came as a surprise when he allowed himself a minute to feel and appreciate it.

That and the surprise of Ivy Rose's faint outline sitting on his bed as he strummed his out-of-practice fingers on the guitar strings. This new peace- one he gave up believing he'd ever feel again.

"Dad, I…I saw Mom. . .and. . .Ivy Rose."

This admission had Pat's fingers constricting against each other. His eyes began to glitter with emotion. Not trusting his voice, he nodded for Trinity to continue.

"They were standing in a beautiful, rainbow light. . . Waiting for me. Both of them perfect. Perfectly healthy, glowing. You…you can't imagine. . . I can't express the overwhelming love I felt." Trinity's eyes skittered to the side. His eyes watered.

"I didn't want to come back, Dad. I only wanted to walk toward them. Pick up Ivy Rose, swing her around like I used to," Trinity bit the inside of his mouth, trying to stifle tears.

"I didn't want to come back," he repeated in a whisper.

Pat allowed his son and himself a minute, cleared his throat and fearful of the answer, croaked, "Why did. . .you, uh. . .return to. . .us?"

The idea of losing Trinity. . . How much loss could a man live through? The loss of his young wife, his only daughter. . .

Pat knew the time would come when Trinity would marry and move out, or maybe move out first, marry later. The thought of that. . . He forced himself to get a grip.

"It was Reilly, wasn't it? Why, Trinity?" Pat recalled his helplessness at Trinity's side in the hospital. His own voice had been useless. Only Reilly's voice kept his son tied by a thread to life. Why? He hadn't known the girl that long. Why?

"Reilly's voice. . .calling me. . .stopped my progress, weighted my feet. . . Picture being called in two different directions at once. I guess. . . I don't know why, but Mom and Ivy Rose seemed to be waving me off- like, 'go back, see you later'.

And hearing Reilly. . . I…I knew she needed me to be here. Sound crazy?"

"No, Son, not at all. I'm glad you felt like you could tell me." Pat was overwrought with gratitude that his youngest son would confide something so utterly personal.

They sat in reflective silence for a bit.

"I hear you playing your guitar some."

"I…I believe Ivy Rose wants me to." Actually, he knew firsthand what his little sister wanted.

Pat wiped an eye, sniffed, "I believe you're right. Maybe you'll come to the family reunion this year?"

Trinity barked a laugh- he'd avoided the party since trying to kill his brother, Pat.

. "We'll see, Dad. You never know."

"So, what's with the girl friends? You decide to become a priest? I mean if that's what you want. . . But the garage. . ."

"Funny, Dad. No, Ryan is my home. I love my job. I love this town. You in a hurry to get rid of me?"

"You know I'm not. I love being around you, Son. It's just that you're a young man, and all of a sudden there is a dearth of girls hanging around. You OK?"

Trinity chuckled, "Everything is in working order, Dad."

"Hmmm. . . You've been spending a lot of time with Reilly. I know you share a special. . .bond. . ."

"You are absolutely right about that," Trinity agreed.

"Son, I'm going to be fatherly for a few minutes, here. Reilly's only what? 15 or 16? You are 23." He'd put off this particular discussion. Found it difficult to address, but. . .

Trinity shrugged, brushed his thick, black hair back, scratched the back of his neck- where a nasty bump once existed.

"I guess I might as well tell you, Dad. I'm going to marry Reilly. Now, before you say anything, I don't care how old she is now, I'll wait." Trinity relaxed into his chair with stolid resolution.

Pat mulled over Trinity's words. Yeah, he could understand what his son was saying, but he didn't feel it was exactly. . .

"Son, there is a difference between feeling gratitude for someone saving your life and being in love with a woman and wanting to love that woman for the rest of your life.

You have to realize Reilly's been uprooted all of her life. A scared little girl. Not that you're chopped liver, but Reilly. . . She'll naturally cling to the first solid thing that enters her life. . .

Reilly is a great girl, please don't misunderstand me, but she needs years to grow. . .to know herself and the possibilities of her own future. I appreciate her tremendously, but she's only a girl. You're a man."

Trinity accepted his dad's advice without rancor. Several nights after he'd returned to his own bed, he'd had a similar conversation with himself.

"I agree with what you're saying, Dad. I am grateful to Reilly, but there is a hell of a lot more feeling I have for her than strictly gratitude. And I think her experiences have made her grow up all too soon in many ways. As for those other girls. . .nothing; I can't even remember having a real moment of fun with any one of them. A passing of time. . . Sex, you know. . ."

He didn't feel he could tell his dad that he could see the ghost of his little sister and that Reilly regularly saw Bridie O'Connair's ghost, but he needed to give his dad something.

"There is a definite connection between us. Do you remember how Mom always made home feel like. . .home? Even though Reilly hasn't had a stable home her whole life- shunted here and there at her mother's whim- when I look in Reilly's eyes, I'm home."

Trinity let the tears roll- the hell with it.

"I've been out with enough girls to know I've never seen, never felt that before," Trinity finished. "Never felt it at all."

"Wow," immense pride in his son basted Pat better than a Thanksgiving turkey.

Reilly, the angel, had brought about these changes in his long-suffering son. Trinity didn't talk about desire, but about home. Wasn't love all about home, after all? His heart ached thinking of his wife; she had indeed made home- home.

"Are you thinking about how Reilly may see you? Puppy love and all that?" Pat hit another nail on the head.

"I'm aware of that, Dad. But, I'm betting Reilly is the smartest cookie in the entire batch. She'll know the difference. I'd bet everything I have on it," Trinity vowed.

"You're quite a bit older than she is. You'll have to give her time, uh. . . You know what I'm talking about?"

Trinity chuckled, relieved, "Yeah, Dad. I can keep my pants zipped." Maybe take up running. Cold showers. . .

"Does Reilly know all of this?"

"I don't believe so. I'm not courting her, yet.

"We'll be friends for now. Mind if I bring her over and watch that old gunslinger movie- the one my namesake is in?"

"I was kind of surprised you didn't invite her and Righteous for chili spaghetti," Pat said. "That cat has the weirdest taste buds for a cat."

Wrench whined at the sound of Righteous' name.

"You really think you can wait for her?" Pat remembered his own early twenties.

"Thinking has nothing to do with it, Dad. She's the one, and I'll wait. Period."

"Hmmm. . . I think I should give you something," Pat rose.

Trinity cocked a brow. Pat retreated to his bedroom, returned with a gift-wrapped box.

"It's not my birthday, Dad," Trinity joked.

"No, I had instructions to give this to you the first time you mentioned marriage- THE girl."

Befuddled, Trinity accepted the light box, sat on the couch, opened the envelope stuck under the lid's ribbon.

He recognized Ivy Rose's diligently perfected handwriting and nearly dropped the box. For a moment, he froze.

Wrench thumped his tail and star-gazed, happily. Trinity followed the dog's eyes. Ivy Rose was excitedly clapping her hands, all smiles at the box in his hands. She patted Wrench's head and the dog lapped thin air. She was as brilliantly obvious to him as Bridie had been when she'd shown herself to him in her garden.

"Trinity?" Pat felt like a peeping Tom.

Trinity glanced to his father and gave him a silly grin. He extracted a slip of paper from the envelope.

Dear Trinity, The girl you're going to marry will love this. If she doesn't, you've made a mistake. Love, Ivy Rose

Trinity's hand brushed at his eyes.

"Dad, how?"

"Before she got really sick, Ivy Rose and I were shopping. She, uh, picked this out and told me we had to have it gift wrapped, and that I was to keep it hidden until the day you mentioned the girl you were going to marry. I have no idea why. A touch of the Irish fey?"

Trinity lifted the box lid and inside, lying on spring-green tissue paper that mimicked the spring grass you'd find its real counterpart on, was a stuffed lamb with black legs and a black face, a pink smile and glossy, gold eyes, small black ears, white curly wool, tiny white tail.

The kind of toy a child would love to hug and curl up with.

'The first thing I loved. . .and lost,' Reilly's words rang in his head.

"Jaysus, Mary and Joseph," he whispered.

Reilly's reaction to the gift- the silent flood of tears, her strangling Trinity's neck- well, it was loads better than the western movie.

Trinity profusely thanked his little sister, fingering the note Reilly had not been privy to, before falling asleep with a great smile on his face.

Ditto, Pat.

38

"Trinity, can I ask you something?" Reilly and Trinity had finished watering the garden in the unseasonable early heat. She'd picked a good deal of the lettuce before it bolted and a few clumps of herbs for drying and cooking.

Wiping the rampant sweat with her elbow, she thought, salad, lots of salad. With all the multi-colored greens, it would be delicious. Especially in this heat.

Trinity, sprawled on the grass pond-side, contemplated shucking his shorts and going swimming. Well, maybe not shucking the shorts part.

"Anything," he eyed her nervousness. "What's up?"

Reilly hesitated, her eyes scouting. Trinity, alerted, rolled to a sitting position, the better to keep an eye on her.

"My mother keeps hinting about my money- my pay from the diner. . ." Reilly avoided Trinity's eyes. Her fingers played feverishly in the grass.

"You didn't give her any, did you?"

The harsh tone of his question had Reilly cringe. I shouldn't have begun this, she thought. The hardness settled like an old, familiar friend on his face- glittering eyes, clenched jaw.

Trinity's thoughts focused on Reilly, her money, and how she never spent a cent on herself. He'd memorized the extent of her wardrobe, for cryin' out loud! Her three pairs of ill-fitting jeans, four long sleeve shirts, two t-shirts. Someday. . .

"No," Reilly slumped, "I told her it was for my college fund. But, she's started with the guilt trips. . . Constantly. . ."

Reilly rushed into the next part, anxious to get to her brainstorm.

"And Dave's worried about keeping all that money in my locker at work. . ."

"Guilt trips? What the hell does she think you should feel guilty about, for God's sake?" Exasperation fueled his anger at the mother. That old feeling of wanting to punch something reared up and taunted him.

"Trinity, it's all right, I'm used to it. I…I think I'm finally strong enough not to give in," and as she said the words, she realized how true they were.

"Used to it? No child should have to get used to that," he swore under his breath.

Reilly bit her lower lip. He thinks of me as a child, she was mortified- a child friend? Why wouldn't he? I am a lot younger than he is.

The braces aided her discomfiture by cutting into her bitten lip and her eyes sought a focal point to keep her from floundering like a fish out of water- she had to get this out.

Trinity saw he was making her uneasy. Better mind what I say, remorselessly ran through his mind. He'd not yet glean all the ramifications to Reilly of his mentioning the 'child' word.

"Reilly, I'm sorry. What were you going to ask me?"

Eyes on a clump of herbs, she asked, "I was thinking. . .uh. . .you have a bank account?" Trinity nodded, wondering where this was going.

"Would you, could you. . .put my money in your bank account?" She'd aimed high, yet she'd prepared for defeat. It was all there in in her cautious eyes, which episodically checked, then refrained from his.

The gist of this question bowled Trinity over. Talk about trust.

"You can't open a savings account?"

"Not as long as I'm a minor. She could conceivably gain access to it." Reilly knew her mother would suffer no compunctions about doing such, and quickly, too.

Trinity gritted his teeth, but could not keep from spitting a foul word. His fists clenched and opened, wishing for an outlet.

The degree of trust she had in him- hard for a man to live up to.

Of course, Reilly believed if she couldn't trust Trinity, she'd probably never trust a living soul, ever again.

"Reilly, it wouldn't be right. I mean. . . I'm flattered that you trust me that much, but it wouldn't be. . . Let me think a minute." There had to be a way to keep that greedy #*#* from. . .

"I've got an idea. I'll open a safety deposit box in my name, but I'll give you the key. That way, nobody gets into that box except you and me, together. You can find a way to hide the key- maybe, at Bridie's. No one would dare take anything from Bridie's. Your money will be safe- no interest, though. Now, how about going for a swim?"

A change of topic- they both needed a diversion and addressing sweaty bodies seemed just the ticket.

"Swim? In there?" Greatly relieved about the money dilemma, Reilly eyed the cat-tail rimmed pond with fearful misgivings.

"Sure! C'mon," he urged with boyish confidence.

"Uh, I don't swim," Reilly reluctantly informed.

"Good, I'll teach you. C'mon."

"Uh, I. . ." Reilly's scaredy-cat eyes swept from Trinity to the pond.

"What are you afraid of? If you trust me with your money, believe me, you can trust me with a swim lesson," he held out his hand, still grinning encouragement.

"I'm. . .just. . .afraid. When I was a kid, one of my mother's boyfriends thought it was funny to throw me into a pool. . . And. . ." Reilly shivered with nightmarish recall. How frightened she'd been, sinking under the water, sucking in the chlorine stench. . .

"The bastard didn't think it might be more fun to teach a kid to swim," Trinity was beside himself. He didn't want to pile on the sympathy though; he wanted to bring her out of her fear-freeze. Help her. . .to overcome another obstacle which she should never have been subjected to. Damn all the damned roadblocks! Helping her would keep him from throttling imaginary sons of. . .in his head.

"OK, watch me. I'll show you how deep it is," Trinity pulled off his sweaty t-shirt, ruefully left his jean shorts on and waded into the pond.

Ivy Rose and Bridie appeared at Reilly's side.

'Will you look at the chest on yer man, Trinity! Saints be praised!' Bridie ardently goggled with continuous 'oohs' and 'ahs'.

Reilly did as Bridie advised. And caught her breath. Only recently, with Trinity's continued presence, did Reilly begin to think of him as other than a friend. How could she help herself? What girl wouldn't dream of having Trinity O'Ryan, with his strong body and mind and deep blue eyes, for a boyfriend?

Once these thoughts strayed into her imagination, Reilly tried to downplay all possibility of anything beyond friendship. He was merely grateful. . . She was a good cook. . .and too young. . .

Someone like Trinity with someone like her? A great looking young man with a kid that looked like her? He was only being kind because. . .

'Stop that,' Bridie shouted at her. 'You're forgetting your lesson about clinging to. . .'

"I know- the fall of the hammer. Negativity. It's just. . .I…I love being with him. . .and his dad," Reilly added, wistfully. Silly girl, she thought, waiting for Bridie to get after her again.

'Of course, you do, Sweetlin'. I do, too. And I can only appreciate him the more when the two of you are together. . .' Bridie's words were for Reilly alone, but Trinity could see the two ghosts.

"Hey, Reilly! Not to interrupt, Bridie, sorry. Look, this section is only three and a half feet deep. C'mon! You can walk around with me. It's cool!" He returned his sister's windmill waving.

"What about snapping turtles?"

Trinity rolled his eyes, "I won't let them hurt you. C'mon!" Ivy Rose gave her a playful smile, and regaled Reilly with how good a swimmer her big brother was- Trinity was privy to the accolades.

He winked at Ivy Rose, and had to purposefully mind his eyes as the water showed him exactly what Reilly was made of. Good thing the water is cold, he thought. Sheesh! I'll never sleep tonight. . .

After a stroll in the cool, spring-fed waters which stayed below her chest, except when Trinity upended and dove, splashing her entire body, Reilly and Trinity let the sun dry them.

Ivy Rose had pestered Reilly for days to ask Trinity to. . .

"Trinity, would you teach me. . .to play guitar?"

"If you agree to some real swim lessons," he qualified.

With Ivy Rose gigging her, to Trinity's delight, she reluctantly agreed.

"Has Bridie told you about her musical skills?" He admired how Bridie played coy, sure if she'd been alive, her face would resemble her pink roses.

"Bridie played harp and fiddle. Pert near up to the day she left us, uh, on a physical plane. Some of her speed, pardon me, Bridie," she ushered him to continue. "Some of her speed was eventually impaired with the fiddle, but the sight of Bridie at the weekly ceili. . . Amazing! And she loved to dance. But I guess you can see that."

Bridie kicked up her heels, flitted above the pond as if she had the fiddle in her hands and danced to the music of bees and frogs.

Even Wrench and Righteous, who had diligently escaped the water shed from their people, were enchanted at Bridie's frolic- their heads swung right, left and up and down.

Bridie beckoned for Ivy Rose to join her and Trinity and Reilly watched, clapping as if to keep time.

"I wish I could have seen and heard her play."

"When Bridie played harp last. . . Gosh, she must have been well into her 100's, there wasn't a dry eye in the pub. The lady was the star of Ryan. She played the strings like a musical actress, haunting, yearning, sad, uplifting. . . She made you feel every note." Trinity mentally rehearsed Bridie's last performance at the pub.

"You know, I'm sure we have videos, somewhere. . ."

Trinity lay in bed that night, arms behind his head, thinking about Reilly. Ivy Rose hovered cross-legged in mid-air, giggling girlishly.

He found it difficult to think in amorous terms with his little sister, ghost or no, chortling. Darned if he didn't think she knew exactly what he was thinking of. And that would not be a good thing.

'It's not hard to guess,' she clapped her hands.

"Ivy Rose, do you remember privacy? How you hated it when I burst in on you in the bathroom?"

'Why, Trinity?'

"I'm trying to establish. . ."

'I don't watch you in the bathroom, or with those other girls, even if I didn't like any of them. You should find out when Reilly's birthday is,' she suggested.

"I'll ask her," that was really a good idea. Now, why didn't I think of that?

'It would be better if you were sneaky about it. She would feel weird about telling you,' Ivy Rose said.

"Weird, why?" Trinity hadn't a clue.

'She doesn't think she's worth your attention, or a present, either.'

How does a kid know that sort of thing? Trinity wondered, and even worse were the implications of this particular unsettling announcement- he sat up, completely perturbed.

"Doesn't think she's worth. . . How do you know this?"

'I watch her when you're together. And sometimes I can hear her thoughts,' Ivy Rose shrugged, like it was no big deal.

Trinity found this even more confounding, thinking of his own recent thoughts.

"You can read her thoughts?" He had to clarify this.

'I guess it's more like understanding her expressions. . .' the little girl ghost shrugged.

"You don't read my mind, do you?" He recalled Reilly's tentative entry through the cattails and into the pond.

Her rolled up jeans. How he wished she'd had a swim suit on. Get a better look at her without those baggy clothes.

How she startled, and then laughed when she felt the fish swim by her legs, tickling her with their fins.

That glimpse of perfect legs. . . When she'd slipped and he'd saved her from a total drenching immersion, the feel of her in his arms. . . When he upended and dove, splashing her and the result on that wet chest. . .

In freeing his heart from the overwhelming anger and grief over the loss of his little sister, Reilly had forged an irrevocable weld between them, but gratitude had nothing to do with his current feelings.

The fact he could also see Ivy Rose whenever he wanted was like adding nuts to a dip cone- immensely satisfying and magically wondrous.

His male brain strayed once more to what Reilly might look like in a swim suit and. . . How old was she? How long would he have to wait out the siren-hold she had on him? He understood exactly how frustrated those ancient Greek sailors felt.

Ivy Rose somersaulted in fits of laughter.

Oh, boy. . . "Ivy Rose?"

"Bridie, I know it's silly, but I…I love him," Reilly confided to her ghostly friend.

'It's never silly to love, Sweetlin'.'

"I wish I…I wish he'd notice. . .me," she whispered.

'Notice? Yer man's not blind, Dearie. Being friends is a more important part of love than any other,' Bridie remarked kindly, yet authoritatively.

"Are you thinking of THE O'Ryan? You loved him, didn't you?"

'Now, just where might you be gettin' yer ideas?'

"I saw a picture of him in an old photo album Trinity showed me. He looks like Mick O'Ryan- the one you're always staring at when he eats at the diner."

'Well, well,' Bridie flitted about, flustered. Regaining a lick of composure, 'Aye, I loved him. We were friends. He was married and that was all there could be,' Bridie's younger-looking face wore a wistful veil.

"Did it break your heart?"

'Not exactly. We're still friends.'

"Oh," Reilly hadn't thought about THE O'Ryan and Bridie on the other side.

'You'd best get some rest, Dearie. I'm sure your dreams will be full,' Bridie kissed her goodnight.

"What if Trinity doesn't, or can't feel the same way about me?"

'You may still love him. Live for today, Reilly, remember?'

Reilly nodded, her thoughts verging in other directions. When Trinity caught her as she slipped, the whole world seemed to spin. What would it be like to have him for her own. . .boyfriend?

Heavens! I'm just a kid with braces, but. . . He said he'd open a safety deposit box for me.

He also referred to me as a child, she silently moaned.

And my lamb. . .which Righteous curled up against by her pillow. It was so hot in her room. Too hot for the kitten to snuggle beside her.

"Bridie, why doesn't my mother love me?"

Bridie froze, shell-shocked. If her tear ducts actually worked on the other side, the room would have been deluged.

The ghost drifted beside Reilly. Her whisper of an arm rested about the girl's shoulder. Righteous stood on hind legs, pawed at Reilly's arm, trilling empathy.

Longing for contact, Reilly leaned in and caught herself before tumbling through the ghostly form. She placed the kitten on her lap; Righteous peered up with intent love in her eyes, and reared up to buss the girl's chin with kitten kisses.

'I wish I could give you a proper hug, Sweetlin'. Your mother is too busy bein' a kid, herself, to think about others. If she's lucky, she'll grow up in time to understand things like love, and havin' a grand, grand daughter such as yourself.

Even if she never shows it, on some level, believe me, she cares for you. I love you, Dearest. Your grandparents and your aunt love you. Righteous does. And the folks of Ryan, the ones who know you, all love you. Love yourself, Reilly. Let your heart love yourself.'

39

Sad. . .S…Steamy. . .Son-of-a-gun. The last was a copout, technically.

Such a long time since she'd used this particular coping mechanism. Or the others. Even her fingernails threatened to present themselves, beseech for nail clippers, if it weren't for all the dishes she washed in the diner keeping them relatively soft.

Months had passed and her tongue and brain had forgotten how to ramble off the three words in quick succession. My brain is probably just tired, she dodged.

Providence kept churning out the early heat and humidity. What would summer be like?

No wonder I feel dewy, disgruntled, down. There, that was better.

How could a person sleep in a trailer closet in this type of heat with no air conditioning? Three times, she'd asked her mother about the lack of locks on her bedroom door and the bathroom door and the non-existent air conditioning in her room.

Her mother's response was typical, "Reilly, Chet works all day. He doesn't want to come home to more work."

Reilly gave up and prayed for a respite from the heat. Just another day. . . Just another day, she silently reiterated.

Stop it, Reilly, she suddenly about-faced and mentally kicked herself.

Next to Reilly in the rumbling, deep cherry red Camaro, Trinity furtively glanced at his passenger. Bridie, lying across the dash, frowned and 'tsk, tsk'ed.'

"You're awful quiet this morning," Trinity ventured into the silence. He wondered what Bridie was up to. Funny thing, looking through a person to see the road ahead. Would he ever get used to this? He kind of hoped not.

"Sorry, I…I couldn't sleep."

From the tone of her voice, Trinity figured he'd let her take a quick nap on the way to the diner. He'd find something to cheer her up after work.

If anything, Reilly seemed even more subdued when Trinity pushed open the door to the diner to look for her. Martie hailed him as she sipped coffee.

"You ready? No hurry," he quickly added. Not for anything would he exhibit impatience to this hard-working, young girl.

She simply nodded, grabbed her ever-present backpack, and exited as he held the clanging door for her. He opened the Camaro's passenger door and she slid in.

Ivy Rose perched above the gear shift in her transparent pink shorts and matching top- her favorite clothes. She eyed Reilly, who leaned back into the comfortable seat and closed her eyes. Her fingers held the strap of her backpack resting at her feet.

Trinity put the key in the ignition, but Ivy Rose stopped him from starting the car. His little sister pointed her thumb at Reilly.

"Reilly, what's going on? You're not yourself, and we're not moving until you tell me. I thought we were better friends than this.

Shoot, if we can discuss death and ghosts," Ivy Rose's face beamed megawatts, "We should be able to talk about anything."

Trinity turned full force to Reilly, his left arm rested on the steering wheel. Even though he could see Reilly perfectly well through his sister, he made a hitching motion for Ivy Rose to get in the backseat.

"Reilly?" Trinity leaned in close until his breath rustled the strands of Reilly's hair which had escaped her headband.

"Earth to Reilly," he whispered, enjoying this close-up look at perfect skin. A freckle at the corner of her mouth. . .he'd not noticed that before. His mouth involuntarily picked that moment to water at the proximity of pink, female lips- Reilly's lips.

Yes, it had been awhile since he'd indulged.

Reilly's eyes flew open- inches separated her from Trinity's face.

"Oh!" she exclaimed, surprised, flustered, embarrassed and desperately hoping her breath wasn't fatal.

"You going to tell me what's bothering you or are we going to sit here the rest of the day? I don't know about you, but I feel as if I've sweated my quotient for the day," Trinity affably remarked.

Reilly was momentarily struck speechless with Trinity's big, dark blue eyes searching her.

A streak of black grease created a double eyebrow over his left eye. The dark shadow of his impending beard about his strong jaws, the dimple. . .

"Reilly, I'm waiting," his lips twitched. What if I up and kissed her right now?

Reilly bit the inside of her mouth, "I'm just tired." She ducked her eyes from his scrutiny.

"Nah, there's something else. C'mon."

"I'm just being a baby," Reilly's lower lip quivered. "It's nothing, nothing." Please don't cry, she hollered at herself.

"You know, I don't pretend to know everything about girls, but I for damn sure know if a girl says it's nothing, it's certainly something."

Reilly tried to look everywhere but at Trinity, until his fingers caught her chin and forced her to face him. In the heat of the Camaro, sun blaring down on them, they were both well-sweated.

"We're going to suffer dehydration, soon," Trinity warned. "And I'd just as soon never see the inside of a hospital again."

"It's my birthday, today," she whispered, closed her eyes and bit hard on her lower lip to stave off tears. Her mother usually forgot her birthday, but her aunt generally called first thing and sent a card, except she hadn't.

'Happy Birthdays!' and high-pitched squeals erupted from the back seat as Bridie and Ivy Rose issued a fanfare of congratulations and ghostly hugs and kisses.

"Why in the world didn't you tell me?" Trinity asked, floored. In his family, everyone warned everyone else of impending birthdays. No chance of forgetting one, and who'd want to, anyway? The O'Ryans enjoyed celebrating each other's special days, and lots of other days, too.

Ivy Rose smirked a superior look at her brother. 'I told you so, I told you so, I told you so,' child-like, she berated Trinity.

Brows raised, he gave his sister a big brother stare which said, hush already.

"C'mon," he opened his door.

"What?" Reilly balked as Trinity got out of his prized, muscle car and opened her door.

"I can't believe you didn't tell me. As I recall, I gave you plenty of notice about my birthday, and how much I loved chocolate layer cake. Jaysus, Mary and Joseph, Woman!"

Trinity pulled her out of the car when she sat like a stone. He looked up and down the street. Good, he thought, it's early yet.

"How old are you?" He'd never asked her before- hoped she wasn't 14, 15, 16. . . How long could he realistically wait? Forever if he had too, but he'd rather not have to.

One look at her flushed face, a rosy-pink, those sweet green eyes which tripped him up every time. . . Yes, forever, if he had to.

Hmmm. . . Lately, he'd not really noticed, but she'd been avoiding looking directly at him. Darned if she wasn't doing it right now. And what exactly did that mean?

Well, either she really liked him and was too shy, or she didn't like him. . .that way. Not a betting man, Trinity still laid odds it was the first. Had to be. Two people couldn't go through what they had. . . Before the day was over, he'd know for sure.

"How old, Baby?" he teased.

"17," Reilly mumbled.

"Hallelujah!" he bellowed.

Puzzled, Reilly daringly crawled out from her shell. "How old did you think I was?"

Trinity shrugged, faking nonchalance, "I was hoping you were closer to 18 than not.

C'mon, how do you feel about getting your ears pierced? I'd like to get you something special for your birthday."

"You don't have to. . ." but she was cut off with a stern glare of forbearance, which stopped her in her tracks. Trinity's right brow rose.

"Uh. . .pierced, as in needles?" Reilly remembered the stitches in her arm- the needle. . .the sick feeling. . .

Bridie raised her eyes heavenward and pushed Reilly into Trinity's chest.

Reilly stumbled; Trinity caught her; Ivy Rose clapped and jumped up and down like a jack-in-the-box. Trinity winked at Bridie over Reilly's head as he fastened his arm about her waist and led her on.

Mrs. Whistler of the local jewelry store agreed to pierce the fearful Reilly's ears.

"Dear, you pick out a pair you like," the woman set out trays of earrings on the glass counter top.

As Reilly studied tiny gold hoops and birthstone earrings, Ivy Rose waved Trinity further down the counter, pointing furiously.

When Reilly turned to see where Trinity was going, Bridie slapped/penetrated the counter to draw the girl's attention back to the task at hand.

With Reilly's back to Trinity, he caught Mrs. Whistler's eye and pointed into the glass case. The casually, but colorfully dressed, surprised saleswoman sent her brows ceiling-bound as she drew out Trinity's choice.

She placed the price tag in his hand with a silent question. Trinity was by no means a big spender.

Other than the Camaro, which he'd mostly restored by himself, he'd never laid out much cash.

With Ivy Rose skipping up and down the glass cases, and Reilly oblivious, Trinity smiled acquiescence at Mrs. Whistler, who pocketed the price tag.

"Hey, Reilly, how about these?" Trinity approached Reilly, who was experiencing great difficulty making a decision, mostly because she didn't want Trinity to spend any money on her.

'You'll like these, Reilly, they look like flowers,' Ivy Rose, with Bridie in cahoots, oohed and aahed over Trinity's selection.

Indeed, the silver-colored petals of the earrings, with a sizeable crystal in their midst, did resemble roses.

"What kind of a stone is this?" Reilly asked the store owner.

Mrs. Whistler was warned off by Trinity's slight shake of the head.

"They're. . .a…a type of crystal, dear. In the sun. . .uh, they'll create rainbows." Mrs. Whistler had always admired young Trinity O'Ryan- he'd always been extra patient with her when she had a problem with her car. She liked all of the O'Ryans, but at this particular moment, she didn't think she'd ever admired a young man more.

"There, dear, what do you think?" The woman handed her a mirror.

Trinity had spun story after funny story as Mrs. Whistler prepared and pierced Reilly's ears.

Bridie and Ivy Rose had danced the polka across the jewelry counter with a hilarious rendition of a can-can thrown in to boot- Trinity had the devil of a time keeping a straight face- thankfully, Mrs. Whistler remained intent on the operation at hand, er, ear. And it happened so fast, Reilly didn't even flinch.

She gazed into the mirror, pulled stray strands of hair out of the way and her eyes watered.

"They're beautiful," she murmured. "Thank you, Trinity. Thank you, very much."

Reilly's eyes weren't the only ones experiencing dew. "Happy Birthday, Reilly," Mrs. Whistler patted her hand and offered a few instructions.

"OK, where would you like to go tonight?"

"Go?"

"I guess, maybe, I didn't phrase that quite right. I'd like to take you out on a date. Will you go out with me? Tonight? For your birthday?" Trinity held her hand and pulled her around to face him.

"You want to go out with me?" Reilly's jaw dropped.

Trinity flexed his t-shirt clad chest, which earned whistles from a couple of girls window shopping.

"Sure, after I get cleaned up. I know," he mused. "I know where we'll go."

Reilly racked her brains. She couldn't go out on a date- not with the clothes she had.

"Uh. . . I'd really like to. . .uh. . .buy some new clothes. Something n...nice to wear," she stammered.

"Great! I know just the place." Trinity ushered her into a shop down a side street. It was filled with up-to-date fashions in all price ranges, most of them made by local women. Cottage industry was alive and well in the town of Ryan.

Reilly had never thought of herself as having a nervous personality- fearful, yes, but not skittish.

Her mother often acted erratically- hence, all the moves. Perhaps being uprooted at the drop of a hat for years had given her an immunity of sorts to excitable attacks. Uncomplaining, she simply resignedly accepted, became an introvert in response to her changeable life circumstances, and quietly hoarded her fears- until now. . .with Bridie's intervention.

Why, then, had she dropped the soap three times, got shampoo in her eyes, slipped in the tub- nearly falling, got dressed and forgot to brush her teeth? She felt her heart thumping as if she'd been in a race. Running around in fruitless circles, picking up this, dropping that. . . What is wrong with me?

Her mother had left a note on the kitchen counter: Chet and I are visiting friends for the weekend. Be back Sunday night. Be good. Ha! Ha!

Nothing about her birthday.

At least, the sink was clear of filth.

I'm going on a date, Reilly thought! My first date! She checked her birthday earrings every few seconds.

Without Chet and her mother in the dump, Reilly had decided to use the air conditioned master bath. Unlike the cracked mirror in the bathroom allotted to her, the master suite had plenty light and several mirrors.

"Aren't they beautiful, Bridie?"

'They certainly are. Yer man, Trinity, has good taste. I noticed him helpin' you pick out those lovely clothes, too.'

Trinity had swept through the shop while Reilly was relegated to the changing room. He'd put together several outfits for her to try on. Dresses, pants and blouses. . .

She refused to be talked into a sundress, which miffed Bridie, and especially disappointed Ivy Rose, who'd been clamoring for her brother to choose the peach and lace sundress.

'It will look great on her,' Ivy Rose whined.

"I know it will, sis, but, hell, you're the one who told me how self-conscious she is," he kept his voice tucked into a light blue top. Talking to a ghost was a covert adventure in itself.

'Well, buy it anyway,' Ivy Rose grumbled.

Of course, this was all unbeknownst to Reilly, who shuffled in and out of various dresses, shirts and slacks and capris. The final decision, approved by all, was a pair of white zip-up the side jeans, which fitted her all the way to her ankles and a turquoise blouse with a modest round neckline, three-quarter sleeves and a scalloped hem which fell at the jeans waistband. Rhinestone sandals completed the outfit.

Trinity had the sundress wrapped and asked for it to be delivered to the garage on Monday. A surprise for another day.

Reilly brushed out her drying hair. For some reason, her hair wasn't as lanky and plain as she'd always thought it.

'It looks especially lovely with the sun streaks, Sweetlin'. You've got a bit of natural curl, too.' Bridie perched on the mirrored dresser, eyeing Reilly as if she were her own daughter- preparing for her first date with a most likeable, young blade.

Reilly picked up her mother's perfume, Chanel #5, and set it back down.

'Good girl, you don't need that. Yer own healthy skin is all you need to drive a man wild.'

Reilly's face blanched at Bridie's impertinent suggestion. "Uh, wild?"

'Just a figure of speech, lass,' Bridie winked.

"Bridie, do you think Trinity is. . .just being nice? This isn't a real date?" Reilly's spirits gathered on the elevator- waiting for the choice- up or down.

'By the looks of those earrings, Sweetlin', he's very serious about this date; got an eye for you, is the old expression,' Bridie confided.

"What?" But a knock at the door had Reilly scampering off, half tripping in her haste, forgetting all about what Bridie said. The ghost floated happily in her wake.

"Damn, you look good," Trinity appraised his date with alacrity.

The light turquoise perfectly complimented Reilly's fair skin and light-streaked, nut brown hair.

Trinity minded his eyes didn't get carried away on their perusal of Reilly's form. Now that he could actually see said form. And he was extremely pleased.

"Thank you, you look great, too," she admired his white dress shirt, sleeves turned back heightening the effect of the dark hair swirling on his muscular forearms. The shirt was tucked into fitted, black jeans.

Trinity opened the trailer door for her and Reilly grabbed her backpack.

"Should have got you a purse," he mused, "Instead of carrying around that big, old bag."

"Oh," Reilly blushed, ducked her head, slid into the Camaro.

Trinity recognized he'd said something inappropriate. Come to think of it, she always carried that old bag with her. He let the Camaro rumble. Ivy Rose eyed him disapprovingly from the back seat.

"Reilly, I didn't mean to. . . Why do you take that backpack with you all the time?"

"Habit, I guess," embarrassed, she fingered the straps of the bag resting between her legs.

"Habit? I don't follow."

"Inside are the things I don't want to lose: some clothes, cards Bridie gave me, her letter to me, my lamb. . . I…I left her sweaters and the cape at her house. Uh, you see. . . My mother, uh, when she says it's time to go. . . Well, I don't get a chance to pack my things. So, I figure if I have this with me all the time. . . This is the longest we've been in one place. . . It's kinda scary," Reilly shyly admitted.

The spirit elevator hit ground floor with an inaudible thud.

The hardness Trinity thought he'd experienced the last of had him mentally cursing and gritting his teeth.

He popped open the glove compartment, drew out a tablet and pen, wrote out a few lines, handed it to Reilly.

"This is my cell phone number, my dad's cell, the garage number and Kate's number, as well as my house number. If you ever disappear on me. . .at least, I'll know why. You call any one of these numbers, anytime. Call collect. And I don't care if she carts you off to Timbuktu, I'll come after you. If you want me to. I'll bring you back here, Reilly, or anywhere you want to go. . ." Trinity broke off, startled by the sentient surge choking his throat.

Ivy Rose and Bridie were holding each other in the back seat. Reilly tentatively accepted the paper from her date, gently folded it and hid it inside the zipper pocket inside the backpack. All the while trying not to cry.

Trinity tilted her chin up to find her Irish green eyes swimming. How had he held himself back from the depths of those tear-curtained eyes?

"I love you, Reilly," he whispered. "When you're ready, I'll give you that home you've always wanted. I promise."

He cradled her upper body to his chest while she silently cried into his neck.

"The best fish and chips in the state, or any other state, are right here," Trinity and Reilly, hand in hand, walked to O'Ryan's Pub after he'd parked the Camaro in a suitable parking slot.

Reilly hesitated as Trinity made to follow another couple into the Pub. He sensed her consternation, and set down his guitar.

"I know what you're thinking. This is not a bar, as you know bars to be. This is considered a Public House as in the old country- a family place. Folks get together here after work. Families come here for supper, and to listen to music. Saturday is fish and chips night and the weekly ceili.

My Uncle Mick doesn't allow any shenanigans, and believe me he's big enough to discourage the wrong sort from ever walking in, let alone causing a ruckus. Trust me," Trinity urged.

Reilly felt ghostly hands pushing her from behind.

"OK," she tried to smile.

"Dia duit, Trinity!" A booming voice hailed the Irish greeting as the young mechanic pulled Reilly in, sporting his guitar case with the other hand.

"Brilliant!" Mick O'Ryan jumped over the bar and rushed to his nephew, slapping him on the back with enough force to knock a normal man off his feet. "Brilliant," he repeated.

"Been a long time, Uncle Mick."

"Too damn long, me lad, too damn long," his uncle elaborately agreed.

Reilly heard Bridie gasp as Mick O'Ryan took both of Reilly's hands in his, cocked his friendly face with its thick black hair and lively brown eyes, winked at her blushing cheeks and asked, "Is this yer lady, m'lad?"

"Mo ghra milis daor, Uncle, and I'll thank you to keep yer roving eyes to yer self," Trinity was not altogether joking with his relative as he switched into Irish and Irish English.

Mick's brows rose, amazed at Trinity's announcement.

Reilly hadn't caught the whole phrase, and wondered what Trinity had said.

"The best seat in the house for this young rake and his lass," he guided them through the single, long room to a booth near a small stage.

Greetings from the nearly full pub rang out as they advanced.

"Reilly! Trinity!" And whispers of, "He's got his guitar," raced about. "Hope he sings!" Reilly heard the excitement in the patrons' voices.

Trinity could sing, too?

Martie and Dave, sitting with a few diner regulars, and other familiar faces called greetings.

Trinity put his guitar on the stage, and sat next to Reilly in a booth.

"You'll be havin' fish and chips, I'm supposin'? A pint for you, lad?"

Trinity gave Reilly a peculiar look, leaned to her ear, "Do you trust me?"

The thought of Trinity drinking had Reilly involuntarily shuddering.

'Sweetlin' there's a big difference between a man who drinks and a man who has a pint. Yer a smart girl, don't let me down,' Bridie tapped the old, scarred wooden table as Ivy Rose Riverdanced on the stage in gleeful anticipation.

"Yes, Trinity, I do," Reilly caught her breath at the huge smile Trinity bestowed on her.

"Half a pint with my dinner, if you please, and a couple of lemonades?" He raised a questioning brow at Reilly who hesitantly smiled and squeezed Trinity's hand in hers.

The O'Ryan clan, those not working on frying fish and chips outside under a canopy, pulled up the few remaining unattended chairs. Someone ran upstairs to find more seats. A fire marshal might have complained at the overly crowded Pub, except he and the resident firemen were among the Saturday night patrons.

"Is it always like this?" Reilly rubbed shoulders with Trinity on her right and Kate on her left.

"Pretty much so," Pat Sr. offered. "Except, I bet a few phone calls went out. I'm sure my youngest son hasn't told you of the extent of his musical expertise."

"I…I thought I heard someone say something about his singing," Reilly responded.

"Just wait," Trinity's dad enigmatically said. Finally, he thought, winging a prayer to all the saints for the angel they'd sent.

Trinity devoured his cod log and chips and half of Reilly's. She was impressed with the outlay of the Saturday night specials. Half pound logs of battered fish, and chips- thick, homemade French fries- and cole slaw loaded large platters. Folks quit their seats, hastened out back to retrieve their meals and upon returning, grabbed weighty glass pints of Guinness from an inexhaustible supply of frothing mugs on the bar.

Once the dining wound down, Mick blocked the view of his nephew carrying a. . .

"Happy Birthday to you. . ." The Pub erupted in the birthday song as Trinity carried a white sheet cake with decorative, red icing roses toward Reilly.

He walked slowly so the candles might retain their flames.

The town of Ryan loved celebrations and they'd taken to Reilly. Hadn't she brought desserts back to the diner? Great desserts! Hadn't she put the create-your-own burger on the Tuesday and Thursday menu? Hadn't she saved Trinity O'Ryan from certain death? And wasn't she the sweetest thing?

The Pub customers sang wholeheartedly to Reilly's great surprise and chagrin. Bridie dipped her fingers in the Guinness glasses, and brazenly baptized all the singers.

'Benedictions and birthdays go together,' she winked at Reilly, and sent a special froth-laden spat at The O'Ryan. As far as Bridie was concerned, Mick, being the spitting image of her old friend, and better yet, he owned a pub, was The O'Ryan.

Mick swiped the foam from his cheek, looked around for the mischievous culprit, burst out laughing, and licked his finger.

"Happy Birthday, mo ghra milis daor," Trinity set the cake with its 17 lit candles in front of Reilly.

A silence so pervasive you might have heard a ghost float about descended as the Irish speakers translated Trinity's words in their heads.

'Make a wish, Reilly,' Ivy Rose tickled Reilly. She closed her eyes, wished, and blew out the candles.

The Pub erupted anew. A passerby would have thought the Irish won the world soccer tournament from the din of joviality thundering within.

Pat Sr. finished his cake, struggled through the crowd, and returned with a beribboned box.

"From the rest of the O'Ryans," he indicated his other son and Kate.

Shyly, Reilly accepted the box. Kate held it while she opened it. A fanciful, white sun hat with a huge peach and turquoise bow and ribbon band peeked out of layers of tissue paper.

Reilly remembered the hat from the Ryan's Regalia Shop. And the price tag that kept her from buying it. She'd been enchanted by how the hat looked on her. Apparently, Trinity had, too.

Teary-eyed at all the attention and kindness, she looked to him.

"Well, let's show them just who this hat was made for," he placed it on her head, tilted it slightly, to appreciative applause.

Flashes burst as Kate began taking pictures. Ivy Rose waved into the camera, and Bridie leaned in to kiss Reilly's cheek.

I wonder if the ghosts will show up in the pictures, Reilly mused, a bit slap-happy.

"Honey, here's a little something from us," Martie handed her a small, wrapped package.

Reilly was afraid she'd drop the little box, her hands were shaking so.

"We see you checking the time when you get to work, noticed you didn't have a watch. . ." A petite, silver watch band graced a pink mother-of-pearl face with silver numbers. "It's waterproof, too. No need to take it off washing dishes," Martie winked.

"Thanks, Martie and Dave. Thank you, Pat, Pat and Kate," Reilly eyed each gift giver with sincere gratitude.

"Time for some music, before we all get to blubbering! Jaysus, Mary and Joseph, I've seen less tears at a wake," The O'Ryan spouted off.

"I wonder why that is," Pat Sr. smirked.

"Could have something to do with the Guinness," a patron joked, as another summoned a round for the house.

Trinity and three other musicians took the stage- one a thin, gray-haired man, beret askew, who blew a few notes on a harmonica; another, a flagrant redheaded young man with his accordion and the last, Pat Sr. himself, checking the tuning on a mandolin.

"Hey, Trinity! Nice to see you where you belong, lad-outside the garage, I mean," a catcall from the back had many others echoing their agreement amidst congenial laughter.

"Thanks for the vote of confidence, Lester," Trinity grinned into the mic. He adjusted his guitar strap, thumbed the strings, listening for a discordant note.

"Pardon, if I'm not up to snuff. I've been. . .out of practice for. . .quite some time." He regarded Reilly who was intently listening to Ivy Rose even as both ghost and girl had him in their headlights.

'My brother used to play here every Saturday, Reilly. I'm so glad you came,' the little girl ghost clasped Reilly like a warm breeze.

'Now, lass, you're about to hear as fine a musician as any Ireland ever produced,' Bridie affirmed. 'And my old homeland is the birthplace of many- no boast, just fact.'

"Until I've composed a suitable serenade for my lass," Trinity winked at Reilly, whose heart was fit to explode with a happiness she'd never experienced, "I'll stick with this. I wish Bridie could be here with us. Excuse me, let me amend that, I'm sure Bridie is with us." Pointedly, he nodded at Bridie.

'Better believe it, lad,' Bridie hallooed, kicking up her jubilant, mucker-clad heels.

Trinity counted off his fellow musicians, and his clear, deep, melodious voice courted the words of the traditional Irish ballad, STAR OF THE COUNTY DOWN.

'Ooh, my favorite! That lad could sing the souls out of heaven,' Bridie proceeded to dance atop unaware patrons' heads while Ivy Rose giggled softly, clapping in time, her eyes solely for her brother.

"From Bantry Bay up to Derry Quay and from Galway to Dublin town, no maid I've seen like the sweet colleen that I met in the County Down."

The entire Pub joined in with the chorus- had the old rafters and wood floor creaking along in celebratory delight.

"No pipe I'll smoke, no horse I'll yoke til my plow is a rust-colored brown, til smiling bright by my own fireside sits the Star of the County Down."

Pat Sr. peered at the starry-eyed Reilly. Who'd have believed that little, rail-thin girl, with the haunted eyes, that stood all forlorn in front of Chet's dump, would turn out to be the star of his youngest son's heart?

It wasn't like a double date on a Saturday night with another couple in the backseat of the Camaro unaware of Trinity and Reilly because they were completely involved in their own romance. No, instead, Ivy Rose and Bridie, with their ghostly faces nosily poking forward, hovered in the back of the Camaro.

'Kiss her, Trinity, kiss her,' wide-eyed and clapping her hands, Ivy Rose egged him on.

He ignored his sister. "I want to kiss you," Trinity leaned toward Reilly, settled his eyes gently on her.

She blushed at the intense longing on his face which was equal to the flock of feelings helter-skeltering inside of her. He was going to. . . Do I just close my eyes?

Reilly's awkward stillness caused him to frown, "Would it be weird if I kissed you?"

"Uh, weird?" Two ghosts in the back seat- weird didn't begin to cover it. "Why would you want to?" Reilly was so flustered she wasn't sure what she was saying.

"You don't know a lot about decent guys, do you? Take your time and think about what you're asking." Trinity hadn't dated any shy girls. Usually, he was a bit behind his regular dates' designs.

"You know," he broached her quiet demeanor, "I've never kissed a girl with braces."

"Uh, so I'm. . .like a science experiment?" How could it be this distressing to receive a kiss? Did other girls feel like this on their first dates?

'I'll just cover the little one's eyes and you go ahead and let that fine blade kiss you, Sweetlin.'

"Bridie!" Reilly let fly, aloud.

"Ah, that's it! We have an audience of two cramping your style," Trinity leaned into his seat.

Reilly's cheeks flamed. Oh, God, she thought, now he'll never kiss me. Maybe that's a good thing, but I'd really like him to.

"Ivy Rose," Trinity fastened a big brother look on his feisty, little sister. "Do you remember our talk on privacy?"

'Ah, Trinity,' Ivy Rose grumbled.

"Ivy Rose," Trinity firmly reiterated his warning.

'Oh, all right,' and Ivy Rose stomped her little foot through the gear shift, and vanished.

"Bridie?" he continued.

'Well, I guess I know when three's a crowd,' Bridie harrumphed, and secretly pleased, she also faded away.

"You don't think they'll be mad?" Reilly feared.

Trinity shook his head, "Now, where were we?" He chuckled, tipped Reilly's chin and. . . The world spun. For both of them.

42

Reilly didn't have to rise from bed Sunday morning. She'd floated through the night on clouds. Dreamy, fluffy clouds. Heavenly clouds. This must be how Bridie and Ivy Rose feel, she mused.

Her head still spun magically, her body still tingled. As for her lips. . . Yesterday, she'd not been Reilly Brooke, but some nobody swept up in a whirlwind fairytale. A nobody who became a princess because THE Prince. . .

She hugged her lamb to her body, kissed its pink nose. She twirled, laughing. Trinity had bought her these gorgeous earrings, he'd taken her on a date, he'd sung to her- heck, he'd brought the house down with his guitar playing and singing. Every note he fingered on the strings vibrated in her heart and as for his singing. . . Tears of happiness, something she'd never known, badgered her eyes.

"I almost forgot, ooh," she whispered to Righteous. The kitten's huge, light green eyes danced, watching the erstwhile never-before-seen antics of her live person, and with the slightest of congratulatory meows, she stoically waited for breakfast.

Reilly dug into her backpack. The paper with all of the telephone numbers. . . Hurriedly, she made four copies, checking and rechecking to make sure she'd copied the numbers correctly. She hid each copy in a different place inside her bag. Carefully, she folded her new outfit and put the new clothes and sandals inside, too. The lamb went on top. She hated to close the zipper on its cute face. Compromising, she left it half open.

"I need to memorize these telephone numbers, just in case," she told the waiting kitten. The prospect of having to leave wasn't quite as fear-inducing, now. She had Trinity to talk to, if. . . And Wrench would take care of Righteous.

She was dishing out the kitten's food before she remembered something else- the most important thing of all.

"Righteous, oh Righteous, he...he told me he loves me, and he talked about a home. . ." She cradled the overly-patient kitten in her arms and sniffled into her golden fur. This was not considered acceptable behavior by any hungry cat standard- a shower when food was on the table? What was a kitten to do?

"Meeooow," Righteous protested, and pushed her hind legs against Reilly's body to facilitate escape.

"Happy Birthday, Reilly," the mother belatedly greeted her Monday evening after Trinity dropped her off from work.

"I bought you an outfit. I'm sure your boyfriend will love it," her mother enthused.

Skeptically, Reilly eyed the Walmart bag.

"Go try it on," the mother puffed on a cigarette. Wordlessly, Chet indulged in a reality pawn broker show on TV.

Reilly blushed furiously at her mother's choice of clothes for her birthday present. The attire was much more suited to her mother's taste.

The spaghetti straps on the tank top couldn't be adjusted high enough to make Reilly feel comfortable.

And the Capri pants were much too thin a white material, and thankfully, didn't fit anyway.

She refolded the items, thanked her mother, but said they didn't fit.

"Oh, well, I guess I'll keep them for myself," the mother pulled out the clothes and checked the tank top color against her nail polish.

Reilly saw a card from her aunt lying on the counter. This cheered her up- her aunt hadn't forgotten. Unconsciously, she pushed hair behind her ear, and picked up the opened envelope- of course, this was how her mother had remembered.

"What are those?" The mother's fingers at her ear had her wincing inside; she held her breath against the eau d' cigarette exhaled in her direction.

'Buck up, lass! She can't pull them out of your ears,' Bridie remonstrated from atop the kitchen cabinets while casting derisive glares Chet's way, and waving off the ascending, obnoxious fumes.

"Trinity's birthday present to me," the mortified Reilly murmured.

"Hmmm. . .he certainly laid out the cash," her mother smacked her lips in appreciation.

Reilly pulled away, puzzled, and her mother continued, "Do you know what the stones are?"

"Sure, Mrs. Whistler at the jewelry store said they were a type of crystal. . ." Reilly's voice trailed off when her mother burst out laughing.

"A type of crystal! I guess, you could say that. He didn't tell you? If I'm not mistaken, these are mighty fine diamonds, maybe a half carat apiece," her mother informed the stunned girl.

Reilly felt her whole body heat up. Oh, my goodness, her mind splintered in various directions.

"It seems you are my daughter after all," the mother cackled like an appreciative crow. "Imagine, attracting a stud like Trinity O'Ryan!"

The mother eyed her up and down, snorted. Couldn't figure out what that young man saw in this girl- her daughter. No visible curves. Plain hair, although the highlights from the sun were acceptable. No make-up. Decent eyes, but a mouth full of metal!

The obvious answer to the mother's questions related to her own first encounter with a potential prince charming, and the resultant kick in the gut when his denial of her pregnancy left her knowing there was no such thing as a fairy tale at 15 years of age.

She'd given Reilly the facts of life very early, and blamed her own mother for her impetuous behavior, and where it had landed her- single with a kid.

Reilly cowered under her mother's objectionable appraisal. She pretty well read her mother's mindset. Aghast, grabbing her aunt's card, she hastened to her room.

Bridie's scathing remarks were lost on the mother, but a swift kick at a bag of opened popcorn fired missiles at the woman's face sending her reeling towards Chet who automatically hit the floor- the memory of the Bridie remark freshly burned into his head.

"These are delicious!"

Reilly and Trinity enjoyed a picnic lunch gleaned from Bridie's garden, which she and Trinity tended under Bridie's guidance.

Ivy Rose's skipping up and down the rows, with Wrench and Righteous creating havoc on the physical plane, provided entertainment. Kitten and cohort seemed mindful of not disturbing the vegetables and flowers- which only added to the already hectic game of chase as Bridie was not shy about shouting pending 'comeuppances' if any produce was injured.

'Watch me veggies, you rambunctious lot!' Bridie cautioned, and laughed as Wrench rolled and Righteous leaped over him and a row of peppers.

Trinity had supplemented the greens and tomatoes with fresh mozzarella and a loaf of French bread. He swiped at the tomato seeds and juice trickling down Reilly's chin. Thought better of it, and gently lapped the stream, instead.

"Delicious," he agreed after following the trail to her lips.

'Isn't that sweet?' In a branch of the willow tree which shaded their picnic lunch, Bridie hovered, idly swinging her legs.

Flustered, blushing, tingling, Reilly blanched.

"We're being observed, aren't we?" Trinity didn't bother looking up, but Reilly timidly nodded.

'Dearest, I'm only chaperoning, as is right and proper. I'd be trustin' you, Trinity, except I know a wee bit about men,' Bridie admonished.

Trinity felt his lips twitch with a rejoinder, but held himself in check.

At least, Ivy Rose was skipping about with the butterflies, and not minding his every move- as she'd always wished- now she capably soared as high as the Monarchs.

"Trinity?" Reilly wasn't sure how to broach the subject bothering her.

"What's on your mind, winsome lass? Say, can you make bread like this?"

She nodded, "Sure."

"And your question?"

Reilly dropped her eyes. For a while after Trinity's death experience and the heart to heart talks engendered by that time, she had met his eyes unequivocally. But something had tripped in her chest recently, and the feelings he engendered in her nurtured her shyness, causing her to more often duck his gaze, again- feeling like a very foolish girl.

Trinity noticed, frowned, but donned a patient cap, although he'd thought with her birthday, and especially, after the kiss, they'd moved beyond her overwhelming, demure stage. He refused to allow her to retreat.

"Reilly?" He tipped her chin.

"My mother saw m…my earrings," she began.

Trinity fought the streak of revulsion brought on by the mention of Reilly's mother.

"She didn't ask to borrow them, did she?"

"N…no. It was an accident she saw. . ."

"Reilly, you don't have to hide them. She won't pull them out of your ears," irritated, Trinity tried his best to stay calm and reasonable.

What mother would forget her daughter's birthday, and then upset her about a present from a friend- boyfriend?

He'd gone a bit overboard, but hey, it was his money.

"That's what Bridie said," she murmured.

"Good. So what's the big deal?"

"Are they really diamonds?" Misty, confused eyes waited Trinity's response.

To her surprise, he simply choked on laughter. Shouldn't a girl be tickled to receive diamond earrings? Seeing she was seriously disconcerted, he reflected on the reason. What was she thinking?

'Diamonds mean love,' Ivy Rose, taking a break from the butterflies, whispered in his ear.

"Hmmm. . . Maybe I missed a step," he grinned.

Reilly dropped her eyes to her fingers. Had she made him mad? Why was he chuckling? She felt stupid. Who questioned birthday gifts? Even expensive ones?

"I've a question for you, mo ghra milis daor. Will you be my steady girl?"

'Yay, Trinity! Trinity and Reilly! Yay!' Ivy Rose chanted repeatedly to Reilly's great chagrin. The little girl danced about, a noisy, over-the-moon, whirling dervish.

Bridie rained down willow leaves on their heads. Was this really happening? Perhaps that nobody in the fairytale was, just maybe- her, Reilly Brooke.

"Steady?" she asked, unsteadily. "Me? Are you sure?" Her eyes threatened a dam burst.

"I'm absolutely positive. I've never even considered a purchase such as these," he fondled her ears, "for another girl. So, will you?" He kissed the tip of her nose.

Ivy Rose continued to chorus for her winning team.

"But what about. . .uh. . ."

'She means se…'

"Ivy Rose, privacy, please!" He waited for his teasing, giggling sister to disappear. Then, he glanced up at Bridie.

'Don't mind me, lad,' the older ghost smiled, pretending to mind the soar of a sparrow.

"Please, Bridie," he appealed with dimples on display.

'Very well, behave yourselves,' she mock-huffed, but agreeably vanished.

He returned his attention to Reilly. "Now that we're alone. . . I'm perfectly content to wait- no big deal. You'll not feel any pressure from me. I love you, and I'll wait. Simple."

He knew it wouldn't always be as simple as he inferred, but there were miles to run, cold showers. . .

"Y...you're sure?" Reilly stammered in disbelief.

Trinity winked, "Positive."

A huge smile spread across Reilly's tomato-flavored lips. The dam burst, and the tears rolled. With her heart hammering, she fell into his arms.

"Yes, yes!"

They strolled up and down the rows of vegetables together before leaving- a tired kitten and her exhausted dog friend bringing up the rear.

"It's a shame you only planted, what, 40 tomato plants?" Trinity held Reilly's hand and eyed the ripening tomatoes, heavy on the vines he'd staked up. And the peppers and. . .

"I know, next year, I'll plant double," Reilly agreed.

"Reilly, I was only joking! What are you going to do with all these tomatoes? And the zucchinis- it's like they grow a foot overnight, and all the rest," he spread his hand out to the multitudes of vegetables.

"Dave is going to buy all that his freezer can hold, after making BLT's. Frozen, they'll be good in soups and chili in the winter. I'll sell some of the zucchinis and shred and bag the rest for winter. They're also good in soups, and zucchini bread and I can make stuffed peppers. . ."

"Well, aren't you the little entrepreneur? I remember Bridie's zucchini bread- great stuff."

"She said she'd teach me to can, too, if you'll supervise. We can make salsas and tomato juice. . ."

"Salsa as in salsa and chips? Wow, hadn't thought of that." He quieted for a moment. "You know, it's customary for a bloke to have at least one day off a week?" He seriously accosted his girl. One black brow rose.

Reilly fell into his deep, blue eyes and was struck by. . . "Oh! I'm sorry, Trinity. I guess I...I'm taking advantage of you." Reilly seemed so pitifully contrite, Trinity could have kicked himself.

He gently pulled her into his arms, "I was only teasing you. I like working in this garden, and I love eating the produce. You did say salsa and chips, right?"

Reilly grinned and grimaced as a sharp wire caught.

"Whatever you need my muscles to do," he managed to adjust the offensive wire. All the better to make room for another kiss.

"Bridie, the sun card is right. M…my feelings, my connection to Trinity. . .is real. I…I feel so energized. . .like a flower blooming," Reilly addressed her ghostly friend.

'You've come a long way in a short time, Sweetlin'.'

"Some of my friends are having a pool party. Want to go?"

"Pool. Swimming pool," Reilly shuddered.

Trinity ruffled her hair. "You don't have to swim. You could just get in the pool and walk around. Like we did at Bridie's pond. A swimsuit might be nice." Very nice, he thought.

Reilly was astute enough to realize that Trinity needed to maintain his friendships, and if she were to fit into his life, she'd need to make friends with his friends. So even though the whole idea of a pool party and lots of people pretty well deflated her, not to mention the pool which she had only frightful memories of, she bolstered a smile of enthusiasm and tried to reflect the same in her voice.

"Can I make something to bring?"

Trinity dropped her off early as he had to make an emergency service call at Winchell's farm- problems with his baler.

What am I going to wear? Silly, Reilly told herself, you only have your birthday outfit. No swimsuit in her backpack. She had never owned a suit, not that that had stopped her mother's male friends from throwing her in a pool.

Swim. Scared. Stop it, she trembled.

"You're home early, Reilly," her mother observed, incongruously standing over a sink full of dishes. Lately, her mother had actually been doing minor clean-up at the dump. How strange, Reilly mused.

"I. . . Trinity invited me to a friend's pool party tonight."

Uncharacteristically, her mother actually heard a hint of misgiving in her daughter's response.

"What time is he picking you up?"

"Around 6," Reilly brought a finger to her mouth. A fingernail to chew, but she saw Bridie give her the eye and dropped her hand.

"OK," her mother grabbed the keys, her purse. "Let's go pick out a birthday present you like. You're going to need a bathing suit," she eyed Reilly's jeans and work shoes. "Shorts, sandals and a cover-up, too."

Her mother missed the complete astonishment on Reilly's face- she'd already exited the trailer. Forty five minutes away was a mall- a better selection, her mother stated.

Reilly's mother made suggestions at one of the shops, but her tastes were far too revealing for her daughter.

"Uh, Mom, I…I'd like to find a…a modest swimsuit. I couldn't possibly wear these," Reilly fingered the string bikinis displayed. Her mother vanished down another aisle, and Reilly hoped she'd not made her angry.

"This will be perfect, trust me. Try these on," her mother foisted an armful of materials into Reilly's arms, about faced her daughter and pushed her into a dressing room.

The word trust was not one Reilly used in conjunction with her mother. Too much history to the contrary. And so the girl was utterly amazed at what was presented in the mirror. A simple two piece suit, pair of shorts, midriff top, sarong wraparound and white tennis shoes were rung up.

"Thanks, Mom. I . . . Thanks a lot. That was. . .fun."

It was the only real shopping experience they'd ever shared. Her mother was strangely quiet on the way back to Red Wing.

"I made a big container of salsa." Reilly met Trinity at the door with her backpack and a spare bag containing her swimsuit, sarong and towel and a covered Tupperware bowl.

Trinity stood there like a popsicle on an Arctic winter day. He had a hard time keeping his jaw from falling off his face.

All those nights wondering what the rest of Reilly's legs might look like. . . His dad used to tell him about a movie star, Betty Grable, and her million dollar-insured legs. Well, Reilly outclassed that. His girl's legs' insurance policy, in his opinion, hit the billion dollar mark.

Pale, trim, toned legs- all that diner walking and garden work, led up to a pair of white shorts with side zip. Not short shorts, but the kind that left a good bit to an inquiring imagination. Especially, with their tiny side slits.

Trinity's mind was off and running. Her pale, pink midriff with little cap sleeves, round neck line. . .

God, he thought, if she brought a swimsuit, I'm in deep trouble. Already, his friends, his age and older, kidded him about hanging out with a kid.

"How long you think that's going to last?" JT had vexed him. "You and an underage girl? Jailbait, my friend, jailbait." Savior of his life or not, they all relentlessly annoyed him.

"You look. . ." Trinity lined up his teeth, forced his jaw back in place, "You look. . .deadly," he sighed.

"Deadly?" Reilly blushed furiously. "Is it that bad? I could change. . ."

"Oh, no you don't. Deadly is an Irish expression similar to damn fine."

Reilly felt herself melt, aflame with his perusal.

"I think I better wear my sunglasses. A man could get cataracts looking at you. C'mon, winsome elf."

Trinity, dressed in long, jean shorts and new, white t-shirt, took Reilly's bags, opened the Camaro door and wolf-whistled as she slipped into the passenger seat.

For loaded seconds, he stared at her again before starting the Camaro. With her hair softly pulled back in a ponytail, her earrings shooting rainbows in the still brilliant sun, she looked like any normal, albeit angelic, girl going on a date. No one, right now, would guess how shattering her life had been.

Trinity made a quick stop at the IGA to gather chips, a case of beer for their hosts and bottled water for Reilly and himself. As a driver and especially as her trusted escort, he restricted his already restricted alcohol intake.

Down a maple-lined drive, a pristine ranch house decorated with numerous petunia and pansy baskets and mulched geranium beds, welcomed guests. Country music and the sound of pool action swelled from around the brick house- drawing guests to the fenced backyard.

Attempting to hide her trepidation, Reilly missed a step and tripped alongside Trinity.

He stopped, keenly aware of her anxiety- after all, this would be the first time she met his friends.

"You all right, sweetheart?"

"Sure, new shoes," Reilly blamed her sneakers.

Trinity frowned, "You ever been to a party?"

Reilly didn't think to mention all the parties her mother had. "My birthday party," she hazarded a grin.

Smiling, Trinity foisted the case of beer under one arm, several bags in that hand and placed his free hand at Reilly's waist.

"It'll be OK, Reilly. I'll introduce you around. These guys are all right. Can't vouch for all the girls," he hitched a shoulder. No telling who his single friends had brought as dates.

"Trinity," a short, muscular guy- shirtless- in cargo shorts wended through a crowd of string bikini-clad beauties and beer-in-hand groups of young men.

"Reilly, this is Jeff- JT; this is his place," Trinity introduced.

"Hi! Beautiful flowers," Reilly complimented.

"Thanks, my better half. Hey, Cindy, c'mere."

JT's wife asked Reilly to join her in the kitchen and Trinity shadowed to refrigerate the beer and water.

"Can I help?" Practical, shy Reilly had no idea how to socialize, other than offering to help.

"I'm going to set everything out on the picnic tables and then everyone can help themselves. My house is your house. Sound good?"

Pert Cindy, with her short, curly red hair in a one-piece, yellow swimsuit, showed Reilly where the bathrooms were, and in between several guest interruptive questions and introductions, she tried to get a gist of Trinity's girl.

Timidly, Reilly succinctly answered inquiries and helped Cindy fill the outside tables with snacks, crock pots and other covered bowls.

"The guys wanted to grill out, but I thought chili dogs with shredded cheddar cheese and potato salad would be good and simple. It's so hot out. The water is nice, did you bring a suit?" Cindy asked.

"Uh, yes," Reilly couldn't fib to save her soul. "But I can't swim," she mumbled.

"That's OK- there's a sizeable area between 3 and 4 feet deep. It's a huge pool." Cindy had a feeling Trinity's new girl was completely out of her element.

He confirmed her opinion and intrigued her further by constantly checking on Reilly's whereabouts and asking her in an unobtrusive manner if she were all right.

Cindy and JT had known the O'Ryans their whole lives. Most everyone in Ryan knew everyone else. She'd watched Trinity flit from one girl to the next, each a contender for a beauty pageant. She and JT had seen him at his crazy worst and been bystanders at some of the impromptu fights.

The skirmishes had been downright terrifying. Once, she'd witnessed 6 friends pulling the anger-fueled Trinity off a loud mouth.

Four of those friends sustained injuries. The loud mouth went to the hospital. She knew of Trinity's attack on his brother. It would have come as no surprise to her if Trinity eventually killed someone and ended up in jail.

It was as if he had no control. Didn't care. At a mere glance, he'd flare up and surge in, fists swinging.

His many girls, 'Trinity's groupies', they were called, hadn't a clue as to how to influence him. Some of them seemed to enjoy Trinity's status of toughest man in the county. If it had been the old west, Trinity would be the gunslinger he was named after.

Cindy hadn't experienced close grief yet, but she couldn't fathom how it could turn someone into an impervious warmonger. But this young girl, Reilly, had accomplished the impossible. She'd literally saved his life. . .on more than one front.

Cindy hoped friendship was in store for her and Reilly. Maybe she'd ask then about how the girl had done it. Anyway, Trinity now displayed his old, affable self. And thank God for that.

His eyes were alive and alert- those deep blue, gorgeous eyes that attracted girls like flies to sugar. No more glints of deadly implacability, no more clenched jaw.

For the third time in ten minutes, Trinity strolled to Reilly's side as she helped Cindy.

"She's fine, sheesh! Go play with the boys," Cindy shooed him away. Reilly giggled, self-consciously, and the dismissed Trinity winked and ambled off.

"While the pool is fairly empty, why don't you and I take a dip?" Cindy asked Reilly after introducing her to more guests whose names went in one ear and out the other- except for those she knew from the diner, and at least two girls she'd seen Trinity with at Red Wing.

At Reilly's hesitation, Cindy entreated her, "C'mon, it will feel great, I promise, and the sun's headed down far enough that you and I will be safe from sunburn."

Reilly empathized with Cindy's freckled, white skin- the proverbial bane of redheads. Bridie had not accompanied them to this event- on purpose, no doubt, so she hadn't the ghost to 'push' her. "I did bring my new suit; I guess I might as well put it on."

"No beer, Trinity?"

"Nah, I might have one when I get a sandwich," Trinity had joined his friends.

JT, Sam, Cory, Roy and Zack exchanged glances.

"You and the kid getting along pretty good?" The jibes began.

"Watch it, JT, her name is Reilly," Trinity snaked a warning to the guys.

JT downed half his beer, ruminating. "And you're not. . .?" His eyebrows rose and fell, hinting provocatively.

"Certain subjects are not up for discussion," Trinity gave each of his friends a meaningful look.

"Since when?" Zack quipped, "I remember you and I. . ."

Trinity cut him short, "Since Reilly. Next topic. You guys going to the Dublin. . ."

He lost his friends as their heads swiveled to the pool.

Cindy, in her yellow suit, walked next to Reilly. Her thick, sun-streaked hair resting about her shoulders and half-way down her back did nothing to hinder the glory of her peach halter top and the French-cut bikini bottom- simultaneously modest and exciting.

Trinity's mouth went dry. All the nightly wonderings were nothing compared to the living doll carefully stepping along the concrete walkway to the pool. Those glorious legs, tiny waist, not a spare ounce, small. . .

He didn't feel the elbow gig his side.

"What was that line in TOMBSTONE? You know, Val Kilmer- Doc Holliday, called Wyatt Earp. . .an oak, wasn't it?" JT guffawed.

"Damn, Trinity, you're an oak, all right," Zack choked on his salivating tongue, spewed beer.

Not to be upstaged, Sonja, one of Trinity's ex- 'groupies', waited the opportune moment.

Cindy paused to speak with a friend lying on a raft in the pool's ten foot deep section. Reilly waited for Cindy who was about to introduce her youngest guest when. . .

Sonja deliberately collided with Reilly and shoved her into the clear depths.

Reilly, mouth open as if to scream, wind-milling into the pool, brought Trinity's voice back. As if in slow motion, he'd witnessed the entire 'accidental' deploy.

"NO!" he screamed, a second too late.

The fire of an automatic rifle could have competed with Trinity's bolt to the pool fence, his clearing the hurdle with Olympic skill and his subsequent dive into the water.

The resultant backsplash inundated the raft occupant and upended her as Trinity rose with Reilly in his arms.

Shock struck the guests into momentary, complete silence before a tumultuous din ensued as the oblivious shouted, "What happened?"

Cindy, horrified, searched for the culprit. Reilly had indicated her fear of deep water to her. Who would dare?

Zack, right behind Trinity, accepted Reilly into his arms as Trinity hoisted himself from the pool. Cindy grabbed towels, provided a pillow for Reilly's head.

"Reilly, sweetheart," Trinity pleaded. He started mouth to mouth resuscitation, but Reilly came around quickly-wheezing, coughing and convulsively trembling. Trinity gathered her into his arms and Reilly held on the best she could, crying and quaking.

"You OK, winsome elf?" his hands rubbed up and down her quivering back, trying to dispel her nightmare-pool-moments-come-true.

"I'm so sorry. I didn't know she couldn't swim. . ." All eyes landed hammer blows on Sonja's mockery of remorse.

"You better go," someone advised.

"Yes, leave," Cindy furiously snapped.

Trinity, a trace of granite across his worried features, issued the final ultimatum, "Get your ass out of here, before I forget you're a female."

Sonja hastened her retreat.

"Easy, Reilly, easy. One breath at a time," Trinity was careful to give her breathing room.

Slowly, her shudders subsided. In a ragged voice, she tried to speak, "I...I knew. . .y...you'd come."

"God, Reilly, you are something! You sure you're OK?" he solicitously repeated.

"My nose and. . .th...throat burn," Reilly coughed. "And. . .the taste of chlorine. . .is awful," she attempted to reassure, but didn't release her grip on Trinity.

The others moved away, engaged in relieved small-talk. Trinity gave her a few moments to relax, regain her bearings. Cindy brought her a drink and another dry towel. Red-eyed from her involuntary dunking, she swiped at her eyes, shakily took a drink.

"I'm so sorry that happened," Cindy apologized.

"S'OK," Reilly sniffled.

Trinity witnessed her guard going up. He'd not let her sink into her shell and end this experience with fear as the prominent factor.

"Reilly, do you trust me?"

"Y...yes," she answered.

"Completely?"

Her eyes fastened on his dark blue concerned gaze. She blinked, nodded.

"Then seeing as how we're already wet, will you get in the pool with me? I don't want you to be afraid of anything, especially when you're with me," gently he caressed her jaw line.

Reilly bit her lower lip. Cut it on her braces, winced, shuddered, stared at the still, pool water.

Sensing this was a pivotal moment for both of them, she swallowed hard- that hurt. . .darn chlorine!

At Ivy Rose's impromptu pop-in and suggestion, Trinity ended up playing dolphin with Reilly as he'd done with his sister when she was a tiny swimmer.

Reilly's hands clasped around his neck, her body stretched along his back.

He swam laps in the pool, politely asking Reilly to check her stranglehold on his neck when she got too fearful. Kept swimming until he finally perceived her body relax- a feat of endurance on his part. He'd not done this many laps since. . .

Once she started to giggle in his ear, he figured it was time to get out. With his hands at her waist in the shallow section, he carefully lifted her out of the pool.

"Let's get up a volley ball game in the pool," someone called out after a suitable interval passed from emptying the chili-dog-filled crock pots.

"Trinity's on my team," JT called.

"You want to play, Reilly? You can stay in the shallow end," Trinity leaned into her and nibbled around her earring.

"No, thanks, but I'll be your cheering section," she answered.

'Me, too,' Ivy Rose bounced, clapped and wafted through Reilly attempting a hug.

Tia, Zack's date, also sat out the game. Arrayed in a lounge chair next to Reilly, she decided to play nosey.

All the girls had questions about Trinity's date- she just was not the norm.

Didn't fit in with the rest of Trinity's models. Kind of cute in a goody-goody way, but. . .

"So you and Trinity are an item, huh?"

Reilly felt this girl wasn't really interested in her as a person in her own right, but she nevertheless, politely replied, "He asked me to go steady."

"I guess if you saved someone's life it makes sense they'd want to hang out with you," Tia crossed her tanned legs and cheered her date.

The Reilly of nearly a year ago would have taken this comment to heart and felt horribly out of place, but the Reilly of today, with Bridie's help, had begun to gain a sense of herself. She'd decided to become her own friend- after all, if two ghosts thought she was worth talking to. . . She knew Trinity, and there was no denying the multitude of feelings between them.

She was willing to wait and see if their love was forever. For her part, she firmly believed it was. But she knew she was also very young.

Instinctively, she knew their relationship wasn't solely about gratitude. There was so much more. And if it was only. . . It didn't matter. She loved him. Time would tell.

"Everyone is entitled to their own opinion," Reilly commented to the rude girl next to her.

'That's my Reilly,' Bridie suddenly appeared and tapped her on the head.

44

For once, Trinity eyed with pleasure Reilly's black backpack, knowing it contained not only her favorite possessions, but overnight necessities, too- change of clothes, toothbrush.

He knew the black-faced lamb would be on top and Bridie's fanciful, antique cards safely tucked into a side pocket- he was enormously grateful for Bridie's mentoring, though he didn't fathom all her means. In her arms, head popped up like a prairie dog, was Righteous.

"You're sure Righteous will be OK?"

"Give it a rest, Reilly. It's easier getting you away than getting you to leave this cat- which you're not with 24 hours of the day, anyway."

And just why was that, he wondered to himself? Kate had no problem talking her mother into Reilly's weekend away. Her mother probably hoped Reilly would get pregnant, too, and keep the welfare ball rolling. Not happening, Trinity grinned, and ruffled Righteous' chest hair, receiving a playful bat in reply.

The O'Ryans' neighbor promised to let Wrench out, try to keep Righteous in, and feed and water both. Reilly deposited the kitten in Trinity's home, to Wrench's great satisfaction. She set out bowls of food and water on the kitchen counter, stacked cat food cans, felt inner turmoil.

"You're keepin' yer man waitin', Sweetlin'. Quit that frettin' o'er Righteous and get along with you,' Bridie admonished.

Trinity checked for human observers and waved to Bridie and Ivy Rose.

'We're going too, Trinity,' Ivy Rose excitedly informed him.

Trinity rolled his eyes, why had he expected otherwise? His sister had always enjoyed the festival. There was a county-wide exodus to the Dublin Irish Festival- the second largest cultural celebration in the world. Reilly only agreed to go because the diner was closed, as was most of the town.

"Looks like we're the last to arrive," Trinity revved the engine in his brother, Sean's, driveway.

The Camaro spit out a resounding clamor that car enthusiasts thrilled to hear.

"Will you let me drive the Camaro some day?" Reilly found the temerity to ask.

"Sure, you should have said something," he hit the accelerator again for pure joy.

"I...I thought you might think it wasn't a good idea," she demurred.

"You've done well learning to drive the electric car," he referred to his teaching Reilly to drive. Miss Overly Cautious, he complimented her with. "C'mon," he held the door for her.

"Can the racket, will you? The baby finally got to sleep, thank God," a harried Sean barked out the door- not a good sign.

Reilly grabbed her bag and followed them inside Sean's house. The O'Ryan clan, sans cousins, was gathered quietly in the kitchen. The promised breakfast was nowhere in sight. The air was funereal.

"As I explained to Dad, I can't put you up. . ." Sean, red-eyed and whiskery, in rumpled t-shirt and shorts, started to say.

Pat Jr. interrupted the imminent pseudo-apology, "Brother Sean has acquired rooms for all of us. I'll amend that. A suite for the guys and a room for the lasses," he gave Reilly a welcome kiss on the cheek, which made her blush. Kate and Pat Sr. hugged her in turn.

"We'll have fun," she assured Reilly with a sincere smile.

The original plan had the four Irish cousins- the O'Ryan Rakes, yearly performers at the festival, taking up two of Sean's five bedrooms, Pat, Trinity and his dad in another, and Kate and Reilly sharing the last guest room. But a colicky baby had thwarted that.

"Do you think I should make a tea for the baby?" Reilly asked. She'd been taking lessons from Bridie in herbal medicines- with Bridie's 100-plus years of experience, Reilly was learning fascinating, practical remedies.

"Waste of time. Sean and his wife only believe in doctor's prescriptions. I'm sure they think of Bridie as a hoax or witch or worse," Trinity leaned to whisper in Reilly's ear.

'Hmmph,' annoyed, Bridie skidded a salt shaker across the table with such force it landed on the floor and rolled under a cabinet. Ivy Rose experimented with the pepper shaker without much success- it only toppled. As Bridie made to use it as a second hockey puck, Trinity's hand closed over it.

"To their own detriment, and the baby's," he sought to placate Bridie, feeling sorry for knuckle-heads who would not at least try to see the light.

Kate and the rest of the O'Ryans knew of Reilly's interest in and usage of Bridie's recipes- they just didn't realize that her instruction came by means of personal, ghostly instruction. Trinity had been privy to many of Reilly's classes and had observed with interest.

The salt shaker was forgotten in the melee following high-pitched baby screams.

"Jaysus, Mary and Joseph," Pat Jr. exclaimed. "Sean, either cough up breakfast money or take us out to eat."

Sean ran his fingers through his horribly mussed hair. His wife pleadingly hailed him from the bedroom.

"Take my credit card," he thrust his wallet into his father's surprised hand.

"Now that's more like it; let's go eat," Pat Jr. quipped.

Trinity had made a covert exit after rescuing the pepper shaker, and returned with a beribboned box, which he presented to Reilly.

"Wait a second, you guys," he stayed the exodus.

Perplexed, Reilly questioned Trinity with her eyes.

"It's give-Reilly-a-present-day. Don't bother marking it on a calendar. They're impromptu days you'll be seeing now and again," he grinned at her.

Bridie's tiny brows shot up. Ivy Rose squealed and bounced up and down, 'I love watching people get presents.'

"But, Trinity. . ." Reilly protested, embarrassed.

Trinity placed his index finger on her lips, "Hurry and open it before all of us perish of hunger." It was nearly lunch time.

Peeling away the tissue paper, Reilly found the peach sundress from the Ryan Regalia boutique.

"Wear it for me today?" Trinity grinned, dimples ablaze.

Pat Jr. muttered some nonsense about gift giving and Kate elbowed him with ferocious intent.

"I guess Trinity is the only brother with a romantic side," she griped, not wholly in a kidding fashion.

Pat Sr. added fuel to the fire with, "You may be right about that." His youngest son's actions reminded him of his own overtures to his love.

Pat Jr. knew he'd not heard the end of it. "Hey, the day isn't over," he attempted to save face.

The hotel across from the festival had a huge buffet set out which the O'Ryans besieged as breakfast items were being replaced with lunch items.

"What time do we meet our cousins?"

"Three o'clock, opposite the Dublin Stage. They'll be wanting some of the Old Bag Of Nails fish and chips before playing."

"Think they're up, yet?"

"You kidding- they probably didn't get to bed til the break of day."

"Better put this on, Reilly. You'll burn to a crisp with that halter top tie and exposed shoulders. Not much shade here. Tie the shirt tails around your waist," Kate handed Reilly a white, long sleeve shirt.

"Your hat will protect your face. And I'll tie a green ribbon up with the pink and turquoise one. Can't have a girl with a name like Reilly not wearing green, now can we?"

Each O'Ryan had either an emerald green polo or t-shirt with O'Ryans Garage and telephone number in an arc over the top of THE O'RYAN RAKES, with an askew guitar propped against a can of Guinness.

Kate pointed to Reilly's whiter than white legs and handed her the sunscreen.

"I'll do the honors," Trinity grabbed the tube from her.

"Trinity," Reilly blushed as he knelt before her outside the festival entry, creating a stir among the throngs of people heading to the ticketed entrance.

People of all ages, many sporting t-shirts with quaint or bawdy Irish sayings, politely lined up and gawked at Reilly's legs.

Trinity caught Reilly eyeing a group of guys in kilts, "Don't even think about it, Reilly." His hands massaged her thighs under the mid-thigh length skirts. With fruitless efforts, she tried to keep her skirts intact as the white, lace crinoline under the full peach skirt swished with Trinity's ministrations.

"Now, you," she told him as he rose.

"Me?" He adjusted his green, O'Ryans Garage ball cap. "I've got a hat."

"Lot of good it'll do your ears," Kate swept by to stop her husband and swab his neck and ears and forearms. "Dad," she called, "You're next; you know how the sun is at this shindig."

They strolled through one of the tented markets. Vendors selling Belleek china, kilts, Celtic jewelry- which Pat Jr. and Kate were lost to- Irish wool sweaters, artwork, baskets, dog collars of all sizes with elaborate Celtic designs and matching leashes, a booth of food items imported from Ireland- everything from candy to porridge oats, leather goods, musical instruments-harps, bagpipes. . .

"I thought bagpipes were Scottish," Reilly inquired of Trinity.

"And just where do you think the Scots came up with the idea?" Trinity pulled her close and tried to explain the differences in the two cultures' bagpipes. "Suffice it to say, the Scots thought, poor blokes, they might improve on our pipes. I'll show you when we see different players," he offered as the lengthy explanation drew out.

"I wonder what Bridie did with her harp and fiddle?" Trinity mused as they stopped to watch a woman sitting on a stool with a finely carved harp between her legs. The melody her fingers produced plying the strings was wistfully beautiful.

"Bridie played harp. . . That's right, I think you mentioned it."

"She hasn't told you? Bridie also played fiddle. She. . . Where have they got off to?" It was easy to lose sight of family and friends, not to mention ghosts, in the dense crowds.

"They're headed for that stage over there," Reilly pointed.

"Hmmm. . . I guess ghosts can't technically get lost, but there are nine stages- constant music," he spied Bridie fluttering atop a patron's Guinness, kicking at the foam.

"Nothing sacred," he chortled.

"Nine stages?" Reilly was stunned."

"With different bands, all day. From 11-11, today. This is the second largest event of its kind in the world. Don't know what the first is. We better head over to the Old Bag of Nails, not that the cousins will be on time, but I'm ready for fish and chips. We'll have plenty of time to see the other exhibits. The Irish Wake is a blast. Brian Boru's recreated eleventh century village is interesting. There are workshops, ceili dances, some games," Reilly's head shifted left and right continuously- she didn't want to miss a thing.

She felt special with her hand clasped in Trinity's large calloused hand. He pointed out various Irish dishes like bangers and mash and shepherd's pie, elucidated their composition.

"Celtic Canines?" Reilly stopped.

"You ever see an Irish Wolfhound? Probably the tallest dog in the world. We'll see them later, and real Irish Setters and some others."

They strolled by a line of craftsmen vendors on the way to the meeting point. A leather worker had an array of leather bracelets with intertwined Celtic motifs. One that caught Reilly's eye was a black, one inch wide band with brass buckle, worked edges and interlaced triangles across the center.

"Trinity, do you like this one?" She arrested his walk.

"It's kind of nice, but I'm not really into jewelry. Hard to wear that stuff when you're a mechanic- gets dangerous," he hitched a shoulder.

"But you're not working now. I…I think it would look nice," she dearly wanted to buy him a gift.

Other than something for his car or guitar, Trinity never seemed to want anything. Correction, food was always in vogue.

Trinity cocked his head trying to read her thoughts. He heard a whisper in his ear. Ivy Rose was hanging upside down from the easy-up structure.

'She wants to buy you a gift, and she's right- that would look great on your tanned arm with your black hair.' Ivy Rose swung back and forth, and although it was impossible, Trinity couldn't help but listen for the creak of the canopy heralding its collapse.

"I think I like this one better. It's wider- more for a guy, but. . ."

"I'll take this one," Reilly hailed the Renaissance-clad artist before Trinity could say- I don't want you to spend your money on me.

Surprisingly enough, it felt pretty good on his wrist, and Reilly couldn't help the pleased, goofy grin on her face. And that made it all the more worthwhile.

He wrapped her in an embrace, "Go raibh mile maith agat, mo ghra milis daor," and to the amusement of the passersby he kissed her, thoroughly, until applause sputtered and her knees gave way. Her brain was numb, contrary to the rest of her electrified self, and she forgot to ask him what he'd said.

"Ah, so's this the lass what saved yer sorry arse?" The Irish accent and back-up chortling pulled Trinity out of line at the Old Bag of Nails food booth.

"Why, she's naught but a wee snapper, I'm in me wick!"

"Yer a cradle robber, y'blaggard!"

"Look at 'er legs- make a cat turn backward! Jaaysus!"

Four, black-haired young men fixed their eyes on Reilly until she felt like a zoo specimen. Though not as tall as Trinity, one could easily see the resemblance. They jostled each other to moon-eye and get closer to her.

"Quit yer gawkin', get on side," Trinity curbed his cousins as one tried to put his arm about Reilly and lead her away.

Reilly wondered if her hearing had become impaired. She thought they were speaking English, but she had a hard time deciphering what they were saying- they spoke so fast and with their accents. . .

"Winsome elf, I'd like you to meet Francis Xavier Anthony, better known as Frank, and Michael, and Flicker and Skipper, named after their dad's jobs as a lighthouse keeper and a ferry captain- The O'Ryan Rakes."

"Right you are, lad. Tis a deadly pleasure to make yer acquaintance," all four knelt and made a great to-do of bowing to the ground in loud salaams. "We're tankin' you for savin' this dead-on, no pun meant, lad of ours, we are."

This unscheduled show attracted quite a lot of attention and the gathered crowd wondered who this girl in the broad-brimmed hat was that was being kowtowed to.

Put on the spot, and blushing to beat the band- no pun intended, Reilly greeted the Rakes, "It's nice to meet you. Will you please get up?"

"Gracious, lass. Anytin' for the likes of you," and two of the four, she wasn't sure who, took her elbows and drew her into the line.

"A word of warning," Trinity said to the crew.

"What is it, lad?" Frank, the more temperate and insightful of the four Irishmen, asked.

"Remember how Dad asked you to sort of watch your language around Ivy Rose?" His little sister hovered, all eager ears.

"What?"

"What's that?" Skipper and Flicker put on horrified faces, "D'yer mean we can't say bollocks?"

"Nor gobshite?" And a spewing forth of unrecognizable words, some in Irish, some with a thick enough accent as to be thoroughly unintelligible, rent the air.

A vast number of newcomers honed in, thinking another show was beginning- one that wasn't on the schedule, but sure seemed promising.

Trinity's dad tasted blood trying to keep from laughing. Kate had grabbed her sides and doubled over. Pat Jr. cried in his Guinness.

'Trinity, Reilly and I aren't babies,' Ivy Rose stuck her tongue out at her brother.

Reilly stood spellbound in the incomprehensible fracas. Once an Irishman gets on a roll, you need a finely tuned ear to distinguish all that's said. She eyed the extended O'Ryan clan and wondered what a 'gobshite' was.

"Would you ever go and cultivate yourselves?" Trinity succumbed to loud guffaws.

"Shite, I guess feck is out of order, too?" Frank had the last word as the attendant asked for their orders.

The O'Ryan Rakes hit the huge stage with its stacked-to-the-top-of-the-tent amplifiers amidst a great bustling storm of admirers. Hundreds of occupied tables clapped, stomped, whistled, yelled.

Wiping the sweat from his brow- the temperature hovered at a humid 90- Flicker asked the audience for their cooperation in bringing to the stage his Yank cousin, Trinity O'Ryan.

Over heartily devoured fish and chips, the cousins had beseeched Trinity to sit in with them as he used to. Since Ivy Rose's death, he'd shook it off, but one look at Reilly, Ivy Rose and Bridie, and it didn't take much audience participation to get Trinity making his way to the stage, with a balky Reilly clasped firmly in hand.

"Trinity?" she appealed to him.

"If I'm going up so are you. Look at Bridie and Ivy Rose, watch them, you can dance with them."

"Dance?" She looked at the thousand or more people clamoring for the Rakes to begin. "Oh, no. . ."

"Oh, yes, winsome elf. Up you go," and he lifted her to the stage.

"Friends, this vision of loveliness is Miss Reilly Brooke. We're hopin' to drop the Miss soon. This dear lass saved the life of the finest guitar wielder we know- our American cousin, Trinity O'Ryan!"

And with that introduction and resultant applause, a guitar was thrust into Trinity's hands and the band rocketed.

Accordion, fiddle, pipes and two guitars- Trinity strummed a lively ballad to begin the set until he fit in, and then let his fingers pick the strings like a lead guitar player.

Reilly stood to the side. Indeed, Bridie and Ivy Rose were moving their transparent feet like tap dancers.

Ivy Rose drifted behind Reilly and gave her a push in Bridie's direction. Digging in her heels was pointless, still Reilly hesitated- senses on edge.

Soon the music took over, drawing her, compelling her to respond, and she tried a few steps in time with the uplifting tune, imitating Bridie and Ivy Rose. She dared to glance at the huge crowd and quailed. All those people. . . All that attention. . . But the music forced its way to the forefront of her mind. Who could be immune to this? The entire audience was moving.

A smile broke over Trinity's face, and with Bridie and Ivy Rose providing role models, Reilly's feet answered the lively Irish reel, playing with movements she'd never ventured to try before. Her skirts piped up until she realized, heartily grateful, that the dance steps required hands to remain at sides.

She lost her sense of dread and feeling out of place and just let go. With Bridie and Ivy Rose, a ghost on each side of her, she kicked up, following their lead- reveling in the unfamiliar essence of complete freedom.

Applause thundered as the band struck its last vibrato note. Breathless and bright-eyed, Reilly clapped along. No one noticed Flicker until he knelt before Trinity and extended a fiddle- no one except Bridie, whose ghostly eyes brimmed.

"I didn't know Trinity could play fiddle, too."

'Ah, Sweetlin', I don't believe the stringed instrument's been borned that that lad can't wring the heart out of. Tis so good to have him back to his old self,' Bridie sniffled.

'Reilly, just wait,' Ivy Rose was thoroughly elated, 'no one plays fiddle like my brother. . .well, except for B. . .'

But Reilly didn't catch the last bit as Trinity drew the bow across the stringed instrument under his chin. Catcalls and strident whistles vied with the fiddle's shrill preamble and the band exploded with a quick tempo.

Ivy Rose and Bridie tapped away; then, like chorus line professionals kicked up their heels synchronously, dancing in mid-air with gleeful abandon. Trinity danced and played, circling around Reilly until she imitated his steps.

The pair danced with the symbiotic rhythm of young lovers. Over the crowds' roaring approval, the band increased the tempo and unbelievably, picked it up again. Trinity with his bow hand racing across the fiddle strings eventually ceased dancing, and played, serenading Reilly in an Irish frenzy. Breathless from her dancing efforts, she stood spell-bound by his speed. The O'Ryan Rakes were on fire and burning the audience right along with them.

"Tired, winsome elf?"

"Hmmm," Reilly leaned into Trinity's side as they walked to the hotel.

"I could carry you," he offered.

It was nearly midnight and the gratified crowd slowly dispersed from the festival grounds.

"I'm OK," she murmured, "No, better than OK."

Inside the foyer of the hotel, the cousins headed for the bar.

"C'mon, Trinity! Night's young, and we've a shockin' drooth on us," they called.

"I'm walking Reilly to her room," he answered.

"Kate, lovely Kate, don't leave us. . ."

"You go on, I'm going to bed. Reilly and I are attending the Gaelic mass in the morning. I don't suppose you boys will make it?"

"Ah, well. . . I've got to see a man about a dog," excuse followed excuse. "We'll drink a pint to youse lovely lasses."

Trinity tipped Reilly's chin at room 417.

"Trinity, I had a deadly time. . ." Reilly started to say, but Trinity's lips interrupted and stole her breath.

"I'll see you tomorrow, probably around noon. Tell Kate to keep her cell on."

"Noon?"

Trinity's eyes glittered, "If I know my cousins, we'll close the hotel bar and then find another."

"Oh," she tried to hide the dismay this caused her.

"Good night, Reilly." Trinity turned to go, but something made him stop and turn back.

The look on Reilly's face. Reminiscent of that forlorn, little girl he first met and all the poignancy she'd dredged up. . .

Reilly wanted to say- don't go, don't drink, but Trinity was a man and she had no right. He wanted to party with his cousins. She dropped her wary, misty eyes as Trinity rejoined her.

Of course, you idiot, she's concerned, and why wouldn't she be? Her father died in a bar room brawl; her mother drinks every day; all those drunks at Chet's all the time, her past filled with her mother's drunken boyfriends, nights spent in bar parking lots when she was a baby. . .

"Reilly, sweetheart, will you please look at me?" he softly asked.

Reilly bit her lip, fear in her eyes- remembering, shy, trepidation chafing her insides.

"I may be up all night, but I don't drink as if there's no tomorrow. Never will. I'm not like my cousins, in that regard. I may have a beer, but more than that, I'll enjoy their company, and their slagging on me. I'll keep my eyes on them, keep them out of trouble and make sure they find their way to their beds. Understand?"

Although Reilly tried to keep it in check, a tear escaped, strolled down her cheek and Trinity drew her to him. "Don't be afraid, lass," he crooned.

45

"Want me to walk you in?" Trinity eyed the assortment of pick-ups and other vehicles parked outside Chet's sorry-excuse-for-a-home.

Why didn't the manager make him do something about it? Clean up this part of Red Wing. Poor old Mr. Clark probably couldn't deal with 'encounters'. Trinity hated the idea of Reilly's being in there.

His misgivings, though, couldn't compete with Reilly's. A guy tottered out of the dump, staggered to the back of the trailer and reappeared a minute later- his pants askew.

"Better not," Reilly took a deep breath, glad she'd overridden Trinity's objections and changed into her old clothes before the drive back to the dump. She grabbed her backpack.

"In case I haven't said it lately, I had a wonderful time. Thank you."

He laughed, "Only about 100 times on the way home and another 100 before we left Dublin." He gritted his teeth as another partier lurched around to the back of the dump.

"I'm escorting you in," he growled.

Hurriedly, before Reilly beat him to it, he jumped out of the Camaro and caught her at the steps.

"Hey, remember, I get your door," he gently reminded her.

Reilly was desperately afraid one of Chet's friends might mouth off. She prayed there wouldn't be any trouble, but she had enough experience watching drunks to know the distinct possibilities, and Trinity wore hard again. God, please, she prayed.

Duct tape hanging off its cracked window, the door screeched as Trinity opened it. He followed Reilly into the smoky den. Empty cans and dropped, crushed snacks littered counters, tables and floor space.

Every eye in the room turned to Reilly. She thanked her intuition for giving her the heads-up about donning her old clothes. At least, the bleary-eyed 'eejits', to use one of the Irish terms, wouldn't see something pretty, she thought.

But she was off base in her surmise.

Trinity's resolute stance behind her perked the drunks' curiosity about the non-descript girl- had to be something there for that guy to be interested.

"Trinity, hey man," Chet made nice to the grim-faced mechanic.

A grizzled man with a cigarette hanging from his lower lip rubbed his pot belly preparatory to an ill-advised remark. Chet stopped him.

Of the five men in his trailer, only Deke Tufrow did not know what Trinity was capable of and Chet knew Trinity could destroy them all with ease.

"I'll see you tomorrow, Reilly," he pressed her lower back, watched her, proprietarily, as she walked the gauntlet to her room.

"Reilly, have a good time?" her mother bumped into her in the hall.

"Yes, great. I'm pretty tired."

"Oh, well. . . See you tomorrow." Reilly caught the familiar smell of her mother's preferred drink in passing.

"Trinity, have a beer with us," Chet offered- playing hospitable host.

"No, thanks," he nodded at Reilly's mother.

Back in the Camaro, he whispered, "Bridie, if you can hear me, watch over my girl in that hellhole."

Reilly had to wait her turn for the bathroom. She listened for exiting footsteps, not caring to encounter any of Chet's friends anywhere, anytime, and especially, not in the close confines of the hall. Finally, the coast cleared. She rushed in, brushed her teeth. Her nose wrinkled at the mis-use of the toilet; hurriedly, she double-scrubbed her hands.

Heaven to hell, she murmured, and retreated to her sweatbox cupboard of a bedroom. With due diligence, she braced the old chair under the broken door knob.

I know how those prisoners felt in the old cowboy movies when they were put in solitary confinement outside in a box, she thought. In her long nightshirt, she was soaked in no time.

Sighing, she wished she'd brought a glass of water with her.

Demeaned. Drenched. Dehydrated. Ha! At least, her brain was working.

If she didn't feel quite so tired, she might laugh, or cry. . .

Righteous scrambled to the open window sill. Her tiny claws ticking on the aluminum frame, she perched precariously, sniffed and meowed.

"Hungry? I'm sorry I'm late, but you should have eaten with Wrench." Nevertheless, Reilly got up, opened a can, spooned the contents onto a small plate.

Despite the heat and the racket from down the hall, Righteous couldn't resist the gravy-laden goods. She bounded onto the mattress and onto the chest of drawers, attacking her dinner.

The gold kitten arched her back as Reilly stroked her.

"You enjoyed your time with Wrench while I was gone?"

Righteous trilled and rubbed her body against Reilly, one side then the other. The kitten sat up on her hind legs, softly batted Reilly's chin with her front paws until the girl leaned down to kiss her nose.

"I missed you, too. Someday, Righteous. . .someday. . . Less than a year to go. I promise we'll have our own place and it will be clean and cool in the summer and clean and warm in the winter and we'll sit and eat together."

Reilly adjusted her pillow. It was too hot to cuddle with Righteous or her lamb, so she left the lamb in the backpack, zipper half open. That way she could at least see the black face peeking out. The single small lamp from the chest of drawers threw enough light to dream by and dispel monsters.

'Darlin' Reilly, try to rest, Sweetlin'. Such a grand adventure you've had this weekend,' Bridie manifested.

"Bridie, I had such a wonderful time," Reilly murmured, heavy eyes closing. Heat or no, a body could only stay awake for so long.

A pleasant dream of baking cookies, Irish music playing in the background- tunes she'd heard at the Irish festival. A sense of impending company. Trinity would be here soon. . .

A knocking. . .but Trinity didn't need to knock. . .

The knocking sound grew louder, harder. Reilly's gut twisted.

Intuition barked. Her heart in her throat, she moaned, "Don't answer. . ."

GET OUT! GET OUT! A roar thrust itself between her and her dream.

Reilly's eyes flew open, startled as to her

whereabouts. She was lying in a pool of her own sweat. Righteous snarled, tail flared and flashed back and forth, ears flat back.

That noise. . . Reilly tried to get her bearings, felt weak, fuzzy-headed.

The noise in her dream. . . The chair braced under the door knob rattled, violently. That was not a knock. Pounding. . . Righteous growled as if to attack.

'Reilly, get out, Sweetlin'! Hurry!' Bridie drifted across her vision and sat in the chair, now vibrating from the siege on the other side of the door.

Reilly scrambled, fell, grabbed her backpack, shoved it out the window, eyed the glass opening. Oh, God, she whispered, it's the only way out. She wasn't sure if she'd get through or not- it seemed so small.

"GET AWAY," she screamed several times, to no avail. No one ever heard her, here. She hoisted herself to the opening on tip toes. Her hands went out and she pushed herself through, using the leverage of her hands against the outside of the trailer wall.

Her hips got stuck, the chair broke and the grizzled, chain smoker burst in.

Frantically, Reilly struggled to release the rest of her. Free, almost, yes. . . Mostly hanging out. . . A little bit mo. . .

Only to feel a hand snatch her ankle and begin to pull her back inside.

Reilly kicked out with her free foot, encountered something. Kicked again. . .

Screams turned to croaks- her throat so parched. Kick. . .

The man cursed and gripped her other foot. Reilly screamed as best she could in her parched state, both of her hands madly seeking to try and hold her in place while kicking at her would-be abductor and valiantly still trying to push herself out of the window. . .her body a living pawn in a vile tug-of-war game.

Growling, spitting, Righteous vaulted onto the attacker's head. Claws unsheathed, the kitten relentlessly raked at the drunk's face. Feline talons dug in far enough to guarantee future scars; blood streamed in the wake of their efforts as the angry kitten continued to wage a snarling war of attribution.

"Aaah," Tuff's screams now drowned out Reilly's. He had to lose his grip of the girl or lose his face, as the kitten kept on slashing at his skin. Feline teeth clamped down on his ear, piercing, tearing- remnants of wild heritage fully engaged.

Reilly fell headlong into the wild rosebush upon her sudden release. She tried to protect her face with her hands as best she could. Thorns tore at her exposed skin, but she'd not feel that for a while. Adrenalin and shock drowned other senses.

"Righteous!" She croaked-shouted. The spitting, snarling, screeching and cursing inside. . . How could the kitten survive?

"Righteous! Bridie, please help," she cried, wanting to run to a safe place, but unwilling to leave the kitten.

I'll have to go back in. . .

Her body convulsed uncontrollably- like a shock-induced icy plunge, even though the outside temperature was maintaining its daytime highs in the nineties- not to mention the extreme humidity.

Like a light switch swept off, all sound from within suddenly died. For a second, Reilly dared to hope.

Righteous appeared in the window and flew out like a flying squirrel. Reilly caught the descending kitten just as Nightmare at Red Wing stuck his head out the window. Long, bloodied scratches vied with spit and snot as he cursed, violently enraged.

"I'll get you," his cigarette-marred voice vowed and he started to exit from the window when a small bit of viable brain matter informed him of the impossibility of his pot-bellied form ever fitting through.

The petrified Reilly stalled, root-bound, kitten in arms and backpack hanging from a distressed arm. The face disappeared.

'RUN, REILLY, RUN!'

46

A hammering on the front door stirred four inebriated Irishmen, but not enough to cause them to shift or attempt to figure out why such a racket was being perpetrated.

'Hurry, Trinity, hurry,' Ivy Rose begged, bounding atop her brother, shuffling sheets.

Instantaneously breaking the fog of a deep sleep, Trinity jumped up, tripped over his shoes, pulled on a pair of jeans as he hastened to the door- all the while hollering for his dad. Wrench joined the hullabaloo with full-out barking.

Trinity stumbled over slow-to-rise cousins, fumbled sleepy-eyed with locks, disconnected them and swung open the door, stopping the pounding mid-thud.

"Reilly?" The frightened girl let loose of Righteous and fell into Trinity's chest, completely done-in. Her backpack dropped to the floor.

"Help me, Trinity," she sobbed, pitiably.

"What the. . ." His arms shot around her, supporting her.

His cousins, one by one, struggled to reach sensible frames of mind, and then errantly fell about rising to the occasion to attend the source of the uproar. Wrench tended quietly to Righteous with a solicitous regard for Reilly.

Trinity peered over her head, "Reilly, what's going on?" But he didn't receive an answer right away, as Reilly cried into his bare chest. Nothing outside; he half-carried her inside.

An anger he'd believed was pretty well extinguished in his lifetime, flared up with torrid vengeance.

He loosed Reilly's grip just enough to get her attention.

Her trembling body, her sodden eyes, cries. . . Night shirt?

"What happened, sweetheart?" The deadly tone of his voice couldn't break through to her. He gripped her chin while still supporting her with one hand, "Tell me."

'Reilly, don't let him go! No matter what, don't let him go. Whatever he says, do not let him go,' Bridie's weary warning seeped into her brain.

Oh, God, she silently prayed and fastened her fingers inside Trinity's belt loops, hanging on for all she was worth.

"One. . .of them. . ." she hiccoughed and stuttered, "b...b...broke into. . .m...my. . .room. W...woke. . .m...me. I. . .t...tr...tried. . .to g...get out the w...win...window. . . He g...g...gr...grabbed m...my f...foot. . ."

Fearing the worst, Trinity tried to un-wrap her from him- his entire soul instantaneously bent on destruction. His body electrified with the need to rain hell on anyone who'd dare hurt his girl. He'd kill. . .the son. . .

"Son, what's going on here?" Pat, in a bathrobe, touched Trinity's vibrating shoulder.

"Pat, some bollocks hurt the lass," one of the cousins had defeated his stupor, caught the gist of what had happened and whispered in abject astonishment.

'Don't let go of him, Sweetlin',' Bridie faintly hovered behind Reilly, desperation and exhaustion in her ghostly voice. 'Don't let him go.'

"I'll kill him," Trinity seethed, still attempting to untangle Reilly from his jeans.

"Trinity, I...I got away. . .out the w...window. . . R...Righteous tore off h...his f...face," Reilly, through her sobs, rushed the battered words. Got to keep Trinity calm. . . Must keep him here. . .

"I'm going to tear off his f*** head and. . ." He was unaware of his grip on Reilly's arms hurting her as he tried to put her aside. He had to get out or explode with irate vengeance.

"Trinity, man, get a grip," all four cousins were on full alert now, ready to block Trinity's exit- at definite risk to their own lives.

"GET. . .OUT. . .OF. . .MY. . .WAY," he gritted, forcefully trying to displace Reilly who clung like a tenacious leech.

"Trinity, please hold me. Please don't let me go. Please don't. . .let me go," Reilly begged. Her terror for her own well-being was now replaced by fears for Trinity. Maybe coming here wasn't the best idea, but she had nowhere else to go. And Trinity would, surely, kill that. . .

Totally enervated, she felt herself about to fall. Between the shaking, the terrified after-math of the attack on her, the racing barefoot to Trinity's door, the depletion of her body's fluids, the overwhelming roller coaster of emotions. . . Only adrenalin, fed by the knowledge of what Trinity was capable of, kept her from fainting- the worst possible thing she could do at that moment.

Her knees buckled, only her fingers kept her from sinking to the floor- her fingers and Trinity's arms, which alternately held her and then tried to disengage her. Picking her up, he moved to place her in the recliner and. . .

"Son, listen to me. Reilly. . .Reilly is here and she needs you with her. I'm going back to Chet's and find out just what the hell is going on."

His words weren't penetrating his son's blank look of rage.

"Trinity, don't go off half-cocked- Reilly needs you. You'll destroy her completely if you go. Son? Do you hear me? If you go, Reilly will only suffer more."

The anger draughts swelling Trinity's sails slowly began to ebb, as Reilly's grip and cries and finally his father's words found a chink.

"Reilly?" His father was right. Reilly needed him, more than he needed to. . .

"Trinity, please d…don't let me go," and these words evoked the memory of when she'd stayed death for him. How could a small body tremble with such ferocity?

"You're sure. . .you're sure. . .you're all. . .right?" he whispered.

"I g…got away. Please h…hold me," she creaked, completely tuckered.

"I've got you, love; I've got you," he huskily murmured, with slumping, surrendering countenance.

His father's hand settled on his shoulder, "Take care of her, Son."

"We'll go wit' you, Pat," the cousins volunteered.

"Frank, I'd appreciate it if you'd come with me. The rest of you stay here." Of the four Irishmen, Frank was the most temperate. Pat was not arming for a warpath; Reilly was safe.

Even with Trinity's decision to stay, he wasn't taking any chances on his son changing his mind- eluding the remaining relatives and murdering the ba. . ., even if he deserved it.

"Let me get the lass a glass of water," someone offered.

Trinity sat with Reilly on his lap, his jaws clenched hard enough to crack nuts. His hands absent-mindedly stroked her back.

"Dad, take some bags, get Reilly's things. She's not going back there," he directed, with finality.

Frank pulled a few grocery bags from a drawer, pulled a shirt over his head. Pat hastily threw on clothes and with a last look at Reilly shivering in Trinity's arms, left.

"Here, lass, have a drink." Reilly's fingers shook too much for her to hold the glass.

Trinity took it from her, "Easy, Reilly, drink it slow, sweetheart."

"Looks like yer pretty scratched up t'ere," Flicker nodded at the thorn-inflicted welts bleeding on her legs and arms.

Michael placed a sheet over Reilly's bare legs, covering where her long night shirt had ridden high up her thighs.

Trinity gently fingered the long, weeping scratches. Reilly winced when he touched a particular spot. Looking closely, he swore and extracted a thorn. His senses finally noted something else.

"Reilly, love, you're soaking wet," he murmured.

"N...no air. . .c...conditioning. . .in. . .my room," she stuttered.

The chill in the living room was adding to the toll of the rest of the nightmare, causing her to shiver uncontrollably all over again.

"Jaaysus, Mary and Joseph and all the saints," the cousins chimed together, as Trinity swore under his breath. The heat inside her room without a/c on a day with 90 some degree temperatures, how? Why?

"We better get you into some dry clothes," Trinity lifted her.

"Wh...where's R...Righteous? S...she and B...," she broke off in time, "She. . .sa...saved m...me."

"By the looks of the little darlin', she's gettin' her props," Flicker hitched his thumb.

Righteous sat in Ivy Rose's lap on the coffee table-bathing, paying special attention to her claws and feet. Wrench groveled at the kitten's feet, whining and flicking out his tongue to help with the feline ablutions.

"You're sure you're all right, sweetheart?"

Bridie gave Reilly a significant look.

"He...he didn't get m...me, Trinity," her glazed, truthful, sodden eyes met his.

Trinity closed his eyes in grateful relief. Most of him still needed to beat the sh. . . out of the malefactor, but he'd wait. He rose and carried Reilly into the bathroom.

"I'll get a shirt for you to sleep in, and maybe I can find an old pair of work-out pants," he made to leave the bathroom.

"Don't l…leave m…me, p…please," fright lingered on her tear-streaked face. Not that she didn't believe him, but she didn't fully trust him not to renege on his promise and return to the dump.

"Reilly, I'll never leave you. Here," and he hoisted her back into his arms and carried her to his bedroom, set her on his bed and tossed various clothes around looking for something suitable for her to wear. Settling on the best of a bad lot, he showed her a short-sleeved sweatshirt and sweat-shorts with a draw string waist.

"How about a shower, little one, and I'll tend to those welts?" He tried a conciliatory smile- exceedingly difficult to do.

"W…will y…you stay…with me?" The thought of him seeing her without clothes didn't enter her mind; she only knew not to let him out of her sight.

"I'll stand guard at the door. With my back turned, like in the old westerns, OK?"

"W…will you t…talk to m…me?" Trinity half-smiled at her persistence in keeping him close. He noticed her teeth were chattering.

"Hurry up and get in the tub, before you shiver to death, Reilly. Would you like it if I sing to you while you shower?" He forced a bit of levity.

"Y…yes," she began to strip as he turned his back.

"Flicker, bring some of those Gatorades and a pitcher of water, please," he called down the hall.

Singing while Reilly showered took some doing, but it helped stave off thoughts of what might have happened to Reilly without Bridie and Righteous' intervention. Maybe later, he'd get the full story from Bridie.

'Is Reilly OK, Trinity?' Ivy Rose drifted into view, outside the bathroom door. She craned her neck to see around her big brother.

Trinity stopped his singing, "She's going to be all right, sis, don't worry."

"Trinity?" Reilly frantically cried from the shower. He picked up the song again. An old fighting tune seemed appropriate- THE GARRYOWEN- something to stem his pent-up agitation.

He rifled through the medicine cabinet, dug out hydrogen peroxide and gauze patches for swabbing, bandages, some ointment. . . Cranking on an extra light, he carefully inspected Reilly's torn arms and legs, found two more thorns.

His heart cringed and his anger smoldered at the damage to her skin, superficial or not. Seeing Reilly hurt in any way- a broken fingernail would have qualified- was infinitely worse than receiving the wounds himself. And he would have preferred it if the hurts were his. But to see her frightened, too, acted like arrows thrust into his heart.

"I called Kate. It would be best to have another woman here. . . As far as. . ." Pat shrugged, dropped his head in his hands, demoralized and nauseated from the spectacle he'd witnessed.

Trinity had convinced Reilly to try to sleep. He'd given up his bed to her, unpacked her lamb and left the bed-side lamp on, adjusting it to a lower light setting.

Righteous and Wrench hopped into bed with her. Ivy Rose crooned a lullaby.

Trinity waited the lengthy interval until Reilly's breathing evened before joining his dad.

With Kate's entrance into the O'Ryans' home, Pat and Frank explained what they'd found at Chet's.

The partiers had ostensibly left. The door was unlocked- no sign of Chet or Reilly's mother.

Poking his head into the master bedroom, he saw both of them passed out, fully clothed. Grimacing at the stench of cigarette smoke and vomit, Pat and Frank headed to Reilly's room at the end of the hall.

Torn off one hinge, the door canted half-way into the small, sweltering room. The single window was broken, and sprawled unconscious, half on the bed, was a raucously snoring drunk. His face, twisted to one side, displayed Righteous' art work. A spate of vomit spewed across the mattress. The body was also decorated with bits of clay pottery, and a shamrock plant, its roots peering from what remained of its potting soil, rested on the assailant's ear, sort of a mad cross between a headstone and a trophy.

Pat had motioned for Frank to gather Reilly's things, which filled one bag- her work shoes, three pairs of jeans, seven shirts and a handful of underwear.

A last hint of intuition made Pat cradle the trophy shamrock plant in his hands. No trace of Reilly remained. Frank had bagged the last cans of cat food.

Trinity listened impassively to his dad. At the mention of the shamrock plant, he caught sight of Bridie sitting on the kitchen counter, fondly running her fingers through the three-leafed plant. His father had set it in a bowl with a small amount of water.

Bridie glanced up at Trinity. 'Did you think I'd let some bleedin' eejit hurt the dear girl? I did what I could.'

Trinity dropped his head into his crossed arms. It was 4:20 a.m. Everyone was bone-tired, but certain points had to be cleared up.

"Should we call the police?" Kate ventured.

"If we do, a social worker will get involved. They're liable to take Reilly away," Pat began, massaging the back of his neck.

"She's not going anywhere," Trinity averred.

"I'd like to check on her," Kate rose, her concern torn between Trinity and Reilly.

"She's in my room," he called to Kate.

Kate's heart clenched, watching Reilly sleep- a stuffed lamb in one arm and a kitten curled in the other. Wrench at her feet.

Kitten and dog lifted their heads to view the intruder and determine the trespasser's motive. Satisfied, feline and canine promptly re-drifted off to sleep. Kate clicked off the light and returned to the living room.

"What will her mother think? I wonder."

"You think that woman cares?" Frank asked. "The lass slept in a room with no lock, no a/c. . ."

"She may move away and take Reilly with her after she hears about last night," Kate said.

"Reilly's not going anywhere," Trinity firmly repeated.

"Son, she's an underage. . ."

"If I have to elope with her, she'll not be going with that woman," he answered his dad.

"And where would you go?" His father touched Trinity's knee, alarm in his soul over his volatile, youngest son.

"There are states where 17-year olds can marry," Trinity replied, rubbing his blood-shot eyes.

"But you'd not be able to come back here, with her underage and you 24. . . They might imprison you."

"Then, I'd stay away until she's 18. Whatever I have to do I. . ."

A shrill scream rent the stressed air, making everyone jump to their feet.

Trinity raced to the source, swore at the darkened room and flipped the light switch to reveal pandemonium.

Wrench whining, cowered on the floor. Righteous had fur fluffed out like she'd been electrocuted and Reilly, blankets tangled and tossed about her, was curled in a fetal position in the corner, muffling frightened screams and squeezing her lamb in a panicked fit.

"Reilly, sweetheart," Trinity's arms swept her up and into his lap. "I'm here. It's all right. Everything's all right, I promise." He rubbed her trembling back and smothered the poor lamb as he held Reilly close.

"I…I woke up. . .and. . .it. . .was so black. I didn't. . .kn…know wh…where I w…was. . ." she sobbed into Trinity's neck.

Gently, he soothed her, "It's OK, Kate accidently turned off the light." His heart in his throat, he gulped, kissed the top of her head, "You're where you belong, love, in my arms."

47

"I want to see my daughter," a perfectly made-up woman confronted Frank when he opened the door.

Reilly slept in the safe harbor of Trinity's scent, emanating from his pillow, his sheets and blankets. With Righteous' purring and Wrench's snuffed doggie snores and a great sleeping temperature, she probably could have slept the day away. Several days away.

On a trip to the bathroom, Trinity heard a stirring as three live bodies and a stuffed lamb rearranged themselves in his bed. He stepped in to investigate.

Thankfully, Reilly wasn't suffering nightmares after. . . Trinity took a deep breath and sought to calm himself as Bridie fondly petted his head. He bent to lightly kiss Reilly's forehead.

"Sleep mo ghra milis daor; you're safe from now on, I promise. Sleep all you want," he whispered.

By 11 a.m., the resident O'Ryans and their guests had sequentially risen to nature calls and hunger pangs. If Reilly had her druthers, she would have remained abed the entire day, cocooned in safety, but she knew there would be music to face. Consequences of the previous night. That, and Bridie telling her to 'rise, shine and be strong'.

In vacating his bedroom, Reilly shyly cast about, looking for Trinity, and her stomach let it be known that the smell of coffee and frying bacon was enough of a good morning prelude- her body required food. But deep inside her gut, a familiar sensation lurked, denying that particular necessity.

"Ah, winsome elf," Trinity's chair fell back as he vaulted up to reach her.

Standing in front of her, he tipped her chin and inspected every square inch of visible flesh, starting with her face. A haunted look lingered in her eyes which timidly lowered. He tried to gauge the state of her mind. Guessing would have to suffice, until he got her alone and they could talk.

"You OK, Reilly?" She nodded as well as possible with her chin in the air. "Sorry," he turned her loose.

"Reilly, dear, are you hungry?" Kate called out as she manned the stove and slapped at impatient, roving fingers.

"Ouch, woman," Flicker scowled and sucked at the burn mark the hot spatula had left on his knuckles.

"Serves you right, wait your turn," she chastised him.

"Ah, you can tell this one is married to an O'Ryan," Skipper nodded to Kate. "She's just like me mother."

Reilly eyed the food. Her stomach grumbled, but she felt sure it was not simply with hunger.

"I...I'm not really hungry," she massaged her mid-section.

Trinity pulled a chair out from a cousin's behind, helped Reilly into it, as the unaware cousin sat down-crashed down to the floor, amidst snickers. His bacon was caught on the fly by Wrench and a piece skittering on the floor was cadged by Righteous.

"You've got to eat something," Trinity cautioned. Bridie agreed and pointed to homemade, peppermint tea bags.

"How about a bowl of oats, a slice of toast and some tea?" Pat offered. "It's what I eat when my stomach is off."

'Peppermint tea,' Bride urged from her perch atop a kitchen cabinet.

"OK," Reilly agreed. Distracting topics of conversation punted about. She acted as if she were listening, but her mind was rolling crazily, her gut cringing in anticipation, and she caught herself constantly checking the door. Fear welled up inside her- certain old fears she thought/hoped she'd seen the last of.

The clock registered one before Pat, with Kate accompanying him, bit the bullet and walked back to Chet's. Reilly expressed heavy odds against her mother rising before then.

As it happened, Reilly was off base. Chet and her mother were still abed. Pat was furious. When no one answered his repeated knocking, he slammed the front door into the wall, twice.

Disgusted, his eyes narrowed at the mess left in the kitchen and living room. How could one get used to this? He hammered on Chet's bedroom door. Kate braced herself from the bile rising in her throat. The intruder's snores rattled from Reilly's room.

"What the. . ." Chet rolled over and fell out of bed. He swiped at his crusty lips, bleary eyes and rats' nest hair.

"O'Ryan? What are you doing here?"

"Get Reilly's mother up," Pat demanded, barely masking the ire he endured. Kate rested her hand on his forearm, sympathetically offering support.

Reilly's mother, bedraggled clothes, stumbled toward the company in the doorway. Awkwardly, as she knew she didn't look her best, she swallowed the foul taste in her mouth, frowned and asked, "Is something wrong?"

Pat snorted, resisted the urge to put his fist through a wall and curse.

"You might say that," he gritted. "Do you know where Reilly is?"

"Reilly?" The mother appeared confused. Was this some kind of a joke?

"Yes, Reilly, your daughter," Pat did not resist a swear word this time.

The mother's hands went to her waist in a defensive posture, "In her room, of course." Did he think she was stupid?

"Would you care to check?" Pat swallowed repugnance, but the Irish was up in him and this made it extremely difficult to fully control anger- cursing sufficed, barely.

Kate stepped aside, let the woman pass. She turned down the hall. Nothing hit her that anything was amiss until she stepped fully into the cupboard-excuse for a bedroom that was Reilly's. The half-canted door and broken chair never registered.

But the sight of a guy lying half-sprawled on Reilly's bed, snoring in his own vomit- that got her.

"What the f***!"

She turned into Pat and Kate, rushed by them, headed to the kitchen, side-swiped the befuddled Chet as she returned with a wood-handled broom in her hand.

A motherly vengeance flashed in her eyes as she cannoned through the hall. She does care, flashed through Kate's mind.

"Wait a minute. . . What are you doing?" Chet staggered after her.

"Where's my daughter?" The mother screamed and began thrashing the body occupying her daughter's bed.

Pat stood patiently, arms crossed, enjoying the sight of the insensible male form absorbing enough blows to sufficiently bring his miserable hide to some form of life.

Chet, in a state of shock at the ramifications of what he was witnessing, struggled to pull the broom from his girlfriend's hands. He received a blow to his gut for his efforts.

Tuff, not so tough now, tried to cram his body under the bed in search of safety.

With a particularly vulgar swear word, the mother broke the broom's handle on the backside of Tuff and promptly searched for another weapon.

"Mrs. Brooke," Pat offered into the shit-storm, "Reilly is with us, at my house."

He gave her one chance to ask the appropriate question and when she didn't, he ushered Kate out with choice expletives riding loudly in his wake.

"I'd like to see my daughter," the mother requested of Frank. "Please," she added, as the door remained blocked. Frank glanced over his shoulder and took his time about stepping aside.

Reilly feared this moment. Her body began to tremble and her gut pitched. The guarded eyes were back, shell clamming shut. Trinity smoldered- his Reilly had come so far in the past months; looking at her now with slumped shoulders, haunted eyes. . . It was all he could do to hold himself in line.

Reilly stood as her mother entered the living room, but her knees weren't in a frame of mind to support her. Trinity moved to stand close behind her. One arm snaked protectively around her waist. His shoulders squared and his teeth gritted upon feeling her shiver.

"I've got you, Reilly," he whispered.

For the next few minutes, she'd relish the feel of his arm- the last peace she'd know until she turned 18. Her backpack was ready. This is what ran through her mind. This and all the times when her mother simply announced, 'let's go.'

No time to pack, no time for good-byes. Through the years, Reilly had stopped making friends- too hard to leave, knowing she'd never see them again. Just grab her ever-present backpack and get in the car for the next act of. . .moving on.

Only this time, there would be good-byes. . .extremely painful ones. But not for long. Trinity's phone numbers were inside the backpack and wired into her brain. Bridie said she'd see her. . . God, how she would miss. . .

Reilly's mother inspected every set of condescending

eyes cast her way. No matter, she had on her make-up. She couldn't see Bridie or Ivy Rose, but on some level, she felt she was persona-non-grata to a kitten and a dog- both stood like resolute guardians in front of Reilly.

"Reilly," her mother couldn't ignore the long, red welts on Reilly's bare legs below the cut-off sweat-shorts and those on her arms- the arms Reilly rested atop Trinity's forearm.

Dissembling, as was her natural want, Reilly's mother addressed her audience as equably as speaking of the weather, "I'd like to see my daughter, alone."

The unfriendly contingent reluctantly rose, one by one and slowly made their way outside. Each of the cousins cast a supportive wink Reilly's way. Pat and Kate offered smiles of encouragement. Trinity didn't budge. Neither did Righteous, Wrench or Bridie.

"I said, alone," the mother repeated, ostensibly, totally at-ease. A practiced drama queen loved nothing better than to flaunt her stuff.

Trinity's jaw clenched ever so slightly and there was no mistaking the defiance in his eyes.

"Reilly?" he murmured, questioning. Reilly increased the pressure of her arms on his and leaned into his chest.

"I'm not going anywhere," he seethed.

The mother rolled her eyes, scoffed. "Whatever. Reilly, are you all right?"

"Does she look all right?" Trinity shot back.

Ignoring him, the mother continued, "Why didn't you yell for help?"

'Sweetlin', you hold onto yer man and hold onto herself. Tis thankful, I am, I sent Ivy Rose to the other room. Holler for help, indeed! In the girl's own room, yet! Jaysus, Mary and Joseph, the woman has her gall!' Bridie was not shy about expressing her feelings on the matter.

Reilly barely heard Bridie, her heart was thudding so loud. She thought she might even faint as her breathing became ragged and black shades sidelined her sight. Trinity whispered in her ear. The mother seemed absolutely oblivious to Reilly's distress.

"Holler? I screamed and screamed from the first. . ." her voice cracked.

Reilly's mother took a deep breath, coughed and wished for a cigarette.

"Get your things, let's go," the mother's words- the guillotine descending.

Reilly bit the inside of her lip. Her braces helped in this regard and she tasted blood. In fact, the blood rushed to her head and contrary to the other times, Reilly felt a surge of anger. Why should she be punished? She hadn't done anything wrong!

"I'm not going," she said. Reilly didn't care if her ribs fractured, she held Trinity's arm to her with all her might.

'Good lass,' Bridie cheered.

"Well, if that's the way you feel, I'll try to work things out with Chet. But if not, we're leaving."

"I'm not. . .leaving. . .here," Reilly clarified.

"Right! You're going to shack up with your boyfriend, end up pregnant and on welfare. . ." the mother smirked.

Reilly gulped for air, feeling as if she were drowning.

Trinity answered for her, "Reilly won't make the same sordid mistakes you do."

"Oh, really? And who's going to stop her?" Reilly's mother sneered, her face twisting with a flare of derision.

"I'll protect her."

'And me,' Ivy Rose popped in and grabbed Reilly's hand.

'And I will,' Bridie stood by them.

Righteous laid her ears back- tail twitching, she spit and snarled, and Wrench, not to be outdone, growled menacingly.

Her mother looked askance at the dog and kitten, blinked a couple times.

"Yeah, right! Protect her, huh? You're a walking chick magnet, that irresistible combination of angel and devil! I know your kind. You buy her diamond earrings, talk sweet, get her in your bed or wherever. . ."

"No!" Reilly shouted. "No, it's not like that! It's not like that at all! He hasn't touched me," fury brought Reilly out of her fearful shell.

Trinity loosed his grip as Reilly thrust against his hold. At last, Reilly's mother got the sense she no longer had the upper hand of her daughter, underage or not.

Reilly was. . . She was 17?- the fact deigned to seep in.

Where had all the years gone?

Physically, she couldn't hold Reilly against her will. Legally, well, she couldn't even consider that route, especially, not after last night's fiasco.

She didn't believe for one moment that this. . .stud hadn't had her daughter. Impossible. . . But, had Reilly ever lied?

Reilly watched her mother coming to terms with an unconceived possibility.

"Don't you believe in anything good? Mom?"

48

The mother shook off Reilly's question with, "Just be ready when I come for you." And she stalked out the door.

Reilly collapsed into Trinity's chest. The confrontation with her mother left her shaking to the point that without Trinity's saving arm, she'd have slunk to the ground- a boneless mess.

"It's over, Reilly, come and sit. . ." But Reilly's gut had considerately waited to fully protest. She clutched her stomach with one hand and her mouth with the other and leaning against the hall wall, stumbled to the bathroom.

Trinity held her hair out of the way as she gagged out her travails. Over and over her body bucked, heaving up her small breakfast. He gently wiped her pale face when it seemed there was nothing more to be rid of, and carried her back to the recliner.

The cousins, Pat, his older son and Kate lounged about, trying not to look as concerned as they felt.

"I think. . ." Pat Jr. began, but closed his mouth with the dire warning Trinity shot him.

With all the attention covertly focused on her, added to her painful, grumbling gut, Reilly wanted desperately to hide.

"Trinity," she murmured, "I…I think I'll lie down."

"That's a good idea, Reilly. Try and get some more rest," Kate agreed.

Reilly knew they'd discuss her as soon as she was out of earshot- her future tossed between the O'Ryan clan and her mother.

Either way, she had no more strength- no reserves to discuss anything as innocuous as the weather, let alone her future.

But Trinity had other ideas. He supported her to his room, closed the door behind them.

"Reilly, I know what you're trying to do. I won't let you surrender. Whatever it takes, I'll not let you return to that haunted. . ." he looked at Bridie clicking her heels together while she hovered upon his dresser. "No offense, Bridie."

'None taken, lad.'

"I'll not let you turn back into that haunted, guarded kid I saw picking trash out of the bushes."

"You don't know what it's like drifting from place to place at...at her moment's notice," Reilly searched for her backpack. A streak of panic hit when she didn't see it right away.

Trinity followed her frantic eyes, "Reilly, I put the damn bag in my closet." He pushed open the closet door, "See," he pointed to the shelf above his hanging clothes. Her flagrant relief bothered him no end.

"I told her I wouldn't go, but I have no place to go to," tears streamed.

"She can't make you. . ."

"You don't know her. She can make anyone do anything. She talked the banker out of my inheritance. She can lay a guilt trip a time traveler couldn't deal with. She. . ."

"Nonsense. Look, I know about suffering, sweetheart," his heart contracted. "You stood up to her. Stay here, Reilly. It's that simple, just stay here. But if you feel you can't, I'll visit you, come get you. . . You call the shots. Just remember, I love you. She can't take you far enough that I won't come for you."

Reilly buried her face in her hands. Trinity deplored the sensation of helplessness. "Bridie," he appealed to the ghost.

'Leave us for a bit, lad,' Bridie reassured Trinity as Reilly sank into herself- curled on his bed, covered up, groped for her lamb and closed her eyes.

Outside, Wrench whined to be let in and Righteous scratched at the door, meowing. Door ajar, Trinity turned to leave with a parting, loving glance at his girl- allowing the animals entry in his stead.

Bridie mentally counted to ten once Trinity left. 'Reilly, bring out the cards. You'll be more inclined to listen if the cards give you something to think about first.'

"I...I'd rather not, Bridie. I'd just like to sleep. . ."

'Of course, you would. But that's the old route. I'll ask you one more time to bring out the cards. My energies have been mightily tried dealing with that bleedin' bollocks- what with dancin' like an eruptin' volcano in the chair blockin' the door and bustin' a perfectly good pot over his head last night. Ghosts do not have unlimited powers to physically rearrange things in the living world.'

'Can I help, Bridie?' Ivy Rose walked through her brother's closed door.

'I'm afraid not, little one. If you would please give us a few minutes?'

Ivy Rose drifted toward the door, quietly compliant, but stopped short.

'Reilly, please get up, Trinity is so sad. He doesn't know how to help you,' Ivy Rose implored the silently weeping Reilly before she disappeared through the door.

"Down, despair, de. . ."

'STOP IT!' Bridie raised her voice in a commanding tone worthy of a general.

Reilly smothered her tears, wiped at her quivering lips, winced as her lower lip caught against her braces. The taste of blood and Bridie's reprimand had her sitting up, repentant and querulous, but still shaken.

"Bridie, if I have to go. . .we'll still be able to talk, like you said?" Reilly reflected on all the things she'd miss, even resolutely knowing she'd find her way back in less than ten months.

Would Trinity wait? There were so many pretty girls without 'issues'. She felt her heart creak.

Bridie sighed with exaggerated impatience.

'Sweetlin', there are ghosts who are bound to people as Ivy Rose is bound to her brother. Other ghosts are viable in particular places. I am an independent ghost. If you call me, I will be there for you, as I've told you before. Now, no more tangents. No more borrowin' trouble. No more forecastin' a future when you do not have that expertise. Draw the cards out. Allow them to spit out what you need to learn.'

Reverently, Reilly retrieved her backpack and drew the old deck from its drawstring pouch. She found a modicum of solace in shuffling, as if the cards were singing to her. When she intuited the correct time for cutting them, she found her fingers accepting the divisions offered.

Her hand hovered over the three cuts until one sang its prominence. She overturned the deck's selection.

A gold-haired woman with a determined look, clad in a linen tunic with leggings and brown leather boots, stood in a green field.

About her neck was a gold Celtic torc. On her wrist- a matching bracelet.

Odd designs were drawn on her cheeks. In her hand rested a sword that would have seemed too big for her, but the woman carried it with ease in an 'en guarde' position.

At her feet, eyeing the ground was a small, gray animal- a badger. Reilly had only seen a badger's picture once, but intuitively, she knew this animal with its white and dark face.

'Tell me what you see, Dearest,' Bridie instructed.

"The woman looks ready to fight," easy to see, thought Reilly.

'Go on.'

"She is standing her ground. She looks rather formidable. Am I supposed to stay here? Fight my mother?"

'You tell me, lass.' As ever, Bridie refused to 'tell' Reilly- the mystery was hers to decipher.

Reilly set the card in her palm for a minute and then she turned it over and back again.

"It's not about simply fighting in a physical sense," Reilly paused.

She recalled the day her mother had brought her to Red Wing Trailer Court. She thought back on all her accumulated fears: the insecurity of having no roots, no safe haven to call her own, her mother's shuffling her from house to house with all the boyfriends- most of them not friendly to a reserved kid, the lack of funds, lack of time to have friends or a pet or even- she lifted her eyes to the stuffed lamb Trinity had given her (he'd told her Ivy Rose had picked it out for his future girl)-a toy to keep through childhood, the dirt, bugs, drunks, lies. . .

She also remembered her grandparents, good times with them, and the love they'd imbued her with for cooking and gardening. Briefly, she cast weary thoughts over the dirty trailer Chet owned and the bugs and the lack of locks or a/c, trying to sleep in a sweltering closet, the attack, Righteous, Bridie, Trinity. . .

"I have to fight not to return to the girl I used to be. I have to fight myself, my not retreating into myself, hiding in my dreams. . . It's hard, Bridie," Reilly choked on a sob.

'Life is not always easy,' Bridie sympathized. 'The more trials you come through- still standing, the greater your strength; your inner strength requires testing to grow. Weakness is not allowin' yourself to make it through the rough spots, to keep on, to persevere intact and strengthen.

Over time, you learn to believe, to know, there is nothing you can not work through. Build on what you've learned over the past months.

Refuse to surrender to defeat- to crawl into your old shell again. Take everything you've learned and be the stronger for it.'

Bridie watched Reilly absorb her words and shore up her backbone. The girl pushed her hair back from her eyes.

"What about this animal?" Reilly gently fingered the picture.

'Ah, you'd not be knowin' the significance of that one. A badger is grounded and can stand against overwhelmin' odds. He is courageous. If he retreats into the ground for a period of time, it's not to dissolve in despair, but to rise and fight again in the moment he chooses.

Through determination and courage, he uses the energies of the earth and being grounded to move forward.

A warrior grows spiritually by remaining clear and calm through adverse circumstances. She does not surrender to her fears, but puts them in perspective, acknowledges their existence, plans accordingly, and moves ahead.'

Reilly traced the figure of the sword-wielding woman and the badger at her feet. "I must not lock myself back inside the tower."

'There's my girl,' Bridie congratulated Reilly and patted her hair.

"Thank you, Bridie. I…I will try to make you proud of me," Reilly's lips experimented with a smile of sorts.

'I'm already proud of you, Reilly. I want you to be proud of you.'

49

Reilly took a short nap after talking with Bridie. She rose with a plan in mind, resigned that no matter what happened in the next few days, she would face it with calm fortitude. Her future was in her hands, she would deal with it. As hard as it might be to do.

Shedding the safety of Trinity's sweat-shorts and shirt, she looked to her own clothes which he'd placed on his dresser. It was weird seeing her underclothes folded on his dresser. She tried not to think of what he thought of her old cotton underwear. In the mirror, she took a long, last, admiring look at her birthday earrings. It wasn't fair to him.

She asked Trinity if they might talk, alone, maybe at Bridie's. Skeptical of what she had in mind, he agreed, retrieved the Camaro keys and despite his brother's 'we need to talk about all of this', Trinity nodded at his dad and guided Reilly into the passenger seat of his muscle car.

The short drive was silent and heavy with portent. He had the distinct feeling he wouldn't like what was coming, but he kept hold on his patience. He knew what he wanted and nothing and nobody could take her from him.

With arms holding her stomach, Reilly walked to the willow-hidden picnic table, admiring the fruitful harvest on the way. Sad to think, it might not be put to good use, sad to think about. . .

"Trinity," she began, once they were seated facing each other. "I'm sorry I've been such a baby."

"Reilly, no one thinks you're a baby, least of all, me."

Trinity wanted to hold her, but Reilly had set up the distance. Instead, he grinned, "You can always be my baby."

Reilly bit the inside of her mouth. Don't cry, she mentally berated herself- don't cry anymore. Gathering her thoughts, she laid them out.

"If I. . .if I have to leave here. . ."

Trinity started to object, but Reilly's fingers settled on his fingers to forego him.

"If I leave here, I…I will come back when I'm 18. Until then, it's not fair to you. . ." she began to take out her earrings.

He caught her hands and held them captive in his.

"You will leave those earrings in. They're yours whether you stay or go. They are yours, do you understand? They are safe in your ears. And I…I got you this, too."

On her ring finger he placed a silver Claddagh ring. "The hands represent friendship, the heart- love, and the crown is for loyalty. Worn this way with the heart facing yours, it tells the world, you are my girl, you are taken. This ring is where it belongs," as my heart is safe in your hands, he instinctively knew. "I was going to save it for. . ." he shrugged.

"You don't have to go. She has no power over you," he continued.

"She's my mother, regardless of what that really means, but you're right, she has no power over me any longer. I know what I want of my life."

"Tell me, Reilly," he lifted her hands, opened them and kissed her palms. "Tell me what you want."

Reilly looked around at the peaceful surroundings, "I want a home like Bridie's, with land to garden. I want to learn everything she'll teach me. I'd like to help people the way she did. I want to work in a small town, here in Ryan," she hitched a shoulder. "At the diner, if they'll let me come back. . ."

"Is that all?" Trinity's eyes clouded, was she giving up on their being together?

"No," Reilly blushed, "but in ten months, maybe you'll find someone else. . ." She tore her eyes away, blinked impending tears she could not control.

Trinity put both of her hands in one of his and his other hand brought her chin to face him.

"I should probably be magnanimous and say you're too young to settle for me without dating other guys, but I'm not feeling that unselfish."

Without hesitation, Trinity confidently continued, "You feel like Bridie's home is a home- a haven to you. My heart feels at home with you. I feel, positively, that we're supposed to be together and I'll not let go of that."

A corner of his mouth tilted up. A dimple came into play. More than anything, Reilly wanted to touch that endearing Trinity trait.

"I love you, Trinity. Nothing will change that. I'm much older than you believe. Seventeen is just a number," she averred.

Trinity's heart somersaulted. This was the first time she'd said that she loved him. And she hadn't ducked her eyes when she said it. Those deep green eyes with their velvet sincerity. His grin turned into a full-blown smile.

"What about college?" he asked, trying to cover all bases.

"I don't need college for what I want to do. The University of Bridie O'Connair is most instructive," Reilly chuckled.

'Here, here,' Bridie crowed her approval.

"What about you, Trinity? Are you happy enough here? I…I mean with the garage and all?"

"Yeah, I am, I'm the Mr. Fix-It. Cars, tractors- anything that runs- I can repair. Heck, I've had women bring me sewing machines. I see moving things in my head and. . .I just know how to fix 'em. It's a gift, what can I say?"

Reilly felt herself begin to relax. She could do this. Her system was grateful for the opportunity.

"OK, now that we've cleared up a few things and discussed one possibility- your leaving, let's talk about the more likely prospect of your staying," one black brow rose, playing peek-a-boo with his thick, black hair. Deep blue eyes gleamed.

"I. . .," Reilly didn't know what to say.

Ivy Rose piped up as she floated down through the swaths of weeping willow branches, 'You can have my room, Reilly.'

Trinity cocked his head, waiting for Reilly's response.

"Uh. . ." she blushed, thinking of sleeping that close to Trinity for ten months.

Ivy Rose leaned in to whisper in Trinity's ear, 'She's worried about se. . .'

"Ivy Rose," Trinity barked. "Privacy, please!" How did his ten year old sister come up with this?

Ivy Rose giggled as she evaporated.

"Are you worried about. . ." how did he genteelly approach the subject weighing on her mind? "Furthering our physical relationship?" That ought to do it; he mentally patted himself on the back.

Reilly flushed rose-red. In fact, her face would have been lost in one of Bridie's roses. They had not participated in anything more than hand-holding, an arm about her waist, chaste kisses. He treated her very gently. And she was glad, not sure she was ready for more.

"Would it be difficult for you. . .uh. . .with me in the next room? I don't want you to be uh. . .uncomfortable," Reilly continued to blush, sure she'd become a human pyre.

Trinity softly chuckled, leaned in and kissed the tip of her nose.

"My mother taught me to keep a tidy bathroom. I'm toilet trained- you'll find the seat is always down and you'll have plenty of hot water as I'll keep myself in check with cold showers," he offered, congenially. "The wait will be worth it," he whispered, sultrily.

Reilly found it hard to breathe. "What will people uh. . . think?"

"The gossip hotline, courtesy of Wilt Winters in #12, has already been apprised that you were attacked last night and ran screaming to my door," he informed her.

"#12?" Reilly gulped.

"Yeah, he had his dog outside at 3a.m., heard you scream, saw you run by. My dad couldn't get past him without an explanation. This town cares about you. If a few residents talk, don't let it bother you."

"You've more friends than not and I assure you, your friends will champion you. And we'll keep a box of raisins and chocolate milk handy for the eejits." They both laughed in grateful relief, remembering Reilly's suspension from school.

Un-straddling the bench seat, Trinity swept her up, placed her on his knees and leaned against the table top.

"My brother thinks you should stay with Kate and him." In Trinity's book this would not work, but he figured to give Reilly a chance to hear an option. By the look that flitted in her eyes, she didn't care for that option, either.

"If she stays, she stays here," Trinity stopped his older brother before he opened his mouth. "If that's OK with you, Dad?"

Pat Sr. plucked at his mandolin, "We'll work it out." He smiled fatherly at Reilly, cradled in his youngest son's arm. "Just don't you worry, Reilly. Treat this place," he glanced around at his living room fit to burst with O'Ryans from both sides of the pond, "As your own."

"We've got burgers coming off the grill. Dad tried to tell us how to make your create-a-Cajun burger. I hope we've not missed an ingredient," Kate spoke, spatula vacillating in hand.

Flicker and Skipper skeptically and cautiously, contemplated the kitchen weapon prior to, "Lass, they're bleedin' deadly!"

"Bang on!" "Gameball!" "Chiming!" All cousins bragged around mouthfuls.

A slice of onion, attended by burger juice, slid down the side of Michael's mustache. "Bleedin' wicked," he agreed.

Reilly leaned into Trinity, "Is that good?"

The entire clan bowled over laughing. "We have to teach the lass the Irish," one of them suggested.

"Can't have an O'Ryan not knowin' the mother tongue, eh?"

"Too right!" They chorused.

"And we're goin' to have a bit of music after we're gummin' these burgers. Yer man told us you've been learnin' the guitar so you'll be joinin' us, I know," Skipper nodded at an extra guitar.

"Oh. . .uh. . .I don't think so. . . I'd rather. . ." Reilly didn't get a chance to finish as Bridie tugged a lock of her hair and harrumphed.

'Don't be a spoilt sport, Sweetlin'!' Ivy Rose jumped up, down and through the grill, boisterously touting the forthcoming impromptu ceili.

"The music will be good for you. We've already seen you on stage." With all O'Ryan eyes directed her way, Reilly had no choice.

Flicker with accordion, Skipper with his whistle and harmonica, Frank with bodhran and Michael with guitar, spread out on various surfaces.

Pat Sr. perched on a chair, mandolin ready. Trinity showed her which chords they'd use in the first song and with his own guitar, acted as a guide.

Pat Sr. counted them off and Reilly played her first Irish reel with the group. Her fingers stumbled awkwardly, at first, but then she seemed to get the hang of it, let the music wrap her in sprightly Irish reverie and wash away her upsets.

Ivy Rose and Bridie clogged upon the kitchen counter; Kate cajoled her husband, Pat, into dancing in an open two foot square spot. Righteous high-tailed it to the highest cabinet available and Wrench, pawing at his ears, whined when the whistle hit a particularly high note.

"That was fun!" Kate collapsed. "Do the one about the drunken Scotsman," she suggested.

"You know it'd be an O'Ryan woman that'd be after hearin' that un," Flicker winked to Skipper.

Trinity covertly nixed the suggestion, tilting his head at Reilly.

"Right! What were ye tinkin' Kate? We've a babe in our midst, for Jaysus sake!"

"Flick," Trinity remonstrated.

"Lighten up lad, yer mollycoddlin' the lass," Frank advised.

'Drunken Scotsman?' Bridie's brows puzzled. 'I don't believe I'm after knowin' that one.'

Pat Sr. coughed while sorting out his thoughts on the matter. But Kate had the last say, so Reilly blushed at being put on the spot once again, albeit in a different way than being prodded to play.

Trinity rose protectively, letting his height further his warning, "D'ye want yer go, then?"

Kate grabbed his elbow, pulled him back with Reilly's help. Girls recognize fighting words in any language.

"Reilly's a smart girl. Don't go all overly guardian on her," Kate tried to reason with him.

'I know what the song is about; what's wrong with Reilly hearing it?' Ivy Rose queried her brother, immediately stealing the wind from his affronted sails.

"Trinity, it's OK," Reilly purposefully sat in his lap. This calmed him more than anything Kate had to say. He winked speculatively at his sister and his arm swept around Reilly; his chin rested on her shoulder.

Flicker counted them off and the Rakes rent the air. The song wittily described the possibility of what a Scotsman may or may not wear under his kilt. All O'Ryans joined in the curious chorus. Reilly couldn't catch the words fast enough to sing with them, but she found the story provocatively interesting.

The last line about first prize had everyone howling-Bridie most of all. Everyone except Reilly, who was late in interpreting the final line. Her wide-eyed announcement of comprehension had the room rolling all over again. Trinity pulled his blushing girl further into the haven of his arms.

Trinity sang an IRISH ROVERS original tune- THE DEAR LITTLE SHAMROCK SHORE. The wistful tale of being forced to leave Ireland because of greedy circumstances hit too close for Reilly to staunch silently flowing tears.

No one should ever have to leave their home, Reilly firmly believed. And this particular tune let her know she was not alone in the proverbial boat, as all the sentient O'Ryans exhibited some form of turmoil.

"You can tell the lass is Irish," Michael wiped at his own eyes.

"UP AMONG THE HEATHER," Kate called after Trinity tousled Reilly's hair and kissed her forehead.

"I think we've furthered Reilly's education enough for one night," Pat Sr., the father figure, put his foot down.

Irish to the core, the O'Ryans never lacked for tunes about rovers, tars, lost loves, other travesties and drinking and fighting, interspersed with lively reels.

Slated to play for Ryan's International Cealidh Festival, the group practiced their original material tirelessly, and music reigned for the rest of the night. The Guinness drinking was held in check.

Yawning, Reilly waved good night.

"The lass'll be after her scratcher- needin' her zeds," Skipper blew her a kiss.

Reilly thanked Pat Jr. and Kate for their offer of a place to stay, smiled wistfully at Trinity and walked down the hall to bed.

Intermittently, Reilly's mother mulled over Reilly's question. How long had it been since she'd believed in anything good? Even thought of the word- good? Before she became pregnant, when she believed in that. . .?

No, surely it hadn't been that long ago. Reilly. Her daughter, Reilly. Didn't she believe in the goodness of Reilly?

Ms. Brooke had never engaged in self-introspection. Too tedious. Too unproductive. Too thirsty a task.

Chet donned his best display of sweet talking. He preferred not to lose the best looking woman he'd ever seen. The daughter, now, was a whole other ballgame. Good riddance as far as he was concerned. But hell, her mother needn't go. . .

Rising well ahead of everyone the next morning, Reilly left a note saying she'd be picking tomatoes, peppers and zucchinis at Bridie's.

Hoisting her backpack over her shoulder, she quietly made her way through the O'Ryan trailer. Carefully, she stepped over Irishmen in their 'zeds'. Was that the right word?

Righteous padded alongside. If Reilly stopped to observe a breakfasting rabbit, or early bird, the gold kitten made figure eights about her legs, rubbing against Reilly's jeans.

"I won't be able to take you with me, Righteous. I hope you won't forget me. Trinity, his dad and Wrench, will take care of you," she sniffled. Righteous peered up at her, wanting to be picked up. She obliged and the kitten stared at her lovingly, blinking slowly, prior to swathing her jaws against Reilly's mouth. Reilly, eyes glittering, kissed the kitten's nose.

"We'd best get to picking," she steered her thoughts to productivity.

With summer winding down, Reilly made notes to herself about how many tomatoes to take to the diner's freezer and also stock the O'Ryan's chest freezer. Mostly, she now believed she would be staying. More than that, she fervently wished it so.

Inside Bridie's cottage, she opened her hat box which was setting upon a shelf, fingered her wool sweaters and cape- articles too cumbersome to keep in her backpack. They'd keep safe in Bridie's, ready in case. . .no, when she returned.

Reilly felt the soil's moisture content in the house plants' pots, gathered a small clay pot to replant the shamrock trophy. She checked the hiding place of her and Trinity's safety deposit box key. Safe. Bridie would keep it all safe.

In locking the door behind her, she felt compelled to take a detour, ever mindful for the sound of her mother's car.

Unshaven and irritable, Trinity muscled the Camaro down Bridie's lane. There was no telling what time Reilly had left and perturbation couldn't begin to describe his state of mind.

That is, until he parked the Camaro, strode around the stone house toward the garden and saw not a single indication of Reilly's presence.

No bags of picked vegetables, no black backpack- it wasn't in his house, either, he'd checked. No cat, no Reilly, no Bridie, not even Ivy Rose. . .

No ghost is good news, was not Trinity's first summation. Surely, at least his sister would tell him if Reilly. . .

"Reilly," he called. Other than a few birds griping about his loud presence, there was no response.

"Reilly!" Louder this time. Nothing. What if her mother had picked her up?

A familiar tightness in his chest- the one Reilly had tamed- drew rein. His jaw clenched to the point of pain. Trinity swore aloud. Agitation metamorphosed into agonizing possibilities.

"Reilly?"

With 30 acres to search, Trinity began to run. Along the pond side he called, intently scrutinizing for signs. He startled a pair of ducks with their near grown brood, upset a chipmunk atop the picnic table. But no Reilly. The woods. . .

The deer trails in the woods were meant for animals that brambles and twining vines didn't deter. They weren't geared for humans to traverse in a hurry. A strong breeze grew fierce as clouds to the west darkened and hurtled east.

"Great, a thunderstorm, just great," Trinity cursed.

"Reilly," he shouted, urgently. Where the devil was Ivy Rose?

He skirted several eroded areas, stepped on available stones in the deep creek, jumped to the other side, missed, slid into the cold, spring-fed waters and cursed again.

Finding a likely set of roots, he pulled himself to the opposite bank.

"Reilly," the wind tore his call and sent it hurtling without any power. Trinity had never been an astute woods walker and with the crash of thunder heralding a downpour, he frantically eyed every bit of underbrush, hoping for a clue.

Finding a high spot, he looked around- loose debris, flapping brush and the onset of rain. Where was she? Was she even here? Why hadn't he thought to see if her mother's rattle-trap car was still parked at the trailer court before rushing off to Bridie's half-cocked?

Stupid, he castigated himself. Rounding an ancient glacial deposit of topsy-turvy boulders, he caught a glimpse of movement. There. A hint of golden fur.

"Reilly?" The hill of rock blocked the disadvantageous wind and also his calls.

Reilly stumbled out of a crevasse. The dying last syllable of her name had her peering around. Righteous flew toward Trinity, as if he were the second coming.

"Reilly, damn't," Trinity's long strides descended a stack of fossil-laden rock.

"What are you doing out here? You had me worried half to death," he exhaled with tremendous relief, pulled her into a tight embrace and bending down, he sidled his face alongside hers.

Reilly gently pushed at Trinity's impervious chest, "You're scratching me."

"Sorry," he fingered his stubbly jaws. "But. . ."

The heavens opened up, closing off communication as thunder timbered a belting aria and lightning sizzled.

Righteous mewled to be carried, preferably undercover, and the soon sodden couple, kitten held fast, hurried as best they could to the car.

The creek gave them a final baptism before they dashed across the meadow and slid into the Camaro.

"Reilly. . ."

"I'm sorry, Trinity, I hoped to pick vegetables and get back to start breakfast before everyone got up. I got sidetracked in the woods. . ."

"Don't ever disappear on me again," his wet hair plastered black streaks across his worried face. He freed Righteous' clutching claws from his shoulders and faced Reilly, "Promise?"

51

Like all astute predators, worries over Reilly's uncertain, immediate future, stalked each recess of her mind, seeking a weakness. But Reilly stood fast, thinking of the badger. Her new mantra of '10 months- no surrender', stayed on the tip of her tongue. Not to mention Bridie's ghosting about and Ivy Rose's skipping in and out of her peripheral vision.

Trinity's constant presence and the rest of the O'Ryan clan doing their utmost to engage Reilly in various interests- most of which were heartily discouraged by Trinity as they involved rather bawdy pub tunes and Irish curse words- kept her from the verge of floundering.

Reilly tried to stave off Trinity's watching her like a hawk by explaining that the norm for her mother was to suddenly appear and say 'let's go', but this time Reilly had all of his numbers memorized and she would call as soon as possible. If she left. The finale was not decided, yet.

This did not ease his anxious solicitude, and the following days she was out of his sight only for most of her sleeping hours. Periodically, Trinity would sub-consciously rise in the night and stand by his door, wrapped in contemplation over the beat of his heart resting in his bed.

After the weekend's Cealidh contest, his cousins would head back to Dublin, Ireland. He'd already made plans, with Ivy Rose's approval, to redecorate his little sister's room in whatever fashion Reilly wanted- something to look forward to.

Trinity had not resigned himself to the actual possibility of Reilly's leaving. He refused to countenance her prolonged absence.

"Son, you should get some rest. Come hell or high water, we're going to work tomorrow. God knows what this place will look like with your cousins unsupervised."

Trinity ruefully smiled and rolled a shoulder in acknowledgement of his father's truthful speculation. His Irish cousins were a carousing bunch of rascals- respectful, but wild, and they could put away Guinness faster than a body could pour a pint down the drain- a sacrilege to an Irishman.

Trinity's uncle had driven them home from the pub this night. It took Trinity, his dad and uncle, to bring the staggering, raucous cousins into the house, and several warnings about Reilly's sleeping to settle them.

"C'mon, Son," Pat laid a hand on Trinity's shoulder. In many ways, his youngest son had more strength and sensitivity than the rest of the O'Ryans put together.

"Reilly has a code of honor and integrity far removed from her mother. It's hard to believe the two are related," his dad voiced aloud their mindset.

Trinity ran a hand through his hair, giving him a second to steady his voice. "Dad, I know she's the one for me. It's a matter of wait and see if she really understands that I'm the one for her. Too much going on right now for her to think straight. You know, she tried to give back the earrings and the Claddagh ring. She was worried I might want to see another girl."

"Try to get some rest. Like you said, in ten months she'll be 18 and mistress of her own future. Wait and see."

Privately, Pat believed his son had jumped the gun by gifting Reilly such an expensive present as diamond earrings, but he trusted Trinity was man enough to live with his own decisions. He'd certainly never spent money like that before Reilly. Well, maybe excepting the Camaro.

It took three days for Reilly's mother to pack, sidestepping the begging Chet all the while. In a way, she didn't care to leave. Chet had been fun. But finally that half-canted door to Reilly's room decided the matter- the door Chet hadn't got around to fixing.

Conveniently, she forgot about the door's never having had a lock and the lack of a/c. . .

Three days before she went looking for her daughter.

Reilly balked at the idea of being baby-sat by Trinity and his dad, especially at the O'Ryans' garage.

"It's not like that, Reilly, sheesh!" Really, it was, but. . . An idea of how to save the scene flew through Trinity's head and he grabbed it. Perfect! Especially with the diner closed for summer vacation.

"Look, we have all this backlog of bookwork. Receipts need to be tallied and registered in our account book and then filed. I hate that stuff," he told her.

Pat hid a smirk and side-stepped the set-up- Trinity did hate bookwork.

"Well," Reilly paused, looking around at the cousins' bodies splayed on floor, couch and chairs. She certainly couldn't see herself hanging out with them all day- not that Trinity would allow that, Reilly felt sure.

"I could do the paperwork, I think. You'll have to show me."

"Good. C'mon, finish your breakfast. We have to get to the garage. The answering machine is fit to blow up with all the calls requiring service and. . .never mind. Dad, you ready?" Trinity looked around.

"The da's been gone tomall," Frank informed him.

"Right. Well, don't burn down the gaff, alright?"

'I'll keep an eye on the lads,' Bridie winked.

Reilly giggled at the idea of Bridie's babysitting the Irish cousins. And what, exactly, would her ghostly friend do if one of them stepped out of line? Might be worth it to stick around and watch.

Righteous curled around her legs and she bent to kiss the kitten's nose. Wrench finagled his way in for some loving, too.

"Always remember, Righteous, I'll come back. I will come back," she whispered. Trinity took her bag and they headed to the Camaro.

It didn't take long for Reilly to catch up with the O'Ryans' paperwork.

Once finished, she ambled into the 2-bay garage and offered to help in other ways- if they could think of something for her to do.

Trinity put her to work handing him sockets, all the while explaining what he was doing with Mr. Flynn's transmission overhaul.

"Break time," Pat called, wiping his hands. "Son, you want to pick up some sandwiches at the IGA deli?"

"Sure, Dad. C'mon, Reilly. Boy, will I be glad when the diner's open again." As they exited the garage, Reilly picked up her backpack.

"Leave it. We're just going a few blocks over," he told her. But Reilly shook her head, no. Trinity sighed, aggravated for the life Reilly had led, the lack of any real security.

The guttural din of an all-too-familiar car trolled Main Street and parked along the curb to intercept the young couple.

"Reilly?" Her mother stepped out- dressed as if she were attending a summer's BBQ party in her white lace midriff top, Capris and high-heeled sandals. Reilly's perfectly made-up mother pageant-walked toward her daughter.

Trinity slid his arms around her waist, anchoring her to him, protectively. The mother did a quick appraisal of the 'chick magnet'.

She'd used her life to study and know people, once she'd parted ways with innocence. It was easy to read people- all the better to get what you wanted from them. And she'd mastered her technique.

For the first time in a long time, if ever, she really studied her daughter. By the guarded look in Reilly's eyes and her shy leaning into the 'chick magnet's' chest. . .

Yes, the mother did believe the local bad boy had a serious thing for Reilly. Serious enough that he'd not pushed her into. . .

"I'd like to speak to my daughter, alone." The first order of pernicious business was to separate him from Reilly.

"I don't think so," Trinity replied, scornfully. Reilly's mother sent him a look that had sundered males in the past. Trinity didn't waver. Not a single iota. Another tactic was called for.

"Reilly?"

"Trinity, it's OK," she patted his grease-marked forearm.

"All right, mo ghra milis daor, but I'm keeping close."

"What? Do you think I'll hurt my own daughter?"

"Now that's a great question for you to ask yourself," Trinity retorted.

The mother's face flamed. Trinity winked at the startled Reilly who'd never seen her mother blush, or act the least bit discomfited, either. Trinity sauntered two store fronts ahead, and leaned against the old, Victorian brick building, his eyes glued on Reilly.

"Just who does he think he is?" Reilly's mother searched for a cigarette, remembered she'd left her purse in the car. "Let's go, Reilly."

Reilly didn't move and that was another first for the mother. Discounting the other day in the O'Ryans' trailer. But that was all right, the mother hadn't been truly ready then.

She used a different tone, "Are you coming?"

"Where?" Reilly tremulously asked as fear gurgled, seeking an outlet.

"I spoke with Sarah. We'll stay with her for a while. Let's get your money."

The money. Of course. The most important part.

A burgeoning independence flared, phoenix-like, within Reilly- dread died suddenly in its tracks.

"No." Reilly stopped nervously fingering her backpack. She'd made up her mind. The mother readied the final stroke.

"No?" Reilly's mother looked to Trinity and back to her daughter. "So, you've made up your mind, then?" The guilt trip's death throes ground to a halt before delivery.

"Yes."

"I see," and all at once, the mother did see, at least a dawning glimpse.

And what she saw tormented her with. . .regret? She studied Trinity again. His eyes never left Reilly. His arms crossed, ready to slay dragons for her. Now, where did that come from? The mother frowned, bewildered.

Her own prince charming had been a lying toad. Of course, nobody warned her about princes in toads' clothes and she probably wouldn't have listened if they had said something. She'd been totally bowled over by the hoopla her 15-year old looks had garnered her. Boys fell at her feet, until she, stupid girl, fell herself.

Good. That word. Reilly. If the mother had done anything right in her whole life, it was birthing Reilly. She licked her lips. Would have pursed them, but that caused wrinkles, as did the frown she quickly smoothed out.

"Reilly," a hint of heartbreak furrowed through her chest.

She tapped at her neckline to still the chaos assailing her.

As if from a distance, she watched one of her hands reach out and touch Reilly's chin, fondled the light skin, and mother and daughter stood transfixed. Eye to eye for a sincere piquant moment in time.

"I. . ." Reilly's mother felt a tear coming. She never cried. "I don't know who you are, Reilly. All these years, and. . . I know you're my daughter. . .but, I don't. . .know you." She dropped her trembling hand and her eyes surrendered the field.

Was this another ploy? Tears? Her mother?

"Mom?" Reilly had never seen her mother like this. If this was an act, but no, her intuition told her that her mother was in a process of discovery. A huge, emotional discovery.

"All right, Reilly. Will you call your aunt? She'll be worried, no matter what I tell her. Remember Gerald Jordan?"

Reilly nodded. The only one of her mother's boyfriends who had talked to her about school and her interests. The only one of her mother's boyfriends who did not drink and had probably really cared for her mother- if he'd only been given a chance. But he was also the only one who would not put up with her mother's foolish behavior.

"He called, asking about me. I...I guess it's time. . .I made my own living. Welfare's been cut off with you working. So. . . I'm. . . Could you lend your mother a few dollars, Reilly?"

With Reilly slowly pulling something out of her pocket, Trinity re-entered the picture.

"Reilly?"

"It's OK, Trinity." And he saw that in one way, she was right.

Reilly only had a twenty on her, a leftover from the Irish Festival. She handed it to her mother.

"I'm staying here," Reilly stated.

Disappointed at the small amount, her mother unfolded and refolded it twice.

"Well," she looked to her daughter once more. "Maybe sometime we can get together. I'd like. . .to get to know you. Once I get to know who the hell I am," her mother conceded with a heavy sigh.

"I'd l...like that, Mom. I'll c...call you," Reilly's voice trembled with fervid emotional overtures.

"OK, Reilly," her mother smoothed Reilly's hair, tears threatened her mascaraed eyes.

Reilly's own eyes watered. Her mother kissed her forehead and turned to go.

"Uh, Ms. Brooke," Trinity pulled out some crumpled bills. "Here. There's about $200, take it."

Reilly's mother put on one of her sunny, male-killer smiles. Somehow, the imminent tears defeated the planned effect.

"I'll pay you back," she said.

"No, it's a gift. I'll bring Reilly to see you whenever she wants," Trinity's arm encircled Reilly's waist to pull her close.

His heart ached at her trembling pathos. Reilly's mother dug a mauve-colored fingernail into Trinity's chest.

"Don't," she warned, "Don't disappoint her."

Resolutely, Trinity curtly bowed his head, "I don't intend to."

And Reilly's mother left with a coughing trail of pipe-belching smoke.

Reilly turned and broke down, sobbing uncontrollably into Trinity's chest.

"Reilly? Sweetheart?" At odds, he held her. He didn't want to, but he had to ask, "Reilly, do you want to go with her? I…I'll take you."

She shook her head, gained a moment's respite from her travail, and endeavored to explain, "My…my mom's been the only constant. . .inconstant my whole life."

"Ah, Reilly, I…I think I understand." Trinity let her cry herself out as concerned passersby offered to help in any way.

52

"Now that we have our house back," Pat scanned a strangely quiet living room. With the boisterous cousins on their way home to Ireland, Pat had directed Trinity and Reilly to stay at the dining room table for a few minutes after supper.

"I'm a little out of my league, here, but as I'm the only one of us who is a father, I'm going to lay down a few rules." He looked pointedly between Trinity and Reilly.

"Reilly, I want you to feel like you are a member of this family and not a paying boarder. Trinity and I are capable of cleaning up after ourselves. We appreciate your cooking efforts, but you are not our servant." Pat proceeded to divvy up chores and cooking schedules.

"Now, for the hard part," Pat rocked his clasped hands on the table top. "No dating during the week. Dates on Friday or Saturday- not both days. And they will end with Reilly being home by midnight- no exceptions."

Reilly, who had never had a list of rules to abide by, was fascinated. Trinity, on the other hand, wasn't overly pleased with the one date a week rule, but by the look on his dad's face, he'd best keep that to himself.

"There will be no excessive demonstrations of affection in this house," Pat ordered. "Or anywhere else," he hurriedly added.

Trinity barked a laugh at this, "Don't worry, Dad. I'll treat Reilly like my little sister." He turned his head and winked at Ivy Rose, all ears, cavorting on the couch.

Pat reminisced on Trinity's and Ivy Rose's relationship.

"Uh, Son? Rethink the wrestling and piggy-back rides in the house."

Trinity rolled his eyes; Reilly waited for more. As far as she was concerned this was great- how a real family acted.

"I guess that about covers it. Reilly, I trust you to attend school and finish all your homework. Our computer is at your disposal. Uh, if I think of anything else, I'll let the two of you know. Oh, one more thing- I prefer both of you not be in the same bedroom at the same time. Any questions? Let's get the dishes done."

Reflecting on his family, Pat rose slowly to leave the table. He'd not seen Ivy Rose grow into her teens, and with his wife gone to God, he felt sure he'd be needing advice.

It didn't take Reilly long to pick up on the O'Ryan routine. Extra-observant, because she didn't want to be in the way, Reilly learned the men liked a quick, simple dinner after a long, work day. The grill was often used, and Reilly contrived to make side dishes to go with the grilled entrees. On the weekends, she cooked more substantial meals like chicken and dumplings or roasts with mashed potatoes and vegetables. And of course, a dessert.

Trinity and Reilly shared a bathroom and as they both preferred showers/baths before bedtime, Reilly recommended tossing a coin. But Trinity magnanimously offered her the tub first. Usually, he found something to do outside when he heard her turn on the shower. Hard to keep some pictures from forming in his mind. . . Ten months and counting. . .

Reilly let go some of her savings after getting comfortable using a bathroom with a working lock, not that she felt it was necessary with the O'Ryans, but accidents could happen. She purchased lilac-scented bubble bath. Trinity teased her about his smelling like a girl in the scented mist lingering in the bathroom, to her blushing and Pat's amusement.

"Reilly, that was too d…too good. You're going to fatten us up," Pat said, not altogether joking.

Reilly had fidgeted during dinner; Pat seemed unaware, but not Trinity.

"What's up, winsome elf?"

"Uh," Reilly blushed, licked her lips. She hated to ask for anything. Ivy Rose whispered in his ear.

"C'mon, spit it out," he urged.

"Well, uh. . . I need to harvest Bridie's apples and dig potatoes before the next rain," she murmured.

"Dad, you didn't realize we were taking in a slave driver, did you? When did you plant potatoes?" Trinity thought back- couldn't place it.

"Sometimes you napped on Sundays and I. . ." Reilly shrugged, embarrassed.

"Martie's right, you are the Energizer Bunny. Sheesh! C'mon, I'm yours to command," Trinity winked. "Dad?"

"Well, I can honestly say I've never dug potatoes," Pat hedged.

"I used to dig them up with my grandpa. It's kind of like a treasure hunt. You never know what you'll find," Reilly's eyes gleamed so eagerly the men couldn't help but reciprocate with a semblance of zeal.

"You do realize our freezer and cupboards are nearly full," Pat intimated.

"That's OK, Bridie has a root cellar," Reilly responded as both the O'Ryans rolled their eyes.

Once school had started, Reilly continued taking the bus in the morning and riding home with Pat and Trinity at night, after her shift at the diner. In the evening, the TV generally stayed on the Western Channel. Happily, the three shared a devotion to the old western serials, like THE VIRGINIAN, MAVERICK and HAVE GUN WILL TRAVEL. Reilly had watched the shows with her grandparents when she was very little, and watching them now gave her a feeling of family familiarity.

She enjoyed watching the movie with Trinity's namesake again. The only resemblance, other than a dimple, was the respect the two men secured.

"You're sure you don't mind being here alone?" Trinity and his dad were on a bowling league. And both worried about leaving her alone.

"Sure, it's not like I'm really alone," she petted Wrench on the head. Righteous swatted at Trinity from the kitchen counter. Ivy Rose and Bridie bid goodbyes.

"Girls night," Trinity mused softly, so his dad wouldn't hear. "Poor Wrench."

"Pat, do you have any books that I could read?"

"There's a case in my bedroom. Help yourself," Pat replied.

Twice Trinity called her from the bowling alley. The other guys heckled him for being a mother hen. It was after 11 when they returned to find Reilly asleep on the couch. Trinity carried her to bed, thinking of the day when. . . He covered her gently, kissed her forehead, left the light on a dim setting and let the door stay ajar for Wrench and Righteous to enter and exit.

"I see she found the old Seckatary Hawkins books. Fast reader. Looks like she finished STONER'S BOY and started THE GRAY GHOST. I used to love these- got them from my dad. All of you kids enjoyed them, too, as I remember," Pat thumbed through the well-worn pages, appreciating the sketches of the chubby Seckatary and the boys' antics as members of the Fair and Square Club.

"I remember imitating some of their exploits. . . And the trouble I got into," Trinity chuckled. "Hope Reilly doesn't get any ideas."

"I don't know. Maybe we should play at your brother's house," Trinity's dad murmured, surreptitiously checking the hall for Reilly's whereabouts.

"Dad, for crying out loud, you think I'm overprotective," Trinity snickered.

"We'll be playing poker and drinking beer. . ."

"You think we're going to tip Reilly into the ranks of the depraved?" Trinity scoffed.

He, too, wondered about the beer drinking, but believed after the cousins' visit, Reilly should realize there was nothing to get out-of-joint about.

"After the fiasco at Chet's, I don't want Reilly to. . ."

"What's up, Pat? You don't want me to. . ."

"Reilly, there you are. It's like having a ghost in the house- you're so quiet," Pat flushed.

Trinity stifled a chuckle, turned his head and rolled his eyes at Ivy Rose, who giggled and gave Reilly a thumbs-up. His dad was right though, the definition of unobtrusive should contain a photo of Reilly- but old habits probably took a long time to be laid to rest.

"We're staging our monthly poker game Saturday night, winsome elf. Beer and aces," Trinity tousled her hair.

"Would you like me to make a pot of chili or stew or something?" Reilly smoothed down her hair which caused Trinity to playfully ruffle it again. She swatted at him, equally playful, and he smiled in surprise. How far Reilly had come, he reflected.

"Uh, thanks, but the guys bring the food- won't be as good as yours, but that's how we do it," Pat explained. "House supplies the cards and table, guests bring the food."

"And beer," Trinity shuddered, giving Reilly a horrified stare.

Reilly checked her inner sensibility about the beer. The O'Ryans were worlds apart from the drunks she'd grown up with, and it was imperative she not interfere with their lives because of her past.

"I have papers to work on and other things. I'll stay out of your way. If I could take the computer to my room?"

"Honey, we don't want you to feel like you have to go to ground. This is your home," Pat said.

"It's fine, Pat, really. I do have homework," scholarly and ghostly, Reilly thought. Bridie had given her some lessons, too.

"You're sure you are OK with it?" Pat felt as if he might have inadvertently hurt the girl's feelings.

"Absolutely, have fun."

"Maybe Reilly might like to play," Trinity stirred the stew.

"I'm afraid your cousins didn't have time to teach me a whole lot about poker. Maybe some other time," Reilly gathered the laptop.

Trinity had an emergency run at Mr. Jasper's farm-stove out, and with Thanksgiving coming. . . When the local appliance man was unavailable, the people of Ryan weren't shy about calling their Mr. Fix-It genius.

Reilly kept Trinity's plate on a warm setting. Her thoughts were on helping Kate with the up-coming family dinner as she bustled around in the kitchen, making lists of needed ingredients.

Pat, at ease in his recliner, turned the TV on low and eyed Reilly at the kitchen counter. She put her pen down. Something in those huddled shoulders, slightly quivering. . .

"Reilly?" Believing he heard a choking sob, he rose, concerned.

"Reilly? Honey? What's wrong?"

Reilly wiped at her eyes, "Nothing. Everything. . . You are all so nice to me. Everything is clean and neat. And you're a good family. And. . . I don't think I've ever thanked you enough for letting me stay h…here," she hiccoughed.

Hesitantly, Pat put his arms about her. If she'd been Ivy Rose, he'd do the same. He patted her back, stifled his own feelings.

"Reilly, you are a wonderful, added joy to our home. We love having you as a member of our family."

"I'm s…s…sorry, Pat."

"Hey, it's all right," Pat searched for a distraction-hated to see a girl cry, always had. "How about some ice cream? I'll dip. And I know I bought some chocolate syrup and caramel, too," he opened cabinets, drawing out bowls and toppings.

His actions were so overwhelmingly exuberant as he searched for the chocolate and caramel, Reilly's sniffles soon turned to giggles.

"You're sure it's OK?" Reilly asked Trinity for the umpteenth time. She didn't really think she wanted to go. . .

"Reilly, Reilly, Reilly, what am I going to do with you?" He had a few ideas, but they'd not meet with his dad's approval, especially his own rule about treating Reilly like a little sister.

Reilly blushed under the intensity of his riveted eyes.

"Now that you are part of the O'Ryan clan," Pat pretended to indulge in his newspaper, grinning all the while, "You've got to learn to speak up for what you want, and accept, without misgivings, what's offered."

Trinity's dimple popped into play, "Oh, and be subject to a little teasing, too."

"Is that all?" Reilly gulped. If you looked up the definition of devastatingly attractive in a dictionary, Trinity's picture would be there. He made her feel like a princess lost in a fairytale.

He leaned in and kissed her forehead, "For right now. Are you ready, then?"

Trinity frowned in concentration as she nodded. "Do you have make-up on?"

"A…a little m…mascara and l…lip gloss," she blushed.

"Hmm. . ."

"You don't like it?"

"Makes your eyes stand out even more. I hope you won't slather any more on. I want to kiss you and not some chemicals. C'mon, we've got a 2-plus hour drive ahead."

Christmas Eve, and Trinity was driving the nervous Reilly to visit her aunt and mother.

Reilly fidgeted and plucked at her cape. He tried to engage her in conversation, knowing her apprehension was rampant under the circumstances. She needed to remember she would be going home with him. And that was for certain.

"That was really cool, your digging up the Seckatary Hawkins' website. Imagine, they're printing some stories that were never put out in book form. Dad's going to love his present. He never asks for anything, so those books are going to be a great surprise. I caught him reading the old stories again. When he finishes with STONER'S BOY, I'm going to read them again in order, too."

"I had a club membership card made out in his name. You know, I like those boys' stories. As I read them, I picture you and your dad when you were little boys and all the mischief and adventures you must have had," Reilly began to relax.

Trinity regaled her with a few anecdotes involving rival gangs, building tree houses, falling out of Bridie's apple trees when they shouldn't have been there in the first place and. . .

"We didn't have caves or rivers to canoe on, but we had great swimming holes in the creek alongside Bridie's and grapevine ropes to swing out on. Once she caught us skinny dipping. . . Oops, hey, Bridie."

'Hey your own self, young man,' Bridie's arched brows spoke volumes.

"I'm going to stop for a coffee. You want a juice or something?" He pulled into a gas station/market.

"No, thanks," she smiled at him.

Trinity handed her an orange juice anyway. That lip gloss was looking. . .all too edible.

"Have I told you lately that I love you?" Their fingers sizzled as Reilly accepted the bottle from him. His eyes fastened on hers.

"It's OK, uh. . ."

"You best not be wasting time thinking about Gina making like a fool over me in the IGA. You are the only girl for me. If you think I've been a little on the shy side with you recently, it's only because close proximity to you fires me up and I'm not wanting to self-incinerate," Trinity stroked her naturally rosy cheek, and surrendering his resistance, leaned over to taste the damned lip gloss.

Bridie harrumphed in the back seat, but Ivy Rose issued a 'kiss her, again' to her big brother.

"Uh, we better get going," he started the car.

Reilly leaned back and closed her eyes, trying to get her breath to return. What would happen when he. . . Breathe, she told herself before she jumped out of her skin.

Thoughts inundated her on the imminent arrival at her aunt's, but luckily, her gut remained at peace. Why am I so nervous? They can't make me stay. For good measure she repeated it like a mantra, 'they can't make me stay'.

While Reilly napped, Trinity mentally ticked off the recent changes in her.

She was still quiet as a ghost, silently drifting around Trinity's home- sort of like the two passengers in the backseat of the old Ford Escort- the winter car.

Bridie and Ivy Rose played an odd version of ghostly peek-a-boo, popping in and out of view.

If Trinity hadn't grown used to their talented antics he might have swerved once or twice as one or the other reappeared upside down or sideways. Good thing ghostly skirts stayed put, regardless. The thought of Bridie's underdrawers. . . Best not to think along those lines.

'Watch yer self, you young rapscallion,' Bridie preened, reading his thoughts, and swished her skirt through the rear view mirror.

Back to the changes in Reilly. A safe topic. The biggest single change was that she no longer clung to that damned, black bag; he sure didn't miss its absence at Reilly's feet. Which meant she had gained a measure of security.

He recalled the first date after she moved in. He fussed to be sure she had everything, without being explicit. No sense getting to the concert and having to turn around. But Reilly knew what he'd hinted at and she simply smiled at him. Her black lamb waited on her pillow and the bag's new role was hauling fresh vegetables and other sundry articles from Bridie's.

Reilly had even made a couple of friends at school. Trinity and his dad were direct beneficiaries of a cookie bake-off night for a benefit. Imagine, three girls baking cookies. Hey, somebody had to sample the merchandise.

Reilly's frugal wardrobe had slowly expanded. Trinity relished her dressing up for their once-a-week dates, usually spent at his uncle's pub for the ceili. She'd even sat in with the players and surprised all of them with her voice. My Reilly, he mused. How lucky can a guy get?

"Here we are, sweetheart," Trinity woke her, and trotted around to open her door. He liked the gallantry she brought out in him. My Reilly, my lady, he grinned.

Retrieving a large wrapped box of baked goodies for her cousins, he held out his hand. Hesitating, she fingered the envelopes she carried.

"C'mon, winsome elf. I've got you, and it's only for a few hours," he encouraged with a wink.

Aunt Sarah flung open the door of the brick Cape Cod before Reilly and Trinity reached the first step.

"Reilly, gosh, look at you!" Reilly received a long, bear hug, complete with tears.

"Aunt Sarah, this is. . ."

"Trinity O'Ryan. Wow! Might I hug you, too?" Without waiting for an answer she swept him into an embrace. Trinity patted her back, conciliatorily.

With her perfectly streaked, expertly cut gold hair, the aunt had several inches over Reilly's doll-like mother; the sisters would be head-turners wherever they went.

"Gary, Steve, Reilly is here," her aunt called forth her boys.

"Mom," two pre-teen boys in jeans and t-shirts wailed. "The TV is acting up again."

"Probably the cable. What do you have to say to Reilly?"

"Hey, Reilly! What's up?" The boys quickly returned to more important matters. "It's not the cable, Mom," they griped.

Aunt Sarah sighed in exasperation.

"I'm pretty good with electronics. Would you like me to take a look?" Trinity offered.

"It might be our only chance at peace," she agreed. "Boys, you be sure to thank Trinity for helping whether he's able to fix it or not," she commanded, as Trinity chuckled and followed the boys into the living room.

"Aunt Sarah, where's Mom?" Reilly hesitated, afraid of thinking the worst.

"She'll be back soon. She's out with Gerald. Last minute stops. Your Trinity is gorgeous! And Reilly, I hardly recognize you! You've blossomed into a beautiful, young lady. I swear, if I'd seen you out somewhere I would not have known it was you," her aunt stated while she gave Reilly a head to toe going over. Reilly blushed and fidgeted over her aunt's compliments.

"Is Mom doing all right?" Reilly was reluctant to ask for particulars. But maybe this was the best time to find out.

"You'll be surprised to hear she's actually begun to grow up. It's hard to say, but I think the welfare check made it too easy for her to stay idle. She's working part-time at the salon, getting her high school diploma and attending AA meetings. Enough about her. You'll see the difference. Are you happy?"

No need to ask.

The pretty hair held back from lively eyes. The clothes. . . Sarah wiped at her eyes. Reilly finally had the happiness, a sense of self-esteem and security she deserved.

"Yes, I am," Reilly surprised herself by saying it aloud and fully recognizing the absolute truth of it.

She perched on a stool at the kitchen island. "I...I feel like I'm home in Ryan. I've a great job and...and I made some friends. . ."

"And a stud for a boyfriend! Are those THE earrings? I heard a lot about them. Are you being safe?" Her aunt lowered her voice.

Caught off guard, Reilly's face flared. "Aunt Sarah, it's not like that."

Her aunt had reservations along those lines, but the truth of her niece's innocence was plain to see. Reilly had never lied and as for smarts. . .

"So Trinity is taking care of you?"

Reilly nodded, shrugging her shoulders, trying not to stare at the ghosts. Bridie and Ivy Rose were peeking into cabinets without opening them and skipping through the house, oohing and aahing over her aunt's tremendous Christmas displays and rotund, overly-ornamented tree.

"He treats me like I'm gold," Reilly's eyes misted.

Trinity's arms swept silently around her and he kissed the top of her head. "You are much better than gold," he ardently avowed.

Timers went off and her aunt forcibly withdrew her attention from the young couple to attend dinner preparations.

"Can I help?" Reilly asked, gently disengaging from Trinity's arms.

"No, Honey, just talk to me. How's the TV?"

"Notice how quiet the boys are?" Trinity quipped.

"Reilly, I may kidnap him," her aunt teased.

"Aunt Sarah, is Mom nice to Gerald?"

"Oh, yes. He doesn't take any sh… He doesn't cater to her like those other goons," her aunt gladly confided.

"I always liked him," Reilly admitted, hopefully.

Reilly's mother and Gerald made it back as Trinity placed the turkey on its platter. Gerald helped her mother out of her coat as Reilly tentatively approached them.

"Hi, Reilly," her mother seemed just as hesitant at hello as Reilly felt.

"Hi, Mom, Gerald." Reilly looked up at the tall, sandy-haired man in a tweed jacket- the same man who'd befriended the Brookes years ago.

At that time, her mother had been more interested in male conquests than grown-up relationships, so Gerald had intelligently, but regretfully, backed away. He'd not only cared for the mother, he'd also wanted to be a father to Reilly.

"This can't be the same Reilly of four years ago?" His eyes twinkled in amazed pleasure. "Reilly, you are beautiful!"

At the male attention focusing on his girl, Trinity left off dinner arrangements and sauntered over.

"Trinity," Reilly's mother introduced Gerald. "Honey, this is. . ."

"Her fiancé," Trinity finished. Reilly's eyes popped, as did the adults. What was Trinity saying? She noticed a slight tick at his jaw. The hardness. . . Did he think. . .?

"Pleased to meet you, Trinity," Gerald offered his hand.

Remembering Gerald's inquisitiveness concerning new, economical inventions, Reilly piped up, after recovering some aplomb over Trinity's revelation, "Trinity has converted his Ford Escort into a hybrid car. It gets 100 miles to the gallon," she gigged him to shake hands, which he promptly did.

"Serious?" Gerald asked, immediately intrigued.

Non-committal, Trinity nodded, realizing he'd jumped the gun- this man was different from the mother's norm.

"Could I take a look?" Gerald rubbed his hands together, eagerly anticipating, just like a kid presented with a wished-for toy.

"Come and eat, you boys can look at cars later. Sheesh!"

After their turkey dinner, Aunt Sarah prompted the gift exchange, mindful of Reilly and Trinity's short time to visit.

"Mom, these are. . .beautiful," Reilly had unwrapped two leather-bound journals. The spines on the books were embossed with vines and wreaths of flowers plied the front covers. Reilly's mother nervously plucked at her tights.

"I...I thought with all the gardening you've been doing, you might like to record your efforts from year to year. New things you might learn," her mother attempted to explain, sans confidence.

'Give her a hug, Sweetlin', she's tryin',' Bridie whispered into Reilly's numbed brain.

Reilly rose and mother and daughter came together in a flurry of limbs, blushes, giggles and tears- a long overdue first for the two of them.

Reilly sat close to her mother, terribly pleased that a wonderful new future, for both of them, seemed to be in the works.

"This goes along with them," her aunt proposed, handing her a package.

Inside were colored pencils- 200 bright shades. "You used to like to draw, I remember. You can draw your favorite flowers and vegetables in the journal."

"Thanks, Aunt Sarah," Reilly admiringly fingered the colorful pencils.

Gary and Steve dug into their box of cookies with a, "We sure miss your cookies, Reilly."

Reilly also had a box of cookies for Gerald, and massage gift certificates for her aunt and mother. The two sisters were thrilled- something they'd enjoy doing together.

Trinity and Gerald had finagled their escape to check out Trinity's vehicle modifications. Aunt Sarah ushered the boys out of the room and joined them- leaving Reilly and her mother a bit of private time.

"You ready, winsome elf? Gotta get you home before Santa Claus comes."

"You have to go already? We heard you play guitar. . ." the boys, too-late, realized something better than TV might exist.

"I'll be back," Trinity assured them.

"What kind of music do you play?"

"I prefer traditional Irish tunes. . ."

"But he can play anything after hearing it just once," Reilly complimented her beau.

"Including rock?" Gary challenged.

Trinity modestly shrugged an assent. "You know, Reilly can play, too," he blurted, and was visually castigated and elbowed for his remark.

"Hurt yourself, sweetheart?" The adults laughed as Trinity kissed her elbow; the cousins groaned and made faces.

"Merry Christmas, everybody," Trinity hailed. Hugs and promises were exchanged.

Reilly's mother tried to hand Trinity a folded bill. "Part of what I owe you," she quietly said.

"Keep it, Ms. Brooke, as I said before, it's a gift. Merry Christmas." He didn't have to force the fond expression he gave her. It seemed she had come a long way, too.

"You are the real thing, aren't you?"

Trinity simply looked over at Gerald, "He's the real deal, too."

He wrapped Reilly in her cape, and with a last thank you to Reilly's aunt, they stepped out into large flakes of snow dancing in the last light of a late afternoon.

"Looks like a white Christmas."

54

"Are you going to ask him?" Reilly and Tracy stopped to read a poster advertising the high school Sadie Hawkins Dance.

"It's girls' choice, you know?" Tracy persisted in pestering her quiet friend. "C'mon, if I can ask a boy after just moving here- and you know how shy I am, you can certainly ask him."

"I don't think so. I don't really know how to dance, and I can't see Trinity wanting to go to a high school dance," Reilly fumbled with her text books. She was glad for Tracy, but as for herself. . .

"Corrie's telling everybody that she's going to ask Trinity. She's told everyone that she's had the hots for him ever since her sister married Trinity's big brother." Tracy figured this information ought to get Reilly moving.

"That's OK, I. . .he told my mother and aunt he's my fiancé," Reilly honestly believed she was safe from Corrie's competition. For the life of her, she couldn't see Trinity with anyone like Corrie. And she trusted in his avowed love for her.

"Really?" Tracy squealed loud enough to attract the other students into stopping to check out the reason.

"My Claddagh ring has new significance," Reilly held up her ring finger, but Tracy displayed her ignorance of what two hands holding a crowned heart meant.

"If the crown is closest to the wearer's heart, it means friendship. If the heart is closest to my heart. . ."

She tipped her tiny silver ring showing the hands holding a heart topped with a filigreed crown. The whole, beautiful idea of the ring put her close to tears.

"Well, shoot! We knew he was in love with you. How could he not be? So, are you, like, uh. . .getting married? When?" Tracy shot rapid-fire questions.

Reilly laughed. She still surprised herself at the unfamiliar sound hearkening from her mouth.

"Not yet. Too soon. We better get to class," Reilly moved off in a happy reverie. She couldn't ask him, could she?

Reilly holed up in her room after supper, claiming homework.

But instead she pulled out Bridie's cards from their silk, drawstring pouch.

They now rested on her bedside table. Reilly no longer feared for her possessions. She even took off her watch when she slept, but the earrings remained in place. Delicately, she shuffled the old cards over and over until Bridie 'tut, tutted'.

'You can't learn if you block your brain, Sweetlin',' Bridie advised.

Reilly cut the cards three times, stacked them and turned over the top card, working on the energy inherent in the ancient deck as well as her intuition. At times she wondered if there existed any separation between what the cards indicated and how her own sixth sense worked. A question for Bridie, later.

A lady with a coronet of stars in royal blue robes, which emphasized her womanly figure, stood on a verdant green field.

The moon shone on one side of her head and the sun on the other. In her arms began a waterfall of bounty which overflowed to her feet- it included apples and many flowers Reilly had already learned of. The Lady.

Reilly studied the card. What did it mean to her? She knew there were many hidden meanings in all the various facets portrayed in the picture card. Many of these were indecipherable to Reilly without Bridie's help.

Think overall, not specifically, Bridie had cautioned her initially.

'Tell me Sweetlin'.' The ghost perched on air inches above the bed's footboard.

"This lady is a grown woman. An earth mother, I assume, because of all the flowers, fruits and vegetables. I like to garden, but it's. . . I'm growing up, Bridie and it's a little scary. Lately, the way Trinity looks at me. . . Like he's waiting. . ." Reilly shivered with all the implications of Trinity's recent perusals of her.

'Embrace yourself, Reilly. Recognize that you are loved; take pleasure in your great health, the bounties that God has bestowed on you. You care for everyone around you. Care for yourself. Ground yourself now, and know your body is a precious gift waiting to experience all the wonders. . .' Bridie figured this was the talk her mother should have given Reilly, instead of 'you'll either make it or you won't' accompanied by a porno magazine.

'Dearest, you have enough smarts and patience to act when you should, and wait when you need to. Connect with your body.'

'If you have concerns, tell yer young man. Friendship implies sharing confidences. That does not end because a ring becomes a pledge. I'll leave you to study, Sweetlin'.' Bridie floated teasingly around the swatting Righteous for a second and then vanished, blowing a kiss in her wake.

"Reilly?" A knock on her door disrupted her thinking. Suspicioning Reilly had something weighing on her mind, Trinity determinedly knocked again. He'd get to the bottom. . .of whatever.

Reilly opened the door, glanced back at her lesson card, took a deep breath, smiled up at Trinity, "Would you go to the Sadie Hawkins Dance with me?"

Trinity laughed, relieved, "Of course, winsome elf. Is that what was bothering you?"

Part of it, she thought.

The theme of the dance was Down Home Country. Attendees dressed accordingly; those who met with the approval of the gate keepers got in free. Those lacking in spirit were charged.

The school gym had straw bales grouped for seats, a bluegrass band dressed in denim overalls and straw hats and all the BBQ sandwiches, chips and cole slaw one could eat. For dessert- hand-cranked ice cream.

Trinity absolutely refused to don a straw hat and overalls. Pat dug out his grandfather's wool workpants and jacket, a chambray shirt and a newsboy cap, which Trinity jauntily cocked to the right atop his head. To complete the ensemble, Pat also found an old pair of work boots. And a camera.

Reilly broke out of her shy mode and called Kate for advice. Taken by surprise, but pleased, Kate closeted herself with Reilly.

"They've been in there for an hour," Trinity griped.

"Son, they ARE girls, and isn't this Reilly's first dance?"

Trinity perched on the arm rest of the couch, scratched his thigh- the old wool itched.

"Holy smokes!" Pat exclaimed.

Trinity's eyes lit up and he licked his lips. Reilly.
. .

Kate had recommended a square dancing outfit. Red gingham bodice had a modest, rounded neckline trimmed in white lace which sported a red bow and short, puffed, lace-trimmed sleeves. From her waist, numerous lace petticoats flared the short, red-checked skirt. On her feet, Mary Janes and lace-trimmed bobby socks. Kate had tied Reilly's hair from her face with a red and white ribbon band with a bow on her crown.

Reilly's eyes were only for Trinity's reaction. Slowly, he rose. His advance to her was even slower.

"If you ain't cuter than a speckled pup, and the prettiest sight I've ever seen," Trinity gently took her hand and twirled her, admiring her legs.

Passing muster at the entry, Trinity and Reilly, hand in hand, met up with Tracy and her date Jim, and Bridget and Wayne. Trinity guided Reilly through the dancing semantics of blue grass music, patiently ignoring her stepping on his steel-toe work boots.

Actually, except for her being abashed and grabbing his shoulder when she stepped on his toes, he never felt a thing.

When a slow dance came up, he positioned her hands. As she stood further from him than he liked, Trinity's hand resting at her waist surreptitiously slipped down her rump just long enough to pull her closer.

Speechless, she blushed up at him.

"Now, isn't this better?" he asked as his hand went back to her waist.

Reilly wasn't sure if her heart could stand to continue its hammering. This close to his body. . . She felt as if she were being electrocuted. Her skin tingled, her lungs crackled for air, her legs wobbled. His smile, eyes, hands, kept her afloat-in some kind of Bluegrass fantasy-land.

The end of the slow song signaled the band's break time. Trinity, Reilly and her friends joined the line for sandwiches, amiably conversing as they waited their turn at the buffet.

Corrie, in a slinky, non-country halter dress, confronted Trinity.

"Will you dance with me, Trinity?" If she'd batted her eyes to go with her sultry voice and out-of-place dress, Trinity would have burst out laughing.

"No, thanks, I've got a date," he brushed her off. They'd reached the buffet table. But some people don't know when to take 'no' for an answer.

"You're not tired of your live-in slut, yet?" Corrie cocked her hip to block Reilly's picking up a plate. Mortified, Reilly stood dumbfounded.

Trinity smoked, "You are one messed up spoiled rotten chick! I can't believe you're Kate's sister. I think I'll have a talk with your dad about washing your mouth out with soap. If I weren't a man. . ."

'Being a ghost, I have no such compunctions,' Bridie proceeded to dump a thick, juicy helping of Sloppy Joe, sans bun, atop Corrie's moussed hair.

'Take that, Miss Potty Mouth!' The ghost admired her handiwork. 'I do believe I have as much fun being a ghost as in me 'physical' days,' she gloated, and for good measure dolloped another spoonful atop the slack-jawed, flabbergasted Corrie.

Trinity cracked-up. Reilly was alternately stabbed by the comment and floored by Bridie's reprisal. She was pulled away from the spectacle by loving hands.

"You'd better not mind that witch, winsome elf," Trinity's hand rested at her waist, aware of the possibility of Reilly's crumbling. But Reilly held firm.

Corrie, on the other hand, wailed, couldn't find the source of her attack, sputtered at the sauce trolling down her face and tried to move away, but Ivy Rose had wound a loose length of baling twine about her ankles, and Corrie stumbled and fell into the arms of the audience of other students, who hastily pushed her off. Whatever had happened, it might be catching; they exchanged puzzled, but amused looks.

"Bridie, you're a wonder. I'm not entirely sure about your influence on my little sister, though," Trinity winked at Ivy Rose.

'She better never say a bad thing about my sister,' Ivy Rose boasted, scornfully.

55

Trinity parked the car at the O'Ryan home at 11:30. Only the porch lantern provided any light. He presumed his dad had gone to bed. Not that Trinity intended to brook the midnight curfew, but a few minutes alone with his beautiful date. . .

He'd been proud of his continued restraint. He'd kept the kisses chaste, innocent. Driving him crazy. . .

It started off that way. Innocent. Trinity's lips gently touched hers, top lip, bottom, sweet. . . Aggravated with the gear shift's intrusion, he lifted Reilly and placed her on his lap.

Fortunately or not, her skirts rode up as he hefted her over the gear shift handle. Reilly's hands went to readjust her dress, but Trinity stopped her, and brought her hands to his chest.

His kisses trailed to her ears, her neck, flitted up and down along the pulse racing in her veins.

"Reilly, you smell so good. Delicious Reilly," he whispered.

One calloused hand rested on her bare thigh. He'd been right about the fire business; he was burning up. Reilly tried to return Trinity's kisses, but these kisses were different; his mouth claimed hers and then, his hands. . . What were they doing?

She began to shiver. Too many nerve endings singing at once. Her hands remained at his chest, on the soft chambray- a barrier she was only vaguely aware of. A guard against. . .

Trinity's head dipped to her neckline.

A hand slowly stroked up her leg, another on its own course, climbing. . .

Reilly felt she was falling. No longer herself. Stricken by. . . No control. . . Wanting, yet. . .

No! Her trembling increased as a tad of sensibility threatened her composure. "Tr…Trinity," she moaned; weak as she'd become in the frenzy of cell-shattering, she pushed at his obdurate chest. "Trinity. . .p…please." She was not ready for this!

An overwhelming desire roared through Trinity's body.

"Trinity. . ." Was his hand moving under her skirt? "Trin…Trinity p…p…please," a tiny voice from far off. . .

He slammed back into his right mind.

"Reilly?" The state of her quivering body brought him instantly alert- a bucket of ice water on a sizzling, summer day.

"Reilly? Sweetheart, are you cold?" The only reply was her moaning, quaking and bowed head. "Reilly, it's all right, it's all right."

Her reaction to his slightly overcrossing the line scared him. What, did she think he'd actually. . .? Here, in a car. . .

"Reilly, talk to me. Talk to me, tell me. . . I'm sorry I…I got a little carried away. Talk to me, mo ghra milis daor."

He spied the extent of his roving hand. Removing the culprit, he smoothed her skirts down. What else would Reilly think? She had no experience of. . .petting.

"Reilly, don't hide from me. Don't be afraid. Tell me what you're thinking, please," he begged, contrite.

Dear God, don't let me lose her, he prayed, as he castigated himself with, 'you damned idiot'.

"I…I didn't know. . .it would be so p…powerful," he barely heard her say.

"Love is very powerful," he softly admitted, to himself as much as to her. He held her hands in his, tenderly.

"This is how g…girls get into. . .trouble," she pulled away, trying to put distance between them.

"Is that what you think? That I…I would get you in trouble?" Trinity was thoroughly dismayed. "Reilly, I swear to you, we won't make love until we're both ready. And we will certainly not have kids until we're both ready," he rushed on as he felt her constructing a barricade between them.

"Look, I found the literature Kate gave you about birth control. I don't want you taking any chemicals- no pills. I'll take care of the protection. You have to believe me. I'll never hurt you. I know we're not ready to be parents. This, tonight. . ." he exhaled heavily.

Remorse knocked at his heart. You, idiot, he ranted! Of course, Reilly wouldn't understand the difference between kissing-v-heavy petting-v-full blown sex. Reilly hadn't a clue. Bleedin' eejit, he angrily reproached himself.

"Bridie doesn't want me to take pills, either," her eyes would not meet his.

"Good. There are enough side effects to scare the hell out of me. I'll take care of birth control. But, Reilly, I wasn't headed that way tonight. I. . ."

He reflected on their previous kisses. Simple. Quick. Granted, he'd been a little too zealous tonight, but. . .

Something else occurred to him. Never in all the times he'd pulled her into his arms for a kiss, since they'd been a steady couple, had she ever placed her arms around his neck. Her hands always stayed between them. Walls set up between his heart and hers.

"Reilly, are you afraid of me?" He dreaded the answer. If he'd ruined this, he'd never get over it.

"I…I think I'm more afraid of myself. I…I didn't want you to stop. . ., but I was. . .also afraid you might not," he caught the crackling sound of near tears.

He lifted her chin and felt like crying himself as tears welled in her eyes. He'd done this to her. . . No, her past was the main culprit, flaunting itself, haunting her; his approach tonight had only brought it to the forefront again.

"Do you trust me, Reilly?" Fearfully, she inclined her head. "I promise we will not go all the way without your complete awareness and agreement. I look forward to you wanting me as much as I want you. There's nothing wrong with desire, especially when it's tied to the love I have for you. Do you believe me?"

"It's. . .scary," she whispered.

"Do you want to talk to Bridie or Kate?"

"No," she shook her head, "only you."

Thank God, he sighed. He hadn't completely screwed up, if she still wanted to talk to him.

"Forget about getting pregnant. It's not going to happen. Let your body relax and enjoy my touch. Put your arms around my neck, drop the barriers."

"I…I'll wait for you to initiate the next kisses we share, OK?" He'd probably have to hog-tie himself, but maybe if he held off, she might let herself relax.

"I'm s…sorry, Trinity."

"Sweetheart, there's nothing to be sorry about. I didn't mean to scare you," his worried eyes scorched her.

A shaky hand reached up to touch his cheek. "C…could we. . .try again?" she stuttered.

He turned his lips into her palm. More than anything he wanted to comply, but the porch light flickered. Curfew.

"You want to talk about it, Son?" Trinity had walked Reilly to her room and then slouched out to the porch. That old clenched jaw was back in place. Whatever had struck his youngest son had struck him hard.

He didn't think Trinity would confide in him. He'd never done so after Ivy Rose. All those years of massive hurt and suffering overtly disguised as tremendous, volatile, pent-up anger escalating into violence.

"She's afraid, Dad. Afraid of. . .natural things." Pat waited for more. "I…I got a little carried away. . .not like you're thinking. She's afraid to let herself go."

"Do you think that episode at Chet's. . .?" Pat let it hang.

"I think it's probably a combination of that, growing up with sex not meaning anything, no motherly affection, no idea of husband and wife role models, and the fear of pregnancy the way her mother experienced it."

"I trust you've got that last one covered?"

"Definitely," Trinity vowed.

"Give her time, Son. Will she talk to you?"

"Yeah, she does, thank God. Or I'd really feel like an s.o.b."

"Then just be patient. Keep the communication lines open."

"Bridie, I failed miserably," Reilly cried into her pillow. "He wants me and I'm scared to show him how I feel. Scared to let go."

Bridie stroked Reilly's hair. 'Sweetlin', it's another bit to put behind you. You and yer man talked, eh?'

Reilly nodded. "I'm such a mess," she managed.

'Nonsense. A smart girl waits 'til she's ready, and a smart man gives her room. I'm bettin' both of you have the smarts. Now, stop yer caterwauling and give another gander at the card that chose you. There's nothing wrong with a body responding to another's for the sake of love. Pleasure is not wrong if it's thoughtful. Only mindless pleasure is against nature.'

"Mornin', Reilly," Pat greeted her, putting down his newspaper.

"Good morning, Pat," Reilly studied Trinity's empty chair.

"Trinity went fishing," Pat said.

"Oh, I didn't know," she glumly said.

"Freezer was getting low on fish," Pat replied, doing his best not to give anything away. But Reilly looked all too dejected.

It was late Tuesday when Trinity returned. He, JT and Pat, had acquired a pretty good catch of Walleye.

His head was clear and despite his dad's eyeing his walk down the hall, he knocked on Reilly's door. Upon her response, he stepped in to the lighted room. When would she ever feel safe enough to sleep in the dark? Trinity wasn't sure if he could sleep in a lighted room. Oh well, something to deal with when the time came.

Reilly rolled out of a dream to find it wasn't a dream at all. She hastily removed her braces' head gear.

"Trinity," she sat up, disturbing the sleeping arrangements of one cat, one dog and one lamb.

Although he'd missed her terribly and wanted to hold her something fierce, he sat on the side of her bed, quietly. His hands rested on his thighs.

"You're not mad at me, are you?" she whispered. Please don't let him be mad at me, she prayed.

"Lord, no! Not at all," he gently reassured her. "Reilly, I want you to 'live' every second of your life with greedy anticipation, joy and gratitude. Not dread. I want you to take pleasure in every moment we're together, as I do. My world exists because you're here. Share it with me. Don't be afraid. I love you, mo ghra milis daor." The intensity of his deep blue eyes saturated her with his love.

'Rightly, well done, lad,' Bridie sniffled silently in the background.

"What does that mean? I…I've heard you say it before and I. . .keep forgetting to ask," she returned his gaze without flinching.

"My dear, sweet love, Reilly," Trinity kept his aching arms at his sides. He would stick to his guns and let her initiate. Please, God, let her. . .

"Trinity," she whispered, nearly crying in relief and happiness. Awkwardly, she threw her arms around his neck. Barely, he refrained from responding. Barely. God, she smelled good and clean.

With her hands in place around his neck, fingering his longish hair, she faced him, unmindful of her bare legs escaping the blankets. All focus on Trinity, her friend, her. . .

With the crowned lady in the back of her head, where she'd been as a kind of urgent reminder for days, Reilly really looked at Trinity. Eyes to eyes. Closer than close. Open soul to open soul.

"I love you, Trinity, mo ghra milis daor," she whispered.

She let the allure of his mouth draw hers. But it was Reilly's lips that fluttered first upon his. Trinity maintained the tight rein on his body until he felt her completely relax into her kissing him. Her fingers playing in his hair at the nape of his neck- igniting nerve endings. . .

Ever so slowly, he began to match her. The pent-up flood of fears in Reilly's chest released her- shattered into oblivion. Her heart soared. She pulled Trinity closer. Closer until close was not close enough. . .

"A hem," Pat coughed outside the door. He was surprised to be answered with a spate of giggles, instead of a flurry of disengagement.

With the decline of winter, Trinity helped Reilly prepare for her driver's test. He had to ask the backseat drivers to stay home as too many cautious instructions discombobulated the new driver.

Easily passing her test and with a wondrous sense of accomplishment, Reilly celebrated by doing spring cleaning at Bridie's and then at the O'Ryans' home. She encouraged Trinity and his dad to give her a few hours, alone. Pat, not giving a fig newton for what dust might reside where, was inclined to say 'leave it' but Reilly stood her ground.

'We need cleaning music,' Ivy Rose popped in as Reilly had finished up all the rooms except for the kitchen.

"What do you suggest?" Reilly asked. And so it happened that Trinity and his dad stepped into the trailer to find Reilly belting out, with Aretha Franklin in the background, the words to RESPECT. For safety, Wrench and Righteous had removed themselves to the far side of the living room and watched the incredulous behavior of their beloved humans- the one on the physical plane and the other two angels.

In Trinity's old cut-off sweat shorts and a raggedy t-shirt, Reilly swiveled her hips in imitation of Ivy Rose's dancing above her, while she scrubbed the counter.

'Like this, Bridie,' Ivy Rose tutored the traditional-minded ghost.

The Irishwoman had a difficult time with the Soul Train extravaganza. Her body had never moved like that. With great overemphasis, Ivy Rose stuck out her pink shorts-clad hips.

'Dearie, I'm not sure it's legal to move like that,' Bridie nevertheless tried and fell through herself for her efforts- a ghostly somersault of sorts. Rising with a snort of glee, she was game to try again.

Reilly hit a high wail and Pat dropped a 6-pack. Stunned at the errant sound, she swung around. The soul-like cry died on her lips as her face flamed in embarrassment.

"Don't let me interrupt," Pat sidled around the dance floor, amusement plastering his face.

Aghast, Reilly clapped her hands to her cheeks, unaware that her one hand still held a sponge full of cleanser. Trinity couldn't stop laughing- at the ghostly dance display and Reilly. . . Damn, that girl could sing! And God, but his life would never be dull, Saints be praised!

"I see you've been keeping secrets from me sweetheart," his deep blue eyes twinkled.

"Uh. . .uh. . .," Reilly stammered. Trinity wiped the Comet cleanser from her face.

"With a voice like that, I'm going to have you singing more often," he leaned down and kissed the tip of her nose.

56

Trinity knew better, but hey, his little sister had always loved and looked forward to birthdays. So had every girl he'd ever dated. Hints about potential presents ran rampant as 'that' day approached.

Try to get Reilly to indulge in a little, wistful, present-longing- right, not happening. Trinity considered himself to be pretty observant. If Reilly wouldn't hint, he'd surprise. With every ounce of his being he hoped she'd be pleasantly surprised.

"Looking forward to your birthday? The big 18," he let out his dimples with a beaming smile.

A momentary lapse of the watering can at Bridie's and the pensive look on her face had Trinity thinking, 'uh, oh.' Reilly shrugged.

"C'mere, winsome elf," Trinity absolved her from the watering can, led her to Bridie's high-sided couch. He knelt before her, "Tell me."

Reilly looked at everything but Trinity, tried to smile, "I'm sorry, I'm being such a baby."

"Always my baby," he fondled her knee.

'Tell him,' Bridie commanded.

"It seems scary, turning 18, being an adult with responsibilities. . . Even though I always thought I wanted. . ." she bit at her lower lip.

"Reilly, all of your life, you've acted more like an adult than a child. As for responsibilities, you've got a job, you're graduating, you've a savings account and you have plans for your life. What's so different? What's scary?"

She fiddled with her fingers for a minute, trying to put her feelings into words.

"For the past months, for the longest period of time in my life. . .I've felt like part of a family. Secure, in a clean home with good people. Cooking for you and your dad. Taking care of you when you had the flu. . ."

Trinity grinned ruefully, "Which you didn't catch."

"Only because of Bridie's remedies, and you recovered in record time," she continued to fiddle with her fingers.

"Unfortunately. I kind of enjoyed having you at my beck and call. Tell me the rest." Though he pretty well guessed.

"Once I'm 18, it will all change," she murmured.

Ah, yes. As he'd assumed. That 'change' word. "Nonsense, you'll always be part of the O'Ryan family."

Reilly shook her head. "I'll open my own bank account. I do have a job, but I'll have to. . ." she closed her eyes, sighed resignedly, "get my own apartment."

"Bulls…!" he exploded.

"I can't stay with you and your dad. . ."

"You can and will stay as long as you want to," he objected. Forever, he thought. Only he had a different objective in mind.

"Reilly, turning 18 doesn't mean you have to rush into anything. You got it?" Trinity caressed her cheek with his calloused fingers. "Reilly, do you understand what I'm saying?"

For a moment, she just lost herself in his warm, loving eyes. What would happen to 'them'? "OK."

"Good. I want you to always be comfortable talking to me about anything. Ivy Rose! Sheesh!" His little sister had pestered him by whispering in his ear as he was talking.

"I mean anything. Ivy Rose wants you to know that," Trinity actually blushed, a first for him, that he could recall, "It was me that told her about. . .the birds and the bees."

Reilly's mouth flew open. Astounded, she began to giggle, then, full-blown gales of laughter. Did he think she needed a lesson in how babies came about? She might be naïve about the process, but she did know the mechanics. Mechanics! Clutching her sides, she laughed harder and pretty soon everyone in the room was doubled over in raucous merriment.

"Miss Brooke," an elegantly attired, white-haired gentleman with merry brown eyes strode into his mahogany-paneled office and shook Reilly's tentative hand.

"Seamus O'Flynn at your service. Thank you for meeting me this morning."

Reilly had come awake on her eighteenth birthday to the strong scent of chocolate. The O'Ryans' coffee splurge couldn't conceal the redolence of Reilly's favorite sweet.

"I smell chocolate," she announced as the siren-scent drew her to the kitchen. Huh, no chocolate in sight!

"Happy Birthday, sweetheart," Trinity greeted her with a quick kiss.

"Happy Birthday, Reilly," Pat gave her a hug.

Reilly peered around, "Thanks. Don't you smell chocolate?"

"You're imagining things," Trinity said, trying to keep a straight face. But when Reilly began opening cabinets. . .

"If you keep a woman from chocolate, Trinity, she's liable to tear the place apart," Pat warned.

"All right," Trinity carefully brought out a three layer chocolate cake from the oven.

"Oh, my!" Reilly's eyes widened, she licked her lips.

"You have to eat your breakfast first," he held the cake just out of her reach. "And then we'll light the candles."

Reilly had the day off and the O'Ryans' garage was closed. Sunday.

"You have an appointment at Mr. O'Flynn's office at 11:30," Pat stated.

"Who? I don't understand."

"We don't either. Seamus was rather mysterious in his request. I promised I'd have you there," Trinity told her.

"Reilly, may I call you Reilly? Let me congratulate you on your birthday and your imminent graduation. I know you're curious as to why I've asked you here."

The lawyer eyed Trinity, "I'm not sure, but I should speak to you alone. . ."

Trinity had taken a chair next to Reilly across from the attorney. Bridie floated to O'Flynn's desk and spun his favorite pen.

"I'll take that as an affirmative for Trinity's presence?" The pen abruptly stopped its spinning, to the surprise of Reilly and Trinity, who cast covert looks at the grinning ghost.

"I'm the trustee for Bridie's estate. By the way, you've been a remarkably diligent young caretaker. But I'd expect nothing less from Bridie's recommendation."

Reilly looked from Bridie to the attorney. "Can you see her?" she was almost afraid to ask.

"Hmmm," he reticently allowed, "she makes herself known." He gingerly picked up his pen and quickly replaced it on his desk blotter.

"As of today, you are the new trustee of Bridie's estate," he stated.

Reilly felt cold chills pierce her clothes. Supernatural needles shocked her. Trinity had squared his shoulders, stunned. He watched Bridie watching his girl.

Mr. O'Flynn went on to explain how months before Bridie 'left', they'd drawn up the necessary papers. He had to actually physically determine the existence of a Reilly Brooke before the trust could be completed.

Trinity frowned. What would this mean for the future he had in mind?

"For your lifetime, Bridie's cottage and land are at your disposal. As long as you use them with her ideas in mind. Of course, I'll be here to advise on the particulars and to keep the financial aspects viable. As for you, young man, if you would be so kind as to call at my house at your earliest convenience, Bridie has left a harp and violin to your care."

Trinity's shock couldn't compete with Reilly's, but nevertheless it was there.

Blinking his eyes, he sought Bridie's and sincerely thanked her.

'Ah, me lad, only you could do the sweet things justice. I'll be expectin' to hear some delightful sounds soon,' her almost youthful countenance fondly regarded Trinity.

The attorney presented Reilly with a tally of Bridie's assets. Reilly began to shiver as the lawyer's words finally penetrated her stupefied state.

'Sweetlin', snap out of it. You are the daughter I'd have had if things had been different. I'm passing on to you my home to use as your own. I saw you, and knew you would love my cottage and fruitful lands long before you walked up my drive and asked about sweaters.'

"B...b...but," Reilly stammered.

Trinity and O'Flynn looked at her with concern. Neither had been privy to Bridie's address to Reilly.

"Sweetheart, take a drink," Trinity held a glass of water for her and put his arm about her.

'Happy Birthday, me dearest girl. I'll always be around to teach and advise you. But it belongs to you, now.'

Trinity and Pat presented Reilly with her birthday gift before heading out to a steak restaurant for dinner.

"This is. . .mine?" The day's surprises were threatening to overwhelm Reilly's modest equilibrium. Righteous jumped on to the hood while Wrench was heartily discouraged from following suit.

"I've converted it for you. Your own hybrid. A 2003 Cavalier." Trinity hitched his thumbs in his dress pants' pockets.

Reilly stared between him and Pat, Wrench and Righteous and the car- a dark, forest green, 2-door coupe with perfect interior.

"I…I. . ."

"Speechless. You know the present's good when a woman is left speechless," Pat mused, picturing Reilly at the lawyer's office. Now there was a monumental surprise present.

"It's really a combination birthday and graduation present, if that's OK?" Trinity asked.

With the sun's benediction on her in her sundress, Bridie and Ivy Rose cavorting in square dance steps atop her new car's sun roof and smiling beatifically on her, Reilly succumbed to tears of happiness.

Later that evening, after a congenial birthday get-together at the restaurant with Kate and both Pats, Dave and Martie, Ivy Rose and Bridie, Trinity suggested a stroll around Bridie's, er, Reilly's new home.

The stars held court. Trinity scanned the grounds. The small, stone cottage- all moonlit- a fantasy stage.

"Will you be lonely here?" he fretted.

Ivy Rose giggled; Bridie knock-knocked on his head.

"I…I won't really be alone, but. . ."

Trinity hitched his shoulders at the ghosts, "I suppose not. It's a regular girls' slumber party," his jaw tightened in remorseful expectation. "When will you move in? I mean it will take all of ten minutes to move all your belongings."

"D…don't you like it here?" Reilly asked, abject at the tone of his voice, horrified she'd done something wrong.

"Yeah, yeah, I like it here fine," he tersely replied.

Reilly was puzzled. The day had been like a script out of a dream, but now. . .

This wasn't quite how he'd planned it- he'd banked his savings for another surprise- for a home for both of them.

'Trinity, aren't you going to stay?' Ivy Rose had never been shy around her big brother.

"Did she just say what I think she said?" Trinity frowned.

"You said we had to wait until I was 18," Reilly's face was afire with embarrassment. "Don't you want me anymore. . .now. . .that. . ." she broke off.

"Reilly," he tilted her chin up. Her dewy eyes spit droplets. "I love you." He glanced around at Bridie's cottage, eyed Bridie and Ivy Rose sitting on the single gable- an expectant, ghostly audience.

"Would you excuse us, ladies?"

'Why, Trinity?' Ivy Rose asked. But Bridie winked at him, and escorted the inquisitive, giggling girl away.

I hope all this doesn't make a difference, he thought. Maybe it will all be for the best. He'd always loved coming here. . .

Trinity fell to his knees. Unfortunately, he missed the grass and hit the rock-lined path. Stifling a curse and fending Reilly off with a raised hand, he grappled with a pocket and pulled out. . .

"Reilly, I. . . Will you marry me?"

Many of the formally invited guests at Reilly's and Trinity's wedding, the more intuitive ones, were treated to fleeting glimpses here and there, of a host of long-passed on O'Ryans and friends, in their appropriate, period attire.

They danced and mingled, appreciatively eyed the buffet with misgivings and the tiered wedding cake. Lovingly, they hovered and bestowed ghostly blessings on the newest O'Ryan couple.

Reilly noticed Bridie impatiently peering around and watched her friend's face turn radiant at the appearance of a familiar looking gentleman, bedecked in the sartorial splendor of his day.

"Is that THE O'Ryan?" Reilly asked.

The youthful Bridie merely smiled and held out her hand. The image of Trinity's uncle wafted to her with a loving smile on his mustached face.

'But of course, Sweetlin', who else would escort me on this most auspicious day?'

"But I thought, him being married and all. . ."

THE O'Ryan bowed to Bridie and Reilly and Trinity, who kept his arm about his new bride's waist. THE O'Ryan did have a reputation, after all.

The handsome gentleman winked, delightedly, at Ivy

Rose cavorting within a cloud of rose petals flitting and fluttering in her circular wake about the two couples, tilted his head at Trinity, 'Only until my true love came along, lad.'

'You see, Reilly,' Bridie explained, 'in heaven you're married to your soul mate- at whatever age you choose.' Her eyes spoke the world of feelings she'd always had for the love of her life.

In a curtsy of roses, Bridie was lifted up and embraced by THE O'Ryan.

Trinity and Reilly danced their first dance as husband and wife in company with the illustrious pair.

'They're a lovely couple, eh, my Pat?'

"Yes, my dearest, they are perfect together, as you and I are," Pat Sr. replied to his wife. "Ivy Rose, Bridie, and all the rest agree, my love."

'Definitely. Bridie looks so very young and happy with her man,' she smiled and rested her arm about her husband, her cheek comfortably upon his bicep.

"Who is the lovely lady next to your dad, Trinity?" Reilly watched her new husband gulp, startled.

"My mother," he whispered. The lovely woman waved, beamed angelically, full of love for her youngest son and Reilly- the girl who returned life to his shattered soul.

"Isn't it wonderful, all of these new friends?" Reilly indicated their ghostly guests, many of whom she had yet to be introduced to, along with the ones in their 'physicals'.

Trinity's eyes lit upon his bride. Brows rose over deep, gleaming, blue eyes, "How is it, Reilly, that you're not afraid of ghosts?"

Her eyes glistened, "My first friend was Bridie."

"Hmm. . . It will make for interesting family get-togethers that's for sure," and he swept her around the floor to a slow Irish tune.

Trinity carried his lass across the threshold of Bridie's cottage. He'd implored Bridie and Ivy Rose for privacy this night, but Wrench and Righteous had foregone the wedding celebration, and had waited impatiently at Bridie's.

With his love curled onto his chest, the happy Wrench and Righteous curled upon their feet, the lullaby of his heart entrancing her, Reilly issued one more surprise.

"Trinity, turn off the light."

He rolled her onto her back, ignored the feline and canine complaints, eyed the dimly lit room.

"Are you sure? I mean, I'm OK with it."

Her fingers lovingly stroked the hair from his eyes. "I'm sure," she smiled.

"All right, then, Fearless," and he gently tugged the light's chain.

Lisa Annette Powell

Thankful acknowledgements

All the skeletons in my closet

The muses that fascinate my world

Pam, for the godfather of all possums

All who asked- 'when is the next one coming?' and
'what is it about?'

Dave and Zella of Pearl's Diner, my first employers, who
taught me so much

The grand, colorful customers of our Ma's Kettle restaurant

The great band THE IRISH ROVERS

For Irish interested parties: go to Ireland, rent a car, get
lost, and especially, enjoy the west coast and traditional
music played in pubs

The second largest cultural festival- the Dublin Irish
Festival- is a celebration of the Irish and is held in
Dublin, Ohio in August

Special thanks to Brian, the computer genius

Correspondents welcome at the CatSkill Trilogy Facebook site
or at: lisaannettepowell@gmail.com

Thanks for sharing your time with me

In Venice with my hero

www.ingramcontent.com/pod-product-compliance
Lightning Source LLC
Chambersburg PA
CBHW062017170626

46813CB00001B/196